RETIEF: THE DIRTY DOZEN

©2020 Positronic Publishing

Cover Image © Can Stock Photo / Catmando

Hardcover ISBN 13: 978-1-5154-4516-6
Trade Paperback ISBN 13: 978-1-5154-4517-3

Retief: The Dirty Dozen

Keith Laumer

ACKNOWLEDGMENTS

"The Frozen Planet" originally appeared in Worlds of If Science Fiction, September 1961.

"Gambler's World" originally appeared in Worlds of If, November 1961.

"The Yillian Way" originally appeared in Worlds of If, January 1962.

"The Madman From Earth" originally appeared in Worlds of If Science Fiction, March 1962.

"Retief of the Red-Tape Mountain" originally appeared in Worlds of If Science Fiction, May 1962.

"Aide Memoire" originally appeared in Worlds of If Science Fiction, July 1962.

"Cultural Exchange" originally appeared in Worlds of If Science Fiction, September 1962.

"The Desert and the Stars" originally appeared in Worlds of If Science Fiction, November 1962.

"Saline Solution" originally appeared in Worlds of If Science Fiction, March 1963.

"Mightiest Qorn" originally appeared in *Worlds of If Science Fiction*, July 1963.

"The Governor of Glave" originally appeared in Worlds of If Science Fiction, November 1963.

"Diplomat-at-Arms" originally appeared in *Fantastic Science Fiction Stories*, January 1960.

CONTENTS

The Frozen Planet 6

Gambler's World 33

The Yillian Way 55

The Madman from Earth 70

Retief of the Red-Tape Mountain 96

Aide Memoire 111

Cultural Exchange 129

The Desert and the Stars 147

Saline Solution 166

Mightiest Qorn 183

The Governor of Glave 202

Diplomat-at-Arms 229

THE FROZEN PLANET

"It is rather unusual," Magnan said, "to assign an officer of your rank to courier duty, but this is an unusual mission."

Retief sat relaxed and said nothing. Just before the silence grew awkward, Magnan went on.

"There are four planets in the group," he said. "Two double planets, all rather close to an unimportant star listed as DRI-G 33987. They're called Jorgensen's Worlds, and in themselves are of no importance whatever. However, they lie deep in the sector into which the Soetti have been penetrating.

"Now—" Magnan leaned forward and lowered his voice—"we have learned that the Soetti plan a bold step forward. Since they've met no opposition so far in their infiltration of Terrestrial space, they intend to seize Jorgensen's Worlds by force."

Magnan leaned back, waiting for Retief's reaction. Retief drew carefully on his cigar and looked at Magnan. Magnan frowned.

"This is open aggression, Retief," he said, "in case I haven't made myself clear. Aggression on Terrestrial-occupied territory by an alien species. Obviously, we can't allow it."

Magnan drew a large folder from his desk.

"A show of resistance at this point is necessary. Unfortunately, Jorgensen's Worlds are technologically undeveloped areas. They're farmers or traders. Their industry is limited to a minor role in their economy—enough to support the merchant fleet, no more. The war potential, by conventional standards, is nil."

Magnan tapped the folder before him.

"I have here," he said solemnly, "information which will change that picture completely." He leaned back and blinked at Retief.

*

"All right, Mr. Councillor," Retief said. "I'll play along; what's in the folder?"

Magnan spread his fingers, folded one down.

"First," he said. "The Soetti War Plan—in detail. We were fortunate enough to make contact with a defector from a party of renegade Terrestrials who've been advising the Soetti." He folded another finger. "Next, a battle plan for the Jorgensen's people, worked out by the Theory group." He wrestled a third finger down. "Lastly; an Utter Top Secret schematic for conversion of a standard anti-acceleration field into a potent weapon—a development our systems people have been holding in reserve for just such a situation."

"Is that all?" Retief said. "You've still got two fingers sticking up."

Magnan looked at the fingers and put them away.

"This is no occasion for flippancy, Retief. In the wrong hands, this information could be catastrophic. You'll memorize it before you leave this building."

"I'll carry it, sealed," Retief said. "That way nobody can sweat it out of me."

Magnan started to shake his head.

"Well," he said. "If it's trapped for destruction, I suppose—"

"I've heard of these Jorgensen's Worlds," Retief said. "I remember an agent, a big blond fellow, very quick on the uptake. A wizard with cards and dice. Never played for money, though."

"Umm," Magnan said. "Don't make the error of personalizing this situation, Retief. Overall policy calls for a defense of these backwater worlds. Otherwise the Corps would allow history to follow its natural course, as always."

"When does this attack happen?"

"Less than four weeks."

"That doesn't leave me much time."

"I have your itinerary here. Your accommodations are clear as far as Aldo Cerise. You'll have to rely on your ingenuity to get you the rest of the way."

"That's a pretty rough trip, Mr. Councillor. Suppose I don't make it?"

Magnan looked sour. "Someone at a policy-making level has chosen to put all our eggs in one basket, Retief. I hope their confidence in you is not misplaced."

"This antiac conversion; how long does it take?"

"A skilled electronics crew can do the job in a matter of minutes. The Jorgensens can handle it very nicely; every other man is a mechanic of some sort."

Retief opened the envelope Magnan handed him and looked at the tickets inside.

"Less than four hours to departure time," he said. "I'd better not start any long books."

"You'd better waste no time getting over to Indoctrination," Magnan said.

Retief stood up. "If I hurry, maybe I can catch the cartoon."

"The allusion escapes me," Magnan said coldly. "And one last word. The Soetti are patrolling the trade lanes into Jorgensen's Worlds; don't get yourself interned."

"I'll tell you what," Retief said soberly. "In a pinch, I'll mention your name."

"You'll be traveling with Class X credentials," Magnan snapped. "There must be nothing to connect you with the Corps."

"They'll never guess," Retief said. "I'll pose as a gentleman."

"You'd better be getting started," Magnan said, shuffling papers.

"You're right," Retief said. "If I work at it, I might manage a snootful by takeoff." He went to the door. "No objection to my checking out a needler, is there?"

Magnan looked up. "I suppose not. What do you want with it?"

"Just a feeling I've got."

"Please yourself."

"Some day," Retief said, "I may take you up on that."

II

Retief put down the heavy travel-battered suitcase and leaned on the counter, studying the schedules chalked on the board under the legend "ALDO CERISE—INTERPLANETARY." A thin clerk in a faded sequined blouse and a plastic snakeskin cummerbund groomed his fingernails, watching Retief from the corner of his eye.

Retief glanced at him.

The clerk nipped off a ragged corner with rabbitlike front teeth and spat it on the floor.

"Was there something?" he said.

"Two twenty-eight, due out today for the Jorgensen group," Retief said. "Is it on schedule?"

The clerk sampled the inside of his right cheek, eyed Retief. "Filled up. Try again in a couple of weeks."

"What time does it leave?"

"I don't think—"

"Let's stick to facts," Retief said. "Don't try to think. What time is it due out?"

The clerk smiled pityingly. "It's my lunch hour," he said. "I'll be open in an hour." He held up a thumb nail, frowned at it.

"If I have to come around this counter," Retief said, "I'll feed that thumb to you the hard way."

The clerk looked up and opened his mouth. Then he caught Retief's eye, closed his mouth and swallowed.

"Like it says there," he said, jerking a thumb at the board. "Lifts in an hour. But you won't be on it," he added.

Retief looked at him.

8

"Some . . . ah . . . VIP's required accommodation," he said. He hooked a finger inside the sequined collar. "All tourist reservations were canceled. You'll have to try to get space on the Four-Planet Line ship next—"

"Which gate?" Retief said.

"For . . . ah . . . ?"

"For the two twenty-eight for Jorgensen's Worlds," Retief said.

"Well," the clerk said. "Gate 19," he added quickly. "But—"

Retief picked up his suitcase and walked away toward the glare sign reading *To Gates 16-30.*

"Another smart alec," the clerk said behind him.

*

Retief followed the signs, threaded his way through crowds, found a covered ramp with the number 228 posted over it. A heavy-shouldered man with a scarred jawline and small eyes was slouching there in a rumpled gray uniform. He put out a hand as Retief started past him.

"Lessee your boarding pass," he muttered.

Retief pulled a paper from an inside pocket, handed it over.

The guard blinked at it.

"Whassat?"

"A gram confirming my space," Retief said. "Your boy on the counter says he's out to lunch."

The guard crumpled the gram, dropped it on the floor and lounged back against the handrail.

"On your way, bub," he said.

Retief put his suitcase carefully on the floor, took a step and drove a right into the guard's midriff. He stepped aside as the man doubled and went to his knees.

"You were wide open, ugly. I couldn't resist. Tell your boss I sneaked past while you were resting your eyes." He picked up his bag, stepped over the man and went up the gangway into the ship.

A cabin boy in stained whites came along the corridor.

"Which way to cabin fifty-seven, son?" Retief asked.

"Up there." The boy jerked his head and hurried on. Retief made his way along the narrow hall, found signs, followed them to cabin fifty-seven. The door was open. Inside, baggage was piled in the center of the floor. It was expensive looking baggage.

RETIEF: THE DIRTY DOZEN

Retief put his bag down. He turned at a sound behind him. A tall, florid man with an expensive coat belted over a massive paunch stood in the open door, looking at Retief. Retief looked back. The florid man clamped his jaws together, turned to speak over his shoulder.

"Somebody in the cabin. Get 'em out." He rolled a cold eye at Retief as he backed out of the room. A short, thick-necked man appeared.

"What are you doing in Mr. Tony's room?" he barked. "Never mind! Clear out of here, fellow! You're keeping Mr. Tony waiting."

"Too bad," Retief said. "Finders keepers."

"You nuts?" The thick-necked man stared at Retief. "I said it's Mr. Tony's room."

"I don't know Mr. Tony. He'll have to bull his way into other quarters."

"We'll see about you, mister." The man turned and went out. Retief sat on the bunk and lit a cigar. There was a sound of voices in the corridor. Two burly baggage-smashers appeared, straining at an oversized trunk. They maneuvered it through the door, lowered it, glanced at Retief and went out. The thick-necked man returned.

"All right, you. Out," he growled. "Or have I got to have you thrown out?"

Retief rose and clamped the cigar between his teeth. He gripped a handle of the brass-bound trunk in each hand, bent his knees and heaved the trunk up to chest level, then raised it overhead. He turned to the door.

"Catch," he said between clenched teeth. The trunk slammed against the far wall of the corridor and burst.

Retief turned to the baggage on the floor, tossed it into the hall. The face of the thick-necked man appeared cautiously around the door jamb.

"Mister, you must be—"

"If you'll excuse me," Retief said, "I want to catch a nap." He flipped the door shut, pulled off his shoes and stretched out on the bed.

*

Five minutes passed before the door rattled and burst open.

Retief looked up. A gaunt leathery-skinned man wearing white ducks, a blue turtleneck sweater and a peaked cap tilted raffishly over one eye stared at Retief.

"Is this the joker?" he grated.

The thick-necked man edged past him, looked at Retief and snorted, "That's him, sure."

"I'm captain of this vessel," the first man said. "You've got two minutes to haul your freight out of here, buster."

10

"When you can spare the time from your other duties," Retief said, "take a look at Section Three, Paragraph One, of the Uniform Code. That spells out the law on confirmed space on vessels engaged in interplanetary commerce."

"A space lawyer." The captain turned. "Throw him out, boys."

Two big men edged into the cabin, looking at Retief.

"Go on, pitch him out," the captain snapped.

Retief put his cigar in an ashtray, and swung his feet off the bunk.

"Don't try it," he said softly.

One of the two wiped his nose on a sleeve, spat on his right palm, and stepped forward, then hesitated.

"Hey," he said. "This the guy tossed the trunk off the wall?"

"That's him," the thick-necked man called. "Spilled Mr. Tony's possessions right on the deck."

"Deal me out," the bouncer said. "He can stay put as long as he wants to. I signed on to move cargo. Let's go, Moe."

"You'd better be getting back to the bridge, Captain," Retief said. "We're due to lift in twenty minutes."

The thick-necked man and the Captain both shouted at once. The Captain's voice prevailed.

"—twenty minutes . . . uniform Code . . . gonna do?"

"Close the door as you leave," Retief said.

The thick-necked man paused at the door. "We'll see you when you come out."

III

Four waiters passed Retief's table without stopping. A fifth leaned against the wall nearby, a menu under his arm.

At a table across the room, the Captain, now wearing a dress uniform and with his thin red hair neatly parted, sat with a table of male passengers. He talked loudly and laughed frequently, casting occasional glances Retief's way.

A panel opened in the wall behind Retief's chair. Bright blue eyes peered out from under a white chef's cap.

"Givin' you the cold shoulder, heh, Mister?"

"Looks like it, old-timer," Retief said. "Maybe I'd better go join the skipper. His party seems to be having all the fun."

"Feller has to be mighty careless who he eats with to set over there."

11

"I see your point."

"You set right where you're at, Mister. I'll rustle you up a plate."

Five minutes later, Retief cut into a thirty-two ounce Delmonico backed up with mushrooms and garlic butter.

"I'm Chip," the chef said. "I don't like the Cap'n. You can tell him I said so. Don't like his friends, either. Don't like them dern Sweaties, look at a man like he was a worm."

"You've got the right idea on frying a steak, Chip. And you've got the right idea on the Soetti, too," Retief said. He poured red wine into a glass. "Here's to you."

"Dern right," Chip said. "Dunno who ever thought up broiling 'em. Steaks, that is. I got a Baked Alaska coming up in here for dessert. You like brandy in yer coffee?"

"Chip, you're a genius."

"Like to see a feller eat," Chip said. "I gotta go now. If you need anything, holler."

Retief ate slowly. Time always dragged on shipboard. Four days to Jorgensen's Worlds. Then, if Magnan's information was correct, there would be four days to prepare for the Soetti attack. It was a temptation to scan the tapes built into the handle of his suitcase. It would be good to know what Jorgensen's Worlds would be up against.

Retief finished the steak, and the chef passed out the baked Alaska and coffee. Most of the other passengers had left the dining room. Mr. Tony and his retainers still sat at the Captain's table.

As Retief watched, four men arose from the table and sauntered across the room. The first in line, a stony-faced thug with a broken ear, took a cigar from his mouth as he reached the table. He dipped the lighted end in Retief's coffee, looked at it, and dropped it on the tablecloth.

The others came up, Mr. Tony trailing.

"You must want to get to Jorgensen's pretty bad," the thug said in a grating voice. "What's your game, hick?"

Retief looked at the coffee cup, picked it up.

"I don't think I want my coffee," he said. He looked at the thug. "You drink it."

The thug squinted at Retief. "A wise hick," he began.

With a flick of the wrist, Retief tossed the coffee into the thug's face, then stood and slammed a straight right to the chin. The thug went down.

Retief looked at Mr. Tony, still standing open-mouthed.

"You can take your playmates away now, Tony," he said. "And don't bother to come around yourself. You're not funny enough."

Mr. Tony found his voice.

"Take him, Marbles!" he growled.

The thick-necked man slipped a hand inside his tunic and brought out a long-bladed knife. He licked his lips and moved in.

Retief heard the panel open beside him.

"Here you go, Mister," Chip said. Retief darted a glance; a well-honed french knife lay on the sill.

"Thanks, Chip," Retief said. "I won't need it for these punks."

Thick-neck lunged and Retief hit him square in the face, knocking him under the table. The other man stepped back, fumbling a power pistol from his shoulder holster.

"Aim that at me, and I'll kill you," Retief said.

"Go on, burn him!" Mr. Tony shouted. Behind him, the captain appeared, white-faced.

"Put that away, you!" he yelled. "What kind of—"

"Shut up," Mr. Tony said. "Put it away, Hoany. We'll fix this bum later."

"Not on this vessel, you won't," the captain said shakily. "I got my charter to consider."

"Ram your charter," Hoany said harshly. "You won't be needing it long."

"Button your floppy mouth, damn you!" Mr. Tony snapped. He looked at the man on the floor. "Get Marbles out of here. I ought to dump the slob."

He turned and walked away. The captain signaled and two waiters came up. Retief watched as they carted the casualty from the dining room.

The panel opened.

"I usta be about your size, when I was your age," Chip said. "You handled them pansies right. I wouldn't give 'em the time o' day."

"How about a fresh cup of coffee, Chip?" Retief said.

"Sure, Mister. Anything else?"

"I'll think of something," Retief said. "This is shaping up into one of those long days."

*

"They don't like me bringing yer meals to you in yer cabin," Chip said. "But the cap'n knows I'm the best cook in the Merchant Service. They won't mess with me."

13

"What has Mr. Tony got on the captain, Chip?" Retief asked.

"They're in some kind o' crooked business together. You want some more smoked turkey?"

"Sure. What have they got against my going to Jorgensen's Worlds?"

"Dunno. Hasn't been no tourists got in there fer six or eight months. I sure like a feller that can put it away. I was a big eater when I was yer age."

"I'll bet you can still handle it, Old Timer. What are Jorgensen's Worlds like?"

"One of 'em's cold as hell and three of 'em's colder. Most o' the Jorgies live on Svea; that's the least froze up. Man don't enjoy eatin' his own cookin' like he does somebody else's."

"That's where I'm lucky, Chip. What kind of cargo's the captain got aboard for Jorgensen's?"

"Derned if I know. In and out o' there like a grasshopper, ever few weeks. Don't never pick up no cargo. No tourists any more, like I says. Don't know what we even run in there for."

"Where are the passengers we have aboard headed?"

"To Alabaster. That's nine days' run in-sector from Jorgensen's. You ain't got another one of them cigars, have you?"

"Have one, Chip. I guess I was lucky to get space on this ship."

"Plenty o' space, Mister. We got a dozen empty cabins." Chip puffed the cigar alight, then cleared away the dishes, poured out coffee and brandy.

"Them Sweaties is what I don't like," he said.

Retief looked at him questioningly.

"You never seen a Sweaty? Ugly lookin' devils. Skinny legs, like a lobster; big chest, shaped like the top of a turnip; rubbery lookin' head. You can see the pulse beatin' when they get riled."

"I've never had the pleasure," Retief said.

"You prob'ly have it perty soon. Them devils board us nigh ever trip out. Act like they was the Customs Patrol or somethin'."

There was a distant clang, and a faint tremor ran through the floor.

"I ain't superstitious ner nothin'," Chip said. "But I'll be triple-damned if that ain't them boarding us now."

Ten minutes passed before bootsteps sounded outside the door, accompanied by a clicking patter. The doorknob rattled, then a heavy knock shook the door.

"They got to look you over," Chip whispered. "Nosy damn Sweaties."

"Unlock it, Chip." The chef opened the door.

"Come in, damn you," he said.

A tall and grotesque creature minced into the room, tiny hoof-like feet tapping on the floor. A flaring metal helmet shaded the deep-set compound eyes, and a loose mantle flapped around the knobbed knees. Behind the alien, the captain hovered nervously.

"Yo' papiss," the alien rasped.

"Who's your friend, Captain?" Retief said.

"Never mind; just do like he tells you."

"Yo' papiss," the alien said again.

"Okay," Retief said. "I've seen it. You can take it away now."

"Don't horse around," the captain said. "This fellow can get mean."

The alien brought two tiny arms out from the concealment of the mantle, clicked toothed pincers under Retief's nose.

"Quick, soft one."

"Captain, tell your friend to keep its distance. It looks brittle, and I'm tempted to test it."

"Don't start anything with Skaw; he can clip through steel with those snappers."

"Last chance," Retief said. Skaw stood poised, open pincers an inch from Retief's eyes.

"Show him your papers, you damned fool," the captain said hoarsely. "I got no control over Skaw."

*

The alien clicked both pincers with a sharp report, and in the same instant Retief half-turned to the left, leaned away from the alien and drove his right foot against the slender leg above the bulbous knee-joint. Skaw screeched and floundered, greenish fluid spattering from the burst joint.

"I told you he was brittle," Retief said. "Next time you invite pirates aboard, don't bother to call."

"Jesus, what did you do! They'll kill us!" the captain gasped, staring at the figure flopping on the floor.

"Cart poor old Skaw back to his boat," Retief said. "Tell him to pass the word. No more illegal entry and search of Terrestrial vessels in Terrestrial space."

"Hey," Chip said. "He's quit kicking."

The captain bent over Skaw, gingerly rolled him over. He leaned close and sniffed.

"He's dead." The captain stared at Retief. "We're all dead men," he said. "These Soetti got no mercy."

"They won't need it. Tell 'em to sheer off; their fun is over."

"They got no more emotions than a blue crab—"

"You bluff easily, Captain. Show a few guns as you hand the body back. We know their secret now."

"What secret? I—"

"Don't be no dumber than you got to, Cap'n," Chip said. "Sweaties die easy; that's the secret."

"Maybe you got a point," the captain said, looking at Retief. "All they got's a three-man scout. It could work."

He went out, came back with two crewmen. They hauled the dead alien gingerly into the hall.

"Maybe I can run a bluff on the Soetti," the captain said, looking back from the door. "But I'll be back to see you later."

"You don't scare us, Cap'n," Chip said. "Him and Mr. Tony and all his goons. You hit 'em where they live, that time. They're pals o' these Sweaties. Runnin' some kind o' crooked racket."

"You'd better take the captain's advice, Chip. There's no point in your getting involved in my problems."

"They'd of killed you before now, Mister, if they had any guts. That's where we got it over these monkeys. They got no guts."

"They act scared, Chip. Scared men are killers."

"They don't scare me none." Chip picked up the tray. "I'll scout around a little and see what's goin' on. If the Sweaties figure to do anything about that Skaw feller they'll have to move fast; they won't try nothin' close to port."

"Don't worry, Chip. I have reason to be pretty sure they won't do anything to attract a lot of attention in this sector just now."

Chip looked at Retief. "You ain't no tourist, Mister. I know that much. You didn't come out here for fun, did you?"

"That," Retief said, "would be a hard one to answer."

IV

Retief awoke at a tap on his door.

"It's me, Mister. Chip."

"Come on in."

The chef entered the room, locking the door.

"You shoulda had that door locked." He stood by the door, listening, then turned to Retief.

"You want to get to Jorgensen's perty bad, don't you, Mister?"

"That's right, Chip."

"Mr. Tony give the captain a real hard time about old Skaw. The Sweaties didn't say nothin'. Didn't even act surprised, just took the remains and pushed off. But Mr. Tony and that other crook they call Marbles, they was fit to be tied. Took the cap'n in his cabin and talked loud at him fer half a hour. Then the cap'n come out and give some orders to the Mate."

Retief sat up and reached for a cigar.

"Mr. Tony and Skaw were pals, eh?"

"He hated Skaw's guts. But with him it was business. Mister, you got a gun?"

"A 2mm needler. Why?"

"The orders cap'n give was to change course fer Alabaster. We're by-passin' Jorgensen's Worlds. We'll feel the course change any minute."

Retief lit the cigar, reached under the mattress and took out a short-barreled pistol. He dropped it in his pocket, looked at Chip.

"Maybe it was a good thought, at that. Which way to the Captain's cabin?"

*

"This is it," Chip said softly. "You want me to keep an eye on who comes down the passage?"

Retief nodded, opened the door and stepped into the cabin. The captain looked up from his desk, then jumped up.

"What do you think you're doing, busting in here?"

"I hear you're planning a course change, Captain."

"You've got damn big ears."

"I think we'd better call in at Jorgensen's."

"You do, huh?" the captain sat down. "I'm in command of this vessel," he said. "I'm changing course for Alabaster."

"I wouldn't find it convenient to go to Alabaster," Retief said. "So just hold your course for Jorgensen's."

"Not bloody likely."

"Your use of the word 'bloody' is interesting, Captain. Don't try to change course."

The captain reached for the mike on his desk, pressed the key.

"Power Section, this is the captain," he said. Retief reached across the desk, gripped the captain's wrist.

"Tell the mate to hold his present course," he said softly.

"Let go my hand, buster," the captain snarled. Eyes on Retief's, he eased a drawer open with his left hand, reached in. Retief kneed the drawer. The captain yelped and dropped the mike.

"You busted it, you—"

"And one to go," Retief said. "Tell him."

"I'm an officer of the Merchant Service!"

"You're a cheapjack who's sold his bridge to a pack of back-alley hoods."

"You can't put it over, hick."

"Tell him."

The captain groaned and picked up the mike. "Captain to Power Section," he said. "Hold your present course until you hear from me." He dropped the mike and looked up at Retief.

"It's eighteen hours yet before we pick up Jorgensen Control. You going to sit here and bend my arm the whole time?"

Retief released the captain's wrist and turned to the door.

"Chip, I'm locking the door. You circulate around, let me know what's going on. Bring me a pot of coffee every so often. I'm sitting up with a sick friend."

"Right, Mister. Keep an eye on that jasper; he's slippery."

"What are you going to do?" the captain demanded.

Retief settled himself in a chair.

"Instead of strangling you, as you deserve," he said, "I'm going to stay here and help you hold your course for Jorgensen's Worlds."

The captain looked at Retief. He laughed, a short bark.

"Then I'll just stretch out and have a little nap, farmer. If you feel like dozing off sometime during the next eighteen hours, don't mind me."

Retief took out the needler and put it on the desk before him.

"If anything happens that I don't like," he said, "I'll wake you up. With this."

*

"Why don't you let me spell you, Mister?" Chip said. "Four hours to go yet. You're gonna hafta be on yer toes to handle the landing."

"I'll be all right, Chip. You get some sleep."

"Nope. Many's the time I stood four, five watches runnin', back when I was yer age. I'll make another round."

Retief stood up, stretched his legs, paced the floor, stared at the repeater instruments on the wall. Things had gone quietly so far, but the landing would be another matter. The captain's absence from the bridge during the highly complex maneuvering would be difficult to explain . . . .

The desk speaker crackled.

"Captain, Officer of the Watch here. Ain't it about time you was getting up here with the orbit figures?"

Retief nudged the captain. He awoke with a start, sat up.

"Whazzat?" He looked wild-eyed at Retief.

"Watch officer wants orbit figures," Retief said, nodding toward the speaker.

The captain rubbed his eyes, shook his head, picked up the mike. Retief released the safety on the needler with an audible click.

"Watch Officer, I'll . . . ah . . . get some figures for you right away. I'm . . . ah . . . busy right now."

"What the hell you talking about, busy?" the speaker blared. "You ain't got them figures ready, you'll have a hell of a hot time getting 'em up in the next three minutes. You forgot your approach pattern or something?"

"I guess I overlooked it," the Captain said, looking sideways at Retief. "I've been busy."

"One for your side," Retief said. He reached for the captain.

"I'll make a deal," the captain squalled. "Your life for—"

Retief took aim and slammed a hard right to the captain's jaw. He slumped to the floor.

Retief glanced around the room, yanked wires loose from a motile lamp, trussed the man's hands and feet, stuffed his mouth with paper and taped it.

Chip tapped at the door. Retief opened it and the chef stepped inside, looking at the man on the floor.

"The jasper tried somethin', huh? Figured he would. What we goin' to do now?"

"The captain forgot to set up an approach, Chip. He outfoxed me."

"If we overrun our approach pattern," Chip said, "we can't make orbit at Jorgensen's on automatic. And a manual approach—"

"That's out. But there's another possibility."

Chip blinked. "Only one thing you could mean, Mister. But cuttin' out in a lifeboat in deep space is no picnic."

"They're on the port side, aft, right?"

Chip nodded. "Hot damn," he said. "Who's got the 'tater salad?"

"We'd better tuck the skipper away out of sight."

"In the locker."

The two men carried the limp body to a deep storage chest, dumped it in, closed the lid.

"He won't suffercate. Lid's a lousy fit."

Retief opened the door went into the corridor, Chip behind him.

"Shouldn't oughta be nobody around now," the chef said. "Everybody's mannin' approach stations."

*

At the D deck companionway, Retief stopped suddenly.

"Listen."

Chip cocked his head. "I don't hear nothin'," he whispered.

"Sounds like a sentry posted on the lifeboat deck," Retief said softly.

"Let's take him, Mister."

"I'll go down. Stand by, Chip."

Retief started down the narrow steps, half stair, half ladder. Halfway, he paused to listen. There was a sound of slow footsteps, then silence. Retief palmed the needler, went down the last steps quickly, emerged in the dim light of a low ceilinged room. The stern of a five-man lifeboat bulked before him.

"Freeze, you!" a cold voice snapped.

Retief dropped, rolled behind the shelter of the lifeboat as the whine of a power pistol echoed off metal walls. A lunge, and he was under the boat, on his feet. He jumped, caught the quick-access handle, hauled it down. The outer port cycled open.

Feet scrambled at the bow of the boat. Retief whirled and fired. The guard rounded into sight and fell headlong. Above, an alarm bell jangled. Retief stepped on a stanchion, hauled himself into the open port. A yell rang, then the clatter of feet on the stair.

"Don't shoot, Mister!" Chip shouted.

"All clear, Chip," Retief called.

"Hang on. I'm comin' with ya!"

Retief reached down, lifted the chef bodily through the port, slammed the lever home. The outer door whooshed, clanged shut.

"Take number two, tie in! I'll blast her off," Chip said. "Been through a hundred 'bandon ship drills . . . . "

Retief watched as the chef flipped levers, pressed a fat red button. The deck trembled under the lifeboat.

"Blew the bay doors," Chip said, smiling happily. "That'll cool them jaspers down." He punched a green button.

"Look out, Jorgensen's!" With an ear-splitting blast, the stern rockets fired, a sustained agony of pressure . . . .

Abruptly, there was silence. Weightlessness. Contracting metal pinged loudly. Chip's breathing rasped in the stillness.

"Pulled nine G's there for ten seconds," he gasped. "I gave her full emergency kick-off."

"Any armament aboard our late host?"

"A popgun. Time they get their wind, we'll be clear. Now all we got to do is set tight till we pick up a R and D from Svea Tower. Maybe four, five hours."

"Chip, you're a wonder," Retief said. "This looks like a good time to catch that nap."

"Me too," Chip said. "Mighty peaceful here, ain't it?"

There was a moment's silence.

"Durn!" Chip said softly.

Retief opened one eye. "Sorry you came, Chip?"

"Left my best carvin' knife jammed up 'tween Marbles' ribs," the chef said. "Comes o' doin' things in a hurry."

V

The blonde girl brushed her hair from her eyes and smiled at Retief.

"I'm the only one on duty," she said. "I'm Anne-Marie."

"It's important that I talk to someone in your government, Miss," Retief said.

The girl looked at Retief. "The men you want to see are Tove and Bo Bergman. They will be at the lodge by night-fall."

"Then it looks like we go to the lodge," Retief said. "Lead on, Anne-Marie."

"What about the boat?" Chip asked.

"I'll send someone to see to it tomorrow," the girl said.

"You're some gal," Chip said admiringly. "Dern near six feet, ain't ye? And built, too, what I mean."

They stepped out of the door into a whipping wind.

"Let's go across to the equipment shed and get parkas for you," Anne-Marie said. "It will be cold on the slopes."

"Yeah," Chip said, shivering. "I've heard you folks don't believe in ridin' ever time you want to go a few miles uphill in a blizzard."

"It will make us hungry," Anne-Marie said. "Then Chip will cook a wonderful meal for us all."

Chip blinked. "Been cookin' too long," he muttered. "Didn't know it showed on me that way."

Behind the sheds across the wind-scoured ramp abrupt peaks rose, snow-blanketed. A faint trail led across white slopes, disappearing into low clouds.

"The lodge is above the cloud layer," Anne-Marie said. "Up there the sky is always clear."

It was three hours later, and the sun was burning the peaks red, when Anne-Marie stopped, pulled off her woolen cap and waved at the vista below.

"There you see it," she said. "Our valley."

"It's a mighty perty sight," Chip gasped. "Anything this tough to get a look at ought to be."

Anne-Marie pointed. "There," she said. "The little red house by itself. Do you see it, Retief? It is my father's home-acre."

Retief looked across the valley. Gaily painted houses nestled together, a puddle of color in the bowl of the valley.

"I think you've led a good life there," he said.

Anne-Marie smiled brilliantly. "And this day, too, is good."

Relief smiled back. "Yes," he said. "This day is good."

"It'll be a durn sight better when I got my feet up to that big fire you was talking about, Annie," Chip said.

They climbed on, crossed a shoulder of broken rock, reached the final slope. Above, the lodge sprawled, a long low structure of heavy logs, outlined against the deep-blue twilight sky. Smoke billowed from stone chimneys at either end, and yellow light gleamed from the narrow windows, reflected on the snow. Men and women stood in groups of three or four, skis over their shoulders. Their voices and laughter rang in the icy air.

Anne-Marie whistled shrilly. Someone waved.

"Come," she said. "Meet all my friends."

A man separated himself from the group, walked down the slope to meet them.

"Anne-Marie," he called. "Welcome. It was a long day without you." He came up to them, hugged Anne-Marie, smiled at Retief.

"Welcome," he said. "Come inside and be warm."

They crossed the trampled snow to the lodge and pushed through a heavy door into a vast low-beamed hall, crowded with people, talking, singing, some sitting at long plank tables, others ringed around an eight-foot fireplace at the far side of the room. Anne-Marie led the way to a bench near the fire. She made introductions and found a stool to prop Chip's feet near the blaze.

Chip looked around.

"I never seen so many perty gals before," he said delightedly.

"Poor Chip," one girl said. "His feet are cold." She knelt to pull off his boots. "Let me rub them," she said.

A brunette with blue eyes raked a chestnut from the fire, cracked it and offered it to Retief. A tall man with arms like oak roots passed heavy beer tankards to the two guests.

"Tell us about the places you've seen," someone called. Chip emerged from a long pull at the mug, heaving a sigh.

"Well," he said. "I tell you I been in some places . . . . "

Music started up, rising above the clamor.

"Come, Retief," Anne-Marie said. "Dance with me."

Retief looked at her. "My thought exactly," he said.

*

Chip put down his mug and sighed. "Derned if I ever felt right at home so quick before," he said. "Just seems like these folks know all about me." He scratched behind his right ear. "Annie must o' called 'em up and told 'em our names an' all." He lowered his voice.

23

"They's some kind o' trouble in the air, though. Some o' the remarks they passed sounds like they're lookin' to have some trouble with the Sweaties. Don't seem to worry 'em none, though."

"Chip," Retief said, "how much do these people know about the Soetti?"

"Dunno," Chip said. "We useta touch down here, regler. But I always jist set in my galley and worked on ship models or somethin'. I hear the Sweaties been nosin' around here some, though."

Two girls came up to Chip. "Hey, I gotta go now, Mister," he said. "These gals got a idea I oughta take a hand in the kitchen."

"Smart girls," Retief said. He turned as Anne-Marie came up.

"Bo Bergman and Tove are not back yet," she said. "They stayed to ski after moonrise."

"That moon is something," Retief said. "Almost like day-light."

"They will come soon, now. Shall we go out to see the moonlight on the snow?"

Outside, long black shadows fell like ink on silver. The top of the cloud layer below glared white under the immense moon.

"Our sister world, Gota," Anne-Marie said. "Nearly as big as Svea. I would like to visit it someday, although they say it's all stone and ice."

"Anne-Marie," Retief said, "how many people live on Jorgensen's Worlds?"

"About fifteen million, most of us here on Svea. There are mining camps and ice-fisheries on Gota. No one lives on Vasa and Skone, but there are always a few hunters there."

"Have you ever fought a war?"

Anne-Marie turned to look at Retief.

"You are afraid for us, Retief," she said. "The Soetti will attack our worlds, and we will fight them. We have fought before. These planets were not friendly ones."

"I thought the Soetti attack would be a surprise to you," Retief said. "Have you made any preparation for it?"

"We have ten thousand merchant ships. When the enemy comes, we will meet them."

Retief frowned. "Are there any guns on this planet? Any missiles?"

Anne-Marie shook her head. "Bo Bergman and Tove have a plan of deployment—"

"Deployment, hell! Against a modern assault force you need modern armament."

"Look!" Anne-Marie touched Retief's arm. "They're coming now."

Two tall grizzled men came up the slope, skis over their shoulders. Anne-Marie went forward to meet them, Retief at her side.

The two came up, embraced the girl, shook hands with Retief, put down their skis.

"Welcome to Svea," Tove said. "Let's find a warm corner where we can talk."

*

Retief shook his head, smiling, as a tall girl with coppery hair offered a vast slab of venison.

"I've caught up," he said, "for every hungry day I ever lived."

Bo Bergman poured Retief's beer mug full.

"Our captains are the best in space," he said. "Our population is concentrated in half a hundred small cities all across the planet. We know where the Soetti must strike us. We will ram their major vessels with unmanned ships. On the ground, we will hunt them down with small-arms."

"An assembly line turning out penetration missiles would have been more to the point."

"Yes," Bo Bergman said. "If we had known."

"How long have you known the Soetti were planning to hit you?"

Tove raised his eyebrows.

"Since this afternoon," he said.

"How did you find out about it? That information is supposed in some quarters to be a well-guarded secret."

"Secret?" Tove said.

Chip pulled at Retief's arm.

"Mister," he said in Retief's ear. "Come here a minute."

Retief looked at Anne-Marie, across at Tove and Bo Bergman. He rubbed the side of his face with his hand.

"Excuse me," he said. He followed Chip to one side of the room.

"Listen!" Chip said. "Maybe I'm goin' bats, but I'll swear there's somethin' funny here. I'm back there mixin' a sauce knowed only to me and the devil and I be dog if them gals don't pass me ever dang spice I need, without me sayin' a word. Come to put my souffle in the oven—she's already set, right on the button at 350. An' just now I'm settin' lookin' at one of 'em bendin' over a tub o' apples—snazzy little brunette name of Leila—derned if she don't turn around and say—" Chip gulped.

"Never mind. Point is . . . . " His voice nearly faltered. "It's almost like these folks was readin' my mind!"

Retief patted Chip on the shoulder.

"Don't worry about your sanity, Old Timer," he said. "That's exactly what they're doing."

VI

"We've never tried to make a secret of it," Tove said. "But we haven't advertised it, either."

"It really isn't much," Bo Bergman said. "Not a mutant ability, our scholars say. Rather, it's a skill we've stumbled on, a closer empathy. We are few, and far from the old home world. We've had to learn to break down the walls we had built around our minds."

"Can you read the Soetti?" Retief asked.

Tove shook his head. "They're very different from us. It's painful to touch their minds. We can only sense the sub-vocalized thoughts of a human mind."

"We've seen very few of the Soetti," Bo Bergman said. "Their ships have landed and taken on stores. They say little to us, but we've felt their contempt. They envy us our worlds. They come from a cold land."

"Anne-Marie says you have a plan of defense," Retief said. "A sort of suicide squadron idea, followed by guerrilla warfare."

"It's the best we can devise, Retief. If there aren't too many of them, it might work."

Retief shook his head. "It might delay matters—but not much."

"Perhaps. But our remote control equipment is excellent. And we have plenty of ships, albeit unarmed. And our people know how to live on the slopes—and how to shoot."

"There are too many of them, Tove," Retief said. "They breed like flies and, according to some sources, they mature in a matter of months. They've been feeling their way into the sector for years now. Set up outposts on a thousand or so minor planets—cold ones, the kind they like. They want your worlds because they need living space."

"At least, your warning makes it possible for us to muster some show of force, Retief," Bo Bergman said. "That is better than death by ambush."

"Retief must not be trapped here," Anne-Marie said. "His small boat is useless now. He must have a ship."

"Of course," Tove said. "And—"

"My mission here—" Retief said.

"Retief," a voice called. "A message for you. The operator has phoned up a gram."

Retief unfolded the slip of paper. It was short, in verbal code, and signed by Magnan.

"You are recalled herewith," he read. "Assignment canceled. Agreement concluded with Soetti relinquishing all claims so-called Jorgensen system. Utmost importance that under no repeat no circumstances classified intelligence regarding Soetti be divulged to locals. Advise you depart instanter. Soetti occupation imminent."

Retief looked thoughtfully at the scrap of paper, then crumpled it and dropped it on the floor. He turned to Bo Bergman, took a tiny reel of tape from his pocket.

"This contains information," he said. "The Soetti attack plan, a defensive plan instructions for the conversion of a standard anti-acceleration unit into a potent weapon. If you have a screen handy, we'd better get started. We have about seventy-two hours."

*

In the Briefing Room at Svea Tower, Tove snapped off the projector.

"Our plan would have been worthless against that," he said. "We assumed they'd make their strike from a standard in-line formation. This scheme of hitting all our settlements simultaneously, in a random order from all points—we'd have been helpless."

"It's perfect for this defensive plan," Bo Bergman said. "Assuming this antiac trick works."

"It works," Retief said. "I hope you've got plenty of heavy power lead available."

"We export copper," Tove said.

"We'll assign about two hundred vessels to each settlement. Linked up, they should throw up quite a field."

"It ought to be effective up to about fifteen miles, I'd estimate," Tove said. "If it works as it's supposed to."

A red light flashed on the communications panel. Tove went to it, flipped a key.

"Tower, Tove here," he said.

"I've got a ship on the scope, Tove," a voice said. "There's nothing scheduled. ACI 228 by-passed at 1600 . . . . "

"Just one?"

"A lone ship, coming in on a bearing of 291/456/653. On manual, I'd say."

"How does this track key in with the idea of ACI 228 making a manual correction for a missed automatic approach?" Retief asked.

Tove talked to the tower, got a reply.

"That's it," he said.

"How long before he touches down?"

Tove glanced at a lighted chart. "Perhaps eight minutes."

"Any guns here?"

Tove shook his head.

"If that's old 228, she ain't got but the one 50mm rifle," Chip said. "She cain't figure on jumpin' the whole planet."

"Hard to say what she figures on," Retief said. "Mr. Tony will be in a mood for drastic measures."

"I wonder what kind o' deal the skunks got with the Sweaties," Chip said. "Prob'ly he gits to scavenge, after the Sweaties kill off the Jorgensens."

"He's upset about our leaving him without saying good-bye, Chip," Retief said. "And you left the door hanging open, too."

Chip cackled. "Old Mr. Tony don't look so good to the Sweaties now, hey, Mister?"

Retief turned to Bo Bergman.

"Chip's right," he said. "A Soetti died on the ship, and a tourist got through the cordon. Tony's out to redeem himself."

"He's on final now," the tower operator said. "Still no contact."

"We'll know soon enough what he has in mind," Tove said.

"Let's take a look."

Outside, the four men watched the point of fire grow, evolve into a ship ponderously settling to rest. The drive faded and cut; silence fell.

*

Inside the Briefing Room, the speaker called out. Bo Bergman went inside, talked to the tower, motioned to the others.

"—over to you," the speaker was saying. There was a crackling moment of silence; then another voice.

"—illegal entry. Send the two of them out. I'll see to it they're dealt with."

Tove flipped a key. "Switch me direct to the ship," he said.

"Right."

"You on ACI 228," Tove said. "Who are you?"

"What's that to you?"

"You weren't cleared to berth here. Do you have an emergency aboard?"

"Never mind that, you," the speaker rumbled. "I tracked the bird in. I got the lifeboat on the screen now. They haven't gone far in nine hours. Let's have 'em."

"You're wasting your time," Tove said.

There was a momentary silence.

"You think so, hah?" the speaker blared. "I'll put it to you straight. I see two guys on their way out in one minute, or I open up."

"He's bluffin'," Chip said. "The popgun won't bear on us."

"Take a look out the window," Retief said.

In the white glare of the moonlight, a loading cover swung open at the stern of the ship, dropped down and formed a sloping ramp. A squat and massive shape appeared in the opening, trundled down onto the snow-swept tarmac.

Chip whistled. "I told you the Captain was slippery," he muttered. "Where the devil'd he git that at?"

"What is it?" Tove asked.

"A tank," Retief said. "A museum piece, by the look of it."

"I'll say," Chip said. "That's a Bolo *Resartus*, Model M. Built mebbe two hunderd years ago in Concordiat times. Packs a wallop, too, I'll tell ye."

The tank wheeled, brought a gun muzzle to bear in the base of the tower.

"Send 'em out," the speaker growled. "Or I blast 'em out."

"One round in here, and I've had a wasted trip," Retief said. "I'd better go out."

"Wait a minute, Mister," Chip said. "I got the glimmerin's of a idear."

"I'll stall them," Tove said. He keyed the mike.

"ACI 228, what's your authority for this demand?"

"I know that machine," Chip said. "My hobby, old-time fightin' machines. Built a model of a *Resartus* once, inch to the foot. A beauty. Now, lessee . . . . "

VII

The icy wind blew snow crystals stingingly against Retief's face.

"Keep your hands in your pockets, Chip," he said. "Numb hands won't hack the program."

"Yeah." Chip looked across at the tank. "Useta think that was a perty thing, that *Resartus*," he said. "Looks mean, now."

"You're getting the target's-eye view," Retief said. "Sorry you had to get mixed up in this, Old Timer."

"Mixed myself in. Durn good thing, too." Chip sighed. "I like these folks," he said. "Them boys didn't like lettin' us come out here, but I'll give 'em credit. They seen it had to be this way, and they didn't set to moanin' about it."

"They're tough people, Chip."

"Funny how it sneaks up on you, ain't it, Mister? Few minutes ago we was eatin' high on the hog. Now we're right close to bein' dead men."

"They want us alive, Chip."

"It'll be a hairy deal, Mister," Chip said. "But t'hell with it. If it works, it works."

"That's the spirit."

"I hope I got them fields o' fire right—"

"Don't worry. I'll bet a barrel of beer we make it."

"We'll find out in about ten seconds," Chip said.

As they reached the tank, the two men broke stride and jumped. Retief leaped for the gun barrel, swung up astride it, ripped off the fur-lined leather cap he wore and, leaning forward, jammed it into the bore of the cannon. The chef sprang for a perch above the fore scanner antenna. With an angry *whuff!* anti-personnel charges slammed from apertures low on the sides of the vehicle. Retief swung around, pulled himself up on the hull.

"Okay, Mister," Chip called. "I'm going under." He slipped down the front of the tank, disappeared between the treads. Retief clambered up, took a position behind the turret, lay flat as it whirled angrily, sonar eyes searching for its tormentors. The vehicle shuddered, backed, stopped, moved forward, pivoted.

Chip reappeared at the front of the tank.

"It's stuck," he called. He stopped to breathe hard, clung as the machine lurched forward, spun to the right, stopped, rocking slightly.

"Take over here," Retief said. He crawled forward, watched as the chef pulled himself up, slipped down past him, feeling for the footholds between the treads. He reached the ground, dropped on his back, hitched himself under the dark belly of the tank. He groped, found the handholds, probed with a foot for the tread-jack lever.

The tank rumbled, backed quickly, turned left and right in a dizzying sine curve. Retief clung grimly, inches from the clashing treads.

The machine ground to a halt. Retief found the lever, braced his back, pushed. The lever seemed to give minutely. He set himself again, put both feet against the frozen bar and heaved.

With a dry rasp, it slid back. Immediately two heavy rods extended themselves, moved down to touch the pavement, grated. The left track creaked as the weight went off it. Suddenly the tank's drive raced, and Retief grabbed for a hold as the right tread clashed, heaved the fifty-ton machine forward. The jacks screeched as they scored the tarmac, then bit in. The tank pivoted, chips of pavement flying. The jacks extended, lifted the clattering left track clear of the surface as the tank spun like a hamstrung buffalo.

The tank stopped, sat silent, canted now on the extended jacks. Retief emerged from under the machine, jumped, pulled himself above the anti-personnel apertures as another charge rocked the tank. He clambered to the turret, crouched beside Chip. They waited, watching the entry hatch.

Five minutes passed.

"I'll bet Old Tony's givin' the chauffeur hell," Chip said.

The hatch cycled open. A head came cautiously into view in time to see the needler in Retief's hand.

"Come on out," Retief said.

The head dropped. Chip snaked forward to ram a short section of steel rod under the hatch near the hinge. The hatch began to cycle shut, groaned, stopped. There was a sound of metal failing, and the hatch popped open.

Retief half rose, aimed the needler. The walls of the tank rang as the metal splinters ricocheted inside.

"That's one keg o' beer I owe you, Mister," Chip said. "Now let's git outa here before the ship lifts and fries us."

*

"The biggest problem the Jorgensen's people will have is decontaminating the wreckage," Retief said.

Magnan leaned forward. "Amazing," he said. "They just keep coming, did they? Had they no inter-ship communication?"

31

"They had their orders," Retief said. "And their attack plan. They followed it."

"What a spectacle," Magnan said. "Over a thousand ships, plunging out of control one by one as they entered the stress-field."

"Not much of a spectacle," Retief said. "You couldn't see them. Too far away. They all crashed back in the mountains."

"Oh." Magnan's face fell. "But it's as well they did. The bacterial bombs—"

"Too cold for bacteria. They won't spread."

"Nor will the Soetti," Magnan said smugly, "thanks to the promptness with which I acted in dispatching you with the requisite data." He looked narrowly at Retief. "By the way, you're sure no ... ah ... message reached you after your arrival?"

"I got something," Retief said, looking Magnan in the eye. "It must have been a garbled transmission. It didn't make sense."

Magnan coughed, shuffled papers. "This information you've reported," he said hurriedly. "This rather fantastic story that the Soetti originated in the Cloud, that they're seeking a foothold in the main Galaxy because they've literally eaten themselves out of subsistence—how did you get it? The one or two Soetti we attempted to question, ah .... " Magnan coughed again. "There was an accident," he finished. "We got nothing from them."

"The Jorgensens have a rather special method of interrogating prisoners," Retief said. "They took one from a wreck, still alive but unconscious. They managed to get the story from him. He died of it."

"It's immaterial, actually," Magnan said. "Since the Soetti violated their treaty with us the day after it was signed. Had no intention of fair play. Far from evacuating the agreed areas, they had actually occupied half a dozen additional minor bodies in the Whate system."

Retief clucked sympathetically.

"You don't know who to trust, these days," he said.

Magnan looked at him coldly.

"Spare me your sarcasm, Mr. Retief," he said. He picked up a folder from his desk, opened it. "By the way, I have another little task for you, Retief. We haven't had a comprehensive wild-life census report from Brimstone lately—"

"Sorry," Retief said. "I'll be tied up. I'm taking a month off. Maybe more."

"What's that?" Magnan's head came up. "You seem to forget—"

"I'm trying, Mr. Councillor," Retief said. "Good-by now." He reached out and flipped the key. Magnan's face faded from the screen. Retief stood up.

"Chip," he said, "we'll crack that keg when I get back." He turned to Anne-Marie. "How long," he said, "do you think it will take you to teach me to ski by moonlight?"

GAMBLER'S WORLD

Retief paused before a tall mirror to check the overlap of the four sets of lapels that ornamented the vermilion cutaway of a First Secretary and Consul.

"Come along, Retief," Magnan said. "The Ambassador has a word to say to the staff before we go in."

"I hope he isn't going to change the spontaneous speech he plans to make when the Potentate impulsively suggests a trade agreement along the lines they've been discussing for the last two months."

"Your derisive attitude is uncalled for, Retief," Magnan said sharply. "I think you realize it's delayed your promotion in the Corps."

Retief took a last glance in the mirror. "I'm not sure I want a promotion," he said. "It would mean more lapels."

Ambassador Crodfoller pursed his lips, waiting until Retief and Magnan took places in the ring of Terrestrial diplomats around him.

"A word of caution only, gentlemen," he said. "Keep always foremost in your minds the necessity for our identification with the Nenni Caste. Even a hint of familiarity with lower echelons could mean the failure of the mission. Let us remember that the Nenni represent authority here on Petreac. Their traditions must be observed, whatever our personal preferences. Let's go along now. The Potentate will be making his entrance any moment."

Magnan came to Retief's side as they moved toward the salon.

"The Ambassador's remarks were addressed chiefly to you, Retief," he said. "Your laxness in these matters is notorious. Naturally, I believe firmly in democratic principles myself—"

"Have you ever had a feeling, Mr. Magnan, that there's a lot going on here that we don't know about?"

Magnan nodded. "Quite so. Ambassador Crodfoller's point exactly. Matters which are not of concern to the Nenni are of no concern to us."

"Another feeling I get is that the Nenni aren't very bright. Now suppose—"

"I'm not given to suppositions, Retief. We're here to implement the policies of the Chief of Mission. And I should dislike to be in the shoes of a member of the staff whose conduct jeopardized the agreement that will be concluded here tonight."

A bearer with a tray of drinks rounded a fluted column, shied as he confronted the diplomats, fumbled the tray, grabbed and sent a glass crashing to the floor.

34

Magnan leaped back, slapping at the purple cloth of his pants leg. Retief's hand shot out to steady the tray. The servant rolled terrified eyes.

"I'll take one of these, now that you're here," Retief said. He took a glass from the tray, winking at the servant.

"No harm done," he said. "Mr. Magnan's just warming up for the big dance."

A Nenni major-domo bustled up, rubbing his hands politely.

"Some trouble here?" he said. "What happened, Honorables, what, what . . . . "

"The blundering idiot," Magnan spluttered. "How dare—"

"You're quite an actor, Mr. Magnan," Retief said. "If I didn't know about your democratic principles, I'd think you were really mad."

The servant ducked his head and scuttled away.

"Has this fellow . . . . " The major-domo eyed the retreating bearer.

"I dropped my glass," Retief said. "Mr. Magnan's upset because he hates to see liquor wasted."

Retief turned to find himself face-to-face with Ambassador Crodfoller.

"I witnessed that," The Ambassador hissed. "By the goodness of Providence, the Potentate and his retinue haven't appeared yet. But I can assure you the servants saw it. A more un-Nenni-like display I would find it difficult to imagine!"

Retief arranged his features in an expression of deep interest.

"More un-Nenni-like, sir?" he said. "I'm not sure I—"

"Bah!" The Ambassador glared at Retief, "Your reputation has preceded you, sir. Your name is associated with a number of the most bizarre incidents in Corps history. I'm warning you; I'll tolerate nothing." He turned and stalked away.

"Ambassador-baiting is a dangerous sport, Retief," Magnan said.

Retief took a swallow of his drink. "Still," he said, "it's better than no sport at all."

"Your time would be better spent observing the Nenni mannerisms. Frankly, Retief, you're not fitting into the group at all well."

"I'll be candid with you, Mr. Magnan. The group gives me the willies."

"Oh, the Nenni are a trifle frivolous, I'll concede," Magnan said. "But it's with them that we must deal. And you'd be making a contribution to the overall mission if you merely abandoned that rather arrogant manner of yours." Magnan looked at Retief critically. "You can't help your height, of course. But couldn't you curve your back just a bit—and possibly assume a more placating expression? Just act a little more . . . . "

"Girlish?"

"Exactly." Magnan nodded, then looked sharply at Retief.

Retief drained his glass and put it on a passing tray.

"I'm better at acting girlish when I'm well juiced," he said. "But I can't face another sorghum-and-soda. I suppose it would be un-Nenni-like to slip the bearer a credit and ask for a Scotch and water."

"Decidedly." Magnan glanced toward a sound across the room.

"Ah, here's the Potentate now!" He hurried off.

Retief watched the bearers coming and going, bringing trays laden with drinks, carrying off empties. There was a lull in the drinking now, as the diplomats gathered around the periwigged Chief of State and his courtiers. Bearers loitered near the service door, eyeing the notables. Retief strolled over to the service door, pushed through it into a narrow white-tiled hall filled with the odors of the kitchen. Silent servants gaped as he passed, watching as he moved along to the kitchen door and stepped inside.

II

A dozen or more low-caste Petreacans, gathered around a long table in the center of the room looked up, startled. A heap of long-bladed bread knives, French knives, carving knives and cleavers lay in the center of the table. Other knives were thrust into belts or held in the hands of the men. A fat man in the yellow sarong of a cook stood frozen in the act of handing a knife to a tall one-eyed sweeper.

Retief took one glance, then let his eyes wander to a far corner of the room. Humming a careless little tune, he sauntered across to the open liquor shelves, selected a garish green bottle and turned unhurriedly back toward the door. The group of servants watched him, transfixed.

As Retief reached the door, it swung inward. Magnan, lips pursed, stood in the doorway.

"I had a premonition," he said.

"I'll bet it was a dandy," Retief said. "You must tell me all about it—in the salon."

"We'll have this out right here," Magnan snapped. "I've warned you!" Magnan's voice trailed off as he took in the scene around the table.

"After you," Retief said, nudging Magnan toward the door.

"What's going on here?" Magnan barked. He stared at the men, started around Retief. A hand stopped him.

"Let's be going," Retief said, propelling Magnan toward the hall.

"Those knives!" Magnan yelped. "Take your hands off me, Retief! What are you men—?"

Retief glanced back. The fat cook gestured suddenly, and the men faded back. The cook stood, arm cocked, a knife across his palm.

"Close the door and make no sound," he said softly.

Magnan pressed back against Retief. "Let's . . . r-run . . . . " he faltered.

Retief turned slowly, put his hands up.

"I don't run very well with a knife in my back," he said. "Stand very still, Magnan, and do just what he tells you."

"Take them out through the back," the cook said.

"What does he mean?" Magnan spluttered. "Here, you—"

"Silence," the cook said, almost casually. Magnan gaped at him, closed his mouth.

Two of the men with knives came to Retief's side and gestured, grinning broadly.

"Let's go, peacocks," one said.

Retief and Magnan silently crossed the kitchen, went out the back door, stopped on command and stood waiting. The sky was brilliant with stars. A gentle breeze stirred the tree-tops beyond the garden. Behind them the servants talked in low voices.

"You go too, Illy," the cook was saying.

"Do it here," another said.

"And carry their damn dead bodies down?"

"Pitch 'em behind the hedge."

"I said the river. Three of you is plenty for a couple of Nenni. We don't know if we want to—"

"They're foreigners, not Nenni. We don't know—"

"So they're foreign Nenni. Makes no difference. I've seen them. I need every man here; now get going."

"What about the big guy? He looks tough."

"Him? He waltzed into the room and didn't notice a thing. But watch the other one."

At a prod from a knife point, Retief moved off down the walk, two of the escort behind him and Magnan, another going ahead to scout the way.

Magnan moved closer to Retief.

"Say," he said in a whisper. "That fellow in the lead; isn't he the one who spilled the drink? The one you took the blame for?"

"That's him, all right. He doesn't seem nervous any more, I notice."

"You saved him from serious punishment," Magnan said. "He'll be grateful; he'll let us go."

"Better check with the fellows with the knives before you act on that."

"Say something to him," Magnan hissed, "Remind him."

THE lead man fell back in line with Retief and Magnan.

"These two are scared of you," he said, grinning and jerking a thumb toward the knife-handlers. "They haven't worked around the Nenni like me; they don't know you."

"Don't you recognize this gentleman?" Magnan said.

"He did me a favor," the man said. "I remember."

"What's it all about?" Retief asked.

"The revolution. We're taking over now."

"Who's 'we'?"

"The People's Anti-Fascist Freedom League."

"What are all the knives for?"

"For the Nenni; and for all you foreigners."

"What do you mean?" Magnan gasped.

"We'll slit all the throats at one time. Saves a lot of running around."

"What time will that be?"

"Just at dawn; and dawn comes early, this time of year. By full daylight the PAFFL will be in charge."

"You'll never succeed," Magnan said. "A few servants with knives! You'll all be caught and killed."

"By who, the Nenni?" the man laughed. "You Nenni are a caution."

"But we're not Nenni—"

"We've watched you; you're the same. You're part of the same blood-sucking class."

"There are better ways to, uh, adjust differences," Magnan said. "This killing won't help you, I'll personally see to it that your grievances are heard in the Corps Courts. I can assure you that the plight of the downtrodden workers will be alleviated. Equal rights for all—"

"These threats won't work," the man said. "You don't scare me."

"Threats? I'm promising *relief* to the exploited classes of Petreac!"

"You must be nuts," the man said. "You trying to upset the system or something?"

"Isn't that the purpose of your revolution?"

"Look, Nenni, we're tired of you Nenni getting all the graft. We want our turn. What good would it do us to run Petreac if there's no loot?"

"You mean you intend to oppress the people? But they're your own group."

"Group, schmoop. We're taking all the chances; we're doing the work. We deserve the payoff. You think we're throwing up good jobs for the fun of it?"

"You're basing a revolt on these cynical premises?"

"Wise up, Nenni. There's never been a revolution for any other reason."

"Who's in charge of this?" Retief said.

"Shoke, the head chef."

"I mean the big boss. Who tells Shoke what all to do?"

"Oh, that's Zorn. Look out, here's where we start down the slope. It's slippery."

"Look," Magnan said. "You."

"My name's Illy."

"Mr. Illy, this man showed you mercy when he could have had you beaten."

"Keep moving. Yeah, I said I was grateful."

"Yes," Magnan said, swallowing hard. "A noble emotion, gratitude. You won't regret it."

"I always try to pay back a good turn," Illy said. "Watch your step now on this sea-wall."

"You'll never regret it," Magnan said.

"This is far enough," Illy motioned to one of the knife men. "Give me your knife, Vug."

The man passed his knife to Illy. There was an odor of sea-mud and kelp. Small waves slapped against the stones of the sea-wall. The wind was stronger here.

"I know a neat stroke," Illy said. "Practically painless. Who's first?"

"What do you mean?" Magnan quavered.

"I *said* I was grateful. I'll do it myself, give you a nice clean job. You know these amateurs; botch it up and have a guy floppin' around, yellin' and spatterin' everybody up."

"I'm first," Retief said. He pushed past Magnan, stopped suddenly, drove a straight punch at Illy's mouth.

THE long blade flicked harmlessly over Retief's shoulder as Illy fell. Retief whirled, leaped past Magnan, took the unarmed servant by the throat and belt, lifted him and slammed him against the third man. Both scrambled, yelped and fell from the sea-wall into the water.

Retief turned back to Illy. He pulled off the man's belt and strapped his hands together.

Magnan found his voice.

"You . . . . we . . . . they . . . . "

"I know," Retief said.

"We've got to get back," Magnan said, "Warn them!"

"We'd never get through the rebel cordon around the palace. And if we did, trying to give an alarm would only set the assassinations off early."

"We can't just . . . . "

"We've got to go to the source; this fellow Zorn. Get him to call it off."

"We'd be killed! At least we're safe here."

Illy groaned and opened his eyes. He sat up.

"On your feet, Illy," Retief said.

Illy looked around. "I'm sick," he said.

"The damp air is bad for you. Let's be going." Retief pulled the man to his feet. "Where does Zorn stay when he's in town?" he demanded.

"What happened? Where's Vug and . . . . "

"They had an accident. Fell in the pond."

Illy gazed down at the restless black water.

"I guess I had you Nenni figured wrong."

"Us Nenni have hidden qualities. Let's get moving before Vug and Slug make it to shore and start it all over again."

"No hurry," Illy said. "They can't swim." He spat into the water. "So long, Vug. So long, Toscin. Take a pull, at the Hell Horn for me." He started off along the sea wall toward the sound of the surf.

"You want to see Zorn, I'll take you to see Zorn," he said. "I can't swim either."

III

"I take it," Retief said, "that the casino is a front for his political activities."

"He makes plenty off it. This PAFFL is a new kick. I never heard about it until maybe a couple months ago."

Retief motioned toward a dark shed with an open door.

"We'll stop here," he said, "long enough to strip the gadgets off these uniforms."

Illy, hands strapped behind his back, stood by and watched as Retief and Magnan removed medals, ribbons, orders and insignia from the formal diplomatic garments.

"This may help some," Retief said, "if the word is out that two diplomats are loose."

"It's a breeze," Illy said. "We see cats in purple and orange tailcoats all the time."

"I hope you're right," Retief said. "But if we're called, you'll be the first to go, Illy."

"You're a funny kind of Nenni," Illy said, eyeing Retief, "Toscin and Vug must be wonderin' what happened to 'em."

"If you think I'm good at drowning people, you ought to see me with a knife. Let's get going."

"It's only a little way now," Illy said. "But you better untie me. Somebody's liable to stick their nose in and get me killed."

"I'll take the chance. How do we get to the casino?"

"We follow this street. It twists around and goes under a couple tunnels. When we get to the Drunkard's Stairs we go up and it's right in front of us. A pink front with a sign like a big Luck Wheel."

"Give me your belt, Magnan," Retief said.

Magnan handed it over.

"Lie down, Illy," Retief said.

The servant looked at Retief.

"Vug and Toscin will be glad to see me," he said. "But they'll never believe me." He lay down. Retief strapped his feet together and stuffed a handkerchief in his mouth.

"Why are you doing that?" Magnan asked. "We need him."

"We know the way. And we don't need anyone to announce our arrival. It's only on three-dee that you can march a man through a gang of his pals with a finger in his back."

Magnan looked at the man. "Maybe you'd better, uh, cut his throat," he said. Illy rolled his eyes.

"That's a very un-Nenni-like suggestion, Mr. Magnan," Retief said. "If we have any trouble finding the casino, I'll give it serious thought."

There were few people in the narrow street. Shops were shuttered, windows dark.

"Maybe they heard about the coup," Magnan said. "They're lying low."

"More likely, they're at the palace picking up their knives."

41

RETIEF: THE DIRTY DOZEN

They rounded a corner, stepped over a man curled in the gutter snoring heavily and found themselves at the foot of a long flight of littered stone steps.

"The Drunkard's Stairs are plainly marked," Magnan sniffed.

"I hear sounds up there," Retief said. "Sounds of merrymaking."

"Maybe we'd better go back."

"Merrymaking doesn't scare me," Retief said. "Come to think of it, I don't know what the word means." He started up, Magnan behind him.

AT the top of the long stair a dense throng milled in the alley-like street.

A giant illuminated roulette wheel revolved slowly above them. A loudspeaker blared the chant of the croupiers from the tables inside. Magnan and Retief moved through the crowd toward the wide-open doors.

Magnan plucked at Retief's sleeve. "Are you sure we ought to push right in like this? Maybe we ought to wait a bit, look around . . . . "

"When you're where you have no business being," Retief said, "always stride along purposefully. If you loiter, people begin to get curious."

Inside, a mob packed the wide, low-ceilinged room, clustered around gambling devices in the form of towers, tables and basins.

"What do we do now?" Magnan asked.

"We gamble. How much money do you have in your pockets?"

"Why . . . a few credits." Magnan handed the money to Retief. "But what about the man Zorn?"

"A purple cutaway is conspicuous enough, without ignoring the tables," Retief said. "We've got a hundred credits between us. We'll get to Zorn in due course, I hope."

"Your pleasure, gents," a bullet-headed man said, eyeing the colorful evening clothes of the diplomats. "You'll be wantin' to try your luck at the Zoop tower, I'd guess. A game for real sporting gents."

"Why . . . ah . . . " Magnan said.

"What's a zoop tower?" Retief asked.

"Out-of-towners, hey?" The bullet-headed man shifted his dope-stick to the other corner of his mouth. "Zoop is a great little game. Two teams of players buy into the pot. Each player takes a lever; the object is to make the ball drop from the top of the tower into your net. Okay?"

"What's the ante?"

"I got a hundred-credit pot workin' now, gents."

Retief nodded. "We'll try it."

The shill led the way to an eight-foot tower mounted on gimbals. Two perspiring men in trade-class pullovers gripped two of the levers that controlled the tilt of the tower. A white ball lay in a hollow in the thick glass platform at the top. From the center, an intricate pattern of grooves led out to the edge of the glass. Retief and Magnan took chairs before the two free levers.

"When the light goes on, gents, work the lever to jack the tower. You got three gears. Takes a good arm to work top gear. That's this button here. The little knob controls what way you're goin'. May the best team win. I'll take the hundred credits now."

*

Retief handed over the money. A red light flashed on, and Retief tried the lever.

It moved easily, with a ratcheting sound. The tower trembled, slowly tilted toward the two perspiring workmen pumping frantically at their levers. Magnan started slowly, accelerated as he saw the direction the tower was taking.

"Faster, Retief," he said. "They're winning."

"This is against the clock, gents," the bullet-headed man said. "If nobody wins when the light goes off, the house takes all."

"Crank it over to the left," Retief said.

"I'm getting tired."

"Shift to a lower gear."

The tower leaned. The ball stirred, rolled into a concentric channel. Retief shifted to middle gear, worked the lever. The tower creaked to a stop, started back upright.

"There isn't any lower gear," Magnan gasped. One of the two on the other side of the tower shifted to middle gear; the other followed suit. They worked harder now, heaving against the stiff levers. The tower quivered, moved slowly toward their side.

"I'm exhausted," Magnan gasped. He dropped the lever, lolled back in the chair, gulping air. Retief shifted position, took Magnan's lever with his left hand.

"Shift it to middle gear," Retief said. Magnan gulped, punched the button and slumped back, panting.

"My arm," he said. "I've injured myself."

The two men in pullovers conferred hurriedly as they cranked their levers; then one punched a button and the other reached across, using his left arm to help.

"They've shifted to high," Magnan said. "Give up, it's hopeless."

"Shift me to high," Retief said. "Both buttons!"

Magnan complied. Retief's shoulders bulged. He brought one lever down, then the other, alternately, slowly at first, then faster. The tower jerked, tilted toward him, farther . . . . The ball rolled in the channel, found an outlet—

Abruptly, both Retief's levers froze.

The tower trembled, wavered and moved back. Retief heaved. One lever folded at the base, bent down and snapped off short. Retief braced his feet, took the other lever with both hands and pulled.

There was a rasp of metal friction, and a loud twang. The lever came free, a length of broken cable flopping into view. The tower fell over as the two on the other side scrambled aside.

"Hey!" Bullet-head yelled. "You wrecked my equipment!"

Retief got up and faced him.

"Does Zorn know you've got your tower rigged for suckers?"

"You tryin' to call me a cheat or something?"

The crowd had fallen back, ringing the two men. Bullet-head glanced around. With a lightning motion, he plucked a knife from somewhere.

"That'll be five hundred credits for the equipment," he said. "Nobody calls Kippy a cheat."

*

Retief picked up the broken lever.

"Don't make me hit you with this, you cheap chiseler."

Kippy looked at the bar.

"Comin' in here," he said indignantly, looking to the crowd for support. "Bustin' up my rig, callin' names . . . . "

"I want a hundred credits," Retief said. "Now."

"Highway robbery!" Kippy yelled.

"Better pay up," somebody called.

"Hit him, mister," someone else said.

A broad-shouldered man with graying hair pushed through the crowd and looked around. "You heard 'em, Kippy. Give," he said.

The shill growled but tucked his knife away. Reluctantly he peeled a bill from a fat roll and handed it over.

The newcomer looked from Retief to Magnan.

"Pick another game, strangers," he said. "Kippy made a little mistake."

"This is small-time stuff," Retief said. "I'm interested in something big."

The broad-shouldered man lit a perfumed dope stick. "What would you call big?" he said softly.

"What's the biggest you've got?"

The man narrowed his eyes, smiling. "Maybe you'd like to try Slam."

"Tell me about it."

"Over here." The crowd opened up, made a path. Retief and Magnan followed across the room to a brightly-lit glass-walled box.

There was an arm-sized opening at waist height. Inside was a hand grip. A two-foot plastic globe a quarter full of chips hung in the center. Apparatus was mounted at the top of the box.

"Slam pays good odds," the man said. "You can go as high as you like. Chips cost you a hundred credits. You start it up by dropping a chip in here." He indicated a slot.

"You take the hand grip. When you squeeze, it unlocks. The globe starts to turn. You can see, it's full of chips. There's a hole at the top. As long as you hold the grip, the bowl turns. The harder you squeeze, the faster it turns. Eventually it'll turn over to where the hole is down, and chips fall out.

"On the other hand, there's contact plates spotted around the bowl. When one of 'em lines up with a live contact, you get quite a little jolt—guaranteed nonlethal. All you've got to do is hold on long enough, and you'll get the payoff."

"How often does this random pattern put the hole down?"

"Anywhere from three minutes to fifteen, with the average run of players. Oh, by the way, one more thing. That lead block up there—" The man motioned with his head toward a one-foot cube suspended by a thick cable. "It's rigged to drop every now and again. Averages five minutes. A warning light flashes first. You can take a chance; sometimes the light's a bluff. You can set the clock back on it by dropping another chip—or you can let go the grip."

Retief looked at the massive block of metal.

"That would mess up a man's dealing hand, wouldn't it?"

"The last two jokers who were too cheap to feed the machine had to have 'em off. Their arms, I mean. That lead's heavy stuff."

"I don't suppose your machine has a habit of getting stuck, like Kippy's?"

The broad-shouldered man frowned.

"You're a stranger," he said, "You don't know any better."

"It's a fair game, Mister," someone called.

"Where do I buy the chips?"

The man smiled. "I'll fix you up. How many?"

"One."

"A big spender, eh?" The man snickered, but handed over a large plastic chip.

IV

Retief stepped to the machine, dropped the coin.

"If you want to change your mind," the man said, "you can back out now. All it'll cost you is the chip you dropped."

Retief reached through the hole, took the grip. It was leather padded hand-filling. He squeezed it. There was a click and bright lights sprang up. The crowd ah!-ed. The globe began to twirl lazily. The four-inch hole at its top was plainly visible.

"If ever the hole gets in position it will empty very quickly," Magnan said, hopefully.

Suddenly, a brilliant white light flooded the glass cage. A sound went up from the spectators.

"Quick, drop a chip," someone called.

"You've only got ten seconds . . . . "

"Let go!" Magnan yelped.

Retief sat silent, holding the grip, frowning up at the weight. The globe twirled faster now. Then the bright white light winked off.

"A bluff!" Magnan gasped.

"That's risky, stranger," the gray-templed man said.

The globe was turning rapidly now, oscillating from side to side. The hole seemed to travel in a wavering loop, dipping lower, swinging up high, then down again.

"It has to move to the bottom soon," Magnan said. "Slow it down."

"The slower it goes, the longer it takes to get to the bottom," someone said.

There was a crackle and Retief stiffened. Magnan heard a sharp intake of breath. The globe slowed, and Retief shook his head, blinking.

The broad-shouldered man glanced at a meter.

"You took pretty near a full jolt, that time," he said.

The hole in the globe was tracing an oblique course now, swinging to the center, then below.

"A little longer," Magnan said.

"That's the best speed I ever seen on the Slam ball," someone said. "How much longer can he hold it?"

Magnan looked at Retief's knuckles. They showed white against the grip. The globe tilted farther, swung around, then down; two chips fell out, clattered down a chute and into a box.

"We're ahead," Magnan said. "Let's quit."

Retief shook his head. The globe rotated, dipped again; three chips fell.

"She's ready," someone called.

"It's bound to hit soon," another voice added excitedly. "Come on, Mister!"

"Slow down," Magnan said. "So it won't move past too quickly."

"Speed it up, before that lead block gets you," someone called.

The hole swung high, over the top, then down the side. Chips rained out of the hole, six, eight . . . .

"Next pass," a voice called.

The white light flooded the cage. The globe whirled; the hole slid over the top, down, down . . . . A chip fell, two more . . . .

Retief half rose, clamped his jaw and crushed the grip. Sparks flew. The globe slowed, chips spewing. It stopped, swung back, weighted by the mass of chips at the bottom, and stopped again with the hole centered.

Chips cascaded down the chute, filled the box before Retief, spilled on the floor. The crowd yelled.

Retief released the grip and withdrew his arm at the same instant that the lead block slammed down.

"Good lord," Magnan said. "I felt that through the floor."

Retief turned to the broad-shouldered man.

"This game's all right for beginners," he said. "But I'd like to talk a really big gamble. Why don't we go to your office, Mr. Zorn?"

*

"Your proposition interests me," Zorn said, grinding out the stump of his dope stick in a brass ashtray. "But there's some angles to this I haven't mentioned yet."

"You're a gambler, Zorn, not a suicide," Retief said. "Take what I've offered. The other idea was fancier, I agree, but it won't work."

"How do I know you birds aren't lying?" Zorn snarled. He stood up, strode up and down the room. "You walk in here and tell me I'll have a task force on my neck, that the Corps won't recognize my regime. Maybe you're right. But I've got other contacts. They say different." He whirled, stared at Retief.

"I have pretty good assurance that once I put it over, the Corps will have to recognize me as the legal government of Petreac. They won't meddle in internal affairs."

"Nonsense," Magnan spoke up. "The Corps will never deal with a pack of criminals calling themselves—"

"Watch your language, you!" Zorn rasped.

"I'll admit Mr. Magnan's point is a little weak," Retief said. "But you're overlooking something. You plan to murder a dozen or so officers of the Corps Diplomatique Terrestrienne along with the local wheels. The corps won't overlook that. It can't."

"Their tough luck they're in the middle," Zorn muttered.

"Our offer is extremely generous, Mr. Zorn," Magnan said. "The post you'll get will pay you very well indeed. As against the certain failure of your planned coup, the choice should be simple."

Zorn eyed Magnan. "Offering me a job—it sounds phony as hell. I thought you birds were goody-goody diplomats."

"It's time you knew," Retief said. "There's no phonier business in the Galaxy than diplomacy."

"You'd better take it, Mr. Zorn," Magnan said.

"Don't push me, Junior!" Zorn said. "You two walk into my headquarters empty-handed and big-mouthed. I don't know what I'm talking to you for. The answer is no. N-I-X, no!"

"Who are you afraid of?" Retief said softly.

Zorn glared at him.

"Where do you get that 'afraid' routine? I'm top man here!"

"Don't kid around, Zorn. Somebody's got you under their thumb. I can see you squirming from here."

*

"What if I let your boys alone?" Zorn said suddenly. "The Corps won't have anything to say then, huh?"

"The Corps has plans for Petreac, Zorn. You aren't part of them. A revolution right now isn't part of them. Having the Potentate and the whole Nenni caste slaughtered isn't part of them. Do I make myself clear?"

"Listen," Zorn said urgently, pulling a chair around. "I'll tell you guys a few things. You ever heard of a world they call Rotune?"

"Certainly," Magnan said. "It's a near neighbor of yours. Another backward—that is, emergent—"

"Okay," Zorn said. "You guys think I'm a piker, do you? Well, let me wise you up. The Federal Junta on Rotune is backing my play. I'll be recognized by Rotune, and the Rotune fleet will stand by in case I need any help. I'll present the CDT with what you call a *fait accompli*."

"What does Rotune get out of this? I thought they were your traditional enemies."

"Don't get me wrong. I've got no use for Rotune; but our interests happen to coincide right now."

"Do they?" Retief smiled grimly. "You can spot a sucker as soon as he comes through that door out there—but you go for a deal like this!"

"What do you mean?" Zorn looked angrily at Retief. "It's fool-proof."

"After you get in power, you'll be fast friends with Rotune, is that it?"

"Friends, hell! Just give me time to get set, and I'll square a few things with that—"

"Exactly. And what do you suppose they have in mind for you?"

"What are you getting at?"

"Why is Rotune interested in your take-over?"

Zorn studied Retief's face. "I'll tell you why," he said. "It's you birds. You and your trade agreement. You're here to tie Petreac into some kind of trade combine. That cuts Rotune out. Well, we're doing all right out here. We don't need any commitments to a lot of fancy-pants on the other side of the Galaxy."

"That's what Rotune has sold you, eh?" Retief said, smiling.

"Sold, nothing!"

*

Zorn ground out his dope-stick, lit another. He snorted angrily.

"Okay; what's your idea?" he asked after a moment.

"You know what Petreac is getting in the way of imports as a result of the agreement?"

"Sure. A lot of junk."

"To be specific," Retief said, "there'll be 50,000 Tatone B-3 dry washers; 100,000 Glo-float motile lamps; 100,000 Earthworm Minor garden cultivators; 25,000 Veco space heaters; and 75,000 replacement elements for Ford Monomeg drives."

"Like I said. A lot of junk."

Retief leaned back, looking sardonically at Zorn, "Here's the gimmick, Zorn," he said. "The Corps is getting a little tired of Petreac and Rotune carrying on their two-penny war out here. Your privateers have a nasty habit of picking on innocent bystanders. After studying both sides, the Corps has decided Petreac would be a little easier to do business with. So this trade agreement was worked out. The Corps can't openly sponsor an arms shipment to a belligerent. But personal appliances are another story."

"So what do we do—plow 'em under with back-yard cultivators?" Zorn looked at Retief, puzzled. "What's the point?"

"You take the sealed monitor unit from the washer, the repeller field generator from the lamp, the converter control from the cultivator, et cetera, et cetera. You fit these together according to some very simple instructions. Presto! You have one hundred thousand Standard-class Y hand blasters. Just the thing to turn the tide in a stalemated war fought with obsolete arms."

"Good lord!" Magnan said. "Retief, are you—"

"I have to tell him," Retief said. "He has to know what he's putting his neck into."

"Weapons, hey?" Zorn said. "And Rotune knows about it?"

"Sure they know about it. It's not too hard to figure out. And there's more. They want the CDT delegation included in the massacre for a reason. It will put Petreac out of the picture; the trade agreement will go to Rotune; and you and your new regime will find yourselves looking down the muzzles of your own blasters."

Zorn threw his dope-stick to the floor with a snarl.

"I should have smelled something when that Rotune smoothie made his pitch." Zorn looked at his watch.

"I've got two hundred armed men in the palace. We've got about forty minutes to get over there before the rocket goes up."

V

"You'd better stay here on this terrace out of the way until I've spread the word," Zorn said. "Just in case."

"Let me caution you against any . . . ah . . . slip-ups, Mr. Zorn," Magnan said. "The Nenni are not to be molested—"

Zorn looked at Retief.

"Your friend talks too much," he said. "I'll keep my end of it. He'd better keep his."

"Nothing's happened yet, you're sure?" Magnan said.

"I'm sure," Zorn said. "Ten minutes to go. Plenty of time."

"I'll just step into the salon to assure myself that all is well," Magnan said.

"Suit yourself," Zorn said. "Just stay clear of the kitchen, or you'll get your throat cut." He sniffed at his dope-stick. "What's keeping Shoke?" he muttered.

Magnan stepped to a tall glass door, eased it open and poked his head through the heavy draperies. As he moved to draw back, a voice was faintly audible. Magnan paused, head still through the drapes.

"What's going on there?" Zorn rasped. He and Retief stepped up behind Magnan.

"—breath of air, ha-ha," Magnan was saying.

"Well, come along, Magnan!" Ambassador Crodfoller's voice snapped.

Magnan shifted from one foot to the other then pushed through the drapes.

"Where've you been, Mr. Magnan?" The Ambassador's voice was sharp.

"Oh . . . ah . . . a slight accident, Mr. Ambassador."

"What's happened to your shoes? Where are your insignia and decorations?"

"I—ah—spilled a drink on them. Sir. Ah—listen . . . . "

The sound of an orchestra came up suddenly, blaring a fanfare.

Zorn shifted restlessly, ear against the glass.

"What's your friend pulling?" he rasped. "I don't like this."

"Keep cool, Zorn," Retief said. "Mr. Magnan is doing a little emergency salvage on his career."

The music died away with a clatter.

"—My God," Ambassador Crodfoller's voice was faint. "Magnan, you'll be knighted for this. Thank God you reached me. Thank God it's not too late. I'll find some excuse. I'll get a gram off at once."

"But you—"

"It's all right, Magnan. You were in time. Another ten minutes and the agreement would have been signed and transmitted. The wheels would have been put in motion. My career ruined . . . . "

Retief felt a prod at his back. He turned.

"Doublecrossed," Zorn said softly. "So much for the word of a diplomat."

*

Retief looked at the short-barreled needler in Zorn's hand.

"I see you hedge your bets, Zorn," he said.

"We'll wait here," Zorn said, "until the excitement's over inside. I wouldn't want to attract any attention right now."

"Your politics are still lousy, Zorn. The picture hasn't changed. Your coup hasn't got a chance."

"Skip it. I'll take up one problem at a time."

"Magnan's mouth has a habit of falling open at the wrong time—"

"That's my good luck that I heard it. So there'll be no agreement, no guns, no fat job for Tammany Zorn, hey? Well, I can still play it the other way, What have I got to lose?"

With a movement too quick to follow, Retief's hand chopped down across Zorn's wrist. The needler clattered as Zorn reeled, and then Retief's hand clamped Zorn's arm and whirled him around.

"In answer to your last question," Retief said, "your neck."

"You haven't got a chance, doublecrosser," Zorn gasped.

"Shoke will be here in a minute," Retief said. "Tell him it's all off."

"Twist harder, Mister," Zorn said. "Break it off at the shoulder. I'm telling him nothing!"

"The kidding's over, Zorn," Retief said. "Call it off or I'll kill you."

"I believe you," Zorn said. "But you won't have long to remember it."

"All the killing will be for nothing," Retief said. "You'll be dead and the Rotunes will step into the power vacuum."

"So what? When I die, the world ends."

"Suppose I make you another offer, Zorn?"

"Why would it be any better than the last one, chiseler?"

Retief released Zorn's arm, pushed him away, stooped and picked up the needler.

"I could kill you, Zorn. You know that."

"Go ahead!"

Retief reversed the needler, held it out.

"I'm a gambler too, Zorn. I'm gambling you'll listen to what I have to say."

Zorn snatched the gun, stepped back. He looked at Retief.

"That wasn't the smartest bet you ever made, Mister; but go ahead. You've got maybe ten seconds."

"Nobody doublecrossed you, Zorn. Magnan put his foot in it. Too bad. Is that a reason to kill yourself and a lot of other people who've bet their lives on you?"

"They gambled and lost. Tough."

"Maybe you haven't lost yet—if you don't quit."

"Get to the point!"

Retief spoke earnestly for a minute and a half. Zorn stood, gun aimed, listening. Then both men turned as footsteps approached along the terrace. A fat man in a yellow sarong padded up to Zorn.

Zorn tucked the needler in his waistband.

"Hold everything, Shoke," he said. "Tell the boys to put the knives away. Spread the word fast. It's all off."

"I want to commend you, Retief," Ambassador Crodfoller said expansively. "You mixed very well at last night's affair. Actually, I was hardly aware of your presence."

"I've been studying Mr. Magnan's work," Retief said.

"A good man, Magnan. In a crowd, he's virtually invisible."

"He knows when to disappear all right."

"This has been in many ways a model operation, Retief." The Ambassador patted his paunch contentedly. "By observing local social customs and blending harmoniously with the court, I've succeeded in establishing a fine, friendly, working relationship with the Potentate."

"I understand the agreement has been postponed."

The Ambassador chuckled. "The Potentate's a crafty one. Through . . . ah . . . a special study I have been conducting, I learned last night that he had hoped to, shall I say, 'put one over' on the Corps."

"Great heavens," Retief said.

"Naturally, this placed me in a difficult position. It was my task to quash this gambit, without giving any indication that I was aware of its existence."

"A hairy position indeed," Retief said.

"Quite casually, I informed the Potentate that certain items which had been included in the terms of the agreement had been deleted and others substituted. I admired him at that moment, Retief. He took it coolly—appearing completely indifferent—perfectly dissembling his very serious disappointment."

"I noticed him dancing with three girls wearing a bunch of grapes apiece. He's very agile for a man of his bulk."

"You mustn't discount the Potentate! Remember, beneath that mask of frivolity, he had absorbed a bitter blow."

"He had me fooled," Retief said.

"Don't feel badly; I confess at first I failed to sense his shrewdness." The Ambassador nodded and moved off along the corridor.

Retief turned and went into an office. Magnan looked up from his desk.

"Ah," he said. "Retief. I've been meaning to ask you. About the . . . ah . . . blasters. Are you—?"

Retief leaned on Magnan's desk, looked at him.

"I thought that was to be our little secret."

"Well, naturally I—" Magnan closed his mouth, swallowed. "How is it, Retief," he said sharply, "that you were aware of this blaster business, when the Ambassador himself wasn't?"

"Easy," Retief said. "I made it up."

"You what!" Magnan looked wild. "But the agreement—it's been revised! Ambassador Crodfoller has gone on record . . . . "

"Too bad. Glad *I* didn't tell him about it."

*

Magnan leaned back and closed his eyes.

"It was big of you to take all the . . . blame," Retief said, "when the Ambassador was talking about knighting people."

Magnan opened his eyes.

"What about that gambler, Zorn? Won't he be upset?"

"It's all right," Retief said, "I made another arrangement. The business about making blasters out of common components wasn't completely imaginary. You can actually do it, using parts from an old-fashioned disposal unit."

"What good will that do him?" Magnan whispered, looking nervous. "We're not shipping in any old-fashioned disposal units."

"We don't need to," Retief said. "They're already installed in the palace kitchen—and in a few thousand other places, Zorn tells me."

"If this ever leaks . . . . " Magnan put a hand to his forehead.

"I have his word on it that the Nenni slaughter is out. This place is ripe for a change. Maybe Zorn is what it needs."

"But how can we *know?*" Magnan yelped. "How can we be sure?"

"We can't," Retief said. "But it's not up to the Corps to meddle in Petreacs' internal affairs." He leaned over, picked up Magnan's desk lighter and lit a cigar. He blew a cloud of smoke toward the ceiling. "Right?"

Magnan looked at him, nodded weakly. "Right."

"I'd better be getting along to my desk," Retief said. "Now that the Ambassador feels that I'm settling down at last—"

"Retief," Magnan said, "tonight, I implore you. Stay out of the kitchen—no matter what."

Retief raised his eyebrows.

"I know," Magnan said. "If you hadn't interfered, we'd all have had our throats cut. But at least," he added, "we'd have died in accordance with regulations!"

THE YILLIAN WAY

The ceremonious protocol of the Yills was impressive, colorful—and, in the long run, deadly!

I

Jame Retief, vice-consul and third secretary in the Diplomatic Corps, followed the senior members of the terrestrial mission across the tarmac and into the gloom of the reception building. The gray-skinned Yill guide who had met the arriving embassy at the foot of the ramp hurried away. The councillor, two first secretaries and the senior attaches gathered around the ambassador, their ornate uniforms bright in the vast dun-colored room.

Ten minutes passed. Retief strolled across to the nearest door and looked through the glass panel at the room beyond. Several dozen Yill lounged in deep couches, sipping lavender drinks from slender glass tubes. Black-tunicked servants moved about inconspicuously, offering trays. A party of brightly-dressed Yill moved toward the entrance doors. One of the party, a tall male, made to step before another, who raised a hand languidly, fist clenched. The first Yill stepped back and placed his hands on top of his head. Both Yill were smiling and chatting as they passed through the doors.

Retief turned away to rejoin the Terrestrial delegation waiting beside a mound of crates made of rough greenish wood stacked on the bare concrete floor.

As Retief came up, Ambassador Spradley glanced at his finger watch and spoke to the man beside him.

"Ben, are you quite certain our arrival time was made clear?"

Second Secretary Magnan nodded emphatically. "I stressed the point, Mr. Ambassador. I communicated with Mr. T'Cai-Cai just before the lighter broke orbit, and I specifically—"

"I hope you didn't appear truculent, Mr. Magnan," the ambassador said sharply.

"No indeed, Mr. Ambassador. I merely—"

"You're sure there's no VIP room here?" The ambassador glanced around the cavernous room. "Curious that not even chairs have been provided."

"If you'd care to sit on one of these crates—"

"Certainly not." The ambassador looked at his watch again and cleared his throat.

"I may as well make use of these few moments to outline our approach for the more junior members of the staff; it's vital that the entire mission work in harmony

in the presentation of the image. We Terrestrials are a kindly, peace-loving race."
The ambassador smiled in a kindly, peace-loving way.

"We seek only a reasonable division of spheres of influence with the Yill." He
spread his hands, looking reasonable.

"We are a people of high culture, ethical, sincere." The smile was replaced
abruptly by pursed lips.

"We'll start by asking for the entire Sirenian System, and settle for half. We'll
establish a foothold on all the choicer worlds. And, with shrewd handling, in a
century we'll be in a position to assert a wider claim."

The ambassador glanced around. "If there are no questions—"

*

Retief stepped forward. "It's my understanding, Mr. Ambassador, that we hold
the prior claim to the Sirenian System. Did I understand your Excellency to say that
we're ready to concede half of it to the Yill without a struggle?"

Ambassador Spradley looked up at Retief, blinking. The younger man loomed
over him. Beside him, Magnan cleared his throat in the silence.

"Vice-Consul Retief merely means—"

"I can interpret Mr. Retief's remark," the ambassador snapped. He assumed a
fatherly expression.

"Young man, you're new to the Service. You haven't yet learned the team play,
the give-and-take of diplomacy. I shall expect you to observe closely the work of the
experienced negotiators of the mission. You must learn the importance of subtlety."

"Mr. Ambassador," Magnan said, "I think the reception committee is arriving."
He pointed. Half a dozen tall, short-necked Yill were entering through a side door.
The leading Yill hesitated as another stepped in his path. He raised a fist, and the
other moved aside, touching the top of his head perfunctorily with both hands. The
group started across the room toward the Terrestrials. Retief watched as a slender
alien came forward and spoke passable Terran in a reedy voice.

"I am P'Toi. Come this way . . . . " He turned, and the group moved toward the
door, the ambassador leading. As he reached for the door, the interpreter darted
ahead and shouldered him aside. The other Yill stopped, waiting.

The ambassador almost glared, then remembered the image. He smiled and
beckoned the Yill ahead. They milled uncertainly, muttering in the native tongue,
then passed through the door.

The Terran party followed.

"—give a great deal to know what they're saying," Retief overheard as he came up.

"Our interpreter has forged to the van," the ambassador said. "I can only assume he'll appear when needed."

"A pity we have to rely on a native interpreter," someone said.

"Had I known we'd meet this rather uncouth reception," the ambassador said stiffly, "I would have audited the language personally, of course, during the voyage out."

"Oh, no criticism intended, of course, Mr. Ambassador."

"Heavens," Magnan put in. "Who would have thought—"

Retief moved up behind the ambassador.

"Mr. Ambassador," he said, "I—"

"Later, young man," the ambassador snapped. He beckoned to the first councillor, and the two moved off, heads together.

Outside, a bluish sun gleamed in a dark sky. Retief watched his breath form a frosty cloud in the chill air. A broad doughnut-wheeled vehicle was drawn up to the platform. The Yill gestured the Terran party to the gaping door at the rear, then stood back, waiting.

Retief looked curiously at the gray-painted van. The legend written on its side in alien symbols seemed to read "egg nog."

*

The ambassador entered the vehicle, the other Terrestrials following. It was as bare of seats as the Terminal building. What appeared to be a defunct electronic chassis lay in the center of the floor.

Retief glanced back. The Yill were talking excitedly. None of them entered the car. The door was closed, and the Terrans braced themselves under the low roof as the engine started up with a whine of worn turbos.

The van moved off.

It was an uncomfortable ride. Retief put out an arm as the vehicle rounded a corner, just catching the ambassador as he staggered, off-balance. The ambassador glared at him, settled his heavy tri-corner hat and stood stiffly until the car lurched again.

Retief stooped, attempting to see out through the single dusty window. They seemed to be in a wide street lined with low buildings.

They passed through a massive gate, up a ramp, and stopped. The door opened. Retief looked out at a blank gray facade, broken by tiny windows at irregular intervals. A scarlet vehicle was drawn up ahead, the Yill reception committee emerging from it. Through its wide windows Retief saw rich upholstery and caught a glimpse of glasses clamped to a tiny bar.

P'Toi, the Yill interpreter, came forward, gestured to a small door. Magnan opened it, waiting for the ambassador.

As he stepped to it, a Yill thrust himself ahead and hesitated. Ambassador Spradley drew himself up, glaring. Then he twisted his mouth into a frozen smile and stepped aside.

The Yill looked at each other then filed through the door.

Retief was the last to enter. As he stepped inside, a black-clad servant slipped past him, pulled the lid from a large box by the door and dropped in a paper tray heaped with refuse. There were alien symbols in flaking paint on the box. They seemed, Retief noticed, to spell "egg nog."

II

The shrill pipes and whining reeds had been warming up for an hour when Retief emerged from his cubicle and descended the stairs to the banquet hall.

Standing by the open doors, he lit a slender cigar and watched through narrowed eyes as obsequious servants in black flitted along the low wide corridor, carrying laden trays into the broad room, arranging settings on a great four-sided table forming a hollow square that almost filled the room. Rich brocades were spread across the center of the side nearest the door, flanked by heavily decorated white cloths. Beyond, plain white extended to the far side, where metal dishes were arranged on the bare table top.

A richly dressed Yill approached, stepped aside to allow a servant to pass and entered the room.

Retief turned at the sound of Terran voices behind him. The ambassador came up, trailed by two diplomats. He glanced at Retief, adjusted his ruff and looked into the banquet hall.

"Apparently we're to be kept waiting again," he muttered. "After having been informed at the outset that the Yill have no intention of yielding an inch, one almost wonders . . . . "

"Mr. Ambassador," Retief said. "Have you noticed—"

"However," Ambassador Spradley said, eyeing Retief, "a seasoned diplomatist must take these little snubs in stride. In the end—Ah, there, Magnan." He turned away, talking.

Somewhere a gong clanged.

In a moment, the corridor was filled with chattering Yill who moved past the group of Terrestrials into the banquet hall. P'Toi, the Yill interpreter, came up and raised a hand.

"Waitt heere . . . . "

More Yill filed into the dining room to take their places. A pair of helmeted guards approached, waving the Terrestrials back. An immense gray-jowled Yill waddled to the doors and passed through, followed by more guards.

"The Chief of State," Retief heard Magnan say. "The Admirable F'Kau-Kau-Kau."

"I have yet to present my credentials," Ambassador Spradley said. "One expects some latitude in the observances of protocol, but I confess . . . . " He wagged his head.

The Yill interpreter spoke up.

"You now whill lhie on yourr intesstinss, and creep to fesstive board there." He pointed across the room.

"Intestines?" Ambassador Spradley looked about wildly.

"Mr. P'Toi means our stomachs, I wouldn't wonder," Magnan said. "He just wants us to lie down and crawl to our seats, Mr. Ambassador."

"What the devil are you grinning at, you idiot?" the ambassador snapped.

*

Magnan's face fell.

Spradley glanced down at the medals across his paunch.

"This is . . . . I've never . . . . "

"Homage to godss," the interpreter said.

"Oh. Oh, religion," someone said.

"Well, if it's a matter of religious beliefs . . . . " The ambassador looked dubiously around.

"Golly, it's only a couple of hundred feet," Magnan offered.

Retief stepped up to P'Toi.

"His Excellency the Terrestrial Ambassador will not crawl," he said clearly.

"Here, young man! I said nothing—"

"Not to crawl?" The interpreter wore an unreadable Yill expression.

"It is against our religion," Retief said.

"Againsst?"

"We are votaries of the Snake Goddess," Retief said. "It is a sacrilege to crawl." He brushed past the interpreter and marched toward the distant table.

The others followed.

Puffing, the ambassador came to Retief's side as they approached the dozen empty stools on the far side of the square opposite the brocaded position of the Admirable F'Kau-Kau-Kau.

"Mr. Retief, kindly see me after this affair," he hissed. "In the meantime, I hope you will restrain any further rash impulses. Let me remind you I am chief of mission here."

Magnan came up from behind.

"Let me add my congratulations, Retief," he said. "That was fast thinking—"

"Are you out of your mind, Magnan?" the ambassador barked. "I am extremely displeased!"

"Why," Magnan stuttered, "I was speaking sarcastically, of course, Mr. Ambassador. Didn't you notice the kind of shocked little gasp I gave when he did it?"

The Terrestrials took their places, Retief at the end. The table before them was of bare green wood, with an array of shallow pewter dishes.

Some of the Yill at the table were in plain gray, others in black. All eyed them silently. There was a constant stir among them as one or another rose and disappeared and others sat down. The pipes and reeds were shrilling furiously, and the susurration of Yillian conversation from the other tables rose ever higher in competition.

A tall Yill in black was at the ambassador's side now. The nearby Yill fell silent as he began ladling a whitish soup into the largest of the bowls before the Terrestrial envoy. The interpreter hovered, watching.

"That's quite enough," Ambassador Spradley said, as the bowl overflowed. The Yill servant rolled his eyes, dribbled more of the soup into the bowl.

"Kindly serve the other members of my staff," the ambassador said. The interpreter said something in a low voice. The servant moved hesitantly to the next stool and ladled more soup.

*

Retief watched, listening to the whispers around him. The Yill at the table were craning now to watch. The soup ladler was ladling rapidly, rolling his eyes sideways. He came to Retief, reached out with the full ladle for the bowl.

"No," Retief said.

The ladler hesitated.

"None for me," Retief said.

The interpreter came up and motioned to the servant, who reached again, ladle brimming.

"I . . . DON'T . . . LIKE . . . IT!" Retief said, his voice distinct in the sudden hush. He stared at the interpreter, who stared back, then waved the servant away.

"Mr. Retief!" a voice hissed.

Retief looked down at the table. The ambassador was leaning forward, glaring at him, his face a mottled crimson.

"I'm warning you, Mr. Retief," he said hoarsely. "I've eaten sheep's eyes in the Sudan, ka swe in Burma, hundred-year *cug* on Mars and everything else that has been placed before me in the course of my diplomatic career. And, by the holy relics of Saint Ignatz, you'll do the same!" He snatched up a spoon-like utensil and dipped it into his bowl.

"Don't eat that, Mr. Ambassador," Retief said.

The ambassador stared, eyes wide. He opened his mouth, guided the spoon toward it—

Retief stood, gripped the table under its edge and heaved. The immense wooden slab rose and tilted, dishes sliding. It crashed to the floor with a ponderous slam.

Whitish soup splattered across the terrazzo. A couple of odd bowls rolled across the room. Cries rang out from the Yill, mingling with a strangled yell from Ambassador Spradley.

Retief walked past the wild-eyed members of the mission to the sputtering chief. "Mr. Ambassador," he said. "I'd like—"

"You'd like! I'll break you, you young hoodlum! Do you realize—"

"Pleass . . . . " The interpreter stood at Retief's side.

"My apologies," Ambassador Spradley said, mopping his forehead. "My profound apologies."

"Be quiet," Retief said.

"Wha—what?"

"Don't apologize," Retief said. P'Toi was beckoning.

"Pleasse, arll come."

Retief turned and followed him.

The portion of the table they were ushered to was covered with an embroidered white cloth, set with thin porcelain dishes. The Yill already seated there rose, amid babbling, and moved down the table. The black-clad Yill at the end table closed ranks to fill the vacant seats. Retief sat down and found Magnan at his side.

"What's going on here?" the second secretary said angrily.

"They were giving us dog food," Retief said. "I overheard a Yill. They seated us at the bottom of the servants' table—"

"You mean you know their language?"

"I learned it on the way out. Enough, at least."

The music burst out with a clangorous fanfare, and a throng of jugglers, dancers and acrobats poured into the center of the hollow square, frantically juggling, dancing and back-flipping. Black-clad servants swarmed suddenly, heaping mounds of fragrant food on the plates of Yill and Terrestrials alike, pouring a pale purple liquor into slender glasses. Retief sampled the Yill food. It was delicious.

Conversation was impossible in the din. He watched the gaudy display and ate heartily.

III

Retief leaned back, grateful for the lull in the music. The last of the dishes were whisked away, and more glasses filled. The exhausted entertainers stopped to pick up the thick square coins the diners threw.

Retief sighed. It had been a rare feast.

"Retief," Magnan said in the comparative quiet, "what were you saying about dog food as the music came up?"

Retief looked at him. "Haven't you noticed the pattern, Mr. Magnan? The series of deliberate affronts?"

"Deliberate affronts! Just a minute, Retief. They're uncouth, yes, crowding into doorways and that sort of thing . . . . " He looked at Retief uncertainly.

"They herded us into a baggage warehouse at the terminal. Then they hauled us here in a garbage truck—"

"Garbage truck!"

"Only symbolic, of course. They ushered us in the tradesman's entrance, and assigned us cubicles in the servants' wing. Then we were seated with the coolie class sweepers at the bottom of the table."

"You must be . . . . I mean, we're the Terrestrial delegation! Surely these Yill must realize our power."

"Precisely, Mr. Magnan. But—"

With a clang of cymbals the musicians launched a renewed assault. Six tall, helmeted Yill sprang into the center of the floor and paired off in a wild performance, half dance, half combat. Magnan pulled at Retief's arm, his mouth moving.

Retief shook his head. No one could talk against a Yill orchestra in full cry. He sampled a bright red wine and watched the show.

There was a flurry of action, and two of the dancers stumbled and collapsed, their partner-opponents whirling away to pair off again, describe the elaborate pre-combat ritual, and abruptly set to, dulled sabres clashing—and two more Yill were down, stunned. It was a violent dance.

Retief watched, the drink forgotten.

The last two Yill approached and retreated, whirled, bobbed and spun, feinted and postured—and on the instant, clashed, straining chest-to-chest—then broke apart, heavy weapons chopping, parrying, as the music mounted to a frenzy.

Evenly matched, the two hacked, thrust, blow for blow, across the floor, then back, defense forgotten, slugging it out.

And then one was slipping, going down, helmet awry. The other, a giant, muscular Yill, spun away, whirled in a mad skirl of pipes as coins showered—then froze before a gaudy table, raised the sabre and slammed it down in a resounding blow across the gay cloth before a lace and bow-bedecked Yill in the same instant that the music stopped.

In utter silence the dancer-fighter stared across the table at the seated Yill.

With a shout, the Yill leaped up, raised a clenched fist. The dancer bowed his head, spread his hands on his helmet.

Retief took a deep gulp of a pale yellow liqueur and leaned forward to watch. The beribboned Yill waved a hand negligently, spilled a handful of coins across the table and sat down.

The challenger spun away in a screeching shrill of music. Retief caught his eye for an instant as he passed.

And then the dancer stood rigid before the brocaded table—and the music stopped off short as the sabre slammed down before a heavy Yill in ornate metallic coils. The challenged Yill rose and raised a fist. The other ducked his head, put his hands on his helmet. Coins rolled. The dancer moved on.

Twice more the dancer struck the table in ritualistic challenge, exchanged gestures, bent his neck and passed on. He circled the broad floor, sabre twirling, arms darting in an intricate symbolism. The orchestra blared shrilly, unmuffled now by the surf-roar of conversation. The Yill, Retief noticed suddenly, were sitting silent, watching. The dancer was closer now, and then he was before Retief, poised, towering, sabre above his head.

The music cut, and in the startling instantaneous silence, the heavy sabre whipped over and down with an explosive concussion that set dishes dancing on the table-top.

The Yill's eyes held on Retief's. In the silence, Magnan tittered drunkenly. Retief pushed back his stool.

"Steady, my boy," Ambassador Spradley called. Retief stood, the Yill topping his six foot three by an inch. In a motion almost too quick to follow, Retief reached for the sabre, twitched it from the Yill's grip, swung it in a whistling cut. The Yill ducked, sprang back, snatched up a sabre dropped by another dancer.

"Someone stop the madman!" Spradley howled.

Retief leaped across the table, sending fragile dishes spinning.

The other danced back, and only then did the orchestra spring to life with a screech and a mad tattoo of high-pitched drums.

Making no attempt to following the weaving pattern of the Yill bolero, Retief pressed the other, fending off vicious cuts with the blunt weapon, chopping back relentlessly. Left hand on hip, Retief matched blow for blow, driving the other back.

Abruptly, the Yill abandoned the double role. Dancing forgotten, he settled down in earnest, cutting, thrusting, parrying; and now the two stood toe to toe, sabres clashing in a lightning exchange. The Yill gave a step, two, then rallied, drove Retief back, back—

And the Yill stumbled. His sabre clattered, and Retief dropped his point as the other wavered past him and crashed to the floor.

The orchestra fell silent in a descending wail of reeds. Retief drew a deep breath and wiped his forehead.

"Come back here, you young fool!" Spradley called hoarsely.

Retief hefted the sabre, turned, eyed the brocade-draped table. He started across the floor. The Yill sat as if paralyzed.

"Retief, no!" Spradley yelped.

Retief walked directly to the Admirable F'Kau-Kau-Kau, stopped, raised the sabre.

"Not the chief of state," someone in the Terrestrial mission groaned.

Retief whipped the sabre down. The dull blade split the cloth and clove the hardwood table. There was utter silence.

The Admirable F'Kau-Kau-Kau rose, seven feet of obese gray Yill. Broad face expressionless to any Terran eyes, he raised a fist like a jewel-studded ham.

Retief stood rigid for a long moment. Then, gracefully, he inclined his head, placed his finger tips on his temples.

Behind him, there was a clatter as Ambassador Spradley collapsed. Then the Admirable F'Kau-Kau-Kau cried out and reached across the table to embrace the Terrestrial, and the orchestra went mad.

Gray hands helped Retief across the table, stools were pushed aside to make room at F'Kau-Kau-Kau's side. Retief sat, took a tall flagon of coal-black brandy pressed on him by his neighbor, clashed glasses with The Admirable and drank.

IV

Retief turned at the touch on his shoulder.

"The Ambassador wants to speak to you, Retief," Magnan said.

Retief looked across to where Ambassador Spradley sat glowering behind the plain tablecloth.

"Under the circumstances," Retief said, "you'd better ask him to come over here."

"The ambassador?" Magnan's voice cracked.

"Never mind the protocol," Retief said. "The situation is still delicate." Magnan went away.

"The feast ends," F'Kau-Kau-Kau said. "Now you and I, Retief, must straddle the Council Stool."

"I'll be honored, Admirable," Retief said. "I must inform my colleagues."

"Colleagues?" F'Kau-Kau-Kau said. "It is for chiefs to parley. Who shall speak for a king while he yet has tongue for talk?"

"The Yill way is wise," Retief said.

F'Kau-Kau-Kau emptied a squat tumbler of pink beer. "I will treat with you, Retief, as viceroy, since as you say your king is old and the space between worlds is far. But there shall be no scheming underlings privy to our dealings." He grinned a Yill grin. "Afterwards we shall carouse, Retief. The Council Stool is hard and the waiting handmaidens delectable. This makes for quick agreement."

Retief smiled. "The king is wise."

"Of course, a being prefers wenches of his own kind," F'Kau-Kau-Kau said. He belched. "The Ministry of Culture has imported several Terry—excuse me, Retief—Terrestrial joy-girls, said to be top-notch specimens. At least they have very fat watchamacallits."

"The king is most considerate," Retief said.

"Let us to it then, Retief. I may hazard a fling with one of your Terries, myself. I fancy an occasional perversion." F'Kau-Kau-Kau dug an elbow into Retief's side and bellowed with laughter.

Ambassador Spradley hurried to intercept Retief as he crossed to the door at F'Kau-Kau-Kau's side.

"Retief, kindly excuse yourself, I wish a word with you." His voice was icy. Magnan stood behind him, goggling.

"Mr. Ambassador, forgive my apparent rudeness," Retief said. "I don't have time to explain now—"

"Rudeness!" Spradley barked. "Don't have time, eh? Let me tell you—"

"Lower your voice, Mr. Ambassador," Retief said.

Spradley quivered, mouth open, speechless.

"If you'll sit down and wait quietly," Retief said, "I think—"

"You think!" Spradley spluttered.

*

"Silence!" Retief said. Spradley looked up at Retief's face. He stared for a moment into Retief's gray eyes, closed his mouth and swallowed.

"The Yill seem to have gotten the impression I'm in charge," Retief said, "We'll have to keep it up."

"But—but—" Spradley stuttered. Then he straightened. "That is the last straw," he whispered hoarsely. "I am the Terrestrial Ambassador Extraordinary and Minister Plenipotentiary. Magnan has told me that we've been studiedly insulted, repeatedly, since the moment of our arrival. Kept waiting in baggage rooms, transported in refuse lorries, herded about with servants, offered swill at table. Now

I and my senior staff, are left cooling our heels, without so much as an audience while this—this multiple Kau person hobnobs with—with—"

Spradley's voice broke. "I may have been a trifle hasty, Retief, in attempting to restrain you. Blaspheming the native gods and dumping the banquet table are rather extreme measures, but your resentment was perhaps partially justified. I am prepared to be lenient with you." He fixed a choleric eye on Retief.

"I am walking out of this meeting, Mr. Retief. I'll take no more of these deliberate personal—"

"That's enough," Retief snapped. "You're keeping the king waiting. Get back to your chair and sit there until I come back."

Magnan found his voice. "What are you going to do, Retief?"

"I'm going to handle the negotiation," Retief said. He handed Magnan his empty glass. "Now go sit down and work on the Image."

*

At his desk in the VIP suite aboard the orbiting Corps vessel, Ambassador Spradley pursed his lips and looked severely at Vice-Consul Retief.

"Further," he said, "you have displayed a complete lack of understanding of Corps discipline, the respect due a senior agent, even the basic courtesies. Your aggravated displays of temper, ill-timed outbursts of violence and almost incredible arrogance in the assumption of authority make your further retention as an officer-agent of the Diplomatic Corps impossible. It will therefore be my unhappy duty to recommend your immediate—"

There was a muted buzz from the communicator. The ambassador cleared his throat.

"Well?"

"A signal from Sector HQ, Mr. Ambassador," a voice said.

"Well, read it," Spradley snapped. "Skip the preliminaries."

"Congratulations on the unprecedented success of your mission. The articles of agreement transmitted by you embody a most favorable resolution of the difficult Sirenian situation, and will form the basis of continued amicable relations between the Terrestrial States and the Yill Empire. To you and your staff, full credit is due for a job well done. Signed, Deputy Assistant Secretary—"

Spradley cut off the voice impatiently.

He shuffled papers, eyed Retief sharply.

"Superficially, of course, an uninitiated observer might leap to the conclusion that the—ah—results that were produced in spite of these . . . ah . . . irregularities justify the latter." The Ambassador smiled a sad, wise smile. "This is far from the case," he said. "I—"

The communicator burped softly.

"Confound it!" Spradley muttered. "Yes?"

"Mr. T'Cai-Cai has arrived," the voice said. "Shall I—"

"Send him in at once." Spradley glanced at Retief. "Only a two-syllable man, but I shall attempt to correct these false impressions, make some amends . . . . "

The two Terrestrials waited silently until the Yill Protocol chief tapped at the door.

"I hope," the ambassador said, "that you will resist the impulse to take advantage of your unusual position." He looked at the door. "Come in."

T'Cai-Cai stepped into the room, glanced at Spradley, turned to greet Retief in voluble Yill. He rounded the desk to the ambassador's chair, motioned him from it and sat down.

*

"I have a surprise for you, Retief," he said, in Terran. "I myself have made use of the teaching machine you so kindly lent us."

"That's fine. T'Cai-Cai," Retief said. "I'm sure Mr. Spradley will be interested in hearing what we have to say."

"Never mind," the Yill said. "I am here only socially." He looked around the room.

"So plainly you decorate your chamber. But it has a certain austere charm." He laughed a Yill laugh.

"Oh, you are a strange breed, you Terrestrials. You surprised us all. You know, one hears such outlandish stories. I tell you in confidence, we had expected you to be overpushes."

"Pushovers," Spradley said, tonelessly.

"Such restraint! What pleasure you gave to those of us, like myself of course, who appreciated your grasp of protocol. Such finesse! How subtly you appeared to ignore each overture, while neatly avoiding actual contamination. I can tell you, there were those who thought—poor fools—that you had no grasp of etiquette. How gratified we were, we professionals, who could appreciate your virtuosity—when you placed matters on a comfortable basis by spurning the cats'-meat. It was sheer pleasure then, waiting, to see what form your compliment would take."

The Yill offered orange cigars, stuffed one in his nostril.

"I confess even I had not hoped that you would honor our Admirable so signally. Oh, it is a pleasure to deal with fellow professionals, who understand the meaning of protocol!"

Ambassador Spradley made a choking sound.

"This fellow has caught a chill," T'Cai-Cai said. He eyed Spradley dubiously. "Step back, my man. I am highly susceptible.

"There is one bit of business I shall take pleasure in attending to, my dear Retief," T'Cai-Cai went on. He drew a large paper from his reticule. "The Admirable is determined than none other than yourself shall be accredited here. I have here my government's exequatur confirming you as Terrestrial consul-general to Yill. We shall look forward to your prompt return."

Retief looked at Spradley.

"I'm sure the Corps will agree," he said.

"Then I shall be going," T'Cai-Cai said. He stood up. "Hurry back to us, Retief. There is much that I would show you of Yill."

"I'll hurry," Retief said and, with a Yill wink: "Together we shall see many high and splendid things!"

The Madman from Earth

You don't have to be crazy to be an earth diplomat—but on Groac it sure helps!

I

"The Consul for the Terrestrial States," Retief said, "presents his compliments, et cetera, to the Ministry of Culture of the Groacian Autonomy, and with reference to the Ministry's invitation to attend a recital of interpretive grimacing, has the honor to express regret that he will be unable—"

"You can't turn this invitation down," Administrative Assistant Meuhl said flatly. "I'll make that 'accepts with pleasure'."

Retief exhaled a plume of cigar smoke.

"Miss Meuhl," he said, "in the past couple of weeks I've sat through six light-concerts, four attempts at chamber music, and god knows how many assorted folk-art festivals. I've been tied up every off-duty hour since I got here—"

"You can't offend the Groaci," Miss Meuhl said sharply. "Consul Whaffle would never have been so rude."

"Whaffle left here three months ago," Retief said, "leaving me in charge."

"Well," Miss Meuhl said, snapping off the dictyper. "I'm sure I don't know what excuse I can give the Minister."

"Never mind the excuses," Retief said. "Just tell him I won't be there." He stood up.

"Are you leaving the office?" Miss Meuhl adjusted her glasses. "I have some important letters here for your signature."

"I don't recall dictating any letters today, Miss Meuhl," Retief said, pulling on a light cape.

*

"I wrote them for you. They're just as Consul Whaffle would have wanted them."

"Did you write all Whaffle's letters for him, Miss Meuhl?"

"Consul Whaffle was an extremely busy man," Miss Meuhl said stiffly. "He had complete confidence in me."

"Since I'm cutting out the culture from now on," Retief said, "I won't be so busy."

"Well!" Miss Meuhl said. "May I ask where you'll be if something comes up?"

"I'm going over to the Foreign Office Archives."

Miss Meuhl blinked behind thick lenses. "Whatever for?"

Retief looked thoughtfully at Miss Meuhl. "You've been here on Groac for four years, Miss Meuhl. What was behind the coup d'etat that put the present government in power?"

"I'm sure I haven't pried into—"

"What about that Terrestrial cruiser? The one that disappeared out this way about ten years back?"

"Mr. Retief, those are just the sort of questions we *avoid* with the Groaci. I certainly hope you're not thinking of openly intruding—"

"Why?"

"The Groaci are a very sensitive race. They don't welcome outworlders raking up things. They've been gracious enough to let us live down the fact that Terrestrials subjected them to deep humiliation on one occasion."

"You mean when they came looking for the cruiser?"

"I, for one, am ashamed of the high-handed tactics that were employed, grilling these innocent people as though they were criminals. We try never to reopen that wound, Mr. Retief."

"They never found the cruiser, did they?"

"Certainly not on Groac."

Retief nodded. "Thanks, Miss Meuhl," he said. "I'll be back before you close the office." Miss Meuhl's face was set in lines of grim disapproval as he closed the door.

*

The pale-featured Groacian vibrated his throat-bladder in a distressed bleat.

"Not to enter the Archives," he said in his faint voice. "The denial of permission. The deep regret of the Archivist."

"The importance of my task here," Retief said, enunciating the glottal dialect with difficulty. "My interest in local history."

"The impossibility of access to outworlders. To depart quietly."

"The necessity that I enter."

"The specific instructions of the Archivist." The Groacian's voice rose to a whisper. "To insist no longer. To give up this idea!"

"OK, Skinny, I know when I'm licked," Retief said in Terran. "To keep your nose clean."

Outside, Retief stood for a moment looking across at the deeply carved windowless stucco facades lining the street, then started off in the direction of the Terrestrial Consulate General. The few Groacians on the street eyed him furtively, veered to avoid him as he passed. Flimsy high-wheeled ground cars puffed silently along the resilient pavement. The air was clean and cool.

At the office, Miss Meuhl would be waiting with another list of complaints.

Retief studied the carving over the open doorways along the street. An elaborate one picked out in pinkish paint seemed to indicate the Groacian equivalent of a bar. Retief went in.

A Groacian bartender was dispensing clay pots of alcoholic drink from the bar-pit at the center of the room. He looked at Retief and froze in mid-motion, a metal tube poised over a waiting pot.

"To enjoy a cooling drink," Retief said in Groacian, squatting down at the edge of the pit. "To sample a true Groacian beverage."

"To not enjoy my poor offerings," the Groacian mumbled. "A pain in the digestive sacs; to express regret."

"To not worry," Retief said, irritated. "To pour it out and let me decide whether I like it."

"To be grappled in by peace-keepers for poisoning of—foreigners." The barkeep looked around for support, found none. The Groaci customers, eyes elsewhere, were drifting away.

"To get the lead out," Retief said, placing a thick gold-piece in the dish provided. "To shake a tentacle."

"The procuring of a cage," a thin voice called from the sidelines. "The displaying of a freak."

*

Retief turned. A tall Groacian vibrated his mandibles in a gesture of contempt. From his bluish throat coloration, it was apparent the creature was drunk.

"To choke in your upper sac," the bartender hissed, extending his eyes toward the drunk. "To keep silent, litter-mate of drones."

"To swallow your own poison, dispenser of vileness," the drunk whispered. "To find a proper cage for this zoo-piece." He wavered toward Retief. "To show this one in the streets, like all freaks."

"Seen a lot of freaks like me, have you?" Retief asked, interestedly.

"To speak intelligibly, malodorous outworlder," the drunk said. The barkeep whispered something, and two customers came up to the drunk, took his arms and helped him to the door.

"To get a cage!" the drunk shrilled. "To keep the animals in their own stinking place."

"I've changed my mind," Retief said to the bartender. "To be grateful as hell, but to have to hurry off now." He followed the drunk out the door. The other Groaci released him, hurried back inside. Retief looked at the weaving alien.

"To begone, freak," the Groacian whispered.

"To be pals," Retief said. "To be kind to dumb animals."

"To have you hauled away to a stockyard, ill-odored foreign livestock."

"To not be angry, fragrant native," Retief said. "To permit me to chum with you."

"To flee before I take a cane to you!"

"To have a drink together—"

"To not endure such insolence!" The Groacian advanced toward Retief. Retief backed away.

"To hold hands," Retief said. "To be palsy-walsy—"

The Groacian reached for him, missed. A passer-by stepped around him, head down, scuttled away. Retief backed into the opening to a narrow crossway and offered further verbal familiarities to the drunken local, who followed, furious. Retief backed, rounded a corner into a narrow alley-like passage, deserted, silent . . . except for the following Groacian.

Retief stepped around him, seized his collar and yanked. The Groacian fell on his back. Retief stood over him. The downed native half-rose; Retief put a foot against his chest and pushed.

"To not be going anywhere for a few minutes," Retief said. "To stay right here and have a nice long talk."

II

"There you are!" Miss Meuhl said, eyeing Retief over her lenses. "There are two gentlemen waiting to see you. Groacian gentlemen."

"Government men, I imagine. Word travels fast." Retief pulled off his cape. "This saves me the trouble of paying another call at the Foreign Ministry."

"What have you been doing? They seem very upset, I don't mind telling you."

"I'm sure you don't. Come along. And bring an official recorder."

Two Groaci wearing heavy eye-shields and elaborate crest ornaments indicative of rank rose as Retief entered the room. Neither offered a courteous snap of the mandibles, Retief noted. They were mad, all right.

"I am Fith, of the Terrestrial Desk, Ministry of Foreign Affairs, Mr. Consul," the taller Groacian said, in lisping Terran. "May I present Shluh, of the Internal Police?"

"Sit down, gentlemen," Retief said. They resumed their seats. Miss Meuhl hovered nervously, then sat on the edge of a comfortless chair.

"Oh, it's such a pleasure—" she began.

"Never mind that," Retief said. "These gentlemen didn't come here to sip tea today."

"So true," Fith said. "Frankly, I have had a most disturbing report, Mr. Consul. I shall ask Shluh to recount it." He nodded to the police chief.

"One hour ago," The Groacian said, "a Groacian national was brought to hospital suffering from serious contusions. Questioning of this individual revealed that he had been set upon and beaten by a foreigner. A Terrestrial, to be precise. Investigation by my department indicates that the description of the culprit closely matches that of the Terrestrial Consul."

Miss Meuhl gasped audibly.

"Have you ever heard," Retief said, looking steadily at Fith, "of a Terrestrial cruiser, the ISV *Terrific*, which dropped from sight in this sector nine years ago?"

"Really!" Miss Meuhl exclaimed, rising. "I wash my hands—"

"Just keep that recorder going," Retief snapped.

"I'll not be a party—"

"You'll do as you're told, Miss Meuhl," Retief said quietly. "I'm telling you to make an official sealed record of this conversation."

Miss Meuhl sat down.

Fith puffed out his throat indignantly. "You reopen an old wound, Mr. Consul. It reminds us of certain illegal treatment at Terrestrial hands—"

"Hogwash," Retief said. "That tune went over with my predecessors, but it hits a sour note with me."

"All our efforts," Miss Meuhl said, "to live down that terrible episode! And you—"

"Terrible? I understand that a Terrestrial task force stood off Groac and sent a delegation down to ask questions. They got some funny answers, and stayed on to dig around a little. After a week they left. Somewhat annoying to the Groaci, maybe—at the most. If they were innocent."

"IF!" Miss Meuhl burst out.

"If, indeed!" Fith said, his weak voice trembling. "I must protest your—"

*

"Save the protests, Fith. You have some explaining to do. And I don't think your story will be good enough."

"It is for you to explain! This person who was beaten—"

"Not beaten. Just rapped a few times to loosen his memory."

"Then you admit—"

"It worked, too. He remembered lots of things, once he put his mind to it."

Fith rose; Shluh followed suit.

"I shall ask for your immediate recall, Mr. Consul. Were it not for your diplomatic immunity, I should do more—"

"Why did the government fall, Fith? It was just after the task force paid its visit, and before the arrival of the first Terrestrial diplomatic mission."

"This is an internal matter!" Fith cried, in his faint Groacian voice. "The new regime has shown itself most amiable to you Terrestrials. It has outdone itself—"

"—to keep the Terrestrial consul and his staff in the dark," Retief said. "And the same goes for the few terrestrial businessmen you've visaed. This continual round of culture; no social contacts outside the diplomatic circle; no travel permits to visit out-lying districts, or your satellite—"

"Enough!" Fith's mandibles quivered in distress. "I can talk no more of this matter—"

"You'll talk to me, or there'll be a task force here in five days to do the talking," Retief said.

"You can't!" Miss Meuhl gasped.

Retief turned a steady look on Miss Meuhl. She closed her mouth. The Groaci sat down.

"Answer me this one," Retief said, looking at Shluh. "A few years back—about nine, I think—there was a little parade held here. Some curious looking creatures were captured. After being securely caged, they were exhibited to the gentle Groaci public. Hauled through the streets. Very educational, no doubt. A highly cultural show.

"Funny thing about these animals. They wore clothes. They seemed to communicate with each other. Altogether it was a very amusing exhibit.

"Tell me, Shluh, what happened to those six Terrestrials after the parade was over?"

*

Fith made a choked noise and spoke rapidly to Shluh in Groacian. Shluh retracted his eyes, shrank down in his chair. Miss Meuhl opened her mouth, closed it and blinked rapidly.

"How did they die?" Retief snapped. "Did you murder them, cut their throats, shoot them or bury them alive? What amusing end did you figure out for them? Research, maybe? Cut them open to see what made them yell . . . . "

"No!" Fith gasped. "I must correct this terrible false impression at once."

"False impression, hell," Retief said. "They were Terrans! A simple narco-interrogation would get that out of any Groacian who saw the parade."

"Yes," Fith said weakly. "It is true, they were Terrestrials. But there was no killing."

"They're alive?"

"Alas, no. They . . . died."

Miss Meuhl yelped faintly.

"I see," Retief said. "They died."

"We tried to keep them alive, of course. But we did not know what foods—"

"Didn't take the trouble to find out, either, did you?"

"They fell ill," Fith said. "One by one . . . . "

"We'll deal with that question later," Retief said. "Right now, I want more information. Where did you get them? Where did you hide the ship? What happened to the rest of the crew? Did they 'fall ill' before the big parade?"

"There were no more! Absolutely, I assure you!"

"Killed in the crash landing?"

"No crash landing. The ship descended intact, east of the city. The . . . Terrestrials . . . were unharmed. Naturally, we feared them. They were strange to us. We had never before seen such beings."

"Stepped off the ship with guns blazing, did they?"

"Guns? No, no guns—"

"They raised their hands, didn't they? Asked for help. You helped them; helped them to death."

"How could we know?" Fith moaned.

"How could you know a flotilla would show up in a few months looking for them, you mean? That was a shock, wasn't it? I'll bet you had a brisk time of it hiding the ship, and shutting everybody up. A close call, eh?"

"We were afraid," Shluh said. "We are a simple people. We feared the strange creatures from the alien craft. We did not kill them, but we felt it was as well they . . . did not survive. Then, when the warships came, we realized our error. But we feared to speak. We purged our guilty leaders, concealed what had happened, and . . . offered our friendship. We invited the opening of diplomatic relations. We made a blunder, it is true, a great blunder. But we have tried to make amends . . . ."

"Where is the ship?"

"The ship?"

"What did you do with it? It was too big to just walk off and forget. Where is it?"

The two Groacians exchanged looks.

"We wish to show our contrition," Fith said. "We will show you the ship."

"Miss Meuhl," Retief said. "If I don't come back in a reasonable length of time, transmit that recording to Regional Headquarters, sealed." He stood, looked at the Groaci.

"Let's go," he said.

*

Retief stooped under the heavy timbers shoring the entry to the cavern. He peered into the gloom at the curving flank of the space-burned hull.

"Any lights in here?" he asked.

A Groacian threw a switch. A weak bluish glow sprang up.

Retief walked along the raised wooden catwalk, studying the ship. Empty emplacements gaped below lensless scanner eyes. Littered decking was visible within the half-open entry port. Near the bow the words 'IVS Terrific B7 New Terra' were lettered in bright chrome duralloy.

"How did you get it in here?" Retief asked.

"It was hauled here from the landing point, some nine miles distant," Fith said, his voice thinner than ever. "This is a natural crevasse. The vessel was lowered into it and roofed over."

"How did you shield it so the detectors didn't pick it up?"

"All here is high-grade iron ore," Fith said, waving a member. "Great veins of almost pure metal."

Retief grunted. "Let's go inside."

Shluh came forward with a hand-lamp. The party entered the ship.

Retief clambered up a narrow companionway, glanced around the interior of the control compartment. Dust was thick on the deck, the stanchions where acceleration couches had been mounted, the empty instrument panels, the litter of sheared bolts, scraps of wire and paper. A thin frosting of rust dulled the exposed metal where cutting torches had sliced away heavy shielding. There was a faint odor of stale bedding.

"The cargo compartment—" Shluh began.

"I've seen enough," Retief said.

Silently, the Groacians led the way back out through the tunnel and into the late afternoon sunshine. As they climbed the slope to the steam car, Fith came to Retief's side.

"Indeed, I hope that this will be the end of this unfortunate affair," he said. "Now that all has been fully and honestly shown—"

"You can skip all that," Retief said. "You're nine years late. The crew was still alive when the task force called, I imagine. You killed them—or let them die—rather than take the chance of admitting what you'd done."

"We were at fault," Fith said abjectly. "Now we wish only friendship."

"The *Terrific* was a heavy cruiser, about twenty thousand tons." Retief looked grimly at the slender Foreign Office official. "Where is she, Fith? I won't settle for a hundred-ton lifeboat."

*

Fith erected his eye stalks so violently that one eye-shield fell off.

"I know nothing of . . . of . . . . " He stopped. His throat vibrated rapidly as he struggled for calm.

"My government can entertain no further accusations, Mr. Consul," he said at last. "I have been completely candid with you, I have overlooked your probing into matters not properly within your sphere of responsibility. My patience is at an end."

"Where is that ship?" Retief rapped out. "You never learn, do you? You're still convinced you can hide the whole thing and forget it. I'm telling you you can't."

"We return to the city now," Fith said. "I can do no more."

"You can and you will, Fith," Retief said. "I intend to get to the truth of this matter."

Fith spoke to Shluh in rapid Groacian. The police chief gestured to his four armed constables. They moved to ring Retief in.

Retief eyed Fith. "Don't try it," he said. "You'll just get yourself in deeper."

Fith clacked his mandibles angrily, eye stalks canted aggressively toward the Terrestrial.

"Out of deference to your diplomatic status, Terrestrial, I shall ignore your insulting remarks," Fith said in his reedy voice. "Let us now return to the city."

Retief looked at the four policemen. "I see your point," he said.

Fith followed him into the car, sat rigidly at the far end of the seat.

"I advise you to remain very close to your consulate," Fith said. "I advise you to dismiss these fancies from your mind, and to enjoy the cultural aspects of life at Groac. Especially, I should not venture out of the city, or appear overly curious about matters of concern only to the Groacian government."

In the front seat, Shluh looked straight ahead. The loosely-sprung vehicle bobbed and swayed along the narrow highway. Retief listened to the rhythmic puffing of the motor and said nothing.

III

"Miss Meuhl," Retief said, "I want you to listen carefully to what I'm going to tell you. I have to move rapidly now, to catch the Groaci off guard."

"I'm sure I don't know what you're talking about," Miss Meuhl snapped, her eyes sharp behind the heavy lenses.

"If you'll listen, you may find out," Retief said. "I have no time to waste, Miss Meuhl. They won't be expecting an immediate move—I hope—and that may give me the latitude I need."

"You're still determined to make an issue of that incident!" Miss Meuhl snorted. "I really can hardly blame the Groaci. They are not a sophisticated race; they had never before met aliens."

"You're ready to forgive a great deal, Miss Meuhl. But it's not what happened nine years ago I'm concerned with. It's what's happening now. I've told you that it was only a lifeboat the Groaci have hidden out. Don't you understand the implication? That vessel couldn't have come far. The cruiser itself must be somewhere near by. I want to know where!"

"The Groaci don't know. They're a very cultured, gentle people. You can do irreparable harm to the reputation of Terrestrials if you insist—"

"That's my decision," Retief said. "I have a job to do and we're wasting time." He crossed the room to his desk, opened a drawer and took out a slim-barreled needler.

"This office is being watched. Not very efficiently, if I know the Groaci. I think I can get past them all right."

"Where are you going with . . . that?" Miss Meuhl stared at the needler. "What in the world—"

"The Groaci won't waste any time destroying every piece of paper in their files relating to this thing. I have to get what I need before it's too late. If I wait for an official Inquiry Commission, they'll find nothing but blank smiles."

"You're out of your mind!" Miss Meuhl stood up, quivering with indignation. "You're like a . . . a . . . . "

"You and I are in a tight spot, Miss Meuhl. The logical next move for the Groaci is to dispose of both of us. We're the only ones who know what happened. Fith almost did the job this afternoon, but I bluffed him out—for the moment."

Miss Meuhl emitted a shrill laugh. "Your fantasies are getting the better of you," she gasped. "In danger, indeed! Disposing of me! I've never heard anything so ridiculous."

"Stay in this office. Close and safe-lock the door. You've got food and water in the dispenser. I suggest you stock up, before they shut the supply down. Don't let anyone in, on any pretext whatever. I'll keep in touch with you via hand-phone."

"What are you planning to do?"

"If I don't make it back here, transmit the sealed record of this afternoon's conversation, along with the information I've given you. Beam it through on a mayday priority. Then tell the Groaci what you've done and sit tight. I think you'll be all right. It won't be easy to blast in here and anyway, they won't make things worse by killing you. A force can be here in a week."

"I'll do nothing of the sort! The Groaci are very fond of me! You . . . Johnny-come-lately! Roughneck! Setting out to destroy—"

"Blame it on me if it will make you feel any better," Retief said, "but don't be fool enough to trust them." He pulled on a cape, opened the door.

"I'll be back in a couple of hours," he said. Miss Meuhl stared after him silently as he closed the door.

*

It was an hour before dawn when Retief keyed the combination to the safe-lock and stepped into the darkened consular office. He looked tired.

Miss Meuhl, dozing in a chair, awoke with a start. She looked at Retief, rose and snapped on a light, turned to stare.

"What in the world—Where have you been? What's happened to your clothing?"

81

"I got a little dirty. Don't worry about it." Retief went to his desk, opened a drawer and replaced the needler.

"Where have you been?" Miss Meuhl demanded. "I stayed here—"

"I'm glad you did," Retief said. "I hope you piled up a supply of food and water from the dispenser, too. We'll be holed up here for a week, at least." He jotted figures on a pad. "Warm up the official sender. I have a long transmission for Regional Headquarters."

"Are you going to tell me where you've been?"

"I have a message to get off first, Miss Meuhl," Retief said sharply. "I've been to the Foreign Ministry," he added. "I'll tell you all about it later."

"At this hour? There's no one there . . . ."

"Exactly."

Miss Meuhl gasped. "You mean you broke in? You burgled the Foreign Office?"

"That's right," Retief said calmly. "Now—"

"This is absolutely the end!" Miss Meuhl said. "Thank heaven I've already—"

"Get that sender going, woman!" Retief snapped. "This is important."

"I've already done so, Mr. Retief!" Miss Meuhl said harshly. "I've been waiting for you to come back here . . . ." She turned to the communicator, flipped levers. The screen snapped aglow, and a wavering long-distance image appeared.

"He's here now," Miss Meuhl said to the screen. She looked at Retief triumphantly.

"That's good," Retief said. "I don't think the Groaci can knock us off the air, but—"

"I have done my duty, Mr. Retief," Miss Meuhl said. "I made a full report to Regional Headquarters last night, as soon as you left this office. Any doubts I may have had as to the rightness of that decision have been completely dispelled by what you've just told me."

Retief looked at her levelly. "You've been a busy girl, Miss Meuhl. Did you mention the six Terrestrials who were killed here?"

"That had no bearing on the matter of your wild behavior! I must say, in all my years in the Corps, I've never encountered a personality less suited to diplomatic work."

*

The screen crackled, the ten-second transmission lag having elapsed. "Mr. Retief," the face on the screen said, "I am Counsellor Pardy, DSO-1, Deputy Under-secretary for the region. I have received a report on your conduct which makes it mandatory for me to relieve you administratively, vice Miss Yolanda Meuhl, DAO-9. Pending the findings of a Board of Inquiry, you will—"

Retief reached out and snapped off the communicator. The triumphant look faded from Miss Meuhl's face.

"Why, what is the meaning—"

"If I'd listened any longer, I might have heard something I couldn't ignore. I can't afford that, at this moment. Listen, Miss Meuhl," Retief went on earnestly, "I've found the missing cruiser."

"You heard him relieve you!"

"I heard him say he was *going* to, Miss Meuhl. But until I've heard and acknowledged a verbal order, it has no force. If I'm wrong, he'll get my resignation. If I'm right, that suspension would be embarrassing all around."

"You're defying lawful authority! I'm in charge here now." Miss Meuhl stepped to the local communicator.

"I'm going to report this terrible thing to the Groaci at once, and offer my profound—"

"Don't touch that screen," Retief said. "You go sit in that corner where I can keep an eye on you. I'm going to make a sealed tape for transmission to Headquarters, along with a call for an armed task force. Then we'll settle down to wait."

Retief ignored Miss Meuhl's fury as he spoke into the recorder.

The local communicator chimed. Miss Meuhl jumped up, staring at it.

"Go ahead," Retief said. "Answer it."

A Groacian official appeared on the screen.

"Yolanda Meuhl," he said without preamble, "for the Foreign Minister of the Groacian Autonomy, I herewith accredit you as Terrestrial Consul to Groac, in accordance with the advices transmitted to my government direct from the Terrestrial Headquarters. As consul, you are requested to make available for questioning Mr. J. Retief, former consul, in connection with the assault on two peace keepers and illegal entry into the offices of the Ministry for Foreign Affairs."

"Why, why," Miss Meuhl stammered. "Yes, of course. And I do want to express my deepest regrets—"

*

Retief rose, went to the communicator, assisted Miss Meuhl aside.

"Listen carefully, Fith," he said. "Your bluff has been called. You don't come in and we don't come out. Your camouflage worked for nine years, but it's all over now. I suggest you keep your heads and resist the temptation to make matters worse than they are."

"Miss Meuhl," Fith said, "a peace squad waits outside your consulate. It is clear you are in the hands of a dangerous lunatic. As always, the Groaci wish only friendship with the Terrestrials, but—"

"Don't bother," Retief said. "You know what was in those files I looked over this morning."

Retief turned at a sound behind him. Miss Meuhl was at the door, reaching for the safe-lock release . . . .

"Don't!" Retief jumped—too late.

The door burst inward. A crowd of crested Groaci pressed into the room, pushed Miss Meuhl back, aimed scatter guns at Retief. Police Chief Shluh pushed forward.

"Attempt no violence, Terrestrial," he said. "I cannot promise to restrain my men."

"You're violating Terrestrial territory, Shluh," Retief said steadily. "I suggest you move back out the same way you came in."

"I invited them here," Miss Meuhl spoke up. "They are here at my express wish."

"Are they? Are you sure you meant to go this far, Miss Meuhl? A squad of armed Groaci in the consulate?"

"You are the consul, Miss Yolanda Meuhl," Shluh said. "Would it not be best if we removed this deranged person to a place of safety?"

"You're making a serious mistake, Shluh," Retief said.

"Yes," Miss Meuhl said. "You're quite right, Mr. Shluh. Please escort Mr. Retief to his quarters in this building—"

"I don't advise you to violate my diplomatic immunity, Fith," Retief said.

"As chief of mission," Miss Meuhl said quickly, "I hereby waive immunity in the case of Mr. Retief."

Shluh produced a hand recorder. "Kindly repeat your statement, Madam, officially," he said. "I wish no question to arise later."

"Don't be a fool, woman," Retief said. "Don't you see what you're letting yourself in for? This would be a hell of a good time for you to figure out whose side you're on."

"I'm on the side of common decency!"

"You've been taken in. These people are concealing—"

"You think all women are fools, don't you, Mr. Retief?" She turned to the police chief and spoke into the microphone he held up.

"That's an illegal waiver," Retief said. "I'm consul here, whatever rumors you've heard. This thing's coming out into the open, whatever you do. Don't add violation of the Consulate to the list of Groacian atrocities."

"Take the man," Shluh said.

*

Two tall Groaci came to Retief's side, guns aimed at his chest.

"Determined to hang yourselves, aren't you?" Retief said. "I hope you have sense enough not to lay a hand on this poor fool here." He jerked a thumb at Miss Meuhl. "She doesn't know anything. I hadn't had time to tell her yet. She thinks you're a band of angels."

The cop at Retief's side swung the butt of his scatter-gun, connected solidly with Retief's jaw. Retief staggered against a Groacian, was caught and thrust upright, blood running down onto his shirt. Miss Meuhl yelped. Shluh barked at the guard in shrill Groacian, then turned to stare at Miss Meuhl.

"What has this man told you?"

"I—nothing. I refused to listen to his ravings."

"He said nothing to you of some . . . alleged . . . involvement?"

"I've told you!" Miss Meuhl said sharply. She looked at the blood on Retief's shirt.

"He told me nothing," she whispered. "I swear it."

"Let it lie, boys," Retief said. "Before you spoil that good impression."

Shluh looked at Miss Meuhl for a long moment. Then he turned.

"Let us go," he said. He turned back to Miss Meuhl. "Do not leave this building until further advice," he said.

"But . . . I am the Terrestrial consul!"

"For your safety, madam. The people are aroused at the beating of Groacian nationals by an . . . alien."

"So long, Meuhlsie," Retief said. "You played it real foxy."

"You'll . . . lock him in his quarters?" Miss Meuhl said.

"What is done with him is now a Groacian affair, Miss Meuhl. You yourself have withdrawn the protection of your government."

"I didn't mean—"

"Don't start having second thoughts," Retief said. "They can make you miserable."

"I had no choice," Miss Meuhl said. "I had to consider the best interest of the Service."

"My mistake, I guess," Retief said. "I was thinking of the best interests of a Terrestrial cruiser with three hundred men aboard."

"Enough," Shluh said. "Remove this criminal." He gestured to the peace keepers.

"Move along," he said to Retief. He turned to Miss Meuhl.

"A pleasure to deal with you, Madam."

IV

Retief stood quietly in the lift, stepped out at the ground floor and followed docilely down the corridor and across the pavement to a waiting steam car.

One of the peace keepers rounded the vehicle to enter on the other side. Two stooped to climb into the front seat. Shluh gestured Retief into the back seat and got in behind him. The others moved off on foot.

The car started up and pulled away. The cop in the front seat turned to look at Retief.

"To have some sport with it, and then to kill it," he said.

"To have a fair trial first," Shluh said. The car rocked and jounced, rounded a corner, puffed along between ornamented pastel facades.

"To have a trial and then to have a bit of sport," the cop said.

"To suck the eggs in your own hill," Retief said. "To make another stupid mistake."

Shluh raised his short ceremonial club and cracked Retief across the temple. Retief shook his head, tensed—

The cop in the front seat beside the driver turned and rammed the barrel of his scatter-gun against Retief's ribs.

"To make no move, outworlder," he said. Shluh raised his club and carefully struck Retief again. He slumped.

The car swayed, rounded another corner. Retief slid over against the police chief.

"To fend this animal—" Shluh began. His weak voice was cut off short as Retief's hand shot out, took him by the throat and snapped him down onto the floor. As the guard on Retief's left lunged, Retief uppercut him, slamming his head against the door post. He grabbed the scatter-gun as it fell, pushed into the mandibles of the Groacian in the front seat.

"To put your popgun over the seat—carefully—and drop it," he said.

The driver slammed on his brakes, whirled to raise his gun. Retief cracked the gun barrel against the head of the Groacian before him, then swiveled to aim it at the driver.

"To keep your eyestalks on the road," he said. The driver grabbed at the tiller and shrank against the window, watching Retief with one eye, driving with the other.

"To gun this thing," Retief said. "To keep moving."

Shluh stirred on the floor. Retief put a foot on him, pressed him back. The cop beside Retief moved. Retief pushed him off the seat onto the floor.

He held the scatter-gun with one hand and mopped at the blood on his face with the other. The car bounded over the irregular surface of the road, puffing furiously.

"Your death will not be an easy one, Terrestrial," Shluh said in Terran.

"No easier than I can help," Retief said. "Shut up for now, I want to think."

*

The car passed the last of the relief-crusted mounds, sped along between tilled fields.

"Slow down," Retief said. The driver obeyed.

"Turn down this side road."

The car bumped off onto an unpaved surface, threaded its way back among tall stalks.

"Stop here." The car stopped. It blew off steam and sat trembling as the hot engine idled roughly.

Retief opened the door, took his foot off Shluh.

"Sit up," he ordered. "You two in front listen carefully." Shluh sat up, rubbing his throat.

"Three of you are getting out here," Retief said. "Good old Shluh is going to stick around to drive for me. If I get that nervous feeling that the cops are after me, I'll toss him out to confuse them. That will be pretty messy, at high speed. Shluh, tell them to sit tight until dark and forget about sounding any alarms. I'd hate to see your carapace split and spill loveable you all over the pavement."

"To burst your throat sac, evil-smelling beast!" Shluh hissed.

"Sorry, I haven't got one." Retief put the gun under Shluh's ear. "Tell them, Shluh. I can drive myself, in a pinch."

87

RETIEF: THE DIRTY DOZEN

"To do as the foreign one says; to stay hidden until dark," Shluh said.

"Everybody out," Retief said. "And take this with you." He nudged the unconscious Groacian. "Shluh, you get in the driver's seat. You others stay where I can see you."

Retief watched as the Groaci silently followed instructions.

"All right, Shluh," Retief said softly. "Let's go. Take me to Groac Spaceport by the shortest route that doesn't go through the city. And be very careful about making any sudden movements."

*

Forty minutes later, Shluh steered the car up to the sentry-guarded gate in the security fence surrounding the military enclosure at Groac Spaceport.

"Don't yield to any rash impulses," Retief whispered as a crested Groacian soldier came up. Shluh grated his mandibles in helpless fury.

"Drone-master Shluh, Internal Security," he croaked. The guard tilted his eyes toward Retief.

"The guest of the Autonomy," Shluh added. "To let me pass or to rot in this spot, fool?"

"To pass, Drone-master," the sentry mumbled. He was still staring at Retief as the car moved jerkily away.

"You are as good as pegged out on the hill in the pleasure pits now, Terrestrial," Shluh said in Terran. "Why do you venture here?"

"Pull over there in the shadow of the tower and stop," Retief said.

Shluh complied. Retief studied the row of four slender ships parked on the ramp, navigation lights picked out against the early dawn colors of the sky.

"Which of those boats are ready to lift?" Retief demanded.

Shluh swiveled a choleric eye.

"All of them are shuttles; they have no range. They will not help you."

"To answer the question, Shluh, or to get another crack on the head."

"You are not like other Terrestrials! You are a mad dog!"

"We'll rough out a character sketch of me later. Are they all fueled up? You know the procedures here. Did those shuttles just get in, or is that the ready line?"

"Yes. All are fueled and ready for take-off."

"I hope you're right, Shluh. You and I are going to drive over and get in one; if it doesn't lift, I'll kill you and try the next. Let's go."

"You are mad! I have told you—these boats have not more than ten thousand ton-seconds capacity. They are useful only for satellite runs."

"Never mind the details. Let's try the first in line."

Shluh let in the clutch and the steam car clanked and heaved, rolled off toward the line of boats.

"Not the first in line," Shluh said suddenly. "The last is the more likely to be fueled. But—"

"Smart grasshopper," Retief said. "Pull up to the entry port, hop out and go right up. I'll be right behind you."

"The gangway guard. The challenging of—"

"More details. Just give him a dirty look and say what's necessary. You know the technique."

*

The car passed under the stern of the first boat, then the second. There was no alarm. It rounded the third and shuddered to a stop by the open port of the last vessel.

"Out," Retief said. "To make it snappy."

Shluh stepped from the car, hesitated as the guard came to attention, then hissed at him and mounted the steps. The guard looked wonderingly at Retief, mandibles slack.

"An outworlder!" he said. He unlimbered his scatter-gun. "To stop here, meat-faced one."

Shluh froze, turned.

"To snap to attention, litter-mate of drones!" Retief rasped in Groacian. The guard jumped, waved his eye stalks and came to attention.

"About face!" Retief hissed. "Hell out of here—to march!"

The guard tramped off across the ramp. Retief took the steps two at a time, slammed the port shut behind himself.

"I'm glad your boys have a little discipline, Shluh," Retief said. "What did you say to him?"

"I but—"

"Never mind. We're in. Get up to the control compartment."

"What do you know of Groacian naval vessels?"

"Plenty. This is a straight copy from the lifeboat you lads hijacked. I can run it. Get going."

89

Retief followed Shluh up the companionway into the cramped control room.

"Tie in, Shluh," Retief ordered.

"This is insane!" Shluh said. "We have only fuel enough for a one-way transit to the satellite. We cannot enter orbit, nor can we land again! To lift this boat is death—unless your destination is our moon."

"The moon is down, Shluh," Retief said. "And so are we. But not for long. Tie in."

"Release me," Shluh gasped. "I promise you immunity."

"If I have to tie you in myself, I might bend your head in the process."

Shluh crawled onto the couch, strapped in.

"Give it up," he said. "I will see that you are reinstated—with honor! I will guarantee a safe conduct."

"Countdown," Retief said. He threw in the autopilot.

"It is death!" Shluh screeched.

The gyros hummed; timers ticked; relays closed. Retief lay relaxed on the acceleration pad. Shluh breathed noisily, his mandibles clicking rapidly.

"That I had fled in time," Shluh said in a hoarse whisper. "This is not a good death . . . ."

"No death is a good death," Retief said. "Not for a while yet." The red light flashed on in the center of the panel, and abruptly sound filled the universe. The ship trembled, lifted.

Retief could hear Shluh's whimpering even through the roar of the drive.

*

"Perihelion," Shluh said dully. "To begin now the long fall back."

"Not quite," Retief said. "I figure eighty-five seconds to go." He scanned the instruments, frowning.

"We will not reach the surface, of course," Shluh said in Terran. "The pips on the screen are missiles. We have a rendezvous in space, Retief. In your madness, may you be content."

"They're fifteen minutes behind us, Shluh. Your defenses are sluggish."

"Nevermore to burrow in the gray sands of Groac," Shluh said.

Retief's eyes were fixed on a dial face.

"Any time now," he said softly. Shluh counted his eye stalks.

"What do you seek?"

Retief stiffened.

90

"Look at the screen," he said. Shluh looked. A glowing point, off-center, moving rapidly across the grid . . . .

"What—"

"Later!"

Shluh watched as Retief's eyes darted from one needle to another.

"How . . . . "

"For your own neck's sake, Shluh," Retief said, "you'd better hope this works." He flipped the sending key.

"2396 TR-42 G, this is the Terrestrial Consul at Groac, aboard Groac 902, vectoring on you at an MP fix of 91/54/94. Can you read me? Over."

"What forlorn gesture is this?" Shluh whispered. "You cry in the night to emptiness!"

"Button your mandibles," Retief snapped, listening. There was a faint hum of stellar background noise. Retief repeated his call, waited.

"Maybe they hear but can't answer," he muttered. He flipped the key.

"2396, you've got twenty seconds to lock a tractor beam on me, or I'll be past you like a shot of rum past a sailor's bridgework . . . . "

"To call into the void!" Shluh said. "To—"

"Look at the DV screen."

*

Shluh twisted his head, looked. Against the background mist of stars, a shape loomed, dark and inert.

"It is . . . a ship!" Shluh said. "A monster ship!"

"That's her," Retief said. "Nine years and a few months out of New Terra on a routine mapping mission. The missing cruiser—the IVS *Terrific*."

"Impossible!" Shluh hissed. "The hulk swings in a deep cometary orbit."

"Right. And now it's making its close swing past Groac."

"You think to match orbits with the derelict? Without power? Our meeting will be a violent one, if that is your intent."

"We won't hit; we'll make our pass at about five thousand yards."

"To what end, Terrestrial? You have found your lost ship. Then what? Is this glimpse worth the death we die?"

"Maybe they're not dead," Retief said.

"Not dead?" Shluh lapsed into Groacian. "To have died in the burrow of one's youth. To have burst my throat sac ere I embarked with a mad alien to call up the dead."

"2396, make it snappy," Retief called. The speaker crackled heedlessly. The dark image on the screen drifted past, dwindling now.

"Nine years, and the mad one speaking as to friends," Shluh raved. "Nine years dead, and still to seek them."

"Another twenty seconds," Retief said softly, "and we're out of range. Look alive, boys."

"Was this your plan, Retief?" Shluh asked in Terran. "Did you flee Groac and risk all on this slender thread?"

"How long would I have lasted in one of your Groaci prisons?"

"Long and long, my Retief," Shluh hissed, "under the blade of an artist."

Abruptly, the ship trembled, seemed to drag, rolling the two passengers in their couches. Shluh hissed as the restraining harness cut into him. The shuttle boat was pivoting heavily, upending. Crushing acceleration forces built. Shluh gasped and cried out shrilly.

"What ... is ... it?"

"It looks," Retief said, "like we've had a little bit of luck."

V

"On our second pass," the gaunt-faced officer said, "they let fly with something. I don't know how it got past our screens. It socked home in the stern and put the main pipe off the air. I threw full power to the emergency shields, and broadcast our identification on a scatter that should have hit every receiver within a parsec. Nothing. Then the transmitter blew. I was a fool to send the boat down but I couldn't believe, somehow . . . . "

"In a way it's lucky you did, Captain. That was my only lead."

"They tried to finish us after that. But with full power to the screens, nothing they had could get through. Then they called on us to surrender."

Retief nodded. "I take it you weren't tempted?"

"More than you know. It was a long swing out on our first circuit. Then, coming back in, we figured we'd hit. As a last resort I would have pulled back power from the screens and tried to adjust the orbit with the steering jets. But the bombardment was pretty heavy; I don't think we'd have made it. Then we swung past and headed out again. We've got a three year period. Don't think I didn't consider giving up."

"Why didn't you?"

"The information we have is important. We've got plenty of stores aboard. Enough for another ten years, if necessary. Sooner or later, I knew Search Command would find us."

Retief cleared his throat. "I'm glad you stuck with it, Captain. Even a backwater world like Groac can kill a lot of people when it runs amok."

"What I didn't know," the captain went on, "was that we're not in a stable orbit. We're going to graze atmosphere pretty deeply this pass, and in another sixty days we'd be back to stay. I guess the Groaci would be ready for us."

"No wonder they were sitting on this so tight," Retief said. "They were almost in the clear."

"And you're here now," the captain said. "Nine years, and we weren't forgotten. I knew we could count on—"

"It's over now, Captain," Retief said. "That's what counts."

"Home," the captain said. "After nine years . . . . "

*

"I'd like to take a look at the films you mentioned," Retief said. "The ones showing the installations on the satellite."

The captain complied. Retief watched as the scene unrolled, showing the bleak surface of the tiny moon as the *Terrific* had seen it nine years before.

In harsh black and white, row on row of identical hulls cast long shadows across the pitted metallic surface of the satellite. Retief whistled.

"They had quite a little surprise in store. Your visit must have panicked them."

"They should be about ready to go, by now. Nine years . . . . "

"Hold the picture," Retief said suddenly. "What's that ragged black line across the plain there?"

"I think it's a fissure. The crystalline structure—"

"I've got what may be an idea," Retief said. "I had a look at some classified files last night, at the foreign office. One was a progress report on a fissionable stockpile. It didn't make much sense at the time. Now I get the picture. Which is the 'north' end of that crevasse?"

"At the top of the picture."

"Unless I'm badly mistaken, that's the bomb dump. The Groaci like to tuck things underground. I wonder what a direct hit with a fifty mega-ton missile would do to it?"

"If that's an ordnance storage dump," the captain said, "it's an experiment I'd like to try."

"Can you hit it?"

"I've got fifty heavy missiles aboard. If I fire them in direct sequence, it should saturate the defenses. Yes, I can hit it."

"The range isn't too great?"

"These are the de luxe models," the captain smiled balefully. "Video guidance. We could steer them into a bar and park 'em on a stool."

"What do you say we try it?"

"I've been wanting a solid target for a long time," the captain said.

*

Retief waved a hand toward the screen.

"That expanding dust cloud used to be the satellite of Groac, Shluh," he said. "Looks like something happened to it."

The police chief stared at the picture.

"Too bad," Retief said. "But then it wasn't of any importance, was it, Shluh?"

Shluh muttered incomprehensibly.

"Just a bare hunk of iron, Shluh. That's what the foreign office told me when I asked for information."

"I wish you'd keep your prisoner out of sight," the captain said. "I have a hard time keeping my hands off him."

"Shluh wants to help, Captain. He's been a bad boy and I have a feeling he'd like to cooperate with us now. Especially in view of the imminent arrival of a Terrestrial ship, and the dust cloud out there."

"What do you mean?"

"Captain, you can ride it out for another week, contact the ship when it arrives, get a tow in and your troubles are over. When your films are shown in the proper quarter, a task force will come out here. They'll reduce Groac to a sub-technical cultural level, and set up a monitor system to insure she doesn't get any more expansionist ideas. Not that she can do much now, with her handy iron mine in the sky gone."

"That's right; and—"

"On the other hand," Retief said, "there's what I might call the diplomatic approach . . . . "

He explained at length. The captain looked at him thoughtfully.

"I'll go along," he said. "What about this fellow?"

Retief turned to Shluh. The Groacian shuddered, eye stalks retracted.

"I will do it," he said faintly.

"Right," Retief said. "Captain, if you'll have your men bring in the transmitter from the shuttle, I'll place a call to a fellow named Fith at the foreign office." He turned to Shluh. "And when I get him, Shluh, you'll do everything exactly as I've told you—or have terrestrial monitors dictating in Groac City."

*

"Quite candidly, Retief," Counsellor Pardy said, "I'm rather nonplussed. Mr. Fith of the foreign office seemed almost painfully lavish in your praise. He seems most eager to please you. In the light of some of the evidence I've turned up of highly irregular behavior on your part, it's difficult to understand."

"Fith and I have been through a lot together," Retief said. "We understand each other."

"You have no cause for complacency, Retief," Pardy said. "Miss Meuhl was quite justified in reporting your case. Of course, had she known that you were assisting Mr. Fith in his marvelous work, she would have modified her report somewhat, no doubt. You should have confided in her."

"Fith wanted to keep it secret, in case it didn't work out," Retief said. "You know how it is."

"Of course. And as soon as Miss Meuhl recovers from her nervous breakdown, there'll be a nice promotion awaiting her. The girl more than deserves it for her years of unswerving devotion to Corps policy."

"Unswerving," Retief said. "I'll sure go along with that."

"As well you may, Retief. You've not acquitted yourself well in this assignment. I'm arranging for a transfer. You've alienated too many of the local people . . . . "

"But as you said, Fith speaks highly of me . . . . "

"Oh, true. It's the cultural intelligentsia I'm referring to. Miss Meuhl's records show that you deliberately affronted a number of influential groups by boycotting—"

"Tone deaf," Retief said. "To me a Groacian blowing a nose-whistle sounds like a Groacian blowing a nose-whistle."

95

RETIEF: THE DIRTY DOZEN

"You have to come to terms with local aesthetic values," Pardy explained. "Learn to know the people as they really are. It's apparent from some of the remarks Miss Meuhl quoted in her report that you held the Groaci in rather low esteem. But how wrong you were! All the while, they were working unceasingly to rescue those brave lads marooned aboard our cruiser. They pressed on even after we ourselves had abandoned the search. And when they discovered that it had been a collision with their satellite which disabled the craft, they made that magnificent gesture—unprecedented. One hundred thousand credits in gold to each crew member, as a token of Groacian sympathy."

"A handsome gesture," Retief murmured.

*

"I hope, Retief, that you've learned from this incident. In view of the helpful part you played in advising Mr. Fith in matters of procedure to assist in his search, I'm not recommending a reduction in grade. We'll overlook the affair, give you a clean slate. But in future, I'll be watching you closely."

"You can't win 'em all," Retief said.

"You'd better pack up. You'll be coming along with us in the morning." Pardy shuffled his papers together.

"I'm sorry," he said, "that I can't file a more flattering report on you. I would have liked to recommend your promotion, along with Miss Meuhl's."

"That's okay," Retief said. "I have my memories."

Retief of the Red-Tape Mountain

Retief knew the importance of sealed orders—and the need to keep them that way!

"It's true," Consul Passwyn said, "I requested assignment as principal officer at a small post. But I had in mind one of those charming resort worlds, with only an occasional visa problem, or perhaps a distressed spaceman or two a year. Instead, I'm zoo-keeper to these confounded settlers. And not for one world, mind you, but eight!" He stared glumly at Vice-Consul Retief.

"Still," Retief said, "it gives an opportunity to travel—"

"Travel!" the consul barked. "I hate travel. Here in this backwater system particularly—" He paused, blinked at Retief and cleared his throat. "Not that a bit of travel isn't an excellent thing for a junior officer. Marvelous experience."

He turned to the wall-screen and pressed a button. A system triagram appeared: eight luminous green dots arranged around a larger disk representing the primary. He picked up a pointer, indicating the innermost planet.

"The situation on Adobe is nearing crisis. The confounded settlers—a mere handful of them—have managed, as usual, to stir up trouble with an intelligent indigenous life form, the Jaq. I can't think why they bother, merely for a few oases among the endless deserts. However I have, at last, received authorization from Sector Headquarters to take certain action." He swung back to face Retief. "I'm sending you in to handle the situation, Retief—under sealed orders." He picked up a fat buff envelope. "A pity they didn't see fit to order the Terrestrial settlers out weeks ago, as I suggested. Now it is too late. I'm expected to produce a miracle—a rapprochement between Terrestrial and Adoban and a division of territory. It's idiotic. However, failure would look very bad in my record, so I shall expect results."

He passed the buff envelope across to Retief.

"I understood that Adobe was uninhabited," Retief said, "until the Terrestrial settlers arrived."

"Apparently, that was an erroneous impression." Passwyn fixed Retief with a watery eye. "You'll follow your instructions to the letter. In a delicate situation such as this, there must be no impulsive, impromptu element introduced. This approach has been worked out in detail at Sector. You need merely implement it. Is that entirely clear?"

"Has anyone at Headquarters ever visited Adobe?"

"Of course not. They all hate travel. If there are no other questions, you'd best be on your way. The mail run departs the dome in less than an hour."

"What's this native life form like?" Retief asked, getting to his feet.

"When you get back," said Passwyn, "you tell me."

*

The mail pilot, a leathery veteran with quarter-inch whiskers, spat toward a stained corner of the compartment, leaned close to the screen.

"They's shootin' goin' on down there," he said. "See them white puffs over the edge of the desert?"

"I'm supposed to be preventing the war," said Retief. "It looks like I'm a little late."

The pilot's head snapped around. "War?" he yelped. "Nobody told me they was a war goin' on on 'Dobe. If that's what that is, I'm gettin' out of here."

"Hold on," said Retief. "I've got to get down. They won't shoot at you."

"They shore won't, sonny. I ain't givin' 'em the chance." He started punching keys on the console. Retief reached out, caught his wrist.

"Maybe you didn't hear me. I said I've got to get down."

The pilot plunged against the restraint, swung a punch that Retief blocked casually. "Are you nuts?" the pilot screeched. "They's plenty shootin' goin' on fer me to see it fifty miles out."

"The mail must go through, you know."

"Okay! You're so dead set on gettin' killed, you take the skiff. I'll tell 'em to pick up the remains next trip."

"You're a pal. I'll take your offer."

The pilot jumped to the lifeboat hatch and cycled it open. "Get in. We're closin' fast. Them birds might take it into their heads to lob one this way . . . . "

Retief crawled into the narrow cockpit of the skiff, glanced over the controls. The pilot ducked out of sight, came back, handed Retief a heavy old-fashioned power pistol. "Long as you're goin' in, might as well take this."

"Thanks." Retief shoved the pistol in his belt. "I hope you're wrong."

"I'll see they pick you up when the shootin's over—one way or another."

The hatch clanked shut. A moment later there was a jar as the skiff dropped away, followed by heavy buffeting in the backwash from the departing mail boat. Retief watched the tiny screen, hands on the manual controls. He was dropping rapidly: forty miles, thirty-nine . . . .

A crimson blip showed on the screen, moving out.

Retief felt sweat pop out on his forehead. The red blip meant heavy radiation from a warhead. Somebody was playing around with an outlawed but by no means unheard of fission weapon. But maybe it was just on a high trajectory and had no connection with the skiff . . . .

Retief altered course to the south. The blip followed.

He checked instrument readings, gripped the controls, watching. This was going to be tricky. The missile bored closer. At five miles Retief threw the light skiff into maximum acceleration, straight toward the oncoming bomb. Crushed back in the padded seat, he watched the screen, correcting course minutely. The proximity fuse should be set for no more than 1000 yards.

At a combined speed of two miles per second, the skiff flashed past the missile, and Retief was slammed violently against the restraining harness in the concussion of the explosion . . . a mile astern, and harmless.

Then the planetary surface was rushing up with frightening speed. Retief shook his head, kicked in the emergency retro-drive. Points of light arced up from the planet face below. If they were ordinary chemical warheads the skiff's meteor screens should handle them. The screen flashed brilliant white, then went dark. The skiff flipped on its back. Smoke filled the tiny compartment. There was a series of shocks, a final bone-shaking concussion, then stillness, broken by the ping of hot metal contracting.

*

Coughing, Retief disengaged himself from the shock-webbing. He beat out sparks in his lap, groped underfoot for the hatch and wrenched it open. A wave of hot jungle air struck him. He lowered himself to a bed of shattered foliage, got to his feet . . . and dropped flat as a bullet whined past his ear.

He lay listening. Stealthy movements were audible from the left.

He inched his way to the shelter of a broad-boled dwarf tree. Somewhere a song lizard burbled. Whining insects circled, scented alien life, buzzed off. There was another rustle of foliage from the underbrush five yards away. A bush quivered, then a low bough dipped.

Retief edged back around the trunk, eased down behind a fallen log. A stocky man in grimy leather shirt and shorts appeared, moving cautiously, a pistol in his hand.

As he passed, Retief rose, leaped the log and tackled him.

They went down together. The stranger gave one short yell, then struggled in silence. Retief flipped him onto his back, raised a fist—

"Hey!" the settler yelled. "You're as human as I am!"

"Maybe I'll look better after a shave," said Retief. "What's the idea of shooting at me?"

"Lemme up. My name's Potter. Sorry 'bout that. I figured it was a Flap-jack boat; looks just like 'em. I took a shot when I saw something move. Didn't know it was a Terrestrial. Who are you? What you doin' here? We're pretty close to the edge of the oases. That's Flap-jack country over there." He waved a hand toward the north, where the desert lay.

"I'm glad you're a poor shot. That missile was too close for comfort."

"Missile, eh? Must be Flap-jack artillery. We got nothing like that."

"I heard there was a full-fledged war brewing," said Retief. "I didn't expect—"

"Good!" Potter said. "We figured a few of you boys from Ivory would be joining up when you heard. You are from Ivory?"

"Yes. I'm—"

"Hey, you must be Lemuel's cousin. Good night! I pretty near made a bad mistake. Lemuel's a tough man to explain something to."

"I'm—"

"Keep your head down. These damn Flap-jacks have got some wicked hand weapons. Come on . . . . " He moved off silently on all fours. Retief followed. They crossed two hundred yards of rough country before Potter got to his feet, took out a soggy bandana and mopped his face.

"You move good for a city man. I thought you folks on Ivory just sat under those domes and read dials. But I guess bein' Lemuel's cousin you was raised different."

"As a matter of fact—"

"Have to get you some real clothes, though. Those city duds don't stand up on 'Dobe."

Retief looked down at the charred, torn and sweat-soaked powder-blue blazer and slacks.

"This outfit seemed pretty rough-and-ready back home," he said. "But I guess leather has its points."

"Let's get on back to camp. We'll just about make it by sundown. And, look. Don't say anything to Lemuel about me thinking you were a Flap-jack."

"I won't, but—"

Potter was on his way, loping off up a gentle slope. Retief pulled off the sodden blazer, dropped it over a bush, added his string tie and followed Potter.

II

"We're damn glad you're here, mister," said a fat man with two revolvers belted across his paunch. "We can use every hand. We're in bad shape. We ran into the Flap-jacks three months ago and we haven't made a smart move since. First, we thought they were a native form we hadn't run into before. Fact is, one of the boys shot one, thinkin' it was fair game. I guess that was the start of it." He stirred the fire, added a stick.

"And then a bunch of 'em hit Swazey's farm here," Potter said. "Killed two of his cattle, and pulled back."

"I figure they thought the cows were people," said Swazey. "They were out for revenge."

"How could anybody think a cow was folks?" another man put in. "They don't look nothin' like—"

"Don't be so dumb, Bert," said Swazey. "They'd never seen Terries before. They know better now."

Bert chuckled. "Sure do. We showed 'em the next time, didn't we, Potter? Got four."

"They walked right up to my place a couple days after the first time," Swazey said. "We were ready for 'em. Peppered 'em good. They cut and run."

"Flopped, you mean. Ugliest lookin' critters you ever saw. Look just like a old piece of dirty blanket humpin' around."

"It's been goin' on this way ever since. They raid and then we raid. But lately they've been bringing some big stuff into it. They've got some kind of pint-sized airships and automatic rifles. We've lost four men now and a dozen more in the freezer, waiting for the med ship. We can't afford it. The colony's got less than three hundred able-bodied men."

"But we're hanging onto our farms," said Potter. "All these oases are old sea-beds—a mile deep, solid topsoil. And there's a couple of hundred others we haven't touched yet. The Flap-jacks won't get 'em while there's a man alive."

"The whole system needs the food we can raise," Bert said. "These farms we're trying to start won't be enough but they'll help."

"We been yellin' for help to the CDT, over on Ivory," said Potter. "But you know these Embassy stooges."

"We heard they were sending some kind of bureaucrat in here to tell us to get out and give the oases to the Flap-jacks," said Swazey. He tightened his mouth. "We're waitin' for him . . . . "

"Meanwhile we got reinforcements comin' up, eh, boys?" Bert winked at Retief. "We put out the word back home. We all got relatives on Ivory and Verde."

"Shut up, you damn fool!" a deep voice grated.

"Lemuel!" Potter said. "Nobody else could sneak up on us like that."

"If I'd a been a Flap-jack; I'd of et you alive," the newcomer said, moving into the ring of fire, a tall, broad-faced man in grimy leather. He eyed Retief. "Who's that?"

"What do ya mean?" Potter spoke in the silence. "He's your cousin . . . . "

"He ain't no cousin of mine," Lemuel said slowly. He stepped to Retief. "Who you spyin' for, stranger?" he rasped.

*

Retief got to his feet. "I think I should explain—"

A short-nosed automatic appeared in Lemuel's hand, a clashing note against his fringed buckskins.

"Skip the talk. I know a fink when I see one."

"Just for a change, I'd like to finish a sentence," said Retief. "And I suggest you put your courage back in your pocket before it bites you."

"You talk too damned fancy to suit me."

"Maybe. But I'm talking to suit me. Now, for the last time, put it away."

Lemuel stared at Retief. "You givin' me orders . . . ?"

Retief's left fist shot out, smacked Lemuel's face dead center. He stumbled back, blood starting from his nose; the pistol fired into the dirt as he dropped it. He caught himself, jumped for Retief . . . and met a straight right that snapped him onto his back: out cold.

"Wow!" said Potter. "The stranger took Lem . . . in two punches!"

"One," said Swazey. "That first one was just a love tap."

Bert froze. "Hark, boys," he whispered. In the sudden silence a night lizard called. Retief strained, heard nothing. He narrowed his eyes, peered past the fire—

With a swift lunge he seized up the bucket of drinking water, dashed it over the fire, threw himself flat. He heard the others hit the dirt a split second behind him.

102

"You move fast for a city man," breathed Swazey beside him. "You see pretty good too. We'll split and take 'em from two sides. You and Bert from the left, me and Potter from the right."

"No," said Retief. "You wait here. I'm going out alone."

"What's the idea . . . ?"

"Later. Sit tight and keep your eyes open." Retief took a bearing on a treetop faintly visible against the sky and started forward.

*

Five minutes' stealthy progress brought him to a slight rise of ground. With infinite caution he raised himself, risking a glance over an out-cropping of rock.

The stunted trees ended just ahead. Beyond, he could make out the dim contour of rolling desert. Flap-jack country. He got to his feet, clambered over the stone—still hot after a day of tropical heat—and moved forward twenty yards. Around him he saw nothing but drifted sand, palely visible in the starlight, and the occasional shadow of jutting shale slabs. Behind him the jungle was still.

He sat down on the ground to wait.

It was ten minutes before a movement caught his eye. Something had separated itself from a dark mass of stone, glided across a few yards of open ground to another shelter. Retief watched. Minutes passed. The shape moved again, slipped into a shadow ten feet distant. Retief felt the butt of the power pistol with his elbow. His guess had better be right this time . . . .

There was a sudden rasp, like leather against concrete, and a flurry of sand as the Flap-jack charged.

Retief rolled aside, then lunged, threw his weight on the flopping Flap-jack—a yard square, three inches thick at the center and all muscle. The ray-like creature heaved up, curled backward, its edge rippling, to stand on the flattened rim of its encircling sphincter. It scrabbled with prehensile fringe-tentacles for a grip on Retief's shoulders. He wrapped his arms around the alien and struggled to his feet. The thing was heavy. A hundred pounds at least. Fighting as it was, it seemed more like five hundred.

The Flap-jack reversed its tactics, went limp. Retief grabbed, felt a thumb slip into an orifice—

The alien went wild. Retief hung on, dug the thumb in deeper.

"Sorry, fellow," he muttered between clenched teeth. "Eye-gouging isn't gentlemanly, but it's effective . . . . "

The Flap-jack fell still, only its fringes rippling slowly. Retief relaxed the pressure of his thumb; the alien gave a tentative jerk; the thumb dug in.

The alien went limp again, waiting.

"Now we understand each other," said Retief. "Take me to your leader."

*

Twenty minutes' walk into the desert brought Retief to a low rampart of thorn branches: the Flap-jacks' outer defensive line against Terry forays. It would be as good a place as any to wait for the move by the Flap-jacks. He sat down and eased the weight of his captive off his back, but kept a firm thumb in place. If his analysis of the situation was correct, a Flap-jack picket should be along before too long . . . .

A penetrating beam of red light struck Retief in the face, blinked off. He got to his feet. The captive Flap-jack rippled its fringe in an agitated way. Retief tensed his thumb in the eye-socket.

"Sit tight," he said. "Don't try to do anything hasty . . . . " His remarks were falling on deaf ears—or no ears at all—but the thumb spoke as loudly as words.

There was a slither of sand. Another. He became aware of a ring of presences drawing closer.

Retief tightened his grip on the alien. He could see a dark shape now, looming up almost to his own six-three. It looked like the Flap-jacks came in all sizes.

A low rumble sounded, like a deep-throated growl. It strummed on, faded out. Retief cocked his head, frowning.

"Try it two octaves higher," he said.

"Awwrrp! Sorry. Is that better?" a clear voice came from the darkness.

"That's fine," Retief said. "I'm here to arrange a prisoner exchange."

"Prisoners? But we have no prisoners."

"Sure you have. Me. Is it a deal?"

"Ah, yes, of course. Quite equitable. What guarantees do you require?"

"The word of a gentleman is sufficient." Retief released the alien. It flopped once, disappeared into the darkness.

"If you'd care to accompany me to our headquarters," the voice said, "we can discuss our mutual concerns in comfort."

"Delighted."

Red lights blinked briefly. Retief glimpsed a gap in the thorny barrier, stepped through it. He followed dim shapes across warm sand to a low cave-like entry, faintly lit with a reddish glow.

"I must apologize for the awkward design of our comfort-dome," said the voice. "Had we known we would be honored by a visit—"

"Think nothing of it," Retief said. "We diplomats are trained to crawl."

Inside, with knees bent and head ducked under the five-foot ceiling, Retief looked around at the walls of pink-toned nacre, a floor like burgundy-colored glass spread with silken rugs and a low table of polished red granite that stretched down the center of the spacious room, set out with silver dishes and rose-crystal drinking-tubes.

III

"Let me congratulate you," the voice said.

Retief turned. An immense Flap-jack, hung with crimson trappings, rippled at his side. The voice issued from a disk strapped to its back. "You fight well. I think we will find in each other worthy adversaries."

"Thanks. I'm sure the test would be interesting, but I'm hoping we can avoid it."

"Avoid it?" Retief heard a low humming coming from the speaker in the silence. "Well, let us dine," the mighty Flap-jack said at last. "We can resolve these matters later. I am called Hoshick of the Mosaic of the Two Dawns."

"I'm Retief." Hoshick waited expectantly, " . . . of the Mountain of Red Tape," Retief added.

"Take place, Retief," said Hoshick. "I hope you won't find our rude couches uncomfortable." Two other large Flap-jacks came into the room, communed silently with Hoshick. "Pray forgive our lack of translating devices," he said to Retief. "Permit me to introduce my colleagues . . . . "

A small Flap-jack rippled the chamber bearing on its back a silver tray laden with aromatic food. The waiter served the four diners, filled the drinking tubes with yellow wine. It smelled good.

"I trust you'll find these dishes palatable," said Hoshick. "Our metabolisms are much alike, I believe." Retief tried the food. It had a delicious nut-like flavor. The wine was indistinguishable from Chateau d'Yquem.

"It was an unexpected pleasure to encounter your party here," said Hoshick. "I confess at first we took you for an indigenous earth-grubbing form, but we were soon disabused of that notion." He raised a tube, manipulating it deftly with his fringe tentacles. Retief returned the salute and drank.

"Of course," Hoshick continued, "as soon as we realized that you were sportsmen like ourselves, we attempted to make amends by providing a bit of activity for you. We've ordered out our heavier equipment and a few trained skirmishers and soon we'll be able to give you an adequate show. Or so I hope."

"Additional skirmishers?" said Retief. "How many, if you don't mind my asking?"

"For the moment, perhaps only a few hundred. There-after . . . well, I'm sure we can arrange that between us. Personally I would prefer a contest of limited scope. No nuclear or radiation-effect weapons. Such a bore, screening the spawn for deviations. Though I confess we've come upon some remarkably useful sports. The rangerform such as you made captive, for example. Simple-minded, of course, but a fantastically keen tracker."

"Oh, by all means," Retief said. "No atomics. As you pointed out, spawn-sorting is a nuisance, and then too, it's wasteful of troops."

"Ah, well, they are after all expendable. But we agree: no atomics. Have you tried the ground-gwack eggs? Rather a specialty of my Mosaic . . . . "

"Delicious," said Retief. "I wonder. Have you considered eliminating weapons altogether?"

*

A scratchy sound issued from the disk. "Pardon my laughter," Hoshick said, "but surely you jest?"

"As a matter of fact," said Retief, "we ourselves seldom use weapons."

"I seem to recall that our first contact of skirmishforms involved the use of a weapon by one of your units."

"My apologies," said Retief. "The—ah—the skirmishform failed to recognize that he was dealing with a sportsman."

"Still, now that we have commenced so merrily with weapons . . . . " Hoshick signaled and the servant refilled tubes.

"There is an aspect I haven't yet mentioned," Retief went on. "I hope you won't take this personally, but the fact is, our skirmishforms think of weapons as something one employs only in dealing with certain specific life-forms."

"Oh? Curious. What forms are those?"

"Vermin. Or 'varmints' as some call them. Deadly antagonists, but lacking in caste. I don't want our skirmishforms thinking of such worthy adversaries as yourself as varmints."

"Dear me! I hadn't realized, of course. Most considerate of you to point it out." Hoshick clucked in dismay. "I see that skirmishforms are much the same among you as with us: lacking in perception." He laughed scratchily. "Imagine considering us as—what was the word?—varmints."

"Which brings us to the crux of the matter. You see, we're up against a serious problem with regard to skirmishforms. A low birth rate. Therefore we've reluctantly taken to substitutes for the mass actions so dear to the heart of the sportsman. We've attempted to put an end to these contests altogether . . . . "

Hoshick coughed explosively, sending a spray of wine into the air. "What are you saying?" he gasped. "Are you proposing that Hoshick of the Mosaic of the Two Dawns abandon honor . . . . ?"

"Sir!" said Retief sternly. "You forget yourself. I, Retief of the Red Tape Mountain, make an alternate proposal more in keeping with the newest sporting principles."

"New?" cried Hoshick. "My dear Retief, what a pleasant surprise! I'm enthralled with novel modes. One gets so out of touch. Do elaborate."

"It's quite simple, really. Each side selects a representative and the two individuals settle the issue between them."

"I . . . um . . . fear I don't understand. What possible significance could one attach to the activities of a couple of random skirmishforms?"

"I haven't made myself clear," said Retief. He took a sip of wine. "We don't involve the skirmishforms at all. That's quite passe."

"You don't mean . . . ?"

"That's right. You and me."

*

Outside on the starlit sand Retief tossed aside the power pistol, followed it with the leather shirt Swazey had lent him. By the faint light he could just make out the towering figure of the Flap-jack rearing up before him, his trappings gone. A silent rank of Flap-jack retainers were grouped behind him.

"I fear I must lay aside the translator now, Retief," said Hoshick. He sighed and rippled his fringe tentacles. "My spawn-fellows will never credit this. Such a curious turn fashion has taken. How much more pleasant it is to observe the action of the skirmishforms from a distance."

"I suggest we use Tennessee rules," said Retief. "They're very liberal. Biting, gouging, stomping, kneeing and of course choking, as well as the usual punching, shoving and kicking."

"Hmmm. These gambits seem geared to forms employing rigid endo-skeletons; I fear I shall be at a disadvantage."

"Of course," Retief said, "if you'd prefer a more plebeian type of contest . . . . "

"By no means. But perhaps we could rule out tentacle-twisting, just to even it."

"Very well. Shall we begin?"

With a rush Hoshick threw himself at Retief, who ducked, whirled, and leaped on the Flap-jack's back . . . and felt himself flipped clear by a mighty ripple of the alien's slab-like body. Retief rolled aside as Hoshick turned on him; he jumped to his feet and threw a right hay-maker to Hoshick's mid-section. The alien whipped his left fringe around in an arc that connected with Retief's jaw, sent him spinning onto his back . . . and Hoshick's weight struck him.

Retief twisted, tried to roll. The flat body of the alien blanketed him. He worked an arm free, drumming blows on the leathery back. Hoshick nestled closer.

Retief's air was running out. He heaved up against the smothering weight. Nothing budged.

It was like burial under a dump-truck-load of concrete.

He remembered the rangerform he had captured. The sensitive orifice had been placed ventrally, in what would be the thoracic area . . . .

He groped, felt tough hide set with horny granules. He would be missing skin tomorrow . . . if there was a tomorrow. His thumb found the orifice and probed.

The Flap-jack recoiled. Retief held fast, probed deeper, groping with the other hand. If the alien were bilaterally symmetrical there would be a set of ready made hand-holds . . . .

*

There were.

Retief dug in and the Flap-jack writhed, pulled away. Retief held on, scrambled to his feet, threw his weight against the alien and fell on top of him, still gouging. Hoshick rippled his fringe wildly, flopped in terror, then went limp.

Retief relaxed, released his hold and got to his feet, breathing hard. Hoshick humped himself over onto his ventral side, lifted and moved gingerly over to the sidelines. His retainers came forward, assisted him into his trappings, strapped on the translator. He sighed heavily, adjusted the volume.

"There is much to be said for the old system," he said. "What a burden one's sportsmanship places on one at times."

"Great sport, wasn't it?" said Retief. "Now, I know you'll be eager to continue. If you'll just wait while I run back and fetch some of our gougerforms—"

"May hide-ticks devour the gougerforms!" Hoshick bellowed. "You've given me such a sprong-ache as I'll remember each spawning-time for a year."

"Speaking of hide-ticks," said Retief, "we've developed a biterform—"

"Enough!" Hoshick roared, so loudly that the translator bounced on his hide. "Suddenly I yearn for the crowded yellow sands of Jaq. I had hoped . . . ." He broke off, drew a rasping breath. "I had hoped, Retief," he said, speaking sadly now, "to find a new land here where I might plan my own Mosaic, till these alien sands and bring forth such a crop of paradise-lichen as should glut the markets of a hundred worlds. But my spirit is not equal to the prospect of biterforms and gougerforms without end. I am shamed before you . . . ."

"To tell you the truth, I'm old-fashioned myself. I'd rather watch the action from a distance too."

"But surely your spawn-fellows would never condone such an attitude."

"My spawn-fellows aren't here. And besides, didn't I mention it? No one who's really in the know would think of engaging in competition by mere combat if there were any other way. Now, you mentioned tilling the sand, raising lichens—things like that—"

"That on which we dined but now," said Hoshick, "and from which the wine is made."

"The big news in fashionable diplomacy today is farming competition. Now, if you'd like to take these deserts and raise lichen, we'll promise to stick to the oases and vegetables."

Hoshick curled his back in attention. "Retief, you're quite serious? You would leave all the fair sand hills to us?"

"The whole works, Hoshick. I'll take the oases."

Hoshick rippled his fringes ecstatically. "Once again you have outdone me, Retief," he cried. "This time, in generosity."

"We'll talk over the details later. I'm sure we can establish a set of rules that will satisfy all parties. Now I've got to get back. I think some of the gougerforms are waiting to see me."

RETIEF: THE DIRTY DOZEN

IV

It was nearly dawn when Retief gave the whistled signal he had agreed on with Potter, then rose and walked into the camp circle. Swazey stood up.

"There you are," he said. "We been wonderin' whether to go out after you."

Lemuel came forward, one eye black to the cheekbone. He held out a raw-boned hand. "Sorry I jumped you, stranger. Tell you the truth, I thought you was some kind of stool-pigeon from the CDT."

Bert came up behind Lemuel. "How do you know he ain't, Lemuel?" he said. "Maybe he—"

Lemuel floored Bert with a backward sweep of his arm. "Next cotton-picker says some embassy Johnny can cool me gets worse'n that."

"Tell me," said Retief. "How are you boys fixed for wine?"

"Wine? Mister, we been livin' on stump water for a year now. 'Dobe's fatal to the kind of bacteria it takes to ferment likker."

"Try this." Retief handed over a sqat jug. Swazey drew the cork, sniffed, drank and passed it to Lemuel.

"Mister, where'd you get that?"

"The Flap-jacks make it. Here's another question for you: Would you concede a share in this planet to the Flap-jacks in return for a peace guarantee?"

At the end of a half hour of heated debate Lemuel turned to Retief. "We'll make any reasonable deal," he said. "I guess they got as much right here as we have. I think we'd agree to a fifty-fifty split. That'd give about a hundred and fifty oases to each side."

"What would you say to keeping all the oases and giving them the desert?"

Lemuel reached for the wine jug, eyes on Retief. "Keep talkin', mister," he said. "I think you got yourself a deal."

*

Consul Passwyn glanced up at Retief, went on perusing a paper.

"Sit down, Retief," he said absently. "I thought you were over on Pueblo, or Mudflat, or whatever they call that desert."

"I'm back."

Passwyn eyed him sharply. "Well, well, what is it you need, man? Speak up. Don't expect me to request any military assistance, no matter how things are . . . . "

Retief passed a bundle of documents across the desk. "Here's the Treaty. And a Mutual Assistance Pact declaration and a trade agreement."

"Eh?" Passwyn picked up the papers, riffled through them. He leaned back in his chair, beamed.

"Well, Retief. Expeditiously handled." He stopped, blinked at Retief. "You seem to have a bruise on your jaw. I hope you've been conducting yourself as befits a member of the Embassy staff."

"I attended a sporting event," Retief said. "One of the players got a little excited."

"Well . . . it's one of the hazards of the profession. One must pretend an interest in such matters." Passwyn rose, extended a hand. "You've done well, my boy. Let this teach you the value of following instructions to the letter."

Outside, by the hall incinerator drop, Retief paused long enough to take from his briefcase a large buff envelope, still sealed, and drop it in the slot.

AIDE MEMOIRE

The Fustians looked like turtles—but they could move fast when they chose!

Across the table from Retief, Ambassador Magnan rustled a stiff sheet of parchment and looked grave.

"This aide memoire," he said, "was just handed to me by the Cultural Attache. It's the third on the subject this week. It refers to the matter of sponsorship of Youth groups—"

"Some youths," Retief said. "Average age, seventy-five."

"The Fustians are a long-lived people," Magnan snapped. "These matters are relative. At seventy-five, a male Fustian is at a trying age—"

"That's right. He'll try anything—in the hope it will maim somebody."

"Precisely the problem," Magnan said. "But the Youth Movement is the important news in today's political situation here on Fust. And sponsorship of Youth groups is a shrewd stroke on the part of the Terrestrial Embassy. At my suggestion, well nigh every member of the mission has leaped at the opportunity to score a few p—that is, cement relations with this emergent power group—the leaders of the future. You, Retief, as Councillor, are the outstanding exception."

"I'm not convinced these hoodlums need my help in organizing their rumbles," Retief said. "Now, if you have a proposal for a pest control group—"

"To the Fustians this is no jesting matter," Magnan cut in. "This group—" he glanced at the paper—"known as the Sexual, Cultural, and Athletic Recreational Society, or SCARS for short, has been awaiting sponsorship for a matter of weeks now."

"Meaning they want someone to buy them a clubhouse, uniforms, equipment and anything else they need to complete their sexual, cultural and athletic development," Retief said.

"If we don't act promptly," Magnan said, "the Groaci Embassy may well anticipate us. They're very active here."

"That's an idea," said Retief. "Let 'em. After awhile they'll go broke instead of us."

"Nonsense. The group requires a sponsor. I can't actually order you to step forward. However . . . ." Magnan let the sentence hang in the air. Retief raised one eyebrow.

"For a minute there," he said, "I thought you were going to make a positive statement."

112

*

Magnan leaned back, lacing his fingers over his stomach. "I don't think you'll find a diplomat of my experience doing anything so naive," he said.

"I like the adult Fustians," said Retief. "Too bad they have to lug half a ton of horn around on their backs. I wonder if surgery would help."

"Great heavens, Retief," Magnan sputtered. "I'm amazed that even you would bring up a matter of such delicacy. A race's unfortunate physical characteristics are hardly a fit matter for Terrestrial curiosity."

"Well, of course your experience of the Fustian mentality is greater than mine. I've only been here a month. But it's been my experience, Mr. Ambassador, that few races are above improving on nature. Otherwise you, for example, would be tripping over your beard."

Magnan shuddered. "Please—never mention the idea to a Fustian."

Retief stood. "My own program for the day includes going over to the dockyards. There are some features of this new passenger liner the Fustians are putting together that I want to look into. With your permission, Mr. Ambassador . . . ?"

Magnan snorted. "Your pre-occupation with the trivial disturbs me, Retief. More interest in substantive matters—such as working with Youth groups—would create a far better impression."

"Before getting too involved with these groups, it might be a good idea to find out a little more about them," said Retief. "Who organizes them? There are three strong political parties here on Fust. What's the alignment of this SCARS organization?"

"You forget, these are merely teenagers, so to speak," Magnan said. "Politics mean nothing to them . . . yet."

"Then there are the Groaci. Why their passionate interest in a two-horse world like Fust? Normally they're concerned with nothing but business. But what has Fust got that they could use?"

"You may rule out the commercial aspect in this instance," said Magnan. "Fust possesses a vigorous steel-age manufacturing economy. The Groaci are barely ahead of them."

"Barely," said Retief. "Just over the line into crude atomics . . . like fission bombs."

Magnan shook his head, turned back to his papers. "What market exists for such devices on a world at peace? I suggest you address your attention to the less spectacular but more rewarding work of studying the social patterns of the local youth."

"I've studied them," said Retief. "And before I meet any of the local youth socially I want to get myself a good blackjack."

II

Retief left the sprawling bungalow-type building that housed the chancery of the Terrestrial Embassy, swung aboard a passing flat-car and leaned back against the wooden guard rail as the heavy vehicle trundled through the city toward the looming gantries of the shipyards.

It was a cool morning. A light breeze carried the fishy odor of Fusty dwellings across the broad cobbled avenue. A few mature Fustians lumbered heavily along in the shade of the low buildings, audibly wheezing under the burden of their immense carapaces. Among them, shell-less youths trotted briskly on scaly stub legs. The driver of the flat-car, a labor-caste Fustian with his guild colors emblazoned on his back, heaved at the tiller, swung the unwieldy conveyance through the shipyard gates, creaked to a halt.

"Thus I come to the shipyard with frightful speed," he said in Fustian. "Well I know the way of the naked-backs, who move always in haste."

Retief climbed down, handed him a coin. "You should take up professional racing," he said. "Daredevil."

He crossed the littered yard and tapped at the door of a rambling shed. Boards creaked inside. Then the door swung back.

A gnarled ancient with tarnished facial scales and a weathered carapace peered out at Retief.

"Long-may-you-sleep," said Retief. "I'd like to take a look around, if you don't mind. I understand you're laying the bedplate for your new liner today."

"May-you-dream-of-the-deeps," the old fellow mumbled. He waved a stumpy arm toward a group of shell-less Fustians standing by a massive hoist. "The youths know more of bedplates than do I, who but tend the place of papers."

"I know how you feel, old-timer," said Retief. "That sounds like the story of my life. Among your papers do you have a set of plans for the vessel? I understand it's to be a passenger liner."

The oldster nodded. He shuffled to a drawing file, rummaged, pulled out a sheaf of curled prints and spread them on the table. Retief stood silently, running a finger over the uppermost drawing, tracing lines . . . .

"What does the naked-back here?" barked a deep voice behind Retief. He turned. A heavy-faced Fustian youth, wrapped in a mantle, stood at the open door. Beady yellow eyes set among fine scales bored into Retief.

"I came to take a look at your new liner," said Retief.

"We need no prying foreigners here," the youth snapped. His eye fell on the drawings. He hissed in sudden anger.

"Doddering hulk!" he snapped at the ancient. "May you toss in nightmares! Put by the plans!"

"My mistake," Retief said. "I didn't know this was a secret project."

*

The youth hesitated. "It is not a secret project," he muttered. "Why should it be secret?"

"You tell me."

The youth worked his jaws and rocked his head from side to side in the Fusty gesture of uncertainty. "There is nothing to conceal," he said. "We merely construct a passenger liner."

"Then you don't mind if I look over the drawings," said Retief. "Who knows? Maybe some day I'll want to reserve a suite for the trip out."

The youth turned and disappeared. Retief grinned at the oldster. "Went for his big brother, I guess," he said. "I have a feeling I won't get to study these in peace here. Mind if I copy them?"

"Willingly, light-footed one," said the old Fustian. "And mine is the shame for the discourtesy of youth."

Retief took out a tiny camera, flipped a copying lens in place, leafed through the drawings, clicking the shutter.

"A plague on these youths," said the oldster, "who grow more virulent day by day."

"Why don't you elders clamp down?"

"Agile are they and we are slow of foot. And this unrest is new. Unknown in my youth was such insolence."

"The police—"

"Bah!" the ancient rumbled. "None have we worthy of the name, nor have we needed ought ere now."

"What's behind it?"

"They have found leaders. The spiv, Slock, is one. And I fear they plot mischief." He pointed to the window. "They come, and a Soft One with them."

Retief pocketed the camera, glanced out the window. A pale-featured Groaci with an ornately decorated crest stood with the youths, who eyed the hut, then started toward it.

"That's the military attache of the Groaci Embassy," Retief said. "I wonder what he and the boys are cooking up together?"

"Naught that augurs well for the dignity of Fust," the oldster rumbled. "Flee, agile one, while I engage their attentions."

"I was just leaving," Retief said. "Which way out?"

"The rear door," the Fustian gestured with a stubby member. "Rest well, stranger on these shores." He moved to the entrance.

"Same to you, pop," said Retief. "And thanks."

He eased through the narrow back entrance, waited until voices were raised at the front of the shed, then strolled off toward the gate.

*

The second dark of the third cycle was lightening when Retief left the Embassy technical library and crossed the corridor to his office. He flipped on a light. A note was tucked under a paperweight:

"Retief—I shall expect your attendance at the IAS dinner at first dark of the fourth cycle. There will be a brief but, I hope, impressive Sponsorship ceremony for the SCARS group, with full press coverage, arrangements for which I have managed to complete in spite of your intransigence."

Retief snorted and glanced at his watch. Less than three hours. Just time to creep home by flat-car, dress in ceremonial uniform and creep back.

Outside he flagged a lumbering bus. He stationed himself in a corner and watched the yellow sun, Beta, rise rapidly above the low skyline. The nearby sea was at high tide now, under the pull of the major sun and the three moons, and the stiff breeze carried a mist of salt spray.

Retief turned up his collar against the dampness. In half an hour he would be perspiring under the vertical rays of a third-noon sun, but the thought failed to keep the chill off.

116

Two Youths clambered up on the platform, moving purposefully toward Retief. He moved off the rail, watching them, weight balanced.

"That's close enough, kids," he said. "Plenty of room on this scow. No need to crowd up."

"There are certain films," the lead Fustian muttered. His voice was unusually deep for a Youth. He was wrapped in a heavy cloak and moved awkwardly. His adolescence was nearly at an end, Retief guessed.

"I told you once," said Retief. "Don't crowd me."

The two stepped close, slit mouths snapping in anger. Retief put out a foot, hooked it behind the scaly leg of the overaged juvenile and threw his weight against the cloaked chest. The clumsy Fustian tottered, fell heavily. Retief was past him and off the flat-car before the other Youth had completed his vain lunge toward the spot Retief had occupied. The Terrestrial waved cheerfully at the pair, hopped aboard another vehicle, watched his would-be assailants lumber down from their car, tiny heads twisted to follow his retreating figure.

So they wanted the film? Retief reflected, thumbing a cigar alight. They were a little late. He had already filed it in the Embassy vault, after running a copy for the reference files.

And a comparison of the drawings with those of the obsolete Mark XXXV battle cruiser used two hundred years earlier by the Concordiat Naval Arm showed them to be almost identical, gun emplacements and all. The term "obsolete" was a relative one. A ship which had been outmoded in the armories of the Galactic Powers could still be king of the walk in the Eastern Arm.

But how had these two known of the film? There had been no one present but himself and the old-timer—and he was willing to bet the elderly Fustian hadn't told them anything.

At least not willingly . . . .

Retief frowned, dropped the cigar over the side, waited until the flat-car negotiated a mud-wallow, then swung down and headed for the shipyard.

*

The door, hinges torn loose, had been propped loosely back in position. Retief looked around at the battered interior of the shed. The old fellow had put up a struggle.

There were deep drag-marks in the dust behind the building. Retief followed them across the yard. They disappeared under the steel door of a warehouse.

Retief glanced around. Now, at the mid-hour of the fourth cycle, the workmen were heaped along the edge of the refreshment pond, deep in their siesta. He took a multi-bladed tool from a pocket, tried various fittings in the lock. It snicked open.

He eased the door aside far enough to enter.

Heaped bales loomed before him. Snapping on the tiny lamp in the handle of the combination tool, Retief looked over the pile. One stack seemed out of alignment . . . and the dust had been scraped from the floor before it. He pocketed the light, climbed up on the bales, looked over into a nest made by stacking the bundles around a clear spot. The aged Fustian lay in it, on his back, a heavy sack tied over his head.

Retief dropped down inside the ring of bales, sawed at the tough twine and pulled the sack free.

"It's me, old fellow," Retief said. "The nosy stranger. Sorry I got you into this."

The oldster threshed his gnarled legs. He rocked slightly and fell back. "A curse on the cradle that rocked their infant slumbers," he rumbled. "But place me back on my feet and I hunt down the youth, Slock, though he flee to the bottommost muck of the Sea of Torments."

"How am I going to get you out of here? Maybe I'd better get some help."

"Nay. The perfidious Youths abound here," said the old Fustian. "It would be your life."

"I doubt if they'd go that far."

"Would they not?" The Fustian stretched his neck. "Cast your light here. But for the toughness of my hide . . . . "

Retief put the beam of the light on the leathery neck. A great smear of thick purplish blood welled from a ragged cut. The oldster chuckled, a sound like a seal coughing.

"Traitor, they called me. For long they sawed at me—in vain. Then they trussed me and dumped me here. They think to return with weapons to complete the task."

"Weapons? I thought it was illegal!"

"Their evil genius, the Soft One," said the Fustian. "He would provide fuel to the Devil himself."

"The Groaci again," said Retief. "I wonder what their angle is."

"And I must confess, I told them of you, ere I knew their full intentions. Much can I tell you of their doings. But first, I pray, the block and tackle."

Retief found the hoist where the Fustian directed him, maneuvered it into position, hooked onto the edge of the carapace and hauled away. The immense Fustian rose slowly, teetered . . . then flopped on his chest.

Slowly he got to his feet.

"My name is Whonk, fleet one," he said. "My cows are yours."

"Thanks. I'm Retief. I'd like to meet the girls some time. But right now, let's get out of here."

Whonk leaned his bulk against the ponderous stacks of baled kelp, bulldozed them aside. "Slow am I to anger," he said, "but implacable in my wrath. Slock, beware!"

"Hold it," said Retief suddenly. He sniffed. "What's that odor?" He flashed the light around, played it over a dry stain on the floor. He knelt, sniffed at the spot.

"What kind of cargo was stacked here, Whonk? And where is it now?"

Whonk considered. "There were drums," he said. "Four of them, quite small, painted an evil green, the property of the Soft Ones, the Groaci. They lay here a day and a night. At full dark of the first period they came with stevedores and loaded them aboard the barge *Moss Rock*."

"The VIP boat. Who's scheduled to use it?"

"I know not. But what matters this? Let us discuss cargo movements after I have settled a score with certain Youths."

"We'd better follow this up first, Whonk. There's only one substance I know of that's transported in drums and smells like that blot on the floor. That's titanite: the hottest explosive this side of a uranium pile."

III

Beta was setting as Retief, Whonk puffing at his heels, came up to the sentry box beside the gangway leading to the plush interior of the official luxury space barge *Moss Rock*.

"A sign of the times," said Whonk, glancing inside the empty shelter. "A guard should stand here, but I see him not. Doubtless he crept away to sleep."

"Let's go aboard and take a look around."

They entered the ship. Soft lights glowed in utter silence. A rough box stood on the floor, rollers and pry-bars beside it—a discordant note in the muted luxury of the setting. Whonk rummaged in it.

"Curious," he said. "What means this?" He held up a stained cloak of orange and green, a metal bracelet, papers.

"Orange and green," mused Relief. "Whose colors are those?"

"I know not." Whonk glanced at the arm-band. "But this is lettered." He passed the metal band to Retief.

"SCARS," Retief read. He looked at Whonk. "It seems to me I've heard the name before," he murmured. "Let's get back to the Embassy—fast."

Back on the ramp Retief heard a sound . . . and turned in time to duck the charge of a hulking Fustian youth who thundered past him and fetched up against the broad chest of Whonk, who locked him in a warm embrace.

"Nice catch, Whonk. Where'd he sneak out of?"

"The lout hid there by the storage bin," rumbled Whonk. The captive youth thumped fists and toes fruitlessly against the oldster's carapace.

"Hang onto him," said Retief. "He looks like the biting kind."

"No fear. Clumsy I am, yet not without strength."

"Ask him where the titanite is tucked away."

"Speak, witless grub," growled Whonk, "lest I tweak you in twain."

The youth gurgled.

"Better let up before you make a mess of him," said Retief. Whonk lifted the Youth clear of the floor, then flung him down with a thump that made the ground quiver. The younger Fustian glared up at the elder, mouth snapping.

"This one was among those who trussed me and hid me away for the killing," said Whonk. "In his repentance he will tell all to his elder."

"That's the same young squirt that tried to strike up an acquaintance with me on the bus," Retief said. "He gets around."

The youth scrambled to hands and knees, scuttled for freedom. Retief planted a foot on his dragging cloak; it ripped free. He stared at the bare back of the Fustian—

"By the Great Egg!" Whonk exclaimed, tripping the refugee as he tried to rise. "This is no Youth! His carapace has been taken from him!"

Retief looked at the scarred back. "I thought he looked a little old. But I thought—"

"This is not possible," Whonk said wonderingly. "The great nerve trunks are deeply involved. Not even the cleverest surgeon could excise the carapace and leave the patient living."

"It looks like somebody did the trick. But let's take this boy with us and get out of here. His folks may come home."

"Too late," said Whonk. Retief turned.

Three youths came from behind the sheds.

"Well," Retief said. "It looks like the SCARS are out in force tonight. Where's your pal?" he said to the advancing trio. "The sticky little bird with the eye-stalks? Back at his Embassy, leaving you suckers holding the bag, I'll bet."

"Shelter behind me, Retief," said Whonk.

"Go get 'em, old-timer." Retief stooped, picked up one of the pry-bars. "I'll jump around and distract them."

Whonk let out a whistling roar and charged for the immature Fustians. They fanned out . . . and one tripped, sprawled on his face. Retief whirled the metal bar he had thrust between the Fustian's legs, slammed it against the skull of another, who shook his head, turned on Retief . . . and bounced off the steel hull of the *Moss Rock* as Whonk took him in full charge.

Retief used the bar on another head. His third blow laid the Fustian on the pavement, oozing purple. The other two club members departed hastily, seriously dented but still mobile.

Retief leaned on his club, breathing hard. "Tough heads these kids have got. I'm tempted to chase those two lads down, but I've got another errand to run. I don't know who the Groaci intended to blast, but I have a sneaking suspicion somebody of importance was scheduled for a boat ride in the next few hours. And three drums of titanite is enough to vaporize this tub and everyone aboard her."

"The plot is foiled," said Whonk. "But what reason did they have?"

"The Groaci are behind it. I have an idea the SCARS didn't know about this gambit."

"Which of these is the leader?" asked Whonk. He prodded a fallen Youth with a horny toe. "Arise, dreaming one."

"Never mind him, Whonk. We'll tie these two up and leave them here. I know where to find the boss."

*

A stolid crowd filled the low-ceilinged banquet hall. Retief scanned the tables for the pale blobs of Terrestrial faces, dwarfed by the giant armored bodies of the Fustians. Across the room Magnan fluttered a hand. Retief headed toward him. A low-pitched vibration filled the air: the rumble of subsonic Fustian music.

Retief slid into his place beside Magnan. "Sorry to be late, Mr. Ambassador."

"I'm honored that you chose to appear at all," said Magnan coldly. He turned back to the Fustian on his left.

"Ah, yes, Mr. Minister," he said. "Charming, most charming. So joyous."

The Fustian looked at him, beady-eyed. "It is the *Lament of Hatching*," he said; "our National Dirge."

"Oh," said Magnan. "How interesting. Such a pleasing balance of instruments—"

"It is a droon solo," said the Fustian, eyeing the Terrestrial Ambassador suspiciously.

"Why don't you just admit you can't hear it," Retief whispered loudly. "And if I may interrupt a moment—"

Magnan cleared his throat. "Now that our Mr. Retief has arrived, perhaps we could rush right along to the Sponsorship ceremonies."

"This group," said Retief, leaning across Magnan, "the SCARS. How much do you know about them, Mr. Minister?"

"Nothing at all," the huge Fustian elder rumbled. "For my taste, all Youths should be kept penned with the livestock until they grow a carapace to tame their irresponsibility."

"We mustn't lose sight of the importance of channeling youthful energies," said Magnan.

"Labor gangs," said the minister. "In my youth we were indentured to the dredge-masters. I myself drew a muck sledge."

"But in these modern times," put in Magnan, "surely it's incumbent on us to make happy these golden hours."

The minister snorted. "Last week I had a golden hour. They set upon me and pelted me with overripe stench-fruit."

"But this was merely a manifestation of normal youthful frustrations," cried Magnan. "Their essential tenderness—"

"You'd not find a tender spot on that lout yonder," the minister said, pointing with a fork at a newly arrived Youth, "if you drilled boreholes and blasted."

*

"Why, that's our guest of honor," said Magnan, "a fine young fellow! Slop I believe his name is."

"Slock," said Retief. "Eight feet of armor-plated orneriness. And—"

Magnan rose and tapped on his glass. The Fustians winced at the, to them, supersonic vibrations. They looked at each other muttering. Magnan tapped louder. The Minister drew in his head, eyes closed. Some of the Fustians rose, tottered for the doors; the noise level rose. Magnan redoubled his efforts. The glass broke with a clatter and green wine gushed on the tablecloth.

"What in the name of the Great Egg!" the Minister muttered. He blinked, breathing deeply.

"Oh, forgive me," blurted Magnan, dabbing at the wine.

"Too bad the glass gave out," said Retief. "In another minute you'd have cleared the hall. And then maybe I could have gotten a word in sideways. There's a matter you should know about—"

"Your attention, please," Magnan said, rising. "I see that our fine young guest has arrived, and I hope that the remainder of his committee will be along in a moment. It is my pleasure to announce that our Mr. Retief has had the good fortune to win out in the keen bidding for the pleasure of sponsoring this lovely group."

Retief tugged at Magnan's sleeve. "Don't introduce me yet," he said. "I want to appear suddenly. More dramatic, you know."

"Well," murmured Magnan, glancing down at Retief, "I'm gratified to see you entering into the spirit of the event at last." He turned his attention back to the assembled guests. "If our honored guest will join me on the rostrum . . . ?" he said. "The gentlemen of the press may want to catch a few shots of the presentation."

Magnan stepped up on the low platform at the center of the wide room, took his place beside the robed Fustian youth and beamed at the cameras.

"How gratifying it is to take this opportunity to express once more the great pleasure we have in sponsoring SCARS," he said, talking slowly for the benefit of the scribbling reporters. "We'd like to think that in our modest way we're to be a part of all that the SCARS achieve during the years ahead."

Magnan paused as a huge Fustian elder heaved his bulk up the two low steps to the rostrum, approached the guest of honor. He watched as the newcomer paused behind Slock, who did not see the new arrival.

Retief pushed through the crowd, stepped up to face the Fustian youth. Slock stared at him, drew back.

"You know me, Slock," said Retief loudly. "An old fellow named Whonk told you about me, just before you tried to saw his head off, remember? It was when I came out to take a look at that battle cruiser you're building."

RETIEF: THE DIRTY DOZEN

IV

With a bellow Slock reached for Retief—and choked off in mid-cry as the Fustian elder, Whonk, pinioned him from behind, lifting him clear of the floor.

"Glad you reporters happened along," said Retief to the gaping newsmen. "Slock here had a deal with a sharp operator from the Groaci Embassy. The Groaci were to supply the necessary hardware and Slock, as foreman at the shipyards, was to see that everything was properly installed. The next step, I assume, would have been a local take-over, followed by a little interplanetary war on Flamenco or one of the other nearby worlds . . . for which the Groaci would be glad to supply plenty of ammo."

Magnan found his tongue. "Are you mad, Retief?" he screeched. "This group was vouched for by the Ministry of Youth!"

"The Ministry's overdue for a purge," snapped Retief. He turned back to Slock. "I wonder if you were in on the little diversion that was planned for today. When the *Moss Rock* blew, a variety of clues were to be planted where they'd be easy to find . . . with SCARS written all over them. The Groaci would thus have neatly laid the whole affair squarely at the door of the Terrestrial Embassy . . . whose sponsorship of the SCARS had received plenty of publicity."

"The *Moss Rock*?" said Magnan. "But that was—Retief! This is idiotic. Slock himself was scheduled to go on a cruise tomorrow!"

Slock roared suddenly, twisting violently. Whonk teetered, his grip loosened . . . and Slock pulled free and was off the platform, butting his way through the milling oldsters on the dining room floor. Magnan watched, open-mouthed.

"The Groaci were playing a double game, as usual," Retief said. "They intended to dispose of this fellow Slock, once he'd served their purpose."

"Well, don't stand there," yelped Magnan over the uproar. "If Slock is the ring-leader of a delinquent gang . . . !" He moved to give chase.

Retief grabbed his arm. "Don't jump down there! You'd have as much chance of getting through as a jack-rabbit through a threshing contest."

Ten minutes later the crowd had thinned slightly. "We can get through now," Whonk called. "This way." He lowered himself to the floor, bulled through to the exit. Flashbulbs popped. Retief and Magnan followed in Whonk's wake.

In the lounge Retief grabbed the phone, waited for the operator, gave a code letter. No reply. He tried another.

"No good," he said after a full minute had passed. "Wonder what's loose?" He slammed the phone back in its niche. "Let's grab a cab."

*

In the street the blue sun, Alpha, peered like an arc light under a low cloud layer, casting flat shadows across the mud of the avenue. The three mounted a passing flat-car. Whonk squatted, resting the weight of his immense shell on the heavy plank flooring.

"Would that I too could lose this burden, as has the false youth we bludgeoned aboard the *Moss Rock*," he sighed. "Soon will I be forced into retirement. Then a mere keeper of a place of papers such as I will rate no more than a slab on the public strand, with once-daily feedings. And even for a man of high position, retirement is no pleasure. A slab in the Park of Monuments is little better. A dismal outlook for one's next thousand years!"

"You two carry on to the police station," said Retief. "I want to play a hunch. But don't take too long. I may be painfully right."

"What—?" Magnan started.

"As you wish, Retief," said Whonk.

The flat-car trundled past the gate to the shipyard and Retief jumped down, headed at a run for the VIP boat. The guard post still stood vacant. The two Youths whom he and Whonk had left trussed were gone.

"That's the trouble with a peaceful world," Retief muttered. "No police protection." He stepped down from the lighted entry and took up a position behind the sentry box. Alpha rose higher, shedding a glaring blue-white light without heat. Retief shivered. Maybe he'd guessed wrong . . . .

There was a sound in the near distance, like two elephants colliding.

Retief looked toward the gate. His giant acquaintance, Whonk, had reappeared and was grappling with a hardly less massive opponent. A small figure became visible in the melee, scuttled for the gate. Headed off by the battling titans, he turned and made for the opposite side of the shipyard. Retief waited, jumped out and gathered in the fleeing Groaci.

"Well, Yith," he said, "how's tricks? You should pardon the expression."

"Release me, Retief!" the pale-featured alien lisped, his throat bladder pulsating in agitation. "The behemoths vie for the privilege of dismembering me out of hand!"

"I know how they feel. I'll see what I can do . . . for a price."

"I appeal to you," Yith whispered hoarsely. "As a fellow diplomat, a fellow alien, a fellow soft-back—"

"Why don't you appeal to Slock, as a fellow skunk?" said Retief. "Now keep quiet . . . and you may get out of this alive."

The heavier of the two struggling Fustians threw the other to the ground. There was another brief flurry, and then the smaller figure was on its back, helpless.

"That's Whonk, still on his feet," said Retief. "I wonder who he's caught—and why."

Whonk came toward the *Moss Rock* dragging the supine Fustian, who kicked vainly. Retief thrust Yith down well out of sight behind the sentry box. "Better sit tight, Yith. Don't try to sneak off; I can outrun you. Stay here and I'll see what I can do." He stepped out and hailed Whonk.

Puffing like a steam engine Whonk pulled up before him. "Sleep, Retief!" He panted. "You followed a hunch; I did the same. I saw something strange in this one when we passed him on the avenue. I watched, followed him here. Look! It is Slock, strapped into a dead carapace! Now many things become clear."

*

Retief whistled. "So the Youths aren't all as young as they look. Somebody's been holding out on the rest of you Fustians!"

"The Soft One," Whonk said. "You laid him by the heels, Retief. I saw. Produce him now."

"Hold on a minute, Whonk. It won't do you any good—"

Whonk winked broadly. "I must take my revenge!" he roared. "I shall test the texture of the Soft One! His pulped remains will be scoured up by the ramp-washers and mailed home in bottles!"

Retief whirled at a sound, caught up with the scuttling Yith fifty feet away, hauled him back to Whonk.

"It's up to you, Whonk," he said. "I know how important ceremonial revenge is to you Fustians. I will not interfere."

"Mercy!" Yith hissed, eye-stalks whipping in distress. "I claim diplomatic immunity!"

"No diplomat am I," rumbled Whonk. "Let me see; suppose I start with one of those obscenely active eyes—" He reached . . . .

"I have an idea," said Retief brightly. "Do you suppose—just this once—you could forego the ceremonial revenge if Yith promised to arrange for a Groaci Surgical Mission to de-carapace you elders?"

"But," Whonk protested, "those eyes! What a pleasure to pluck them, one by one!"

"Yess," hissed Yith, "I swear it! Our most expert surgeons . . . platoons of them, with the finest of equipment."

"I have dreamed of how it would be to sit on this one, to feel him squash beneath my bulk . . . . "

"Light as a whissle feather shall you dance," Yith whispered. "Shell-less shall you spring in the joy of renewed youth—"

"Maybe just one eye," said Whonk grudgingly. "That would leave him four."

"Be a sport," said Retief.

"Well."

"It's a deal then," said Retief. "Yith, on your word as a diplomat, an alien, a soft-back and a skunk, you'll set up the mission. Groaci surgical skill is an export that will net you more than armaments. It will be a whissle feather in your cap—if you bring it off. And in return, Whonk won't sit on you. And I won't prefer charges of interference in the internal affairs of a free world."

Behind Whonk there was a movement. Slock, wriggling free of the borrowed carapace, struggled to his feet . . . in time for Whonk to seize him, lift him high and head for the entry to the *Moss Rock*.

"Hey," Retief called. "Where are you going?"

"I would not deny this one his reward," called Whonk. "He hoped to cruise in luxury. So be it."

"Hold on," said Retief. "That tub is loaded with titanite!"

"Stand not in my way, Retief. For this one in truth owes me a vengeance."

Retief watched as the immense Fustian bore his giant burden up the ramp and disappeared within the ship.

"I guess Whonk means business," he said to Yith, who hung in his grasp, all five eyes goggling. "And he's a little too big for me to stop."

Whonk reappeared, alone, climbed down.

"What did you do with him?" said Retief. "Tell him you were going to—"

"We had best withdraw," said Whonk. "The killing radius of the drive is fifty yards."

RETIEF: THE DIRTY DOZEN

"You mean—"

"The controls are set for Groaci. Long-may-he-sleep."

*

"It was quite a bang," said Retief. "But I guess you saw it, too."

"No, confound it," Magnan said. "When I remonstrated with Hulk, or Whelk—"

"Whonk."

"—the ruffian thrust me into an alley bound in my own cloak. I'll most certainly complain to the Minister."

"How about the surgical mission?"

"A most generous offer," said Magnan. "Frankly, I was astonished. I think perhaps we've judged the Groaci too harshly."

"I hear the Ministry of Youth has had a rough morning of it," said Retief. "And a lot of rumors are flying to the effect that Youth Groups are on the way out."

Magnan cleared his throat, shuffled papers. "I—ah—have explained to the press that last night's—ah—"

"Fiasco."

"—affair was necessary in order to place the culprits in an untenable position. Of course, as to the destruction of the VIP vessel and the presumed death of, uh, Slop."

"The Fustians understand," said Retief. "Whonk wasn't kidding about ceremonial vengeance."

"The Groaci had been guilty of gross misuse of diplomatic privilege," said Magnan. "I think that a note—or perhaps an Aide Memoire: less formal . . . . "

"The *Moss Rock* was bound for Groaci," said Retief. "She was already in her transit orbit when she blew. The major fragments will arrive on schedule in a month or so. It should provide quite a meteorite display. I think that should be all the *aide* the Groaci's *memoires* will need to keep their tentacles off Fust."

"But diplomatic usage—"

"Then, too, the less that's put in writing, the less they can blame you for, if anything goes wrong."

"That's true," said Magnan, lips pursed. "Now you're thinking constructively, Retief. We may make a diplomat of you yet." He smiled expansively.

"Maybe. But I refuse to let it depress me." Retief stood up. "I'm taking a few weeks off . . . if you have no objection, Mr. Ambassador. My pal Whonk wants to show me an island down south where the fishing is good."

128

"But there are some extremely important matters coming up," said Magnan. "We're planning to sponsor Senior Citizen Groups—"

"Count me out. All groups give me an itch."

"Why, what an astonishing remark, Retief! After all, we diplomats are ourselves a group."

"Uh-huh," Retief said.

Magnan sat quietly, mouth open, and watched as Retief stepped into the hall and closed the door gently behind him.

CULTURAL EXCHANGE

It was a simple student exchange—but Retief gave them more of an education than they expected!

I

Second Secretary Magnan took his green-lined cape and orange-feathered beret from the clothes tree. "I'm off now, Retief," he said. "I hope you'll manage the administrative routine during my absence without any unfortunate incidents."

"That seems a modest enough hope," Retief said. "I'll try to live up to it."

"I don't appreciate frivolity with reference to this Division," Magnan said testily. "When I first came here, the Manpower Utilization Directorate, Division of Libraries and Education was a shambles. I fancy I've made MUDDLE what it is today. Frankly, I question the wisdom of placing you in charge of such a sensitive desk, even for two weeks. But remember. Yours is purely a rubber-stamp function."

"In that case, let's leave it to Miss Furkle. I'll take a couple of weeks off myself. With her poundage, she could bring plenty of pressure to bear."

"I assume you jest, Retief," Magnan said sadly. "I should expect even you to appreciate that Bogan participation in the Exchange Program may be the first step toward sublimation of their aggressions into more cultivated channels."

"I see they're sending two thousand students to d'Land," Retief said, glancing at the Memo for Record. "That's a sizable sublimation."

Magnan nodded. "The Bogans have launched no less than four military campaigns in the last two decades. They're known as the Hoodlums of the Nicodemean Cluster. Now, perhaps, we shall see them breaking that precedent and entering into the cultural life of the Galaxy."

"Breaking and entering," Retief said. "You may have something there. But I'm wondering what they'll study on d'Land. That's an industrial world of the poor but honest variety."

"Academic details are the affair of the students and their professors," Magnan said. "Our function is merely to bring them together. See that you don't antagonize the Bogan representative. This will be an excellent opportunity for you to practice your diplomatic restraint—not your strong point, I'm sure you'll agree."

A buzzer sounded. Retief punched a button. "What is it, Miss Furkle?"

"That—bucolic person from Lovenbroy is here again." On the small desk screen, Miss Furkle's meaty features were compressed in disapproval.

"This fellow's a confounded pest. I'll leave him to you, Retief," Magnan said. "Tell him something. Get rid of him. And remember: here at Corps HQ, all eyes are upon you."

"If I'd thought of that, I'd have worn my other suit," Retief said.

Magnan snorted and passed from view. Retief punched Miss Furkle's button. "Send the bucolic person in."

*

A tall broad man with bronze skin and gray hair, wearing tight trousers of heavy cloth, a loose shirt open at the neck and a short jacket, stepped into the room. He had a bundle under his arm. He paused at sight of Retief, looked him over momentarily, then advanced and held out his hand. Retief took it. For a moment the two big men stood, face to face. The newcomer's jaw muscles knotted. Then he winced.

Retief dropped his hand and motioned to a chair.

"That's nice knuckle work, mister," the stranger said, massaging his hand. "First time anybody ever did that to me. My fault though. I started it, I guess." He grinned and sat down.

"What can I do for you?" Retief said.

"You work for this Culture bunch, do you? Funny. I thought they were all ribbon-counter boys. Never mind. I'm Hank Arapoulous. I'm a farmer. What I wanted to see you about was—" He shifted in his chair. "Well, out on Lovenbroy we've got a serious problem. The wine crop is just about ready. We start picking in another two, three months. Now I don't know if you're familiar with the Bacchus vines we grow . . . ?"

"No," Retief said. "Have a cigar?" He pushed a box across the desk. Arapoulous took one. "Bacchus vines are an unusual crop," he said, puffing the cigar alight. "Only mature every twelve years. In between, the vines don't need a lot of attention, so our time's mostly our own. We like to farm, though. Spend a lot of time developing new forms. Apples the size of a melon—and sweet—"

"Sounds very pleasant," Retief said. "Where does the Libraries and Education Division come in?"

Arapoulous leaned forward. "We go in pretty heavy for the arts. Folks can't spend all their time hybridizing plants. We've turned all the land area we've got into parks and farms. Course, we left some sizable forest areas for hunting and such. Lovenbroy's a nice place, Mr. Retief."

131

"It sounds like it, Mr. Arapoulous. Just what—"

"Call me Hank. We've got long seasons back home. Five of 'em. Our year's about eighteen Terry months. Cold as hell in winter; eccentric orbit, you know. Blue-black sky, stars visible all day. We do mostly painting and sculpture in the winter. Then Spring; still plenty cold. Lots of skiing, bob-sledding, ice skating; and it's the season for woodworkers. Our furniture—"

"I've seen some of your furniture," Retief said. "Beautiful work."

Arapoulous nodded. "All local timbers too. Lots of metals in our soil and those sulphates give the woods some color, I'll tell you. Then comes the Monsoon. Rain—it comes down in sheets. But the sun's getting closer. Shines all the time. Ever seen it pouring rain in the sunshine? That's the music-writing season. Then summer. Summer's hot. We stay inside in the daytime and have beach parties all night. Lots of beach on Lovenbroy; we're mostly islands. That's the drama and symphony time. The theatres are set up on the sand, or anchored off-shore. You have the music and the surf and the bonfires and stars—we're close to the center of a globular cluster, you know . . . . "

"You say it's time now for the wine crop?"

"That's right. Autumn's our harvest season. Most years we have just the ordinary crops. Fruit, grain, that kind of thing; getting it in doesn't take long. We spend most of the time on architecture, getting new places ready for the winter or remodeling the older ones. We spend a lot of time in our houses. We like to have them comfortable. But this year's different. This is Wine Year."

*

Arapoulous puffed on his cigar, looked worriedly at Retief. "Our wine crop is our big money crop," he said. "We make enough to keep us going. But this year . . . . "

"The crop isn't panning out?"

"Oh, the crop's fine. One of the best I can remember. Course, I'm only twenty-eight; I can't remember but two other harvests. The problem's not the crop."

"Have you lost your markets? That sounds like a matter for the Commercial—"

"Lost our markets? Mister, nobody that ever tasted our wines ever settled for anything else!"

"It sounds like I've been missing something," said Retief. "I'll have to try them some time."

Arapoulous put his bundle on the desk, pulled off the wrappings. "No time like the present," he said.

Retief looked at the two squat bottles, one green, one amber, both dusty, with faded labels, and blackened corks secured by wire.

"Drinking on duty is frowned on in the Corps, Mr. Arapoulous," he said.

"This isn't *drinking*. It's just wine." Arapoulous pulled the wire retainer loose, thumbed the cork. It rose slowly, then popped in the air. Arapoulous caught it. Aromatic fumes wafted from the bottle. "Besides, my feelings would be hurt if you didn't join me." He winked.

Retief took two thin-walled glasses from a table beside the desk. "Come to think of it, we also have to be careful about violating quaint native customs."

Arapoulous filled the glasses. Retief picked one up, sniffed the deep rust-colored fluid, tasted it, then took a healthy swallow. He looked at Arapoulous thoughtfully.

"Hmmm. It tastes like salted pecans, with an undercurrent of crusted port."

"Don't try to describe it, Mr. Retief," Arapoulous said. He took a mouthful of wine, swished it around his teeth, swallowed. "It's Bacchus wine, that's all. Nothing like it in the Galaxy." He pushed the second bottle toward Retief. "The custom back home is to alternate red wine and black."

*

Retief put aside his cigar, pulled the wires loose, nudged the cork, caught it as it popped up.

"Bad luck if you miss the cork," Arapoulous said, nodding. "You probably never heard about the trouble we had on Lovenbroy a few years back?"

"Can't say that I did, Hank." Retief poured the black wine into two fresh glasses. "Here's to the harvest."

"We've got plenty of minerals on Lovenbroy," Arapoulous said, swallowing wine. "But we don't plan to wreck the landscape mining 'em. We like to farm. About ten years back some neighbors of ours landed a force. They figured they knew better what to do with our minerals than we did. Wanted to strip-mine, smelt ore. We convinced 'em otherwise. But it took a year, and we lost a lot of men."

"That's too bad," Retief said. "I'd say this one tastes more like roast beef and popcorn over a Riesling base."

"It put us in a bad spot," Arapoulous went on. "We had to borrow money from a world called Croanie. Mortgaged our crops. Had to start exporting art work too. Plenty of buyers, but it's not the same when you're doing it for strangers."

"Say, this business of alternating drinks is the real McCoy," Retief said. "What's the problem? Croanie about to foreclose?"

"Well, the loan's due. The wine crop would put us in the clear. But we need harvest hands. Picking Bacchus grapes isn't a job you can turn over to machinery—and anyway we wouldn't if we could. Vintage season is the high point of living on Lovenbroy. Everybody joins in. First, there's the picking in the fields. Miles and miles of vineyards covering the mountain sides, and crowding the river banks, with gardens here and there. Big vines, eight feet high, loaded with fruit, and deep grass growing between. The wine-carriers keep on the run, bringing wine to the pickers. There's prizes for the biggest day's output, bets on who can fill the most baskets in an hour . . . . The sun's high and bright, and it's just cool enough to give you plenty of energy. Come nightfall, the tables are set up in the garden plots, and the feast is laid on: roast turkeys, beef, hams, all kinds of fowl. Big salads. Plenty of fruit. Fresh-baked bread . . . and wine, plenty of wine. The cooking's done by a different crew each night in each garden, and there's prizes for the best crews.

"Then the wine-making. We still tramp out the vintage. That's mostly for the young folks but anybody's welcome. That's when things start to get loosened up. Matter of fact, pretty near half our young-uns are born after a vintage. All bets are off then. It keeps a fellow on his toes though. Ever tried to hold onto a gal wearing nothing but a layer of grape juice?"

*

"Never did," Retief said. "You say most of the children are born after a vintage. That would make them only twelve years old by the time—"

"Oh, that's Lovenbroy years; they'd be eighteen, Terry reckoning."

"I was thinking you looked a little mature for twenty-eight," Retief said.

"Forty-two, Terry years," Arapoulous said. "But this year it looks bad. We've got a bumper crop—and we're short-handed. If we don't get a big vintage, Croanie steps in. Lord knows what they'll do to the land. Then next vintage time, with them holding half our grape acreage—"

"You hocked the vineyards?"

"Yep. Pretty dumb, huh? But we figured twelve years was a long time."

"On the whole," Retief said, "I think I prefer the black. But the red is hard to beat . . . . "

"What we figured was, maybe you Culture boys could help us out. A loan to see us through the vintage, enough to hire extra hands. Then we'd repay it in sculpture, painting, furniture—"

"Sorry, Hank. All we do here is work out itineraries for traveling side-shows, that kind of thing. Now, if you needed a troop of Groaci nose-flute players—"

"Can they pick grapes?"

"Nope. Anyway, they can't stand the daylight. Have you talked this over with the Labor Office?"

"Sure did. They said they'd fix us up with all the electronics specialists and computer programmers we wanted—but no field hands. Said it was what they classified as menial drudgery; you'd have thought I was trying to buy slaves."

The buzzer sounded. Miss Furkle's features appeared on the desk screen.

"You're due at the Intergroup Council in five minutes," she said. "Then afterwards, there are the Bogan students to meet."

"Thanks." Retief finished his glass, stood. "I have to run, Hank," he said. "Let me think this over. Maybe I can come up with something. Check with me day after tomorrow. And you'd better leave the bottles here. Cultural exhibits, you know."

II

As the council meeting broke up, Retief caught the eye of a colleague across the table.

"Mr. Whaffle, you mentioned a shipment going to a place called Croanie. What are they getting?"

Whaffle blinked. "You're the fellow who's filling in for Magnan, over at MUDDLE," he said. "Properly speaking, equipment grants are the sole concern of the Motorized Equipment Depot, Division of Loans and Exchanges." He pursed his lips. "However, I suppose there's no harm in telling you. They'll be receiving heavy mining equipment."

"Drill rigs, that sort of thing?"

"Strip mining gear." Whaffle took a slip of paper from a breast pocket, blinked at it. "Bolo Model WV/1 tractors, to be specific. Why is MUDDLE interested in MEDDLE's activities?"

"Forgive my curiosity, Mr. Whaffle. It's just that Croanie cropped up earlier today. It seems she holds a mortgage on some vineyards over on—"

"That's not MEDDLE's affair, sir," Whaffle cut in. "I have sufficient problems as Chief of MEDDLE without probing into MUDDLE'S business."

"Speaking of tractors," another man put in, "we over at the Special Committee for Rehabilitation and Overhaul of Under-developed Nations' General Economies have been trying for months to get a request for mining equipment for d'Land through MEDDLE—"

"SCROUNGE was late on the scene," Whaffle said. "First come, first served. That's our policy at MEDDLE. Good day, gentlemen." He strode off, briefcase under his arm.

"That's the trouble with peaceful worlds," the SCROUNGE committeeman said. "Boge is a troublemaker, so every agency in the Corps is out to pacify her. While my chance to make a record—that is, assist peace-loving d'Land—comes to naught." He shook his head.

"What kind of university do they have on d'Land?" asked Retief. "We're sending them two thousand exchange students. It must be quite an institution."

"University? D'Land has one under-endowed technical college."

"Will all the exchange students be studying at the Technical College?"

"Two thousand students? Hah! Two *hundred* students would overtax the facilities of the college."

"I wonder if the Bogans know that?"

"The Bogans? Why, most of d'Land's difficulties are due to the unwise trade agreement she entered into with Boge. Two thousand students indeed!" He snorted and walked away.

*

Retief stopped by the office to pick up a short cape, then rode the elevator to the roof of the 230-story Corps HQ building and hailed a cab to the port. The Bogan students had arrived early. Retief saw them lined up on the ramp waiting to go through customs. It would be half an hour before they were cleared through. He turned into the bar and ordered a beer.

A tall young fellow on the next stool raised his glass.

"Happy days," he said.

"And nights to match."

"You said it." He gulped half his beer. "My name's Karsh. Mr. Karsh. Yep, Mr. Karsh. Boy, this is a drag, sitting around this place waiting . . . . "

"You meeting somebody?"

"Yeah. Bunch of babies. Kids. How they expect—Never mind. Have one on me."

"Thanks. You a Scoutmaster?"

"I'll tell you what I am. I'm a cradle-robber. You know—" he turned to Retief—"not one of those kids is over eighteen." He hiccupped. "Students, you know. Never saw a student with a beard, did you?"

"Lots of times. You're meeting the students, are you?"

The young fellow blinked at Retief. "Oh, you know about it, huh?"

"I represent MUDDLE."

Karsh finished his beer, ordered another. "I came on ahead. Sort of an advance guard for the kids. I trained 'em myself. Treated it like a game, but they can handle a CSU. Don't know how they'll act under pressure. If I had my old platoon—"

He looked at his beer glass, pushed it back. "Had enough," he said. "So long, friend. Or are you coming along?"

Retief nodded. "Might as well."

*

At the exit to the Customs enclosure, Retief watched as the first of the Bogan students came through, caught sight of Karsh and snapped to attention, his chest out.

"Drop that, mister," Karsh snapped. "Is that any way for a student to act?"

The youth, a round-faced lad with broad shoulders, grinned.

"Heck, no," he said. "Say, uh, Mr. Karsh, are we gonna get to go to town? We fellas were thinking—"

"You were, hah? You act like a bunch of school kids! I mean . . . no! Now line up!"

"We have quarters ready for the students," Retief said. "If you'd like to bring them around to the west side, I have a couple of copters laid on."

"Thanks," said Karsh. "They'll stay here until take-off time. Can't have the little dears wandering around loose. Might get ideas about going over the hill." He hiccupped. "I mean they might play hookey."

"We've scheduled your re-embarkation for noon tomorrow. That's a long wait. MUDDLE's arranged theater tickets and a dinner."

"Sorry," Karsh said. "As soon as the baggage gets here, we're off." He hiccupped again. "Can't travel without our baggage, y'know."

"Suit yourself," Retief said. "Where's the baggage now?"

"Coming in aboard a Croanie lighter."

"Maybe you'd like to arrange for a meal for the students here."

"Sure," Karsh said. "That's a good idea. Why don't you join us?" Karsh winked. "And bring a few beers."

"Not this time," Retief said. He watched the students, still emerging from Customs. "They seem to be all boys," he commented. "No female students?"

"Maybe later," Karsh said. "You know, after we see how the first bunch is received."

Back at the MUDDLE office, Retief buzzed Miss Furkle.

"Do you know the name of the institution these Bogan students are bound for?"

"Why, the University at d'Land, of course."

"Would that be the Technical College?"

Miss Furkle's mouth puckered. "I'm sure I've never pried into these details."

"Where does doing your job stop and prying begin, Miss Furkle?" Retief said. "Personally, I'm curious as to just what it is these students are travelling so far to study—at Corps expense."

"Mr. Magnan never—"

"For the present. Miss Furkle, Mr. Magnan is vacationing. That leaves me with the question of two thousand young male students headed for a world with no classrooms for them . . . a world in need of tractors. But the tractors are on their way to Croanie, a world under obligation to Boge. And Croanie holds a mortgage on the best grape acreage on Lovenbroy."

"Well!" Miss Furkle snapped, small eyes glaring under unplucked brows. "I hope you're not questioning Mr. Magnan's wisdom!"

"About Mr. Magnan's wisdom there can be no question," Retief said. "But never mind. I'd like you to look up an item for me. How many tractors will Croanie be getting under the MEDDLE program?"

"Why, that's entirely MEDDLE business," Miss Furkle said. "Mr. Magnan always—"

"I'm sure he did. Let me know about the tractors as soon as you can."

*

Miss Furkle sniffed and disappeared from the screen. Retief left the office, descended forty-one stories, followed a corridor to the Corps Library. In the stacks he thumbed through catalogues, pored over indices.

"Can I help you?" someone chirped. A tiny librarian stood at his elbow.

"Thank you, ma'am," Retief said. "I'm looking for information on a mining rig. A Bolo model WV tractor."

"You won't find it in the industrial section," the librarian said. "Come along." Retief followed her along the stacks to a well-lit section lettered ARMAMENTS. She took a tape from the shelf, plugged it into the viewer, flipped through and stopped at a squat armored vehicle.

"That's the model WV," she said. "It's what is known as a continental siege unit. It carries four men, with a half-megaton/second firepower."

"There must be an error somewhere," Retief said. "The Bolo model I want is a tractor. Model WV M-1—"

"Oh, the modification was the addition of a bulldozer blade for demolition work. That must be what confused you."

"Probably—among other things. Thank you."

Miss Furkle was waiting at the office. "I have the information you wanted," she said. "I've had it for over ten minutes. I was under the impression you needed it urgently, and I went to great lengths—"

"Sure," Retief said. "Shoot. How many tractors?"

"Five hundred."

"Are you sure?"

Miss Furkle's chins quivered. "Well! If you feel I'm incompetent—"

"Just questioning the possibility of a mistake, Miss Furkle. Five hundred tractors is a lot of equipment."

"Was there anything further?" Miss Furkle inquired frigidly.

"I sincerely hope not," Retief said.

III

Leaning back in Magnan's padded chair with power swivel and hip-u-matic concontour, Retief leafed through a folder labelled "CERP 7-602-Ba; CROANIE (general)." He paused at a page headed Industry.

Still reading, he opened the desk drawer, took out the two bottles of Bacchus wine and two glasses. He poured an inch of wine into each and sipped the black wine meditatively.

It would be a pity, he reflected, if anything should interfere with the production of such vintages . . . .

Half an hour later he laid the folder aside, keyed the phone and put through a call to the Croanie Legation. He asked for the Commercial Attache.

"Retief here, Corps HQ," he said airily. "About the MEDDLE shipment, the tractors. I'm wondering if there's been a slip up. My records show we're shipping five hundred units . . . . "

"That's correct. Five hundred."

Retief waited.

"Ah . . . are you there, Retief?"

"I'm still here. And I'm still wondering about the five hundred tractors."

"It's perfectly in order. I thought it was all settled. Mr. Whaffle—"

"One unit would require a good-sized plant to handle its output," Retief said. "Now Croanie subsists on her fisheries. She has perhaps half a dozen pint-sized processing plants. Maybe, in a bind, they could handle the ore ten WV's could scrape up . . . if Croanie had any ore. It doesn't. By the way, isn't a WV a poor choice as a mining outfit? I should think—"

"See here, Retief! Why all this interest in a few surplus tractors? And in any event, what business is it of yours how we plan to use the equipment? That's an internal affair of my government. Mr. Whaffle—"

"I'm not Mr. Whaffle. What are you going to do with the other four hundred and ninety tractors?"

"I understood the grant was to be with no strings attached!"

"I know it's bad manners to ask questions. It's an old diplomatic tradition that any time you can get anybody to accept anything as a gift, you've scored points in the game. But if Croanie has some scheme cooking—"

*

"Nothing like that, Retief. It's a mere business transaction."

"What kind of business do you do with a Bolo WV? With or without a blade attached, it's what's known as a continental siege unit."

"Great Heavens, Retief! Don't jump to conclusions! Would you have us branded as warmongers? Frankly—is this a closed line?"

"Certainly. You may speak freely."

"The tractors are for transshipment. We've gotten ourselves into a difficult situation, balance-of-payments-wise. This is an accommodation to a group with which we have rather strong business ties."

"I understand you hold a mortgage on the best land on Lovenbroy," Retief said. "Any connection?"

"Why . . . ah . . . no. Of course not, ha ha."

"Who gets the tractors eventually?"

"Retief, this is unwarranted interference!"

"Who gets them?"

"They happen to be going to Lovenbroy. But I scarcely see—"

"And who's the friend you're helping out with an unauthorized transshipment of grant material?"

"Why ... ah ... I've been working with a Mr. Gulver, a Bogan representative."

"And when will they be shipped?"

"Why, they went out a week ago. They'll be half way there by now. But look here, Retief, this isn't what you're thinking!"

"How do you know what I'm thinking? I don't know myself." Retief rang off, buzzed the secretary.

"Miss Furkle, I'd like to be notified immediately of any new applications that might come in from the Bogan Consulate for placement of students."

"Well, it happens, by coincidence, that I have an application here now. Mr. Gulver of the Consulate brought it in."

"Is Mr. Gulver in the office? I'd like to see him."

"I'll ask him if he has time."

"Great. Thanks." It was half a minute before a thick-necked red-faced man in a tight hat walked in. He wore an old-fashioned suit, a drab shirt, shiny shoes with round toes and an ill-tempered expression.

*

"What is it you wish?" he barked. "I understood in my discussions with the other ... ah ... civilian there'd be no further need for these irritating conferences."

"I've just learned you're placing more students abroad, Mr. Gulver. How many this time?"

"Two thousand."

"And where will they be going?"

"Croanie. It's all in the application form I've handed in. Your job is to provide transportation."

"Will there be any other students embarking this season?"

"Why ... perhaps. That's Boge's business." Gulver looked at Retief with pursed lips. "As a matter of fact, we had in mind dispatching another two thousand to Featherweight."

"Another under-populated world—and in the same cluster, I believe," Retief said. "Your people must be unusually interested in that region of space."

"If that's all you wanted to know, I'll be on my way. I have matters of importance to see to."

After Gulver left, Retief called Miss Furkle in. "I'd like to have a break-out of all the student movements that have been planned under the present program," he said. "And see if you can get a summary of what MEDDLE has been shipping lately."

Miss Furkle compressed her lips. "If Mr. Magnan were here, I'm sure he wouldn't dream of interfering in the work of other departments. I . . . overheard your conversation with the gentleman from the Croanie Legation—"

"The lists, Miss Furkle."

"I'm not accustomed," Miss Furkle said, "to intruding in matters outside our interest cluster."

"That's worse than listening in on phone conversations, eh? But never mind. I need the information, Miss Furkle."

"Loyalty to my Chief—"

"Loyalty to your pay-check should send you scuttling for the material I've asked for," Retief said. "I'm taking full responsibility. Now scat."

The buzzer sounded. Retief flipped a key. "MUDDLE, Retief speaking . . . . "

Arapoulous's brown face appeared on the desk screen.

"How-do, Retief. Okay if I come up?"

"Sure, Hank. I want to talk to you."

In the office, Arapoulous took a chair. "Sorry if I'm rushing you, Retief," he said. "But have you got anything for me?"

Retief waved at the wine bottles. "What do you know about Croanie?"

"Croanie? Not much of a place. Mostly ocean. All right if you like fish, I guess. We import our seafood from there. Nice prawns in monsoon time. Over a foot long."

"You on good terms with them?"

"Sure, I guess so. Course, they're pretty thick with Boge."

"So?"

"Didn't I tell you? Boge was the bunch that tried to take us over here a dozen years back. They'd've made it too, if they hadn't had a lot of bad luck. Their armor went in the drink, and without armor they're easy game."

Miss Furkle buzzed. "I have your lists," she said shortly.

"Bring them in, please."

*

The secretary placed the papers on the desk. Arapoulous caught her eye and grinned. She sniffed and marched from the room.

"What that gal needs is a slippery time in the grape mash," Arapoulous observed. Retief thumbed through the papers, pausing to read from time to time. He finished and looked at Arapoulous.

"How many men do you need for the harvest, Hank?" Retief inquired.

Arapoulous sniffed his wine glass and looked thoughtful.

"A hundred would help," he said. "A thousand would be better. Cheers."

"What would you say to two thousand?"

"Two thousand? Retief, you're not fooling?"

"I hope not." He picked up the phone, called the Port Authority, asked for the dispatch clerk.

"Hello, Jim. Say, I have a favor to ask of you. You know that contingent of Bogan students. They're traveling aboard the two CDT transports. I'm interested in the baggage that goes with the students. Has it arrived yet? Okay, I'll wait."

Jim came back to the phone. "Yeah, Retief, it's here. Just arrived. But there's a funny thing. It's not consigned to d'Land. It's ticketed clear through to Lovenbroy."

"Listen, Jim," Retief said. "I want you to go over to the warehouse and take a look at that baggage for me."

Retief waited while the dispatch clerk carried out the errand. The level in the two bottles had gone down an inch when Jim returned to the phone.

"Hey, I took a look at that baggage, Retief. Something funny going on. Guns. 2mm needlers, Mark XII hand blasters, power pistols—"

"It's okay, Jim. Nothing to worry about. Just a mix-up. Now, Jim, I'm going to ask you to do something more for me. I'm covering for a friend. It seems he slipped up. I wouldn't want word to get out, you understand. I'll send along a written change order in the morning that will cover you officially. Meanwhile, here's what I want you to do . . . ."

Retief gave instructions, then rang off and turned to Arapoulous.

"As soon as I get off a couple of TWX's, I think we'd better get down to the port, Hank. I think I'd like to see the students off personally."

143

IV

Karsh met Retief as he entered the Departures enclosure at the port.

"What's going on here?" he demanded. "There's some funny business with my baggage consignment. They won't let me see it! I've got a feeling it's not being loaded."

"You'd better hurry, Mr. Karsh," Retief said. "You're scheduled to blast off in less than an hour. Are the students all loaded?"

"Yes, blast you! What about my baggage? Those vessels aren't moving without it!"

"No need to get so upset about a few toothbrushes, is there, Mr. Karsh?" Retief said blandly. "Still, if you're worried—" He turned to Arapoulous.

"Hank, why don't you walk Mr. Karsh over to the warehouse and . . . ah . . . take care of him?"

"I know just how to handle it," Arapoulous said.

The dispatch clerk came up to Retief. "I caught the tractor equipment," he said. "Funny kind of mistake, but it's okay now. They're being off-loaded at d'Land. I talked to the traffic controller there. He said they weren't looking for any students."

"The labels got switched, Jim. The students go where the baggage was consigned. Too bad about the mistake, but the Armaments Office will have a man along in a little while to dispose of the guns. Keep an eye out for the luggage. No telling where it's gotten to."

"Here!" a hoarse voice yelled. Retief turned. A disheveled figure in a tight hat was crossing the enclosure, arms waving.

"Hi there, Mr. Gulver," Retief called. "How's Boge's business coming along?"

"Piracy!" Gulver blurted as he came up to Retief, puffing hard. "You've got a hand in this, I don't doubt! Where's that Magnan fellow?"

"What seems to be the problem?" Retief said.

"Hold those transports! I've just been notified that the baggage shipment has been impounded. I'll remind you, that shipment enjoys diplomatic free entry!"

"Who told you it was impounded?"

"Never mind! I have my sources!"

Two tall men buttoned into gray tunics came up. "Are you Mr. Retief of CDT?" one said.

"That's right."

"What about my baggage!" Gulver cut in. "And I'm warning you, if those ships lift without—"

"These gentlemen are from the Armaments Control Commission," Retief said. "Would you like to come along and claim your baggage, Mr. Gulver?"

"From where? I—" Gulver turned two shades redder about the ears. "Armaments?"

"The only shipment I've held up seems to be somebody's arsenal," Retief said. "Now if you claim this is your baggage . . . . "

"Why, impossible," Gulver said in a strained voice. "Armaments? Ridiculous. There's been an error . . . . "

*

At the baggage warehouse Gulver looked glumly at the opened cases of guns. "No, of course not," he said dully. "Not my baggage. Not my baggage at all."

Arapoulous appeared, supporting the stumbling figure of Mr. Karsh.

"What—what's this?" Gulver spluttered. "Karsh? What's happened?"

"He had a little fall. He'll be okay," Arapoulous said.

"You'd better help him to the ship," Retief said. "It's ready to lift. We wouldn't want him to miss it."

"Leave him to me!" Gulver snapped, his eyes slashing at Karsh. "I'll see he's dealt with."

"I couldn't think of it," Retief said. "He's a guest of the Corps, you know. We'll see him safely aboard."

Gulver turned, signaled frantically. Three heavy-set men in identical drab suits detached themselves from the wall, crossed to the group.

"Take this man," Gulver snapped, indicating Karsh, who looked at him dazedly, reached up to rub his head.

"We take our hospitality seriously," Retief said. "We'll see him aboard the vessel."

Gulver opened his mouth.

"I know you feel bad about finding guns instead of school books in your luggage," Retief said, looking Gulver in the eye. "You'll be busy straightening out the details of the mix-up. You'll want to avoid further complications."

"Ah. Ulp. Yes," Gulver said. He appeared unhappy.

Arapoulous went on to the passenger conveyor, turned to wave.

"Your man—he's going too?" Gulver blurted.

"He's not our man, properly speaking," Retief said. "He lives on Lovenbroy."

"Lovenbroy?" Gulver choked. "But . . . the . . . I . . . . "

"I know you said the students were bound for d'Land," Retief said. "But I guess that was just another aspect of the general confusion. The course plugged into the

145

navigators was to Lovenbroy. You'll be glad to know they're still headed there—even without the baggage."

"Perhaps," Gulver said grimly, "perhaps they'll manage without it."

"By the way," Retief said. "There was another funny mix-up. There were some tractors—for industrial use, you'll recall. I believe you co-operated with Croanie in arranging the grant through MEDDLE. They were erroneously consigned to Lovenbroy, a purely agricultural world. I saved you some embarrassment, I trust, Mr. Gulver, by arranging to have them off-loaded at d'Land."

"D'Land! You've put the CSU's in the hands of Boge's bitterest enemies!"

"But they're only tractors, Mr. Gulver. Peaceful devices. Isn't that correct?"

"That's . . . correct." Gulver sagged. Then he snapped erect. "Hold the ships!" he yelled. "I'm canceling the student exchange—"

His voice was drowned by the rumble as the first of the monster transports rose from the launch pit, followed a moment later by the second, Retief watched them out of sight, then turned to Gulver.

"They're off," he said. "Let's hope they get a liberal education."

V

Retief lay on his back in deep grass by a stream, eating grapes. A tall figure appeared on the knoll above him and waved.

"Retief!" Hank Arapoulous bounded down the slope and embraced Retief, slapping him on the back. "I heard you were here—and I've got news for you. You won the final day's picking competition. Over two hundred bushels! That's a record!"

"Let's get on over to the garden. Sounds like the celebration's about to start."

In the flower-crowded park among the stripped vines, Retief and Arapoulous made their way to a laden table under the lanterns. A tall girl dressed in loose white, and with long golden hair, came up to Arapoulous.

"Delinda, this is Retief—today's winner. And he's also the fellow that got those workers for us."

Delinda smiled at Retief. "I've heard about you, Mr. Retief. We weren't sure about the boys at first. Two thousand Bogans, and all confused about their baggage that went astray. But they seemed to like the picking." She smiled again.

"That's not all. Our gals liked the boys," Hank said. "Even Bogans aren't so bad, minus their irons. A lot of 'em will be staying on. But how come you didn't tell me you were coming, Retief? I'd have laid on some kind of big welcome."

"I liked the welcome I got. And I didn't have much notice. Mr. Magnan was a little upset when he got back. It seems I exceeded my authority."

Arapoulous laughed. "I had a feeling you were wheeling pretty free, Retief. I hope you didn't get into any trouble over it."

"No trouble," Retief said. "A few people were a little unhappy with me. It seems I'm not ready for important assignments at Departmental level. I was shipped off here to the boondocks to get a little more experience."

"Delinda, look after Retief," said Arapoulous. "I'll see you later. I've got to see to the wine judging." He disappeared in the crowd.

"Congratulations on winning the day," said Delinda. "I noticed you at work. You were wonderful. I'm glad you're going to have the prize."

"Thanks. I noticed you too, flitting around in that white nightie of yours. But why weren't you picking grapes with the rest of us?"

"I had a special assignment."

"Too bad. You should have had a chance at the prize."

Delinda took Retief's hand. "I wouldn't have anyway," she said. "I'm the prize."

The Desert and the Stars

The Aga Kaga wanted peace—a piece of everything in sight!

"I'm not at all sure," Under-Secretary Sternwheeler said, "that I fully understand the necessity for your . . . ah . . . absenting yourself from your post of duty, Mr. Retief. Surely this matter could have been dealt with in the usual way—assuming any action is necessary."

"I had a sharp attack of writer's cramp, Mr. Secretary," Retief said. "So I thought I'd better come along in person—just to be sure I was positive of making my point."

"Eh?"

"Why, ah, there were a number of dispatches," Deputy Under-Secretary Magnan put in. "Unfortunately, this being end-of-the-fiscal-year time, we found ourselves quite inundated with reports. Reports, reports, reports—"

"Not criticizing the reporting system, are you, Mr. Magnan?" the Under-Secretary barked.

"Gracious, no," Magnan said. "I love reports."

"It seems nobody's told the Aga Kagans about fiscal years," Retief said. "They're going right ahead with their program of land-grabbing on Flamme. So far, I've persuaded the Boyars that this is a matter for the Corps, and not to take matters into their own hands."

The Under-Secretary nodded. "Quite right. Carry on along the same lines. Now, if there's nothing further—"

"Thank you, Mr. Secretary," Magnan said, rising. "We certainly appreciate your guidance."

"There is a little something further," said Retief, sitting solidly in his chair. "What's the Corps going to do about the Aga Kagans?"

The Under-Secretary turned a liverish eye on Retief. "As Minister to Flamme, you should know that the function of a diplomatic representative is merely to . . . what shall I say . . . ?"

"String them along?" Magnan suggested.

"An unfortunate choice of phrase," the Under-Secretary said. "However, it embodies certain realities of Galactic politics. The Corps must concern itself with matters of broad policy."

"Sixty years ago the Corps was encouraging the Boyars to settle Flamme," Retief said. "They were assured of Corps support."

"I don't believe you'll find that in writing," said the Under-Secretary blandly. "In any event, that was sixty years ago. At that time a foothold against Neo-Concordiatist elements was deemed desirable. Now the situation has changed."

"The Boyars have spent sixty years terraforming Flamme," Retief said. "They've cleared jungle, descummed the seas, irrigated deserts, set out forests. They've just about reached the point where they can begin to enjoy it. The Aga Kagans have picked this as a good time to move in. They've landed thirty detachments of 'fishermen'—complete with armored trawlers mounting 40 mm infinite repeaters—and another two dozen parties of 'homesteaders'—all male and toting rocket launchers."

"Surely there's land enough on the world to afford space to both groups," the Under-Secretary said. "A spirit of co-operation—"

*

"The Boyars needed some co-operation sixty years ago," Retief said. "They tried to get the Aga Kagans to join in and help them beat back some of the saurian wild life that liked to graze on people. The Corps didn't like the idea. They wanted to see an undisputed anti-Concordiatist enclave. The Aga Kagans didn't want to play, either. But now that the world is tamed, they're moving in."

"The exigencies of diplomacy require a flexible policy—"

"I want a firm assurance of Corps support to take back to Flamme," Retief said. "The Boyars are a little naive. They don't understand diplomatic triple-speak. They just want to hold onto the homes they've made out of a wasteland."

"I'm warning you, Retief!" the Under-Secretary snapped, leaning forward, wattles quivering. "Corps policy with regard to Flamme includes no inflammatory actions based on outmoded concepts. The Boyars will have to accommodate themselves to the situation!"

"That's what I'm afraid of," Retief said. "They're not going to sit still and watch it happen. If I don't take back concrete evidence of Corps backing, we're going to have a nice hot little shooting war on our hands."

The Under-Secretary pushed out his lips and drummed his fingers on the desk.

"Confounded hot-heads," he muttered. "Very well, Retief. I'll go along to the extent of a Note; but positively no further."

"A Note? I was thinking of something more like a squadron of Corps Peace Enforcers running through a few routine maneuvers off Flamme."

"Out of the question. A stiffly worded Protest Note is the best I can do. That's final."

Back in the corridor, Magnan turned to Retief. "When will you learn not to argue with Under-Secretaries? One would think you actively disliked the idea of ever receiving a promotion. I was astonished at the Under-Secretary's restraint. Frankly, I was stunned when he actually agreed to a Note. I, of course, will have to draft it." Magnan pulled at his lower lip thoughtfully. "Now, I wonder, should I view with deep concern an act of open aggression, or merely point out an apparent violation of technicalities . . . ."

"Don't bother," Retief said. "I have a draft all ready to go."

"But how—?"

"I had a feeling I'd get paper instead of action," Retief said. "I thought I'd save a little time all around."

"At times, your cynicism borders on impudence."

"At other times, it borders on disgust. Now, if you'll run the Note through for signature, I'll try to catch the six o'clock shuttle."

"Leaving so soon? There's an important reception tonight. Some of our biggest names will be there. An excellent opportunity for you to join in the diplomatic give-and-take."

"No, thanks. I want to get back to Flamme and join in something mild, like a dinosaur hunt."

"When you get there," said Magnan, "I hope you'll make it quite clear that this matter is to be settled without violence."

"Don't worry. I'll keep the peace, if I have to start a war to do it."

*

On the broad verandah at Government House, Retief settled himself comfortably in a lounge chair. He accepted a tall glass from a white-jacketed waiter and regarded the flamboyant Flamme sunset, a gorgeous blaze of vermillion and purple that reflected from a still lake, tinged the broad lawn with color, silhouetted tall poplars among flower beds.

"You've done great things here in sixty years, Georges," said Retief. "Not that natural geological processes wouldn't have produced the same results, given a couple of hundred million years."

"Don't belabor the point," the Boyar Chef d'Regime said. "Since we seem to be on the verge of losing it."

"You're forgetting the Note."

"A Note," Georges said, waving his cigar. "What the purple polluted hell is a Note supposed to do? I've got Aga Kagan claim-jumpers camped in the middle of what used to be a fine stand of barley, cooking sheep's brains over dung fires not ten miles from Government House—and upwind at that."

"Say, if that's the same barley you distill your whiskey from, I'd call that a first-class atrocity."

"Retief, on your say-so, I've kept my boys on a short leash. They've put up with plenty. Last week, while you were away, these barbarians sailed that flotilla of armor-plated junks right through the middle of one of our best oyster breeding beds. It was all I could do to keep a bunch of our men from going out in private helis and blasting 'em out of the water."

"That wouldn't have been good for the oysters, either."

"That's what I told 'em. I also said you'd be back here in a few days with something from Corps HQ. When I tell 'em all we've got is a piece of paper, that'll be the end. There's a strong vigilante organization here that's been outfitting for the last four weeks. If I hadn't held them back with assurances that the CDT would step in and take care of this invasion, they would have hit them before now."

*

"That would have been a mistake," said Retief. "The Aga Kagans are tough customers. They're active on half a dozen worlds at the moment. They've been building up for this push for the last five years. A show of resistance by you Boyars without Corps backing would be an invitation to slaughter—with the excuse that you started it."

"So what are we going to do? Sit here and watch these goat-herders take over our farms and fisheries?"

"Those goat-herders aren't all they seem. They've got a first-class modern navy."

"I've seen 'em. They camp in goat-skin tents, gallop around on animal-back, wear dresses down to their ankles—"

"The 'goat-skin' tents are a high-polymer plastic, made in the same factory that turns out those long flowing bullet-proof robes you mention. The animals are just for show. Back home they use helis and ground cars of the most modern design."

The Chef d'Regime chewed his cigar.

"Why the masquerade?"

"Something to do with internal policies, I suppose."

"So we sit tight and watch 'em take our world away from us. That's what I get for playing along with you, Retief. We should have clobbered these monkeys as soon as they set foot on our world."

"Slow down, I haven't finished yet. There's still the Note."

"I've got plenty of paper already. Rolls and rolls of it."

"Give diplomatic processes a chance," said Retief. "The Note hasn't even been delivered yet. Who knows? We may get surprising results."

"If you expect me to supply a runner for the purpose, you're out of luck. From what I hear, he's likely to come back with his ears stuffed in his hip pocket."

"I'll deliver the Note personally," Retief said. "I could use a couple of escorts—preferably strong-arm lads."

The Chef d'Regime frowned, blew out a cloud of smoke. "I wasn't kidding about these Aga Kagans," he said. "I hear they have some nasty habits. I don't want to see you operated on with the same knives they use to skin out the goats."

"I'd be against that myself. Still, the mail must go through."

"Strong-arm lads, eh? What have you got in mind, Retief?"

"A little muscle in the background is an old diplomatic custom," Retief said.

The Chef d'Regime stubbed out his cigar thoughtfully. "I used to be a pretty fair elbow-wrestler myself," he said. "Suppose I go along . . . ?"

"That," said Retief, "should lend just the right note of solidarity to our little delegation." He hitched his chair closer. "Now, depending on what we run into, here's how we'll play it . . . . "

II

Eight miles into the rolling granite hills west of the capital, a black-painted official air-car flying the twin flags of Chief of State and Terrestrial Minister skimmed along a foot above a pot-holed road. Slumped in the padded seat, the Boyar Chef d'Regime waved his cigar glumly at the surrounding hills.

"Fifty years ago this was bare rock," he said. "We've bred special strains of bacteria here to break down the formations into soil, and we followed up with a program of broad-spectrum fertilization. We planned to put the whole area into crops by next year. Now it looks like the goats will get it."

"Will that scrubland support a crop?" Retief said, eyeing the lichen-covered knolls.

"Sure. We start with legumes and follow up with cereals. Wait until you see this next section. It's an old flood plain, came into production thirty years ago. One of our finest—"

The air-car topped a rise. The Chef dropped his cigar and half rose, with a hoarse yell. A herd of scraggly goats tossed their heads among a stand of ripe grain. The car pulled to a stop. Retief held the Boyar's arm.

"Keep calm, Georges," he said. "Remember, we're on a diplomatic mission. It wouldn't do to come to the conference table smelling of goats."

"Let me at 'em!" Georges roared. "I'll throttle 'em with my bare hands!"

A bearded goat eyed the Boyar Chef sardonically, jaw working. "Look at that long-nosed son!" The goat gave a derisive bleat and took another mouthful of ripe grain.

"Did you see that?" Georges yelled. "They've trained the son of a—"

"Chin up, Georges," Retief said. "We'll take up the goat problem along with the rest."

"I'll murder 'em!"

"Hold it, Georges. Look over there."

A hundred yards away, a trio of brown-cloaked horsemen topped a rise, paused dramatically against the cloudless pale sky, then galloped down the slope toward the car, rifles bobbing at their backs, cloaks billowing out behind. Side by side they rode, through the brown-golden grain, cutting three narrow swaths that ran in a straight sweep from the ridge to the air-car where Retief and the Chef d'Regime hovered, waiting.

Georges scrambled for the side of the car. "Just wait 'til I get my hands on him!"

Retief pulled him back. "Sit tight and look pleased, Georges. Never give the opposition a hint of your true feelings. Pretend you're a goat lover—and hand me one of your cigars."

The three horsemen pulled up in a churn of chaff and a clatter of pebbles. Georges coughed, batting a hand at the settling dust. Retief peeled the cigar unhurriedly, sniffed, at it and thumbed it alight. He drew at it, puffed out a cloud of smoke and glanced casually at the trio of Aga Kagan cavaliers.

"Peace be with you," he intoned in accent-free Kagan. "May your shadows never grow less."

*

The leader of the three, a hawk-faced man with a heavy beard, unlimbered his rifle. He fingered it, frowning ferociously.

"Have no fear," Retief said, smiling graciously. "He who comes as a guest enjoys perfect safety."

A smooth-faced member of the threesome barked an oath and leveled his rifle at Retief.

"Youth is the steed of folly," Retief said. "Take care that the beardless one does not disgrace his house."

The leader whirled on the youth and snarled an order. He lowered the rifle, muttering. Blackbeard turned back to Retief.

"Begone, interlopers," he said. "You disturb the goats."

"Provision is not taken to the houses of the generous," Retief said. "May the creatures dine well ere they move on."

"Hah! The goats of the Aga Kaga graze on the lands of the Aga Kaga." The leader edged his horse close, eyed Retief fiercely. "We welcome no intruders on our lands."

"To praise a man for what he does not possess is to make him appear foolish," Retief said. "These are the lands of the Boyars. But enough of these pleasantries. We seek audience with your ruler."

"You may address me as 'Exalted One'," the leader said. "Now dismount from that steed of Shaitan."

"It is written, if you need anything from a dog, call him 'sir'," Retief said. "I must decline to impute canine ancestry to a guest. Now you may conduct us to your headquarters."

"Enough of your insolence!" The bearded man cocked his rifle. "I could blow your heads off!"

"The hen has feathers, but it does not fly," Retief said. "We have asked for escort. A slave must be beaten with a stick; for a free man, a hint is enough."

"You mock me, pale one. I warn you—"

"Only love makes me weep," Retief said. "I laugh at hatred."

"Get out of the car!"

Retief puffed at his cigar, eyeing the Aga Kagan cheerfully. The youth in the rear moved forward, teeth bared.

"Never give in to the fool, lest he say, 'He fears me,'" Retief said.

"I cannot restrain my men in the face of your insults," the bearded Aga Kagan roared. "These hens of mine have feathers—and talons as well!"

"When God would destroy an ant, he gives him wings," Retief said. "Distress in misfortune is another misfortune."

The bearded man's face grew purple.

Retief dribbled the ash from his cigar over the side of the car.

"Now I think we'd better be getting on," he said briskly. "I've enjoyed our chat, but we do have business to attend to."

The bearded leader laughed shortly. "Does the condemned man beg for the axe?" he enquired rhetorically. "You shall visit the Aga Kaga, then. Move on! And make no attempt to escape, else my gun will speak you a brief farewell."

The horsemen glowered, then, at a word from the leader, took positions around the car. Georges started the vehicle forward, following the leading rider. Retief leaned back and let out a long sigh.

"That was close," he said. "I was about out of proverbs."

"You sound as though you'd brought off a coup," Georges said. "From the expression on the whiskery one's face, we're in for trouble. What was he saying?"

"Just a routine exchange of bluffs," Retief said. "Now when we get there, remember to make your flattery sound like insults and your insults sound like flattery, and you'll be all right."

"These birds are armed. And they don't like strangers," Georges said. "Maybe I should have boned up on their habits before I joined this expedition."

"Just stick to the plan," Retief said. "And remember: a handful of luck is better than a camel-load of learning."

*

The air car followed the escort down a long slope to a dry river bed and across it, through a barren stretch of shifting sand to a green oasis set with canopies.

The armed escort motioned the car to a halt before an immense tent of glistening black. Before the tent armed men lounged under a pennant bearing a lion *couchant* in crimson on a field verte.

"Get out," Blackbeard ordered. The guards eyed the visitors, their drawn sabers catching sunlight. Retief and Georges stepped from the car onto rich rugs spread on the grass. They followed the ferocious gesture of the bearded man through the opening into a perfumed interior of luminous shadows. A heavy odor of incense hung in the air, and the strumming of stringed instruments laid a muted pattern of sound behind the decorations of gold and blue, silver and green. At the far end of the room, among a bevy of female slaves, a large and resplendently clad man with blue-black hair and a clean-shaven chin popped a grape into his mouth. He wiped his fingers negligently on a wisp of silk offered by a handmaiden, belched loudly and looked the callers over.

Blackbeard cleared his throat. "Down on your faces in the presence of the Exalted One, the Aga Kaga, ruler of East and West."

"Sorry," Retief said firmly. "My hay-fever, you know."

The reclining giant waved a hand languidly.

"Never mind the formalities," he said. "Approach."

Retief and Georges crossed the thick rugs. A cold draft blew toward them. The reclining man sneezed violently, wiped his nose on another silken scarf and held up a hand.

"Night and the horses and the desert know me," he said in resonant tones. "Also the sword and the guest and paper and pen—" He paused, wrinkled his nose and sneezed again. "Turn off that damned air-conditioner," he snapped.

He settled himself and motioned the bearded man to him. The two exchanged muted remarks. Then the bearded man stepped back, ducked his head and withdrew to the rear.

"Excellency," Retief said, "I have the honor to present M. Georges Duror, Chef d'Regime of the Planetary government."

"Planetary government?" The Aga Kaga spat grape seeds on the rug. "My men have observed a few squatters along the shore. If they're in distress, I'll see about a distribution of goat-meat."

"It is the punishment of the envious to grieve at anothers' plenty," Retief said. "No goat-meat will be required."

"Ralph told me you talk like a page out of Mustapha ben Abdallah Katib Jelebi," the Aga Kaga said. "I know a few old sayings myself. For example, 'A Bedouin is only cheated once.'"

"We have no such intentions, Excellency," Retief said. "Is it not written, 'Have no faith in the Prince whose minister cheats you'?"

"I've had some unhappy experiences with strangers," the Aga Kaga said. "It is written in the sands that all strangers are kin. Still, he who visits rarely is a welcome guest. Be seated."

III

Handmaidens brought cushions, giggled and fled. Retief and Georges settled themselves comfortably. The Aga Kaga eyed them in silence.

"We have come to bear tidings from the Corps Diplomatique Terrestrienne," Retief said solemnly. A perfumed slave girl offered grapes.

"Modest ignorance is better than boastful knowledge," the Aga Kaga said. "What brings the CDT into the picture?"

"The essay of the drunkard will be read in the tavern," Retief said. "Whereas the words of kings . . . . "

"Very well, I concede the point." The Aga Kaga waved a hand at the serving maids. "Depart, my dears. Attend me later. You too, Ralph. These are mere diplomats. They are men of words, not deeds."

The bearded man glared and departed. The girls hurried after him.

"Now," the Aga Kaga said. "Let's drop the wisdom of the ages and get down to the issues. Not that I don't admire your repertoire of platitudes. How do you remember them all?"

"Diplomats and other liars require good memories," said Retief. "But as you point out, small wisdom to small minds. I'm here to effect a settlement of certain differences between yourself and the planetary authorities. I have here a Note, which I'm conveying on behalf of the Sector Under-Secretary. With your permission, I'll read it."

"Go ahead." The Aga Kaga kicked a couple of cushions onto the floor, eased a bottle from under the couch and reached for glasses.

"The Under-Secretary for Sector Affairs presents his compliments to his Excellency, the Aga Kaga of the Aga Kaga, Primary Potentate, Hereditary Sheik, Emir of the—"

"Yes, yes. Skip the titles."

Retief flipped over two pages.

" . . . and with reference to the recent relocation of persons under the jurisdiction of his Excellency, has the honor to point out that the territories now under settlement comprise a portion of that area, hereinafter designated as Sub-sector Alpha, which, under terms of the Agreement entered into by his Excellency's predecessor, and as referenced in Sector Ministry's Notes numbers G-175846573957-b and X-7584736 c-1, with particular pertinence to that body designated in the Revised Galactic Catalogue, Tenth Edition, as amended, Volume Nine, reel 43, as 54 Cygni Alpha, otherwise referred to hereinafter as Flamme—"

"Come to the point," the Aga Kaga cut in. "You're here to lodge a complaint that I'm invading territories to which someone else lays claim, is that it?" He smiled broadly, offered dope-sticks and lit one. "Well, I've been expecting a call. After all, it's what you gentlemen are paid for. Cheers."

"Your Excellency has a lucid way of putting things," Retief said.

"Call me Stanley," the Aga Kaga said. "The other routine is just to please some of the old fools—I mean the more conservative members of my government. They're still gnawing their beards and kicking themselves because their ancestors dropped science in favor of alchemy and got themselves stranded in a cultural dead end. This charade is supposed to prove they were right all along. However, I've no time to waste in neurotic compensations. I have places to go and deeds to accomplish."

"At first glance," Retief said, "it looks as though the places are already occupied, and the deeds are illegal."

*

The Aga Kaga guffawed. "For a diplomat, you speak plainly, Retief. Have another drink." He poured, eyeing Georges. "What of M. Duror? How does he feel about it?"

Georges took a thoughtful swallow of whiskey. "Not bad," he said. "But not quite good enough to cover the odor of goats."

The Aga Kaga snorted. "I thought the goats were overdoing it a bit myself," he said. "Still, the graybeards insisted. And I need their support."

"Also," Georges said distinctly, "I think you're soft. You lie around letting women wait on you, while your betters are out doing an honest day's work."

The Aga Kaga looked startled. "Soft? I can tie a knot in an iron bar as big as your thumb." He popped a grape into his mouth. "As for the rest, your pious views about the virtues of hard labor are as childish as my advisors' faith in the advantages of primitive plumbing. As for myself, I am a realist. If two monkeys want the same banana, in the end one will have it, and the other will cry morality. The days of my years are numbered, praise be to God. While they last, I hope to eat well, hunt well, fight well and take my share of pleasure. I leave to others the arid satisfactions of self-denial and other perversions."

"You admit you're here to grab our land, then," Georges said. "That's the damnedest piece of bare-faced aggression—"

"Ah, ah!" The Aga Kaga held up a hand. "Watch your vocabulary, my dear sir. I'm sure that 'justifiable yearnings for territorial self-realization' would be more appropriate to the situation. Or possibly 'legitimate aspirations, for self-determination of formerly exploited peoples' might fit the case. Aggression is, by definition, an activity carried on only by those who have inherited the mantle of Colonial Imperialism."

"Imperialism! Why, you Aga Kagans have been the most notorious planet-grabbers in Sector history, you—you—"

"Call me Stanley." The Aga Kaga munched a grape. "I merely face the realities of popular folk-lore. Let's be pragmatic; it's a matter of historical association. Some people can grab land and pass it off lightly as a moral duty; others are dubbed imperialist merely for holding onto their own. Unfair, you say. But that's life, my friends. And I shall continue to take every advantage of it."

"We'll fight you!" Georges bellowed. He took another gulp of whiskey and slammed the glass down. "You won't take this world without a struggle!"

"Another?" the Aga Kaga said, offering the bottle. Georges glowered as his glass was filled. The Aga Kaga held the glass up to the light.

"Excellent color, don't you agree?" He turned his eyes on Georges.

"It's pointless to resist," he said. "We have you outgunned and outmanned. Your small nation has no chance against us. But we're prepared to be generous. You may continue to occupy such areas as we do not immediately require until such time as you're able to make other arrangements."

"And by the time we've got a crop growing out of what was bare rock, you'll be ready to move in," the Boyar Chef d'Regime snapped. "But you'll find that we aren't alone!"

*

"Quite alone," the Aga said. He nodded sagely. "Yes, one need but read the lesson of history. The Corps Diplomatique will make expostulatory noises, but it will accept the *fait accompli*. You, my dear sir, are but a very small nibble. We won't make the mistake of excessive greed. We shall inch our way to empire—and those who stand in our way shall be dubbed warmongers."

"I see you're quite a student of history, Stanley," Retief said. "I wonder if you recall the eventual fate of most of the would-be empire nibblers of the past?"

"Ah, but they grew incautious. They went too far, too fast."

"The confounded impudence," Georges rasped. "Tells us to our face what he has in mind!"

"An ancient and honorable custom, from the time of *Mein Kampf* and the *Communist Manifesto* through the *Porcelain Wall* of Leung. Such declarations have a legendary quality. It's traditional that they're never taken at face value."

159

"But always," Retief said, "there was a critical point at which the man on horseback could have been pulled from the saddle."

"*Could* have been," the Aga Kaga chuckled. He finished the grapes and began peeling an orange. "But they never were. Hitler could have been stopped by the Czech Air Force in 1938; Stalin was at the mercy of the primitive atomics of the west in 1946; Leung was grossly over-extended at Rangoon. But the onus of that historic role could not be overcome. It has been the fate of your spiritual forebears to carve civilization from the wilderness and then, amid tearing of garments and the heaping of ashes of self-accusation on your own confused heads, to withdraw, leaving the spoils for local political opportunists and mob leaders, clothed in the mystical virtue of native birth. Have a banana."

"You're stretching your analogy a little too far," Retief said. "You're banking on the inaction of the Corps. You could be wrong."

"I shall know when to stop," the Aga Kaga said.

"Tell me, Stanley," Retief said, rising. "Are we quite private here?"

"Yes, perfectly so," the Aga Kaga said. "None would dare to intrude in my council." He cocked an eyebrow at Retief. "You have a proposal to make in confidence? But what of our dear friend Georges? One would not like to see him disillusioned."

"Don't worry about Georges. He's a realist, like you. He's prepared to deal in facts. Hard facts, in this case."

The Aga Kaga nodded thoughtfully. "What are you getting at?"

"You're basing your plan of action on the certainty that the Corps will sit by, wringing its hands, while you embark on a career of planetary piracy."

"Isn't it the custom?" the Aga Kaga smiled complacently.

"I have news for you, Stanley. In this instance, neck-wringing seems more in order than hand-wringing."

The Aga Kaga frowned. "Your manner—"

"Never mind our manners!" Georges blurted, standing. "We don't need any lessons from goat-herding land-thieves!"

The Aga Kaga's face darkened. "You dare to speak thus to me, pig of a muck-grubber!"

*

With a muffled curse Georges launched himself at the potentate. The giant rolled aside. He grunted as the Boyar's fist thumped in his short ribs; then he chopped down on Georges' neck. The Chef d'Regime slid off onto the floor as the Aga Kaga bounded to his feet, sending fruit and silken cushions flying.

"I see it now!" he hissed. "An assassination attempt!" He stretched his arms, thick as tree-roots—a grizzly in satin robes. "Your heads will ring together like gongs before I have done with you!" He lunged for Retief. Retief came to his feet, feinted with his left and planted a short right against the Aga Kaga's jaw with a solid smack. The potentate stumbled, grabbed; Retief slipped aside. The Aga Kaga whirled to face Retief.

"A slippery diplomat, by all the houris in Paradise!" he grated, breathing hard. "But a fool. True to your medieval code of chivalry, you attacked singly, a blunder I would never have made. And you shall die for your idiocy!" He opened his mouth to bellow—

"You sure look foolish, with your fancy hair-do down in your eyes," Retief said. "The servants will get a big laugh out of it."

With a choked yell, the Aga Kaga dived for Retief, missed as he leaped aside. The two went to the mat together and rolled, sending a stool skittering. Grunts and curses echoed as the two big men strained, muscles popping. Retief groped for a scissors hold; the Aga Kaga seized his foot, bit hard. Retief bent nearly double, braced himself and slammed the potentate against the rug. Dust flew. Then the two were on their feet, circling.

"Many times have I longed to broil a diplomat over a slow fire," the Aga Kaga snarled. "Tonight will see it come to pass!"

"I've seen it done often at staff meetings," said Retief. "It seems to have no permanent effect."

The Aga Kaga reached for Retief, who feinted left, hammered a right to the chin. The Aga Kaga tottered. Retief measured him, brought up a haymaker. The potentate slammed to the rug—out cold.

*

Georges rolled over, sat up. "Let me at the son of a—" he muttered.

"Take over, Georges," Retief said, panting. "Since he's in a mood to negotiate now, we may as well get something accomplished."

Georges eyed the fallen ruler, who stirred, groaned lugubriously. "I hope you know what you're doing," Georges said. "But I'm with you in any case." He straddled the prone body, plucked a curved knife from the low table and prodded the Aga Kaga's Adam's apple. The monarch opened his eyes.

"Make one little peep and your windbag will spring a leak," Georges said. "Very few historical figures have accomplished anything important after their throats were cut."

"Stanley won't yell," Retief said. "We're not the only ones who're guilty of cultural idiocy. He'd lose face something awful if he let his followers see him like this." Retief settled himself on a tufted ottoman. "Right, Stanley?"

The Aga Kaga snarled.

Retief selected a grape and ate it thoughtfully. "These aren't bad, Georges. You might consider taking on a few Aga Kagan vine-growers—purely on a yearly contract basis, of course."

The Aga Kaga groaned, rolling his eyes.

"Well, I believe we're ready to get down to diplomatic proceedings now," Retief said. "Nothing like dealing in an atmosphere of realistic good fellowship. First, of course, there's the matter of the presence of aliens lacking visas." He opened his briefcase, withdrew a heavy sheet of parchment. "I have the document here, drawn up and ready for signature. It provides for the prompt deportation of such persons, by Corps Transport, all expenses to be borne by the Aga Kagan government. That's agreeable, I assume?" Retief looked expectantly at the purple face of the prone potentate. The Aga Kaga grunted a strangled grunt.

"Speak up, Stanley," Retief said. "Give him plenty of air, Georges."

"Shall I let some in through the side?"

"Not yet. I'm sure Stanley wants to be agreeable."

The Aga Kaga snarled.

"Maybe just a little then, Georges," Retief said judiciously. Georges jabbed the knife in far enough to draw a bead of blood. The Aga Kaga grunted.

"Agreed!" he snorted. "By the beard of the prophet, when I get my hands on you . . . . "

"Second item: certain fields, fishing grounds, et cetera, have suffered damage due to the presence of the aforementioned illegal immigrants. Full compensation will be made by the Aga Kagan government. Agreed?"

*

The Aga Kaga drew a breath, tensed himself; Georges jabbed with the knife point. His prisoner relaxed with a groan. "Agreed!" he grated. "A vile tactic! You enter my tent under the guise of guests, protected by diplomatic immunity—"

"I had the impression we were herded in here at sword point," said Retief. "Shall we go on? Now there's the little matter of restitution for violation of sovereignty, reparations for mental anguish, payment for damaged fences, roads, drainage canals, communications, et cetera, et cetera. Shall I read them all?"

"Wait until the news of this outrage is spread abroad!"

"They'd never believe it," Retief said. "History would prove it impossible. And on mature consideration, I'm sure you won't want it noised about that you entertained visiting dignitaries flat on your back."

"What about the pollution of the atmosphere by goats?" Georges put in. "And don't overlook the muddying of streams, the destruction of timber for camp fires and—"

"I've covered all that sort of thing under a miscellaneous heading," Retief said. "We can fill it in at leisure when we get back."

"Bandits!" the Aga Kaga hissed. "Thieves! Dogs of unreliable imperialists!"

"It is disillusioning, I know," Retief said. "Still, of such little surprises is history made. Sign here." He held the parchment out and offered a pen. "A nice clear signature, please. We wouldn't want any quibbling about the legality of the treaty, after conducting the negotiation with such scrupulous regard for the niceties."

"Niceties! Never in history has such an abomination been perpetrated!"

"Oh, treaties are always worked out this way, when it comes right down to it. We've just accelerated the process a little. Now, if you'll just sign like a good fellow, we'll be on our way. Georges will have his work cut out for him, planning how to use all this reparations money."

The Aga Kaga gnashed his teeth; Georges prodded. The Aga Kaga seized the pen and scrawled his name. Retief signed with a flourish. He tucked the treaty away in his briefcase, took out another.

"This is just a safe-conduct, to get us out of the door and into the car," he said. "Probably unnecessary, but it won't hurt to have it, in case you figure out some way to avoid your obligations as a host."

The Aga Kaga signed the document after another prod from Georges.

"One more paper, and I'll be into the jugular," he said.

*

RETIEF: THE DIRTY DOZEN

"We're all through now," said Retief. "Stanley, we're going to have to run now. I'm going to strap up your hands and feet a trifle; it shouldn't take you more than ten minutes or so to get loose, stick a band-aid on your neck and—"

"My men will cut you down for the rascals you are!"

"By that time, we'll be over the hill," Retief continued. "At full throttle; we'll be at Government House in an hour, and of course I won't waste any time transmitting the treaty to Sector HQ. And the same concern for face that keeps you from yelling for help will insure that the details of the negotiation remain our secret."

"Treaty! That scrap of paper!"

"I confess the Corps is a little sluggish about taking action at times," Retief said, whipping a turn of silken cord around the Aga Kaga's ankles. "But once it's got signatures on a legal treaty, it's extremely stubborn about all parties adhering to the letter. It can't afford to be otherwise, as I'm sure you'll understand." He cinched up the cord, went to work on the hands. The Aga Kaga glared at him balefully.

"To the Pit with the Corps! The ferocity of my revenge—"

"Don't talk nonsense, Stanley. There are several squadrons of Peace Enforcers cruising in the Sector just now. I'm sure you're not ready to make any historical errors by taking them on." Retief finished and stood.

"Georges, just stuff a scarf in Stanley's mouth. I think he'd prefer to work quietly until he recovers his dignity." Retief buckled his briefcase, selected a large grape and looked down at the Aga Kaga.

"Actually, you'll be glad you saw things our way, Stanley," he said. "You'll get all the credit for the generous settlement. Of course, it will be a striking precedent for any other negotiations that may become necessary if you get grabby on other worlds in this region. And if your advisors want to know why the sudden change of heart, just tell them you've decided to start from scratch on an unoccupied world. Mention the virtues of thrift and hard work. I'm confident you can find plenty of historical examples to support you."

"Thanks for the drink," said Georges. "Drop in on me at Government House some time and we'll crack another bottle."

"And don't feel bad about your project's going awry," Retief said. "In the words of the prophet, 'Stolen goods are never sold at a loss.'"

*

"A remarkable about-face, Retief," Magnan said. "Let this be a lesson to you. A stern Note of Protest can work wonders."

"A lot depends on the method of delivery," Retief said.

"Nonsense. I knew all along the Aga Kagans were a reasonable and peace-loving people. One of the advantages of senior rank, of course, is the opportunity to see the big picture. Why, I was saying only this morning—"

The desk screen broke into life. The mottled jowls of Under-Secretary Sternwheeler appeared.

"Magnan! I've just learned of the Flamme affair. Who's responsible?"

"Why, ah . . . I suppose that I might be said—"

"This is your work, is it?"

"Well . . . Mr. Retief did play the role of messenger."

"Don't pass the buck, Magnan!" the Under-Secretary barked. "What the devil went on out there?"

"Just a routine Protest Note. Everything is quite in order."

"Bah! Your over-zealousness has cost me dear. I was feeding Flamme to the Aga Kagans to consolidate our position of moral superiority for use as a lever in a number of important negotiations. Now they've backed out! Aga Kaga emerges from the affair wreathed in virtue. You've destroyed a very pretty finesse in power politics, Mr. Magnan! A year's work down the drain!"

"But I thought—"

"I doubt that, Mr. Magnan, I doubt that very much!" The Under-Secretary rang off.

"This is a fine turn of events," Magnan groaned. "Retief, you know very well Protest Notes are merely intended for the historical record! No one ever takes them seriously."

"You and the Aga Kaga ought to get together," said Retief. "He's a great one for citing historical parallels. He's not a bad fellow, as a matter of fact. I have an invitation from him to visit Kaga and go mud-pig hunting. He was so impressed by Corps methods that he wants to be sure we're on his side next time. Why don't you come along?"

"Hmmm. Perhaps I should cultivate him. A few high-level contacts never do any harm. On the other hand, I understand he lives in a very loose way, feasting and merrymaking. Frivolous in the extreme. No wife, you understand, but hordes of lightly clad women about. And in that connection, the Aga Kagans have some very curious notions as to what constitutes proper hospitality to a guest."

Retief rose, pulled on the powder blue cloak and black velvet gauntlets of a Career Minister.

"Don't let it worry you," he said. "You'll have a great time. And as the Aga Kaga would say, 'Ugliness is the best safeguard of virginity.'"

SALINE SOLUTION

Blast you, Retief! Your violent ways are the disgrace of Earth's diplomatic corps—but your salty jokes are worse!

I

Consul-General Magnan gingerly fingered the heavily rubber-banded sheaf of dog-eared documents. "I haven't rushed into precipitate action on this claim, Retief," he said. "The Consulate has grave responsibilities here in the Belt. One must weigh all aspects of the situation, consider the ramifications. What consequences would arise from a grant of minerals rights on the planetoid to this claimant?"

"The claim looked all right to me," Retief said. "Seventeen copies with attachments. Why not process it? You've had it on your desk for a week."

Magnan's eyebrows went up. "You've a personal interest in this claim, Retief?"

"Every day you wait is costing them money. That hulk they use for an ore-carrier is in a parking orbit piling up demurrage."

"I see you've become emotionally involved in the affairs of a group of obscure miners. You haven't yet learned the true diplomat's happy faculty of non-identification with specifics—or should I say identification with non-specifics?"

"They're not a wealthy outfit, you know. In fact, I understand this claim is their sole asset—unless you want to count the ore-carrier."

"The Consulate is not concerned with the internal financial problems of the Sam's Last Chance Number Nine Mining Company."

"Careful," Retief said. "You almost identified yourself with a specific that time."

"Hardly, my dear Retief," Magnan said blandly. "The implication is mightier than the affidavit. You should study the records of the giants of galactic diplomacy: Crodfoller, Passwyn, Spradley, Nitworth, Sternwheeler, Rumpwhistle. The roll-call of those names rings like the majestic tread of . . . of . . . . "

"Dinosaurs?" Retief suggested.

"An apt simile," Magnan nodded. "Those mighty figures, those armored hides—"

"Those tiny brains—"

Magnan smiled sadly. "I see you're indulging your penchant for distorted facetiae. Perhaps one day you'll learn their true worth."

"I already have my suspicions."

The intercom chimed. Miss Gumble's features appeared on the desk screen.

"Mr. Leatherwell to see you, Mr. Magnan. He has no appointment—"

Magnan's eyebrows went up. "Send Mr. Leatherwell right in." He looked at Retief. "I had no idea Leatherwell was planning a call. I wonder what he's after?" Magnan looked anxious. "He's an important figure in Belt minerals circles. It's important to avoid arousing antagonism, while maintaining non-commitment. You may as well stay. You might pick up some valuable pointers technique-wise."

*

The door swung wide. Leatherwell strode into the room, his massive paunch buckled into fashionable vests of turquoise velvet and hung with the latest in fluorescent watch charms. He extended a large palm and pumped Magnan's flaccid arm vigorously.

"Ah, there, Mr. Consul-General. Good of you to receive me." He wiped his hand absently on his thigh, eyeing Retief questioningly.

"Mr. Retief, my Vice-Consul and Minerals Officer," Magnan said. "Do take a chair, Mr. Leatherwell. In what capacity can I serve today?"

"I am here, gentlemen," Leatherwell said, putting an immense yellow briefcase on Magnan's desk and settling himself in a power rocker, "on behalf of my company, General Minerals. General Minerals has long been aware, gentlemen, of the austere conditions obtaining here in the Belt, to which public servants like yourselves are subjected." Leatherwell bobbed with the pitch of the rocker, smiling complacently at Magnan. "General Minerals is more than a great industrial combine. It is an organization with a heart." Leatherwell reached for his breast pocket, missed, tried again. "How do you turn this damned thing off?" he growled.

Magnan half-rose, peering over Leatherwell's briefcase. "The switch just there—on the arm."

The executive fumbled. There was a *click*, and the chair subsided with a sigh of compressed air.

"That's better." Leatherwell drew out a long slip of blue paper.

"To alleviate the boredom and brighten the lives of that hardy group of Terrestrials laboring here on Ceres to bring free enterprise to the Belt, General Minerals is presenting to the Consulate—on their behalf—one hundred thousand credits for the construction of a Joy Center, to be equipped with the latest and finest in recreational equipment, including a Gourmet Model C banquet synthesizer, a forty-foot sublimation chamber, a five thousand tape library—with a number of choice items unobtainable in Boston—a twenty-foot Tri-D tank and other amenities too numerous to mention." Leatherwell leaned back, beaming expectantly.

"Why, Mr. Leatherwell. We're overwhelmed, of course." Magnan smiled dazedly past the briefcase. "But I wonder if it's quite proper . . . . "

"The gift is to the people, Mr. Consul. You merely accept on their behalf."

"I wonder if General Minerals realizes that the hardy Terrestrials laboring on Ceres are limited to the Consular staff?" Retief said. "And the staff consists of Mr. Magnan, Miss Gumble and myself."

"Mr. Leatherwell is hardly interested in these details, Retief," Magnan cut in. "A public-spirited offer indeed, sir. As Terrestrial Consul—and on behalf of all Terrestrials here in the Belt—I accept with a humble awareness of—"

"Now, there was one other little matter." Leatherwell leaned forward to open the briefcase, glancing over Magnan's littered desktop. He extracted a bundle of papers, dropped them on the desk, then drew out a heavy document and passed it across to Magnan.

"Just a routine claim. I'd like to see it rushed through, as we have in mind some loading operations in the vicinity next week."

"Certainly Mr. Leatherwell."

Magnan glanced at the papers, paused to read. He looked up. "Ah—"

"Something the matter, Mr. Consul?" Leatherwell demanded.

"It's just that—ah—I seem to recall—as a matter of fact . . . . " Magnan looked at Retief. Retief took the papers, looked over the top sheet.

"95739-A. Sorry, Mr. Leatherwell. General Minerals has been anticipated. We're processing a prior claim."

"Prior claim?" Leatherwell barked. "You've issued the grant?"

"Oh, no indeed, Mr. Leatherwell," Magnan replied quickly. "The claim hasn't yet been processed."

"Then there's no difficulty," Leatherwell boomed. He glanced at his finger watch. "If you don't mind, I'll wait and take the grant along with me. I assume it will only take a minute or two to sign it and affix seals and so on?"

"The other claim was filed a full week ago—" Retief started.

"Bah!" Leatherwell waved a hand impatiently. "These details can be arranged." He fixed an eye on Magnan. "I'm sure all of us here understand that it's in the public interest that minerals properties go to responsible firms, with adequate capital for proper development."

169

"Why, ah," Magnan said.

"The Sam's Last Chance Number Nine Mining Company is a duly chartered firm. Their claim is valid."

"I know that hole-in-corner concern," Leatherwell snapped. "Mere irresponsible opportunists. General Minerals has spent millions—millions, I say—of the stockholders' funds in minerals explorations. Are they to be balked in realizing a fair return on their investment because these . . . these . . . adventures have stumbled on a deposit? Not that the property is of any real value, of course," he added. "Quite an ordinary bit of rock. But General Minerals would find it convenient to consolidate its holdings."

"There are plenty of other rocks floating around in the Belt. Why not—"

"One moment, Retief," Magnan cut in. He looked across the desk at his junior with a severe expression. "As Consul-General, I'm quite capable of determining the relative merits of claims. As Mr. Leatherwell has pointed out, it's in the public interest to consider the question in depth."

Leatherwell cleared his throat. "I might state at this time that General Minerals is prepared to be generous in dealing with these interlopers. I believe we would be prepared to go so far as to offer them free title to certain GM holdings in exchange for their release of any alleged rights to the property in question—merely to simplify matters, of course."

"That seems more than fair to me," Magnan glowed.

"The Sam's people have a clear priority," Retief said. "I logged the claim in last Friday."

"They have far from a clear title." Leatherwell snapped. "And I can assure you GM will contest their claim, if need be, to the Supreme Court!"

"Just what holdings did you have in mind offering them, Mr. Leatherwell?" Magnan asked nervously.

Leatherwell reached into his briefcase and drew out a paper.

"2645-P," he read. "A quite massive body. Crustal material, I imagine. It should satisfy these squatters' desire to own real estate in the Belt."

"I'll make a note of that," Magnan said, reaching for a pad.

"That's a Bona Fide offer, Mr. Leatherwell?" Retief asked.

"Certainly!"

"I'll record it as such," Magnan said, scribbling.

"And who knows?" Leatherwell said. "It may turn out to contain some surprisingly rich finds."

"And if they won't accept it?" Retief asked.

"Then I daresay General Minerals will find a remedy in the courts, sir!"

"Oh, I hardly think that will be necessary," Magnan said.

"Then there's another routine matter," Leatherwell said. He passed a second document across to Magnan. "GM is requesting an injunction to restrain these same parties from aggravated trespass. I'd appreciate it if you'd push it through at once. There's a matter of a load of illegally obtained ore involved, as well."

"Certainly Mr. Leatherwell. I'll see to it myself."

"No need for that. The papers are all drawn up. Our legal department will vouch for their correctness. Just sign here." Leatherwell spread out the paper and handed Magnan a pen.

"Wouldn't it be a good idea to read that over first?" Retief said.

*

Leatherwell frowned impatiently. "You'll have adequate time to familiarize yourself with the details later, Retief," Magnan snapped, taking the pen. "No need to waste Mr. Leatherwell's valuable time." He scratched a signature on the paper.

Leatherwell rose, gathered up his papers from Magnan's desk, dumped them into the briefcase. "Riff-raff, of course. Their kind has no business in the Belt."

Retief rose, crossed to the desk, and held out a hand. "I believe you gathered in an official document along with your own, Mr. Leatherwell. By error, of course."

"What's that?" Leatherwell bridled. Retief smiled, waiting. Magnan opened his mouth.

"It was under your papers, Mr. Leatherwell," Retief said. "It's the thick one, with the rubber bands."

Leatherwell dug in his briefcase, produced the document. "Well, fancy finding this here," he growled. He shoved the papers into Retief's hand.

"You're a very observant young fellow." He closed the briefcase with a snap. "I trust you'll have a bright future with the CDT."

"Really, Retief," Magnan said reprovingly. "There was no need to trouble Mr. Leatherwell."

Leatherwell directed a sharp look at Retief and a bland one at Magnan. "I trust you'll communicate the proposal to the interested parties. Inasmuch as time is of the essence of the GM position, our offer can only be held open until 0900

Greenwich, tomorrow. I'll call again at that time to finalize matters. I trust there'll be no impediment to a satisfactory settlement at that time. I should dislike to embark on lengthy litigation."

Magnan hurried around his desk to open the door. He turned back to fix Retief with an exasperated frown.

"A crass display of boorishness, Retief," he snapped. "You've embarrassed a most influential member of the business community—and for nothing more than a few miserable forms."

"Those forms represent somebody's stake in what might be a valuable property."

"They're mere paper until they've been processed!"

"Still—"

"My responsibility is to the Public interest—not to a fly-by-night group of prospectors."

"They found it first."

"Bah! A worthless rock. After Mr. Leatherwell's munificent gesture—"

"Better rush his check through before he thinks it over and changes his mind."

"Good heavens!" Magnan clutched the check, buzzed for Miss Gumble. She swept in, took Magnan's instructions and left. Retief waited while Magnan glanced over the injunction, then nodded.

"Quite in order. A person called Sam Mancziewicz appears to be the principal. The address given is the Jolly Barge Hotel; that would be that converted derelict ship in orbit 6942, I assume?"

Retief nodded. "That's what they call it."

"As for the ore-carrier, I'd best impound it, pending the settlement of the matter." Magnan drew a form from a drawer, filled in blanks, shoved the paper across the desk. He turned and consulted a wall chart. "The hotel is nearby at the moment, as it happens. Take the Consulate dinghy. If you get out there right away, you'll catch them before the evening binge has developed fully."

"I take it that's your diplomatic way of telling me that I'm now a process server." Retief took the papers and tucked them into an inside pocket.

"One of the many functions a diplomat is called on to perform in a small consular post. Excellent experience. I needn't warn you to be circumspect. These miners are an unruly lot—especially when receiving bad news."

"Aren't we all." Retief rose. "I don't suppose there's any prospect of your signing off that claim so that I can take a little good news along, too?"

"None whatever," Magnan snapped. "They've been made a most generous offer. If that fails to satisfy them, they have recourse through the courts."

"Fighting a suit like that costs money. The Sam's Last Chance Mining Company hasn't got any."

"Need I remind you—"

"I know. That's none of our concern."

"On your way out," Magnan said as Retief turned to the door, "ask Miss Gumble to bring in the Gourmet catalog from the Commercial Library. I want to check on the specifications of the Model C Banquet synthesizer."

An hour later, nine hundred miles from Ceres and fast approaching the Jolly Barge Hotel, Retief keyed the skiff's transmitter.

"CDT 347-89 calling Navy FP-VO-6."

"Navy VO-6 here, CDT," a prompt voice came back. A flickering image appeared on the small screen. "Oh, hi there, Mr. Retief. What brings you out in the cold night air?"

"Hello, Henry. I'm estimating the Jolly Barge in ten minutes. It looks like a busy night ahead. I may be moving around a little. How about keeping an eye on me? I'll be carrying a personnel beacon. Monitor it, and if I switch it into high, come in fast. I can't afford to be held up. I've got a big meeting in the morning."

"Sure thing, Mr. Retief. We'll keep an eye open."

*

Retief dropped a ten-credit note on the bar, accepted a glass and a squat bottle of black Marsberry brandy and turned to survey the low-ceilinged room, a former hydroponics deck now known as the Jungle Bar. Under the low ceiling, unpruned *Ipomoea batatas* and *Lathyrus odoratus* vines sprawled in a tangle that filtered the light of the S-spectrum glare panels to a muted green. A six-foot trideo screen, salvaged from the wreck of a Concordiat transport, blared taped music in the style of two centuries past. At the tables, heavy-shouldered men in bright-dyed suit liners played cards, clanked bottles and shouted.

Carrying the bottle and glass, Retief moved across to an empty chair at one of the tables.

"You gentlemen mind if I join you?"

Five unshaven faces turned to study Retief's six foot three, his close cut black hair, his non-commital gray coverall, the scars on his knuckles. A redhead with a broken nose nodded. "Pull up a chair, stranger."

RETIEF: THE DIRTY DOZEN

"You workin' a claim, pardner?"

"Just looking around."

"Try a shot of this rock juice."

"Don't do it, Mister. He makes it himself."

"Best rock juice this side of Luna."

"Say, feller—"

"The name's Retief."

"Retief, you ever play Drift?"

"Can't say that I did."

"Don't gamble with Sam, pardner. He's the local champ."

"How do you play it?"

The black-browed miner who had suggested the game rolled back his sleeve to reveal a sinewy forearm, put his elbow on the table.

"You hook forefingers, and put a glass right up on top. The man that takes a swallow wins. If the drink spills, it's drinks for the house."

"A man don't often win out-right," the redhead said cheerfully. "But it makes for plenty of drinkin'."

Retief put his elbow on the table. "I'll give it a try."

The two men hooked forefingers. The redhead poured a tumbler half full of rock juice, placed it atop the two fists. "Okay, boys. Go!"

The man named Sam gritted his teeth; his biceps tensed, knuckles grew white. The glass trembled. Then it moved—toward Retief. Sam hunched his shoulders, straining.

"That's the stuff, Mister!"

"What's the matter, Sam? You tired?"

The glass moved steadily closer to Retief's face.

"A hundred the new man makes it!"

"Watch Sam! Any minute now . . . . "

The glass slowed, paused. Retief's wrist twitched and the glass crashed to the table top. A shout went up. Sam leaned back with a sigh, massaging his hand.

"That's some arm you got, Mister," he said. "If you hadn't jumped just then . . . . "

"I guess the drinks are on me," Retief said.

*

Two hours later Retief's Marsberry bottle stood empty on the table beside half a dozen others.

174

"We were lucky," Sam Mancziewicz was saying. "You figure the original volume of the planet; say 245,000,000,000 cubic miles. The deBerry theory calls for a collapsed-crystal core no more than a mile in diameter. There's your odds."

"And you believe you've found a fragment of this core?"

"Damn right we have. Couple of million tons if it's an ounce. And at three credits a ton delivered at Port Syrtis, we're set for life. About time, too. Twenty years I've been in the Belt. Got two kids I haven't seen for five years. Things are going to be different now."

"Hey, Sam; tone it down. You don't have to broadcast to every claim jumper in the Belt."

"Our claim's on file at the Consulate," Sam said. "As soon as we get the grant—"

"When's that gonna be? We been waitin' a week now."

"I've never seen any collapsed-crystal metal," Retief said. "I'd like to take a look at it."

"Sure. Come on, I'll run you over. It's about an hour's run. We'll take our skiff. You want to go along, Willy?"

"I got a bottle to go," Willy said. "See you in the morning."

The two men descended in the lift to the boat bay, suited up and strapped into the cramped boat. A bored attendant cycled the launch doors, levered the release that propelled the skiff out and clear of the Jolly Barge Hotel. Retief caught a glimpse of a tower of lights spinning majestically against the black of space as the drive hurled the tiny boat away.

II

Retief's feet sank ankle deep into the powdery surface that glinted like snow in the glare of the distant sun.

"It's funny stuff," Sam's voice sounded in his ear. "Under a gee of gravity, you'd sink out of sight. The stuff cuts diamond like butter—but temperature changes break it down into a powder. A lot of it's used just like this, as an industrial abrasive. Easy to load, too. Just drop a suction line, put on ambient pressure and start pumping."

"And this whole rock is made of the same material?"

"Sure is. We ran plenty of test bores and a full schedule of soundings. I've got the reports back aboard *Gertie*—that's our lighter."

"And you've already loaded a cargo here?"

175

"Yep. We're running out of capital fast. I need to get that cargo to port in a hurry—before the outfit goes into involuntary bankruptcy. With this, that'd be a crime."

"What do you know about General Minerals, Sam?"

"You thinking of hiring on with them? Better read the fine print in your contract before you sign. Sneakiest bunch this side of a burglar's convention."

"They own a chunk of rock known as 2645-P. Do you suppose we could find it?"

"Oh, you're buying it, hey? Sure, we can find it. You damn sure want to look it over good if General Minerals is selling."

Back aboard the skiff, Mancziewicz flipped the pages of the chart book, consulted a table. "Yep, she's not too far off. Let's go see what GM's trying to unload."

*

The skiff hovered two miles from the giant boulder known as 2645-P. Retief and Mancziewicz looked it over at high magnification. "It don't look like much, Retief," Sam said. "Let's go down and take a closer look."

The boat dropped rapidly toward the scarred surface of the tiny world, a floating mountain, glaring black and white in the spotlight of the sun. Sam frowned at his instrument panel.

"That's funny. My ion counter is revving up. Looks like a drive trail, not more than an hour or two old. Somebody's been here."

The boat grounded. Retief and Sam got out. The stony surface was littered with rock fragments varying in size from pebbles to great slabs twenty feet long, tumbled in a loose bed of dust and sand. Retief pushed off gently, drifted up to a vantage point atop an upended wedge of rock. Sam joined him.

"This is all igneous stuff," he said. "Not likely we'll find much here that would pay the freight to Syrtis—unless maybe you lucked onto some Bodean artifacts. They bring plenty."

He flipped a binocular in place as he talked, scanned the riven landscape. "Hey!" he said. "Over there!"

Retief followed Sam's pointing glove. He studied the dark patch against a smooth expanse of eroded rock.

"A friend of mine came across a chunk of the old planetary surface two years ago," Sam said thoughtfully. "Had a tunnel in it that'd been used as a storage depot by the Bodeans. Took out over two ton of hardware. Course, nobody's discovered how the stuff works yet, but it brings top prices."

176

"Looks like water erosion," Retief said.

"Yep. This could be another piece of surface, all right. Could be a cave over there. The Bodeans liked caves, too. Must have been some war—but then, if it hadn't been, they wouldn't have tucked so much stuff away underground where it could weather the planetary breakup."

They descended, crossed the jumbled rocks with light, thirty-foot leaps.

"It's a cave, all right," Sam said, stooping to peer into the five-foot bore. Retief followed him inside.

"Let's get some light in here." Mancziewicz flipped on a beam. It glinted back from dull polished surfaces of Bodean synthetic. Sam's low whistle sounded in Retief's headset.

"That's funny," Retief said.

"Funny, hell! It's hilarious. General Minerals trying to sell off a worthless rock to a tenderfoot—and it's loaded with Bodean artifacts. No telling how much is here; the tunnel seems to go quite a ways back."

"That's not what I mean. Do you notice your suit warming up?"

"Huh? Yeah, now that you mention it."

Retief rapped with a gauntleted hand on the satiny black curve of the nearest Bodean artifact. It clunked dully through the suit "That's not metal," he said. "It's plastic."

"There's something fishy here," Sam said. "This erosion; it looks more like a heat beam."

"Sam," Retief said, turning, "it appears to me somebody has gone to a great deal of trouble to give a false impression here."

*

Sam snorted. "I told you they were a crafty bunch." He started out of the cave, then paused, went to one knee to study the floor. "But maybe they outsmarted themselves. Look here!"

Retief looked. Sam's beam reflected from a fused surface of milky white, shot through with dirty yellow. He snapped a pointed instrument in place on his gauntlet, dug at one of the yellow streaks. It furrowed under the gouge, a particle adhering to the instrument. With his left hand, Mancziewicz opened a pouch clipped to his belt, carefully deposited the sample in a small orifice on the device in the pouch. He flipped a key, squinted at a dial.

"Atomic weight 197.2," he said. Retief turned down the audio volume on his headset as Sam's laughter rang in his helmet.

"Those clowns were out to stick you, Retief," he gasped, still chuckling. "They salted the rock with a cave full of Bodean artifacts—"

"Fake Bodean artifacts," Retief put in.

"They planed off the rock so it would look like an old beach, and then cut this cave with beamers. And they were boring through practically solid gold!"

"As good as that?"

Mancziewicz flashed the light around. "This stuff will assay out at a thousand credits a ton, easy. If the vein doesn't run to five thousand tons, the beers are on me." He snapped off the light. "Let's get moving, Retief. You want to sew this deal up before they get around to taking another look at it."

Back in the boat, Retief and Mancziewicz opened their helmets. "This calls for a drink," Sam said, extracting a pressure flask from the map case. "This rock's worth as much as mine, maybe more. You hit it lucky, Retief. Congratulations." He thrust out a hand.

"I'm afraid you've jumped to a couple of conclusions, Sam," Retief said. "I'm not out here to buy mining properties."

"You're not—then why—but man! Even if you didn't figure on buying . . . . " He trailed off as Retief shook his head, unzipped his suit to reach to an inside pocket, take out a packet of folded papers.

"In my capacity as Terrestrial Vice-Consul, I'm serving you with an injunction restraining you from further exploitation of the body known as 95739-A." He handed a paper across to Sam. "I also have here an Order impounding the vessel *Gravel Gertie II.*"

Sam took the papers silently, sat looking at them. He looked up at Retief. "Funny. When you beat me at Drift and then threw the game so you wouldn't show me up in front of the boys, I figured you for a right guy. I've been spilling my heart out to you like you were my old grandma. An old-timer in the game like me." He dropped a hand, brought it up with a Browning 2mm pointed at Retief's chest.

"I could shoot you and dump you here with a slab over you, toss these papers in the John and hightail it with the load . . . . "

"That wouldn't do you much good in the long run, Sam. Besides you're not a criminal or an idiot."

*

Sam chewed his lip. "My claim is on file in the Consulate, legal and proper. Maybe by now the grant's gone through."

"Other people have their eye on your rock, Sam. Ever meet a fellow called Leatherwell?"

"General Minerals, huh? They haven't got a leg to stand on."

"The last time I saw your claim, it was still lying in the pending file. Just a bundle of paper until it's validated by the Consul. If Leatherwell contests it . . . well, his lawyers are on annual retainer. How long could you keep the suit going, Sam?"

Mancziewicz closed his helmet with a decisive snap, motioned to Retief to do the same. He opened the hatch, sat with the gun on Retief.

"Get out, paper-pusher." His voice sounded thin in the headphones. "You'll get lonesome, maybe, but your suit will keep you alive a few days. I'll tip somebody off before you lose too much weight. I'm going back and see if I can't stir up a little action at the Consulate."

Retief climbed out, walked off fifty yards. He watched as the skiff kicked off in a quickly dispersed cloud of dust, dwindled rapidly away to a bright speck that was lost against the stars. Then he extracted the locator beacon from the pocket of his suit and thumbed the control.

Twenty minutes later, aboard Navy FP-VO-6, Retief pulled off his helmet. "Fast work, Henry. I've got a couple of calls to make. Put me through to your HQ, will you? I want a word with Commander Hayle."

The young naval officer raised the HQ, handed the mike to Retief.

"Vice-Consul Retief here, Commander. I'd like you to intercept a skiff, bound from my present position toward Ceres. There's a Mr. Mancziewicz aboard. He's armed, but not dangerous. Collect him and see that he's delivered to the Consulate at 0900 Greenwich tomorrow.

"Next item: The Consulate has impounded an ore-carrier, *Gravel Gertie II*. It's in a parking orbit ten miles off Ceres. I want it taken in tow." Retief gave detailed instruction. Then he asked for a connection through the Navy switchboard to the Consulate. Magnan's voice answered.

"Retief speaking, Mr. Consul. I have some news that I think will interest you—"

"Where are you, Retief? What's wrong with the screen? Have you served the injunction?"

"I'm aboard the Navy patrol vessel. I've been out looking over the situation, and I've made a surprising discovery. I don't think we're going to have any trouble with

179

the Sam's people; they've looked over the body—2645-P—and it seems General Minerals has slipped up. There appears to be a highly valuable deposit there."

"Oh? What sort of deposit?"

"Mr. Mancziewicz mentioned collapsed crystal metal," Retief said.

"Well, most interesting." Magnan's voice sounded thoughtful.

"Just thought you'd like to know. This should simplify the meeting in the morning.

"Yes," Magnan said. "Yes, indeed. I think this makes everything very simple . . . ."

*

At 0845 Greenwich, Retief stepped into the outer office of the Consular suite.

" . . . fantastic configuration," Leatherwell's bass voice rumbled, "covering literally acres. My xenogeologists are somewhat confused by the formations. They had only a few hours to examine the site; but it's clear from the extent of the surface indications that we have a very rich find here. Very rich indeed. Beside it, 95739-A dwindles into insignificance. Very fast thinking on your part, Mr. Consul, to bring the matter to my attention."

"Not at all, Mr. Leatherwell. After all—"

"Our tentative theory is that the basic crystal fragment encountered the core material at some time, and gathered it in. Since we had been working on—that is, had landed to take samples on the other side of the body, this anomalous deposit escaped our attention completely."

Retief stepped into the room.

"Good morning, gentlemen. Has Mr. Mancziewicz arrived?"

"Mr. Mancziewicz is under restraint by the Navy. I've had a call that he'd be escorted here."

"Arrested, eh?" Leatherwell nodded. "I told you these people were an irresponsible group. In a way it seems a pity to waste a piece of property like 95739-A on them."

"I understood General Minerals was claiming that rock," Retief said, looking surprised.

Leatherwell and Magnan exchanged glances. "Ah, GM has decided to drop all claim to the body," Leatherwell said. "As always, we wish to encourage enterprise on the part of the small operators. Let them keep the property. After all GM has other deposits well worth exploiting." He smiled complacently.

"What about 2645-P? You've offered it to the Sam's group."

"That offer is naturally withdrawn!" Leatherwell snapped.

"I don't see how you can withdraw the offer," Retief said. "It's been officially recorded. It's a Bona Fide contract, binding on General Minerals, subject to—"

"Out of the goodness of our corporate heart," Leatherwell roared, "we've offered to relinquish our legitimate, rightful claim to asteroid 2645-P. And you have the infernal gall to spout legal technicalities! I have half a mind to withdraw my offer to withdraw!"

"Actually," Magnan put in, eyeing a corner of the room, "I'm not at all sure I could turn up the record of the offer of 2645-P. I noted it down on a bit of scratch paper—"

"That's all right," Retief said, "I had my pocket recorder going. I sealed the record and deposited it in the Consular archives."

There was a clatter of feet outside. Miss Gumble appeared on the desk screen. "There are a number of persons here—" she began.

*

The door banged open. Sam Mancziewicz stepped into the room, a sailor tugging at each arm. He shook them loose, stared around the room. His eyes lighted on Retief. "How did you get here . . . ?"

"Look here, Monkeywits or whatever your name is," Leatherwell began, popping out of his chair.

Mancziewicz whirled, seized the stout executive by the shirt front and lifted him onto his tiptoes. "You double-barrelled copper-bottomed oak-lined son-of-a—"

"Don't spoil him, Sam," Retief said casually. "He's here to sign off all rights—if any—to 95739-A. It's all yours—if you want it."

Sam glared into Leatherwell's eyes. "That right?" he grated. Leatherwell bobbed his head, his chins compressed into bulging folds.

"However," Retief went on, "I wasn't at all sure you'd still be agreeable, since he's made your company a binding offer of 2645-P in return for clear title to 95739-A."

Mancziewicz looked across at Retief with narrowed eyes. He released Leatherwell, who slumped into his chair. Magnan darted around his desk to minister to the magnate. Behind them, Retief closed one eye in a broad wink at Mancziewicz.

" . . . still, if Mr. Leatherwell will agree, in addition to guaranteeing your title to 95739-A, to purchase your output at four credits a ton, FOB his collection station—"

Mancziewicz looked at Leatherwell. Leatherwell hesitated, then nodded. "Agreed," he croaked.

181

" . . . and to open his commissary and postal facilities to all prospectors operating in the belt . . . . "

Leatherwell swallowed, eyes bulging, glanced at Manczeiwicz's face. He nodded. "Agreed."

" . . . then I think I'd sign an agreement releasing him from his offer."

Manczeiwicz looked at Magnan.

"You're the Terrestrial Consul-General," he said. "Is that the straight goods?"

Magnan nodded. "If Mr. Leatherwell agrees—"

"He's already agreed," Retief said. "My pocket recorder, you know."

"Put it in writing," Manczeiwicz said.

Magnan called in Miss Gumble. The others waited silently while Magnan dictated. He signed the paper with a flourish, passed it across to Manczeiwicz. He read it, re-read it, then picked up the pen and signed. Magnan impressed the Consular seal on the paper.

"Now the grant," Retief said. Magnan signed the claim, added a seal. Manczeiwicz tucked the papers away in an inner pocket. He rose.

"Well, gents, I guess maybe I had you figured wrong," he said. He looked at Retief. "Uh . . . got time for a drink?"

"I shouldn't drink during office hours," Retief said. He rose. "So I'll take the rest of the day off."

*

"I don't get it," Sam said signalling for refills. "What was the routine with the injunction—and impounding *Gertie*? You could have got hurt."

"I don't think so," Retief said. "If you'd meant business with that Browning, you'd have flipped the safety off. As for the injunction—orders are orders."

"I've been thinking," Sam said. "That gold deposit. It was a plant, too, wasn't it?"

"I'm just a bureaucrat, Sam. What would I know about gold?"

"A double-salting job," Sam said. "I was supposed to spot the phoney hardware—and then fall for the gold plant. When Leatherwell put his proposition to me, I'd grab it. The gold was worth plenty, I'd figure, and I couldn't afford a legal tangle with General Minerals. The lousy skunk! And you must have spotted it and put it up to him."

The bar-tender leaned across to Retief. "Wanted on the phone."

In the booth, Magnan's agitated face stared a Retief.

"Retief, Mr. Leatherwell's in a towering rage! The deposit on 2645-P; it was merely a surface film, barely a few inches thick! The entire deposit wouldn't fill an ore-boat." A horrified expression dawned on Magnan's face. "Retief," he gasped, "what did you do with the impounded ore-carrier?"

"Well, let me see," Retief said. "According to the Space Navigation Code, a body in orbit within twenty miles of any inhabited airless body constitutes a navigational hazard. Accordingly, I had it towed away."

"And the cargo?"

"Well, accelerating all that mass was an expensive business, so to save the taxpayer's credits, I had it dumped."

"Where?" Magnan croaked.

"On some unimportant asteroid—as specified by Regulations." He smiled blandly at Magnan. Magnan looked back numbly.

"But you said—"

"All I said was that there was what looked like a valuable deposit on 2645-P. It turned out to be a bogus gold mine that somebody had rigged up in a hurry. Curious, eh?"

"But you told me—"

"And you told Mr. Leatherwell. Indiscreet of you, Mr. Consul. That was a privileged communication; classified information, official use only."

"You led me to believe there was collapsed crystal!"

"I said Sam had mentioned it. He told me his asteroid was made of the stuff."

Magnan swallowed hard, twice. "By the way," he said dully. "You were right about the check. Half an hour ago Mr. Leatherwell tried to stop payment. He was too late."

"All in all, it's been a big day for Leatherwell," Retief said. "Anything else?"

"I hope not," Magnan said. "I sincerely hope not." He leaned close to the screen. "You'll consider the entire affair as . . . confidential? There's no point in unduly complicating relationships."

"Have no fear, Mr. Consul," Retief said cheerfully. "You won't find me identifying with anything as specific as triple-salting an asteroid."

Back at the table, Sam called for another bottle of rock juice.

"That Drift's a pretty good game," Retief said. "But let me show you one I learned out on Yill . . . ."

MIGHTIEST QORN

Sly, brave and truculent, the Qornt held all humans in contempt—except one!

I

Ambassador Nitworth glowered across his mirror-polished, nine-foot platinum desk at his assembled staff.

"Gentlemen, are any of you familiar with a race known as the Qornt?"

There was a moment of profound silence. Nitworth leaned forward, looking solemn.

"They were a warlike race known in this sector back in Concordiat times, perhaps two hundred years ago. They vanished as suddenly as they had appeared. There was no record of where they went." He paused for effect.

"They have now reappeared—occupying the inner planet of this system!"

"But, sir," Second Secretary Magnan offered. "That's uninhabited Terrestrial territory . . . . "

"Indeed, Mr. Magnan?" Nitworth smiled icily. "It appears the Qornt do not share that opinion." He plucked a heavy parchment from a folder before him, harrumphed and read aloud:

His Supreme Excellency The Qorn, Regent of Qornt, Over-Lord of the Galactic Destiny, Greets the Terrestrials and, with reference to the presence in mandated territory of Terrestrial squatters, has the honor to advise that he will require the use of his outer world on the thirtieth day. Then will the Qornt come with steel and fire. Receive, Terrestrials, renewed assurances of my awareness of your existence, and let Those who dare gird for the contest.

"Frankly, I wouldn't call it conciliatory," Magnan said.

Nitworth tapped the paper with a finger.

"We have been served, gentlemen, with nothing less than an Ultimatum!"

"Well, we'll soon straighten these fellows out—" the Military Attache began.

"There happens to be more to this piece of truculence than appears on the surface," the Ambassador cut in. He paused, waiting for interested frowns to settle into place.

"Note, gentlemen, that these invaders have appeared on terrestrial controlled soil—and without so much as a flicker from the instruments of the Navigational Monitor Service!"

The Military Attache blinked. "That's absurd," he said flatly. Nitworth slapped the table.

"We're up against something new, gentlemen! I've considered every hypothesis from cloaks of invisibility to time travel! The fact is—the Qornt fleets are indetectible!"

*

The Military Attache pulled at his lower lip. "In that case, we can't try conclusions with these fellows until we have an indetectible drive of our own. I recommend a crash project. In the meantime—"

"I'll have my boys start in to crack this thing," the Chief of the Confidential Terrestrial Source Section spoke up. "I'll fit out a couple of volunteers with plastic beaks—"

"No cloak and dagger work, gentlemen! Long range policy will be worked out by Deep-Think teams back at the Department. Our role will be a holding action. Now I want suggestions for a comprehensive, well rounded and decisive course for meeting this threat. Any recommendation?"

The Political Officer placed his fingertips together. "What about a stiff Note demanding an extra week's time?"

"No! No begging," the Economic Officer objected. "I'd say a calm, dignified, aggressive withdrawal—as soon as possible."

"We don't want to give them the idea we spook easily," the Military Attache said. "Let's delay the withdrawal—say, until tomorrow."

"Early tomorrow," Magnan said. "Or maybe later today."

"Well, I see you're of a mind with me," Nitworth nodded. "Our plan of action is clear, but it remains to be implemented. We have a population of over fifteen million individuals to relocate." He eyed the Political Officer. "I want five proposals for resettlement on my desk by oh-eight-hundred hours tomorrow." Nitworth rapped out instructions. Harried-looking staff members arose and hurried from the room. Magnan eased toward the door.

"Where are you going, Magnan?" Nitworth snapped.

"Since you're so busy, I thought I'd just slip back down to Com Inq. It was a most interesting orientation lecture, Mr. Ambassador. Be sure to let us know how it works out."

"Kindly return to your chair," Nitworth said coldly. "A number of chores remain to be assigned. I think you, Magnan, need a little field experience. I want you to get over to Roolit I and take a look at these Qornt personally."

Magnan's mouth opened and closed soundlessly.

"Not afraid of a few Qornt, are you, Magnan?"

"Afraid? Good lord, no, ha ha. It's just that I'm afraid I may lose my head and do something rash if I go."

"Nonsense! A diplomat is immune to heroic impulses. Take Retief along. No dawdling, now! I want you on the way in two hours. Notify the transport pool at once. Now get going!"

Magnan nodded unhappily and went into the hall.

"Oh, Retief," Nitworth said. Retief turned.

"Try to restrain Mr. Magnan from any impulsive moves—in any direction."

II

Retief and Magnan topped a ridge and looked down across a slope of towering tree-shrubs and glossy violet-stemmed palms set among flamboyant blossoms of yellow and red, reaching down to a strip of white beach with the blue sea beyond.

"A delightful vista," Magnan said, mopping at his face. "A pity we couldn't locate the Qornt. We'll go back now and report—"

"I'm pretty sure the settlement is off to the right," Retief said. "Why don't you head back for the boat, while I ease over and see what I can observe."

"Retief, we're engaged in a serious mission. This is not a time to think of sightseeing."

"I'd like to take a good look at what we're giving away."

"See here, Retief! One might almost receive the impression that you're questioning Corps policy!"

"One might, at that. The Qornt have made their play, but I think it might be valuable to take a look at their cards before we fold. If I'm not back at the boat in an hour, lift without me."

"You expect me to make my way back alone?"

"It's directly down-slope—" Retief broke off, listening. Magnan clutched at his arm.

There was a sound of crackling foliage. Twenty feet ahead, a leafy branch swung aside. An eight-foot biped stepped into view, long, thin, green-clad legs with back-bending knees moving in quick, bird-like steps. A pair of immense black-lensed goggles covered staring eyes set among bushy green hair above a great bone-white beak. The crest bobbed as the creature cocked its head, listening.

Magnan gulped audibly. The Qornt froze, head tilted, beak aimed directly at the spot where the Terrestrials stood in the deep shade of a giant trunk.

"I'll go for help," Magnan squeaked. He whirled and took three leaps into the brush.

A second great green-clad figure rose up to block his way. He spun, darted to the left. The first Qornt pounced, grappled Magnan to its narrow chest. Magnan yelled, threshing and kicking, broke free, turned—and collided with the eight-foot alien, coming in fast from the right. All three went down in a tangle of limbs.

Retief jumped forward, hauled Magnan free, thrust him aside and stopped, right fist cocked. The two Qornt lay groaning feebly.

"Nice piece of work, Mr. Magnan," Retief said. "You nailed both of them."

*

"Those undoubtedly are the most bloodthirsty, aggressive, merciless countenances it has ever been my misfortune to encounter," Magnan said. "It hardly seems fair. Eight feet tall *and* faces like that!"

The smaller of the two captive Qornt ran long, slender fingers over a bony shin, from which he had turned back the tight-fitting green trousers.

"It's not broken," he whistled nasally in passable Terrestrial, eyeing Magnan through the heavy goggles, now badly cracked. "Small thanks to you."

Magnan smiled loftily. "I daresay you'll think twice before interfering with peaceable diplomats in future."

"Diplomats? Surely you jest."

"Never mind us," Retief said. "It's you fellows we'd like to talk about. How many of you are there?"

"Only Zubb and myself."

"I mean altogether. How many Qornt?"

The alien whistled shrilly.

"Here, no signalling!" Magnan snapped, looking around.

"That was merely an expression of amusement."

"You find the situation amusing? I assure you, sir, you are in perilous straits at the moment. I *may* fly into another rage, you know."

"Please, restrain yourself. I was merely somewhat astonished—" a small whistle escaped—"at being taken for a Qornt."

"Aren't you a Qornt?"

"I? Great snail trails, no!" More stifled whistles of amusement escaped the beaked face. "Both Zubb and I are Verpp. Naturalists, as it happens."

"You certainly *look* like Qornt."

"Oh, not at all—except perhaps to a Terrestrial. The Qornt are sturdily built rascals, all over ten feet in height. And, of course, they do nothing but quarrel. A drone caste, actually."

"A caste? You mean they're biologically the same as you?"

"Not at all! A Verpp wouldn't think of fertilizing a Qornt."

"I mean to say, you are of the same basic stock—descended from a common ancestor, perhaps."

"We are all Pud's creatures."

"What are the differences between you, then?"

"Why, the Qornt are argumentive, boastful, lacking in appreciation for the finer things of life. One dreads to contemplate descending to *their* level."

"Do you know anything about a Note passed to the Terrestrial Ambassador at Smorbrod?" Retief asked.

*

The beak twitched. "Smorbrod? I know of no place called Smorbrod."

"The outer planet of this system."

"Oh, yes. We call it Guzzum. I had heard that some sort of creatures had established a settlement there, but I confess I pay little note to such matters."

"We're wasting time, Retief," Magnan said. "We must truss these chaps up, hurry back to the boat and make our escape. You heard what they said."

"Are there any Qornt down there at the harbor, where the boats are?" Retief asked.

"At Tarroon, you mean? Oh, yes. Planning some adventure."

"That would be the invasion of Smorbrod," Magnan said. "And unless we hurry, Retief, we're likely to be caught there with the last of the evacuees!"

"How many Qornt would you say there are at Tarroon?"

"Oh, a very large number. Perhaps fifteen or twenty."

"Fifteen or twenty what?" Magnan looked perplexed.

"Fifteen or twenty Qornt."

"You mean that there are only fifteen or twenty individual Qornt in all?"

Another whistle. "Not at all. I was referring to the local Qornt only. There are more at the other Centers, of course."

"And the Qornt are responsible for the ultimatum—unilaterally?"

"I suppose so; it sounds like them. A truculent group, you know. And interplanetary relations *are* rather a hobby of theirs."

Zubb moaned and stirred. He sat up slowly, rubbing his head. He spoke to his companion in a shrill alien clatter of consonants.

"What did he say?"

"Poor Zubb. He blames me for his bruises, since it was my idea to gather you as specimens."

"You should have known better than to tackle that fierce-looking creature," Zubb said, pointing his beak at Magnan.

"How does it happen that you speak Terrestrial?" Retief asked.

"Oh, one picks up all sorts of dialects."

"It's quite charming, really," Magnan said. "Such a quaint, archaic accent."

"Suppose we went down to Tarroon," Retief asked. "What kind of reception would we get?"

"That depends. I wouldn't recommend interfering with the Gwil or the Rheuk; it's their nest-mending time, you know. The Boog will be busy mating—such a tedious business—and of course the Qornt are tied up with their ceremonial feasting. I'm afraid no one will take any notice of you."

"Do you mean to say," Magnan demanded, "that these ferocious Qornt, who have issued an ultimatum to the Corps Diplomatique Terrestrienne—who openly avow their occupied world—would ignore Terrestrials in their midst?"

"If at all possible."

Retief got to his feet.

"I think our course is clear, Mr. Magnan. It's up to us to go down and attract a little attention."

III

"I'm not at all sure we're going about this in the right way," Magnan puffed, trotting at Retief's side. "These fellows Zubb and Slun—Oh, they seem affable enough, but how can we be sure we're not being led into a trap?"

"We can't."

Magnan stopped short. "Let's go back."

"All right," Retief said. "Of course there may be an ambush—"

Magnan moved off. "Let's keep going."

The party emerged from the undergrowth at the edge of a great brush-grown mound. Slun took the lead, rounded the flank of the hillock, halted at a rectangular opening cut into the slope.

"You can find your way easily enough from here," he said. "You'll excuse us, I hope—"

"Nonsense, Slun!" Zubb pushed forward. "I'll escort our guests to Qornt Hall." He twittered briefly to his fellow Verpp. Slun twittered back.

"I don't like it, Retief," Magnan whispered. "Those fellows are plotting mischief."

"Threaten them with violence, Mr Magnan. They're scared of you."

"That's true. And the drubbing they received was well-deserved. I'm a patient man, but there are occasions—"

"Come along, please," Zubb called. "Another ten minutes' walk—"

"See here, we have no interest in investigating this barrow," Magnan announced. "We wish you to take us direct to Tarroon to interview your military leaders regarding the ultimatum!"

"Yes, yes, of course. Qornt Hall lies here inside the village."

"This is Tarroon?"

"A modest civic center, sir, but there are those who love it."

"No wonder we didn't observe their works from the air," Magnan muttered. "Camouflaged." He moved hesitantly through the opening.

The party moved along a wide, deserted tunnel which sloped down steeply, then leveled off and branched. Zubb took the center branch, ducking slightly under the nine-foot ceiling lit at intervals with what appeared to be primitive incandescent panels.

"Few signs of an advanced technology here," Magnan whispered. "These creatures must devote all their talents to warlike enterprise."

Ahead, Zubb slowed. A distant susurration was audible, a sustained high-pitched screeching. "Softly, now. We approach Qornt Hall. They can be an irascible lot when disturbed at their feasting."

"When will the feast be over?" Magnan called hoarsely.

"In another few weeks, I should imagine, if, as you say, they've scheduled an invasion for next month."

"Look here, Zubb." Magnan shook a finger at the tall alien. "How is it that these Qornt are allowed to embark on piratical ventures of this sort without reference to the wishes of the majority?"

"Oh, the majority of the Qornt favor the move, I imagine."

"These few hotheads are permitted to embroil the planet in war?"

"Oh, they don't embroil the planet in war. They merely—"

"Retief, this is fantastic! I've heard of iron-fisted military cliques before, but this is madness!"

"Come softly, now." Zubb beckoned, moving toward a bend in the yellow-lit corridor. Retief and Magnan moved forward.

*

The corridor debouched through a high double door into a vast oval chamber, high-domed, gloomy, paneled in dark wood and hung with tattered banners, scarred halberds, pikes, rusted longswords, crossed spears over patinaed hauberks, pitted radiation armor, corroded power rifles, the immense mummified heads of horned and fanged animals. Great guttering torches in wall brackets and in stands along the length of the long table shed a smoky light that reflected from the mirror polish of the red granite floor, gleamed on polished silver bowls and paper-thin glass, shone jewel-red and gold through dark bottles—and cast long flickering shadows behind the fifteen trolls at the board.

Lesser trolls—beaked, bush-haired, great-eyed—trotted briskly, bird-kneed, bearing steaming platters, stood in groups of three strumming slender bottle-shaped lutes, or pranced an intricate-patterned dance, unnoticed in the shrill uproar as each of the magnificently draped, belted, feathered and jeweled Qornt carried on a shouted conversation with an equally noisy fellow.

"A most interesting display of barbaric splendor," Magnan breathed. "Now we'd better be getting back."

"Ah, a moment," Zubb said. "Observe the Qornt—the tallest of the feasters—he with the head-dress of crimson, purple, silver and pink."

"Twelve feet if he's an inch," Magnan estimated. "And now we really must hurry along—"

"That one is chief among these rowdies. I'm sure you'll want a word with him. He controls not only the Tarroonian vessels but those from the other Centers as well."

"What kind of vessels? Warships?"

"Certainly. What other kind would the Qornt bother with?"

"I don't suppose," Magnan said casually, "that you'd know the type, tonnage, armament and manning of these vessels? And how many units comprise the fleet? And where they're based at present?"

"They're fully automated twenty-thousand-ton all-purpose dreadnaughts. They mount a variety of weapons. The Qornt are fond of that sort of thing. Each of the Qornt has his own, of course. They're virtually identical, except for the personal touches each individual has given his ship."

"Great heavens, Retief!" Magnan exclaimed in a whisper. "It sounds as though these brutes employ a battle armada as simpler souls might a set of toy sailboats!"

Retief stepped past Magnan and Zubb to study the feasting hall. "I can see that their votes would carry all the necessary weight."

"And now an interview with the Qorn himself," Zubb shrilled. "If you'll kindly step along, gentlemen . . . . "

"That won't be necessary," Magnan said hastily, "I've decided to refer the matter to committee."

"After having come so far," Zubb said, "it would be a pity to miss having a cosy chat."

There was a pause.

"Ah . . . Retief," Magnan said. "Zubb has just presented a most compelling argument . . . . "

*

Retief turned. Zubb stood gripping an ornately decorated power pistol in one bony hand, a slim needler in the other. Both were pointed at Magnan's chest.

"I suspected you had hidden qualities, Zubb," Retief commented.

"See here, Zubb! We're diplomats!" Magnan started.

"Careful, Mr. Magnan; you may goad him to a frenzy."

"By no means," Zubb whistled. "I much prefer to observe the frenzy of the Qorn when presented with the news that two peaceful Verpp have been assaulted and kidnapped by bullying interlopers. If there's anything that annoys the Qornt, it's Qornt-like behavior in others. Now step along, please."

"Rest assured, this will be reported!"

"I doubt it."

"You'll face the wrath of Enlightened Galactic Opinion!"

"Oh? How big a navy does Enlightened Galactic Opinion have?"

"Stop scaring him, Mr. Magnan. He may get nervous and shoot." Retief stepped into the banquet hall, headed for the resplendent figure at the head of the table. A trio of flute-players broke off in mid-bleat, staring. An inverted pyramid of tumblers blinked as Retief swung past, followed by Magnan and the tall Verpp. The shrill chatter at the table faded.

Qorn turned as Retief came up, blinking three-inch eyes. Zubb stepped forward, gibbered, waving his arms excitedly. Qorn pushed back his chair—a low, heavily padded stool—and stared unwinking at Retief, moving his head to bring first one great round eye, then the other, to bear. There were small blue veins in the immense fleshy beak. The bushy hair, springing out in a giant halo around the grayish, porous-skinned face, was wiry, stiff, moss-green, with tufts of chartreuse fuzz surrounding what appeared to be tympanic membranes. The tall head-dress of scarlet silk and purple feathers was slightly askew, and a loop of pink pearls had slipped down above one eye.

Zubb finished his speech and fell silent, breathing hard.

Qorn looked Retief over in silence, then belched.

"Not bad," Retief said admiringly. "Maybe we could get up a match between you and Ambassador Sternwheeler. You've got the volume on him, but he's got timbre."

"So," Qorn hooted in a resonant tenor. "You come from Guzzum, eh? Or Smorbrod, as I think you call it. What is it you're after? More time? A compromise? Negotiations? Peace?" He slammed a bony hand against the table. "The answer is no!"

Zubb twittered. Qorn cocked an eye, motioned to a servant. "Chain that one." He indicated Magnan. His eyes went to Retief. "This one's bigger; you'd best chain him, too."

"Why, your Excellency—" Magnan started, stepping forward.

"Stay back!" Qorn hooted. "Stand over there where I can keep an eye on you."

"Your Excellency, I'm empowered—"

"Not here, you're not!" Qorn trumpeted. "Want peace, do you? Well, I don't want peace! I've had a surfeit of peace these last two centuries! I want action! Loot! Adventure! Glory!" He turned to look down the table. "How about it, fellows? It's war to the knife, eh?"

*

There was a momentary silence from all sides.

"I guess so," grunted a giant Qornt in iridescent blue with flame-colored plumes.

Qorn's eyes bulged. He half rose. "We've been all over this," he bassooned. He clamped bony fingers on the hilt of a light rapier. "I thought I'd made my point!"

"Oh, sure, Qorn."

"You bet."

"I'm convinced."

Qorn rumbled and resumed his seat. "All for one and one for all, that's us."

"And you're the one, eh, Qorn?" Retief commented.

Magnan cleared his throat. "I sense that some of you gentlemen are not convinced of the wisdom of this move," he piped, looking along the table at the silks, jewels, beaks, feather-decked crests and staring eyes.

"Silence!" Qorn hooted. "No use your talking to my loyal lieutenants anyway," he added. "They do whatever I convince them they ought to do."

"But I'm sure that on more mature consideration—"

"I can lick any Qornt in the house." Qorn said. "That's why I'm Qorn." He belched again.

A servant came up staggering under a weight of chain, dropped it with a crash at Magnan's feet. Zubb aimed the guns while the servant wrapped three loops around Magnan's wrists, snapped a lock in place.

"You next!" The guns pointed at Retief's chest. He held out his arms. Four loops of silvery-gray chain in half-inch links dropped around them. The servant cinched them up tight, squeezed a lock through the ends and closed it.

"Now," Qorn said, lolling back in his chair, glass in hand. "There's a bit of sport to be had here, lads. What shall we do with them?"

"Let them go," the blue and flame Qornt said glumly.

"You can do better than that," Qorn hooted. "Now here's a suggestion: we carve them up a little—lop off the external labiae and pinnae, say—and ship them back."

"Good lord! Retief, he's talking about cutting off our ears and sending us home mutilated! What a barbaric proposal!"

"It wouldn't be the first time a Terrestrial diplomat got a trimming," Retief commented.

"It should have the effect of stimulating the Terries to put up a reasonable scrap," Qorn said judiciously. "I have a feeling that they're thinking of giving up without a struggle."

"Oh, I doubt that," the blue-and-flame Qornt said. "Why should they?"

Qorn rolled an eye at Retief and another at Magnan. "Take these two," he hooted. "I'll wager they came here to negotiate a surrender!"

"Well," Magnan started.

"Hold it, Mr. Magnan," Retief said. "I'll tell him."

"What's your proposal?" Qorn whistled, taking a gulp from his goblet. "A fifty-fifty split? Monetary reparations? Alternate territory? I can assure you, it's useless. We Qornt *like* to fight."

"I'm afraid you've gotten the wrong impression, your Excellency," Retief said blandly. "We didn't come to negotiate. We came to deliver an Ultimatum."

"What?" Qorn trumpeted. Behind Retief, Magnan spluttered.

"We plan to use this planet for target practice," Retief said. "A new type hell bomb we've worked out. Have all your people off of it in seventy-two hours, or suffer the consequences."

IV

"You have the gall," Qorn stormed, "to stand here in the center of Qornt Hall—uninvited, at that—and in chains—"

"Oh, these," Retief said. He tensed his arms. The soft aluminum links stretched and broke. He shook the light metal free. "We diplomats like to go along with colorful local customs, but I wouldn't want to mislead you. Now, as to the evacuation of Roolit I—"

Zubb screeched, waved the guns. The Qornt were jabbering.

"I told you they were brutes," Zubb shrilled.

Qorn slammed his fist down on the table. "I don't care what they are!" he honked. "Evacuate, hell! I can field eighty-five combat-ready ships!"

"And we can englobe every one of them with a thousand Peace Enforcers with a hundred megatons/second firepower each."

"Retief." Magnan tugged at his sleeve. "Don't forget their superdrive."

"That's all right. They don't have one."

"But—"

"We'll take you on!" Qorn French-horned. "We're the Qorn! We glory in battle! We live in fame or go down in—"

"Hogwash," the flame-and-blue Qorn cut in. "If it wasn't for you, Qorn, we could sit around and feast and brag and enjoy life without having to prove anything."

"Qorn, you seem to be the fire-brand here," Retief said. "I think the rest of the boys would listen to reason—"

"Over my dead body!"

"My idea exactly," Retief said. "You claim you can lick any man in the house. Unwind yourself from your ribbons and step out here on the floor, and we'll see how good you are at backing up your conversation."

*

Magnan hovered at Retief's side. "Twelve feet tall," he moaned. "And did you notice the size of those hands?"

Retief watched as Qorn's aides helped him out of his formal trappings. "I wouldn't worry too much, Mr. Magnan. This is a light-Gee world. I doubt if old Qorn would weigh up at more than two-fifty standard pounds here."

"But that phenomenal reach—"

"I'll peck away at him at knee level. When he bends over to swat me, I'll get a crack at him."

Across the cleared floor, Qorn shook off his helpers with a snort.

"Enough! Let me at the upstart!"

Retief moved out to meet him, watching the upraised backward-jointed arms. Qorn stalked forward, long lean legs bent, long horny feet clacking against the polished floor. The other aliens—both servitors and bejeweled Qornt—formed a wide circle, all eyes unwaveringly on the combatants.

Qorn struck suddenly, a long arm flashing down in a vicious cut at Retief, who leaned aside, caught one lean shank below the knee. Qorn bent to haul Retief from his leg—and staggered back as a haymaker took him just below the beak. A screech went up from the crowd as Retief leaped clear.

Qorn hissed and charged. Retief whirled aside, then struck the alien's off-leg in a flying tackle. Qorn leaned, arms windmilling, crashed to the floor. Retief whirled, dived for the left arm, whipped it behind the narrow back, seized Qorn's neck in a stranglehold and threw his weight backward. Qorn fell on his back, his legs squatted out at an awkward angle. He squawked and beat his free arm on the floor, reaching in vain for Retief.

Zubb stepped forward, pistols ready. Magnan stepped before him.

"Need I remind you, sir," he said icily, "that this is an official diplomatic function? I can brook no interference from disinterested parties."

Zubb hesitated. Magnan held out a hand. "I must ask you to hand me your weapons, Zubb."

"Look here," Zubb began.

"I *may* lose my temper," Magnan hinted. Zubb lowered the guns, passed them to Magnan. He thrust them into his belt with a sour smile, turned back to watch the encounter.

Retief had thrown a turn of violet silk around Qorn's left wrist, bound it to the alien's neck. Another wisp of stuff floated from Qorn's shoulder. Retief, still holding Qorn in an awkward sprawl, wrapped it around one outflung leg, trussed ankle and thigh together. Qorn flopped, hooting. At each movement, the constricting loop around his neck, jerked his head back, the green crest tossing wildly.

"If I were you, I'd relax," Retief said, rising and releasing his grip. Qorn got a leg under him; Retief kicked it. Qorn's chin hit the floor with a hollow clack. He wilted, an ungainly tangle of over-long limbs and gay silks.

Retief turned to the watching crowd. "Next?" he called.

The blue and flame Qornt stepped forward. "Maybe this would be a good time to elect a new leader," he said. "Now, my qualifications—"

"Sit down," Retief said loudly. He stepped to the head of the table, seated himself in Qorn's vacated chair. "A couple of you finish trussing Qorn up for me."

"But we must select a leader!"

"That won't be necessary, boys. I'm your new leader."

*

"As I see it," Retief said, dribbling cigar ashes into an empty wine glass, "you Qornt like to be warriors, but you don't particularly like to fight."

"We don't mind a little fighting—within reason. And, of course, as Qornt, we're expected to die in battle. But what I say is, why rush things?"

"I have a suggestion," Magnan said. "Why not turn the reins of government over to the Verpp? They seem a level-headed group."

"What good would that do? Qornt are Qornt. It seems there's always one among us who's a slave to instinct—and, naturally, we have to follow him."

"Why?"

"Because that's the way it's done."

"Why not do it another way?" Magnan offered. "Now, I'd like to suggest community singing—"

"If we gave up fighting, we might live too long. Then what would happen?"

"Live too long?" Magnan looked puzzled.

"When estivating time comes there'd be no burrows for us. Anyway, with the new Qornt stepping on our heels—"

"I've lost the thread," Magnan said. "Who are the new Qornt?"

"After estivating, the Verpp moult, and then they're Qornt, of course. The Gwil become Boog, the Boog become Rheuk, the Rheuk metamorphosize into Verpp—"

"You mean Slun and Zubb—the mild-natured naturalists—will become warmongers like Qorn?"

"Very likely. 'The milder the Verpp, the wilder the Qorn,' as the old saying goes."

"What do Qornt turn into?" Retief asked.

"Hmmmm. That's a good question. So far, none have survived Qornthood."

"Have you thought of forsaking your warlike ways?" Magnan asked. "What about taking up sheepherding and regular church attendance?"

"Don't mistake me. We Qornt like a military life. It's great sport to sit around roaring fires and drink and tell lies and then go dashing off to enjoy a brisk affray and some leisurely looting afterward. But we prefer a nice numerical advantage. Not this business of tackling you Terrestrials over on Guzzum—that was a mad notion. We had no idea what your strength was."

"But now that's all off, of course," Magnan chirped. "Now that we've had diplomatic relations and all—"

"Oh, by no means. The fleet lifts in thirty days. After all, we're Qornt; we have to satisfy our drive to action."

"But Mr. Retief is your leader now. He won't let you!"

"Only a dead Qornt stays home when Attack day comes. And even if he orders us all to cut our own throats, there are still the other Centers—all with their own leaders. No, gentlemen, the Invasion is definitely on."

"Why don't you go invade somebody else?" Magnan suggested. "I could name some very attractive prospects—outside my sector, of course."

"Hold everything," Retief said. "I think we've got the basis of a deal here . . . . "

V

At the head of a double column of gaudily caparisoned Qornt, Retief and Magnan strolled across the ramp toward the bright tower of the CDT Sector HQ.

Ahead, gates opened, and a black Corps limousine emerged, flying an Ambassadorial flag under a plain square of white.

"Curious," Magnan commented. "I wonder what the significance of the white ensign might be?"

Retief raised a hand. The column halted with a clash of accoutrements and a rasp of Qornt boots. Retief looked back along the line. The high white sun flashed on bright silks, polished buckles, deep-dyed plumes, butts of pistols, the soft gleam of leather.

"A brave show indeed," Magnan commented approvingly. "I confess the idea has merit."

The limousine pulled up with a squeal of brakes, stood on two fat-tired wheels, gyros humming softly. The hatch popped up. A portly diplomat stepped out.

"Why, Ambassador Nitworth," Magnan glowed. "This is very kind of you."

"Keep cool, Magnan," Nitworth said in a strained voice. "We'll attempt to get you out of this."

He stepped past Magnan's out-stretched hand and looked hesitantly at the ramrod-straight line of Qornt, eighty-five strong—and beyond, at the eighty-five tall Qornt dreadnaughts.

"Good afternoon, sir . . . ah, Your Excellency," Nitworth said, blinking up at the leading Qornt. "You are Commander of the Strike Force, I assume?"

"Nope," the Qornt said shortly.

"I . . . ah . . . wish to request seventy-two hours in which to evacuate Headquarters," Nitworth plowed on.

"Mr. Ambassador." Retief said. "This—"

"Don't panic, Retief. I'll attempt to secure your release," Nitworth hissed over his shoulder. "Now—"

"You will address our leader with more respect!" the tall Qornt hooted, eyeing Nitworth ominously from eleven feet up.

"Oh, yes indeed, sir . . . your Excellency . . . Commander. Now, about the invasion—"

"Mr. Secretary," Magnan tugged at Nitworth's sleeve.

"In heaven's name, permit me to negotiate in peace!" Nitworth snapped. He rearranged his features. "Now your Excellency, we've arranged to evacuate Smorbrod, of course, just as you requested—"

"Requested?" the Qornt honked.

"Ah ... demanded, that is. Quite rightly of course. Ordered. Instructed. And, of course, we'll be only too pleased to follow any other instructions you might have."

"You don't quite get the big picture, Mr. Secretary," Retief said. "This isn't—"

"Silence, confound you!" Nitworth barked. The leading Qornt looked at Retief. He nodded. Two bony hands shot out, seized Nitworth and stuffed a length of bright pink silk into his mouth, then spun him around and held him facing Retief.

"If you don't mind my taking this opportunity to brief you, Mr. Ambassador," Retief said blandly. "I think I should mention that this isn't an invasion fleet. These are the new recruits for the Peace Enforcement Corps."

Magnan stepped forward, glanced at the gag in Ambassador Nitworth's mouth, hesitated, then cleared his throat. "We felt," he said, "that the establishment of a Foreign Brigade within the P. E. Corps structure would provide the element of novelty the Department has requested in our recruiting, and at the same time would remove the stigma of Terrestrial chauvinism from future punitive operations."

Nitworth stared, eyes bulging. He grunted, reaching for the gag, caught the Qornt's eye on him, dropped his hands to his sides.

"I suggest we get the troops in out of the hot sun," Retief said. Magnan edged close. "What about the gag?" he whispered.

"Let's leave it where it is for a while," Retief murmured. "It may save us a few concessions."

*

An hour later, Nitworth, breathing freely again, glowered across his desk at Retief and Magnan.

"This entire affair," he rumbled, "has made me appear to be a fool!"

"But we who are privileged to serve on your staff already know just how clever you are," Magnan burbled.

Nitworth purpled. "You're skirting insolence, Magnan," he roared. "Why was I not informed of the arrangements? What was I to assume at the sight of eighty-five war vessels over my headquarters, unannounced?"

"We tried to get through, but our wavelengths—"

"Bah! Sterner souls than I would have quailed at the spectacle!"

"Oh, you were perfectly justified in panicking—"

"I did *not* panic!" Nitworth bellowed. "I merely adjusted to the apparent circumstances. Now, I'm of two minds as to the advisability of this foreign legion idea of yours. Still, it may have merit. I believe the wisest course would be to dispatch them on a long training cruise in an uninhabited sector of space—"

The office windows rattled. "What the devil!" Nitworth turned, stared out at the ramp where a Qornt ship rose slowly on a column of pale blue light. The vibration increased as a second ship lifted, then a third.

Nitworth whirled on Magnan. "What's this! Who ordered these recruits to embark without my permission?"

"I took the liberty of giving them an errand to run, Mr. Secretary," Retief said. "There was that little matter of the Groaci infiltrating the Sirenian System. I sent the boys off to handle it."

"Call them back at once!"

"I'm afraid that won't be possible. They're under orders to maintain total communications silence until completion of the mission."

Nitworth drummed his fingers on the desk top. Slowly, a thoughtful expression dawned. He nodded.

"This may work out," he said. "I *should* call them back, but since the fleet is out of contact, I'm unable to do so, correct? Thus I can hardly be held responsible for any over-enthusiasm in chastising the Groaci."

He closed one eye in a broad wink at Magnan. "Very well, gentlemen, I'll overlook the irregularity this time. Magnan, see to it the Smorbrodian public are notified they can remain where they are. And by the way, did you by any chance discover the technique of the indetectable drive the Qornt use?"

"No, sir. That is, yes, sir."

"Well? Well?"

"There isn't any. The Qornt were there all the while. Underground."

"Underground? Doing what?"

"Hibernating—for two hundred years at a stretch."

*

Outside in the corridor, Magnan came up to Retief, who stood talking to a tall man in a pilot's coverall.

"I'll be tied up, sending through full details on my—our—your recruiting theme, Retief," Magnan said. "Suppose you run into the city to assist the new Verpp Consul in settling in."

"I'll do that, Mr. Magnan. Anything else?"

Magnan raised his eyebrows. "You're remarkably compliant today, Retief. I'll arrange transportation."

"Don't bother, Mr. Magnan. Cy here will run me over. He was the pilot who ferried us over to Roolit I, you recall."

"I'll be with you as soon as I pack a few phone numbers, Retief," the pilot said. He moved off. Magnan followed him with a disapproving eye. "An uncouth sort, I fancied. I trust you're not consorting with his kind socially."

"I wouldn't say that, exactly," Retief said. "We just want to go over a few figures together."

THE GOVERNOR OF GLAVE

The revolution was over and peace restored—naturally Retief expected the worst!

I

Retief turned back the gold-encrusted scarlet cuff of the mess jacket of a First Secretary and Consul, gathered in the three eight-sided black dice, shook them by his right ear and sent them rattling across the floor to rebound from the bulk-head.

"Thirteen's the point," the Power Section Chief called. "Ten he makes it!"

"Oh . . . Mr. Retief," a strained voice called. Retief looked up. A tall thin youth in the black-trimmed gray of a Third Secretary flapped a sheet of paper from the edge of the circle surrounding the game. "The Ambassador's compliments, sir, and will you join him and the staff in the conference room at once?"

Retief rose and dusted his knees. "That's all for now, boys," he said. "I'll take the rest of your money later." He followed the junior diplomat from the ward room, along the bare corridors of the crew level, past the glare panel reading NOTICE—FIRST CLASS ONLY BEYOND THIS POINT, through the chandeliered and draped ballroom and along a stretch of soundless carpet to a heavy door bearing a placard with the legend CONFERENCE IN SESSION.

"Ambassador Sternwheeler seemed quite upset, Mr. Retief," the messenger said.

"He usually is, Pete." Retief took a cigar from his breast pocket. "Got a light?"

The Third Secretary produced a permatch. "I don't know why you smoke those things instead of dope sticks, Mr. Retief," he said. "The Ambassador hates the smell."

Retief nodded. "I only smoke this kind at conferences. It makes for shorter sessions." He stepped into the room. Ambassador Sternwheeler eyed him down the length of the conference table.

"Ah, Mr. Retief honors us with his presence. Do be seated, Retief." He fingered a yellow Departmental despatch. Retief took a chair, puffing out a dense cloud of smoke.

"As I have been explaining to the remainder of my staff for the past quarter-hour," Sternwheeler rumbled, "I've been the recipient of important intelligence." He blinked at Retief expectantly. Retief raised his eyebrows in polite inquiry.

"It seems," Sternwheeler went on, "that there has been a change in regime on Glave. A week ago, the government which invited the dispatch of this mission—and to which we're accredited—was overthrown. The former ruling class has fled into exile. A popular workers' and peasants' junta has taken over."

"Mr. Ambassador," Counsellor Magnan broke in, rising. "I'd like to be the first—" he glanced around the table—"or one of the first, anyway, to welcome the new government of Glave into the family of planetary ruling bodies—"

*

"Sit down, Magnan!" Sternwheeler snapped. "Of course the Corps always recognizes *de facto* sovereignty. The problem is merely one of acquainting ourselves with the policies of this new group—a sort of blue-collar coalition, it seems. In what position that leaves this Embassy I don't yet know."

"I suppose this means we'll spend the next month in a parking orbit," Counsellor Magnan sighed.

"Unfortunately," Sternwheeler went on, "the entire affair has apparently been carried off without recourse to violence, leaving the Corps no excuse to move in—that is, it appears our assistance in restoring order will not be required."

"Glave was one of the old Contract Worlds," Retief said. "What's become of the Planetary Manager General and the technical staff? And how do the peasants and workers plan to operate the atmospheric purification system, the Weather Control station, the tide regulation complexes?"

"I'm more concerned at present with the status of the Mission! Will we be welcomed by these peasants or peppered with buckshot?"

"You say that this is a popular junta, and that the former leaders have fled into exile," Retief said. "May I ask the source?"

"The despatch cites a 'reliable Glavian source'."

"That's officialese for something cribbed from a broadcast news tape. Presumably the Glavian news services are in the hands of the revolution. In that case—"

"Yes, yes, there is the possibility that the issue is yet in doubt. Of course we'll have to exercise caution in making our approach. It wouldn't do to make overtures to the wrong side."

"Oh, I think we need have no fear on that score," the Chief of the Political Section spoke up. "I know these entrenched cliques. Once challenged by an aroused populace, they scuttle for safety—with large balances safely tucked away in neutral banks."

"I'd like to go on record," Magnan piped, "as registering my deep gratification at this fulfillment of popular aspirations—"

"The most popular aspiration I know of is to live high off someone else's effort," Retief said. "I don't know of anyone outside the Corps who's managed it."

*

"Gentlemen!" Sternwheeler bellowed. "I'm awaiting your constructive suggestions—not an exchange of political views. We'll arrive off Glave in less than six hours. I should like before that time to have developed some notion regarding to whom I shall expect to offer my credentials!"

There was a discreet tap at the door; it opened and the young Third Secretary poked his head in.

"Mr. Ambassador, I have a reply to your message—just received from Glave. It's signed by the Steward of the GFE, and I thought you'd want to see it at once . . . . "

"Yes, of course; let me have it."

"What's the GFE?" someone asked.

"It's the revolutionary group," the messenger said, passing the message over.

"GFE? GFE? What do the letters SIGNIFY?"

"Glorious Fun Eternally," Retief suggested. "Or possibly Goodies For Everybody."

"I believe that's 'Glavian Free Electorate'," the Third Secretary said.

Sternwheeler stared at the paper, lips pursed. His face grew pink. He slammed the paper on the table.

"Well, gentlemen! It appears our worst fears have been realized! This is nothing less than a warning! A threat! We're advised to divert course and bypass Glave entirely. It seems the GFE wants no interference from meddling foreign exploiters, as they put it!"

Magnan rose. "If you'll excuse me Mr. Ambassador, I want to get off a message to Sector HQ to hold my old job for me—"

"Sit down, you idiot!" Sternwheeler roared. "If you think I'm consenting to have my career blighted—my first Ambassadorial post whisked out from under me—the Corps made a fool of—"

"I'd like to take a look at that message," Retief said. It was passed along to him. He read it.

"I don't believe this applies to us, Mr. Ambassador."

*

"What are you talking about? It's addressed to me by name!"

"It merely states that 'meddling foreign exploiters' are unwelcome. Meddling foreigners we are, but we don't qualify as exploiters unless we show a profit—and this appears to be shaping up as a particularly profitless venture."

"What are you proposing, Mr. Retief?"

"That we proceed to make planetfall as scheduled, greet our welcoming committee with wide diplomatic smiles, hint at largesse in the offing and settle down to observe the lie of the land."

"Just what I was about to suggest," Magnan said.

"That might be dangerous," Sternwheeler said.

"That's why I didn't suggest it," Magnan said.

"Still it's essential that we learn more of the situation than can be gleaned from official broadcasts," Sternwheeler mused. "Now, while I can't justify risking the entire Mission, it might be advisable to dispatch a delegation to sound out the new regime."

"I'd like to volunteer," Magnan said, rising.

"Of course, the delegates may be murdered—"

"—but unfortunately, I'm under treatment at the moment." Magnan sat down.

"—which will place us in an excellent position, propaganda-wise.

"What a pity I can't go," the Military Attache said. "But my place is with my troops."

"The only troops you've got are the Assistant Attache and your secretary," Magnan pointed out.

"Say, I'd like to be down there in the thick of things," the Political Officer said. He assumed a grave expression. "But of course I'll be needed here, to interpret results."

"I appreciate your attitude, gentlemen," Sternwheeler said, studying the ceiling. "But I'm afraid I must limit the privilege of volunteering for this hazardous duty to those officers of more robust physique, under forty years of age—"

"Tsk. I'm forty-one," Magnan said.

"—and with a reputation for adaptability." His glance moved along the table.

"Do you mind if I run along now, Mr. Ambassador?" Retief said. "It's time for my insulin shot."

Sternwheeler's mouth dropped open.

"Just kidding," Retief said. "I'll go. But I have one request, Mr. Ambassador: no further communication with the ground until I give the all-clear."

KEITH LAUMER

II

Retief grounded the lighter, in-cycled the lock and stepped out. The hot yellow Glavian sun beat down on a broad expanse of concrete, an abandoned service cart and a row of tall ships casting black shadows toward the silent control tower. A wisp of smoke curled up from the shed area at the rim of the field. There was no other sign of life.

Retief walked over to the cart, tossed his valise aboard, climbed into the driver's seat and headed for the operations building. Beyond the port, hills rose, white buildings gleaming against the deep green slopes. Near the ridge, a vehicle moved ant-like along a winding road, a dust trail rising behind it. Faintly a distant shot sounded.

Papers littered the ground before the Operations Building. Retief pushed open the tall glass door, stood listening. Slanting sunlight reflected from a wide polished floor, at the far side of which illuminated lettering over empty counters read IMMIGRATION, HEALTH and CUSTOMS. He crossed to the desk, put the valise down, then leaned across the counter. A worried face under an oversized white cap looked up at him.

"You can come out now," Retief said. "They've gone."

The man rose, dusting himself off. He looked over Retief's shoulder. "Who's gone?"

"Whoever it was that scared you."

"Whatta ya mean? I was looking for my pencil."

"Here it is." Retief plucked a worn stub from the pocket of the soiled shirt sagging under the weight of braided shoulderboards. "You can sign me in as a Diplomatic Representative. A break for you—no formalities necessary. Where can I catch a cab for the city?"

The man eyed Retief's bag. "What's in that?"

"Personal belongings under duty-free entry."

"Guns?"

"No, thanks, just a cab."

"You got no gun?" The man raised his voice.

"That's right, fellows," Retief called out. "No gun; no knife, not even a small fission bomb. Just a few pairs of socks and some reading matter."

RETIEF: THE DIRTY DOZEN

A brown-uniformed man ran from behind the Customs Counter, holding a long-barreled blast-rifle centered on the Corps insignia stitched to the pocket of Retief's powder-blue blazer.

"Don't try nothing," he said. "You're under arrest."

"It can't be overtime parking. I've only been here five minutes."

"Hah!" The gun-handler moved out from the counter, came up to Retief. "Empty out your pockets!" he barked. "Hands overhead!"

"I'm just a diplomat, not a contortionist," Retief said, not moving. "Do you mind pointing that thing in some other direction?"

"Looky here, Mister, I'll give the orders. We don't need anybody telling us how to run our business."

"I'm telling you to shift that blaster before I take it away from you and wrap it around your neck," Retief said conversationally. The cop stepped back uncertainly, lowering the gun.

"Jake! Horny! Pud! come on out!"

Three more brown uniforms emerged from concealment.

"Who are you fellows hiding from, the top sergeant?" Retief glanced over the ill-fitting uniforms, the unshaved faces, the scuffed boots. "Tell you what. When he shows up, I'll engage him in conversation. You beat it back to the barracks and grab a quick bath—"

"That's enough smart talk." The biggest of the three newcomers moved up to Retief. "You stuck your nose in at the wrong time. We just had a change of management around here."

"I heard about it," Retief said. "Who do I complain to?"

"Complain? What about?"

"The port's a mess," Retief barked. "Nobody on duty to receive official visitors! No passenger service facilities! Why, do you know I had to carry my own bag—"

"All right, all right, that's outside my department. You better see the boss."

"The boss? I thought you got rid of the bosses."

"We did, but now we got new ones."

"They any better than the old ones?"

"This guy asks too many questions," the man with the gun said. "Let's let Sozier answer 'em."

"Who's he?"

"He's the Military Governor of the City."

"Now we're getting somewhere," Retief said. "Lead the way, Jake—and don't forget my bag."

*

Sozier was a small man with thin hair oiled across a shiny scalp, prominent ears and eyes like coal chips set in rolls of fat. He glowered at Retief from behind a polished desk occupying the center of a spacious office.

"I warned you off," he snapped. "You came anyway." He leaned forward and slammed a fist down on the desk. "You're used to throwing your weight around, but you won't throw it around here! There'll be no spies pussyfooting around Glave!"

"Looking for what, Mr. Sozier?"

"Call me General!"

"Mind if I sit down?" Retief pulled out a chair, seated himself and took out a cigar. "Curiously enough," he said, lighting up, "the Corps has no intention of making any embarrassing investigations. We deal with the existing government, no questions asked." His eyes held the other's. "Unless, of course, there are evidences of atrocities or other illegal measures."

The coal-chip eyes narrowed. "I don't have to make explanations to you or anybody else."

"Except, presumably, the Glavian Free Electorate," Retief said blandly. "But tell me, General—who's actually running the show?"

A speaker on the desk buzzed. "Hey, Corporal Sozier! Wes's got them two hellions cornered. They're holed up in the Birthday Cake—"

"General Sozier, damn you! and plaster your big mouth shut!" He gestured to one of the uniformed men standing by.

"You! Get Trundy and Little Moe up here—pronto!" He swiveled back to Retief. "You're in luck. I'm too busy right now to bother with you. You get back over to the port and leave the same way you came—and tell your blood-sucking friends the easy pickings are over as far as Glave's concerned. You won't lounge around here living high and throwing big parties and cooking up your dirty deals to get fat on at the expense of the working man."

Retief dribbled ash on Sozier's desk and glanced at the green uniform front bulging between silver buttons.

"Who paid for your potbelly, Sozier?" he inquired carelessly.

Sozier's eyes narrowed to slits. "I could have you shot!"

RETIEF: THE DIRTY DOZEN

"Stop playing games with me, Sozier," Retief rapped. "There's a squadron of Peace Enforcers standing by just in case any apprentice statesmen forget the niceties of diplomatic usage. I suggest you start showing a little intelligence about now, or even Horny and Pud are likely to notice."

*

Sozier's fingers squeaked on the arms of his chair. He swallowed.

"You might start by assigning me an escort for a conducted tour of the capital," Retief went on. "I want to be in a position to confirm that order has been re-established, and that normal services have been restored. Otherwise it may be necessary to send in a Monitor Unit to straighten things out."

"You know you can't meddle with the internal affairs of a sovereign world!"

Retief sighed. "The trouble with taking over your boss's job is discovering its drawbacks. It's disillusioning, I know, Sozier, but—"

"All right! Take your tour! You'll find everything running as smooth as silk! Utilities, police, transport, environmental control—"

"What about Space Control? Glave Tower seems to be off the air."

"I shut it down. We don't need anything and we don't want anything from the outside."

"Where's the new Premier keeping himself? Does he share your passion for privacy?"

The general got to his feet. "I'm letting you take your look, Mr. Big Nose. I'm giving you four hours. Then out! And the next meddling bureaucrat that tries to cut atmosphere on Glave without a clearance gets burned!"

"I'll need a car."

"Jake! You stick close to this bird. Take him to the main power plant, the water works and the dispatch center. Ride him around town and show him we're doing okay without a bunch of leeches bossing us. Then dump him at the port—and see that he leaves."

"I'll plan my own itinerary, thanks. I can't promise I'll be finished in four hours—but I'll keep you advised."

"I warned you—"

"I heard you. Five times. And I only warned you once. You're getting ahead of me." Retief rose, motioned to the hulking guard. "Come on, Jake. We've got a lot of ground to cover before we come back for our dinner."

III

At the curb, Retief held out his hand. "Give me the power cylinder out of your rifle, Jake."

"Huh?"

"Come on, Jake. You've got a nervous habit of playing with the firing stud. We don't want any accidents."

"How do you get it out? They only give me this thing yesterday."

Retief pocketed the cylinder. "You sit in back. I'll drive." He wheeled the car off along a broad avenue crowded with vehicles and lined with flowering palms, behind which stately white buildings reared up into the pale sky.

"Nice looking city, Jake," Retief said conversationally. "What's the population?"

"I dunno. I only been here a year."

"What about Horny and Pud? Are they natives?"

"Whatta ya mean, natives? They're just as civilized as me."

"My boner, Jake. Known Sozier long?"

"Sure. He useta come around to the club."

"I take it he was in the army under the old regime?"

"Yeah—but he didn't like the way they run it. Nothing but band playing and fancy marching. There wasn't nobody to fight."

"Just between us, Jake—where did the former Planetary Manager General go?" Retief watched Jake's heavy face in the mirror. Jake jumped, clamped his mouth shut.

"I don't know nothing."

Half an hour later, after a tour of the commercial center, Retief headed towards the city's outskirts. The avenue curved, leading up along the flank of a low hill.

"I must admit I'm surprised, Jake," Retief said. "Everything seems orderly. No signs of riots or panic. Power, water, communications normal—just as the general said. Remarkable, isn't it, considering that the entire managerial class has packed up and left?"

"You wanta see the Power Plant?" Retief could see perspiration beaded on the man's forehead under the uniform cap.

"Sure. Which way?" With Jake directing, Retief ascended to the ridge top, cruised past the blank white facade of the station.

"Quiet, isn't it?" Retief pulled the car in to the curb. "Let's go inside."

"Huh? Corporal Sozier didn't say nothing—"

211

"You're right, Jake. That leaves it to our discretion."

"He won't like it."

"The corporal's a busy man, Jake. We won't worry him by telling him about it."

Jake followed Retief up the walk. The broad double doors were locked. "Let's try the back."

The narrow door set in the high blank wall opened as Retief approached. A gun barrel poked out, followed by a small man with bushy red hair. He looked Retief over.

"Who's this party, Jake?" he barked.

"Sozier said show him the plant," Jake said.

"What we need is more guys to pull duty, not tourists. Anyway, *I'm* Chief Engineer here. Nobody comes in here 'less I like their looks." Retief moved forward, stood looking down at the redhead. The little man hesitated, then waved him past. "Lucky for you I like your looks." Inside, Retief surveyed the long room, the giant converter units, the massive busbars. Armed men—some in uniform, some in work clothes or loud sport shirts—stood here and there. Other men read meters, adjusted controls or inspected dials.

"You've got more guards than workers," Retief said. "Expecting trouble?"

The redhead bit the corner from a plug of spearmint. He glanced around the plant. "Things is quiet now; but you never know."

"Rather old-fashioned equipment isn't it? When was it installed?"

"Huh? I dunno. What's wrong with it?"

"What's your basic power source, a core sink? Lithospheric friction? Sub-crustal hydraulics?"

"Beats me, Mister. I'm the boss here, not a dern mechanic."

*

A gray-haired man carrying a clipboard walked past, studied a panel, made notes, glanced up to catch Retief's eye, moved on.

"Everything seems to be running normally," Retief remarked.

"Sure. Why not?"

"Records being kept up properly?"

"Sure. Some of these guys, all they do is walk around looking at dials and writing stuff on paper. If it was me, I'd put 'em to work."

Retief strolled over to the gray-haired man, now scribbling before a bank of meters. He glanced at the clipboard.

Power off at sunset. Tell Corasol was scrawled in block letters across the record sheet. Retief nodded, rejoined his guard.

"All right, Jake. Let's have a look at the communications center."

Back in the car, headed west, Retief studied the blank windows of office buildings, the milling throngs in beer bars, shooting galleries, tattoo parlors, billiard halls, pinball arcades, bordellos and half-credit casinos.

"Everybody seems to be having fun," he remarked.

Jake stared out the window.

"Yeah."

"Too bad you're on duty, Jake. You could be out there joining in."

"Soon as the corporal gets things organized, I'm opening me up a place to show dirty tri-di's. I'll get my share."

"Meanwhile, let the rest of 'em have their fun, eh Jake?"

"Look, Mister, I been thinking. Maybe you better gimme back that kick-stick you taken outa my gun . . . ."

"Sorry, Jake; no can do. Tell me, what was the real cause of the revolution? Not enough to eat? Too much regimentation?"

"Naw, we always got plenty to eat. There wasn't none of that regimentation up till I joined up in the corporal's army."

"Rigid class structure, maybe? Educational discrimination?"

Jake nodded. "Yeah, it was them schools done it. All the time trying to make a feller do some kind of class. Big shots. Know it all. Gonna make us sit around and view tapes. Figgered they was better than us."

"And Sozier's idea was you'd take over, and you wouldn't have to be bothered."

"Aw, it wasn't Sozier's idea. He ain't the big leader."

"Where does the big leader keep himself?"

"I dunno. I guess he's pretty busy right now." Jake snickered. "Some of them guys call themselves colonels turned out not to know nothing about how to shoot off the guns."

"Shooting, eh? I thought it was a sort of peaceful revolution. The managerial class were booted out, and that was that."

"I don't know nothing," Jake snapped. "How come you keep trying to get me to say stuff I ain't supposed to talk about? You want to get me in trouble?"

*

213

"Oh, you're already in trouble, Jake. But if you stick with me, I'll try to get you out of it. Where exactly did the refugees head for? How did they leave? Must have been a lot of them; I'd say in a city of this size alone, they'd run into the thousands."

"I don't know."

"Of course, it depends on your definition of a big shot. Who's included in that category, Jake?"

"You know, the slick-talking ones; the fancy dressers; the guys that walk around and tell other guys what to do. We do all the work and they get all the big pay."

"I suppose that would cover scientists, professional men, executives, technicians of all sorts, engineers, teachers—all that crowd."

"Yeah, them are the ones."

"And once you got them out of the way, the regular fellows would have a chance. Chaps that don't spend all their time taking baths and reading books and using big words; good Joes that don't mind picking their noses in public."

"We got as much right as anybody—"

"Jake, who's Corasol?"

"He's—I don't know."

"I thought I overheard his name somewhere."

"Uh, here's the communication center," Jake cut in.

Retief swung into a parking lot under a high blank facade. He set the brake and stepped out.

"Lead the way, Jake."

"Look, Mister, the corporal only wanted me to show you the outside."

"Anything to hide, Jake?"

Jake shook his head angrily and stamped past Retief. "When I joined up with Sozier, I didn't figger I'd be getting in this kind of mess."

"I know, Jake. It's tough. Sometimes it seems like a fellow works harder after he's thrown out the parasites than he did before."

A cautious guard let Retief and Jake inside, followed them along bright-lit aisles among consoles, cables, batteries of instruments. Armed men in careless uniforms lounged, watching. Here and there a silent technician worked quietly.

Retief paused by one, an elderly man in a neat white coverall, with a purple spot under one eye.

"Quite a bruise you've got there," Retief commented heartily. "Power failure at sunset," he added softly. The technician hesitated, nodded and moved on.

Back in the car, Retief gave Jake directions. At the end of three hours, he had seen twelve smooth-running, heavily guarded installations.

"So far, so good, Jake," he said. "Next stop, Sub-station Number Nine." In the mirror, Jake's face stiffened. "Hey, you can't go down there—"

"Something going on there, Jake?"

"That's where—I mean, no. I don't know."

"I don't want to miss anything, Jake. Which way?"

"I ain't going down there," Jake said sullenly.

Retief braked. "In that case, I'm afraid our association is at an end, Jake."

"You mean . . . you're getting out here?"

"No, you are."

"Huh? Now wait a minute, Mister! The corporal said I was to stay with you."

Retief accelerated. "That's settled, then. Which way?"

IV

Retief pulled the car to a halt two hundred yards from the periphery of a loose crowd of brown-uniformed men who stood in groups scattered across a broad plaza, overflowing into a stretch of manicured lawn before the bare, functional facade of sub-station number Nine. In the midst of the besieging mob, Sozier's red face and bald head bobbed as he harangued a cluster of green-uniformed men from his place in the rear of a long open car.

"What's it all about, Jake?" Retief enquired. "Since the parasites have all left peacefully, I'm having a hard time figuring out who'd be holed up in the pumping station—and why. Maybe they haven't gotten the word that it's all going to be fun and games from now on."

"If the corporal sees you over here—"

"Ah, the good corporal. Glad you mentioned him, Jake. He's the man to see." Retief stepped out of the car and started through the crowd. A heavy lorry loaded with an immense tank with the letter H blazoned on its side trundled into the square from a side street, moved up to a position before the building. A smaller car pulled alongside Sozier's limousine. The driver stepped down, handed something to Sozier. A moment later, Sozier's amplified voice boomed across the crowd.

"You in there, Corasol! This is General Sozier, and I'm warning you to come out now or you and your smart friends are in for a big surprise. You think I won't blast you out because I don't want to wreck the planet. You see the tank aboard the lorry that just pulled up? It's full of gas—and I got plenty of hoses out here to pump it inside with. I'll put men on the roof and squirt it in the ventilators."

Sozier's voice echoed and died. The militiamen eyed the station. Nothing happened.

"I know you can hear me, damn you!" Sozier squalled. "You'd better get the doors open and get out here fast!"

Retief stepped to Sozier's side. "Say, Corporal, I didn't know you went in for practical jokes."

Sozier jerked around to gape at Retief.

"What are you doing here!" he burst out. "I told Jake—where is that—"

"Jake didn't like the questions I was asking," Retief said, "so he marched me up here to report to you."

"Jake, you damn fool!" Sozier roared. "I got a good mind—"

*

"I disagree, Sozier," Retief cut in. "I think you're a complete imbecile. Sitting out here in the open yelling at the top of your lungs, for example. Corasol and his party might get annoyed and spray that fancy car you've swiped with something a lot more painful than words."

"Eh?" Sozier's head whipped around to stare at the building.

"Isn't that a gun I see sticking out?"

Sozier dropped. "Where?"

"My mistake. Just a foreign particle on my contact lenses." Retief leaned on the car. "On the other hand, Sozier, most murderers are sneaky about it. I think making a public announcement is a nice gesture on your part. The Monitors won't have any trouble deciding who to hang when they come in to straighten out this mess."

Sozier scrambled back onto his seat. "Monitors?" he snarled. "I don't think so. I don't think you'll be around to do any blabbering to anybody." He raised his voice. "Jake! March this spy over to the sidelines. If he tries anything, shoot him!" He gave Retief a baleful grin. "I'll lay the body out nice and ship it back to your cronies. Accidents will happen, you know. It'll be a week or two before they get around to following up—and by then I'll have this little problem under control."

Jake looked at Retief uncertainly, fingering his empty rifle.

Retief put his hands up. "I guess you got me, Jake," he said. "Careful of that gun, now."

Jake glanced at Sozier, gulped, aimed the rifle at Retief and nodded toward the car. As Retief moved off, a murmur swept across the crowd. Retief glanced back. A turret on the station roof was rotating slowly. A shout rose; men surged away from the building, scuffling for way; Sozier yelled. His car started up, moved forward, horns blaring. As Retief watched, a white stream arced up from the turret, catching the sun as it spanned the lawn, plunged down to strike the massed men in a splatter of spray. It searched across the mob, came to rest on Sozier's car. Uniformed men scrambled for safety as the terrified driver gunned the heavy vehicle. The hose followed the car, dropping a solid stream of water on Sozier, kicking and flailing in the back seat. As the car passed from view, down a side street, water was overflowing the sides.

"The corporal will feel all the better for an invigorating swim in his mobile pool," Retief commented. "By the way, Jake, I have to be going now. It wouldn't be fair to send you back to your boss without something to back up your story that you were outnumbered, so—"

Retief's left fist shot out to connect solidly with Jake's jaw. Jake dropped the gun and sat down hard. Retief turned and headed for the pumping station. The hose had shut down now. A few men were standing, eyeing the building anxiously. Others watched his progress across the square. As Retief passed, he caught scattered comments:

"—seen that bird before."

"—where he's headed."

"—feller Sozier was talking to . . . . "

"Hey, you!"

Retief was on the grass now. Ahead, the blank wall loomed up. He walked on briskly.

"Stop that jasper!" a shout rang out. There was a sharp whine and a black spot appeared on the wall ahead. Near it, a small personnel door abruptly swung inward. Retief sprinted, plunged through the opening as a second shot seared the paint on the doorframe. The door clanged behind him. Retief glanced over the half dozen men confronting him.

"I'm Retief, CDT, acting Charge," he said. "Which of you gentlemen is Manager-General Corasol?"

*

217

Corasol was a tall, wide-shouldered man of fifty, with shrewd eyes, a ready smile, capable-looking hands and an urbane manner. He and Retief sat at a table at one side of the large room, under a maze of piping, tanks and valves. Corasol poured amber fluid into square glass tumblers.

"We spotted you by the blazer," he said. "Baby blue and gold braid stand out in a crowd."

Retief nodded. "The uniform has its uses," he agreed. He tried the drink. "Say, what is this? It's not bad."

"Sugarweed rum. Made from a marine plant. We have plenty of ocean here on Glave; there's only the one continent, you know, and it's useless for agriculture."

"Weather?"

"That's part of it. Glave is moving into what would be a major glaciation if it weren't for a rather elaborate climatic control installation. Then there are the tides. Half the continent would be inundated twice a year when our satellite is at aphelion; there's a system of baffles, locks and deep-water pumps that maintain the shore-line more or less constant. We still keep our cities well inland. Then there are the oxygen generators, the atmosphere filtration complex, vermin control and so on. Glave in its natural state is a rather hostile world."

"I'm surprised that your mines can support it all."

"Oh, they don't." Corasol shook his head. "Two hundred years ago, when the company first opened up Glave, it was economical enough. Quintite was a precious mineral in those days. Synthetics have long since taken over. Even fully automated, the mines barely support the public services and welfare system."

"I seem to recall a reference in the Post Report to the effect that a company petition to vacate its charter had been denied . . . . "

Corasol nodded, smiling wryly. "The CDT seemed to feel that as long as any of the world's residents desired to remain, the Company was constrained to oblige them. The great majority departed long ago, of course. Relocated to other operational areas. Only the untrainables, living off welfare funds—and a skeleton staff of single men to operate the technical installations—have stayed on."

"That explains the mechanics of the recent uprising," Retief said.

The bottle clinked against glasses for a second round. "What about the good corporal?" Retief asked. "Assuming he's a strong swimmer, you should be hearing from him soon."

Corasol glanced at his finger watch. "I imagine he'll be launching his gas attack any minute."

"The prospect doesn't seem to bother you."

"Sozier is a clever enough chap in his own way," Corasol said. "But he has a bad habit of leaping to conclusions. He's gotten hold of a tank of what someone has told him is gas—as indeed it is. Hydrogen, for industrial use. It seems the poor fellow is under the impression that anything masquerading as gas will have a lethal effect."

"He may be right—if he pumps it in fast enough."

"Oh, he won't be pumping it. Not after approximately five minutes from now."

"Hmmm. I think I'm beginning to see the light. 'Power off at sunset.'"

Corasol nodded. "I don't think he realizes somehow that all his vehicles are operating off broadcast power."

"Still, he has a good-sized crowd of hopefuls with him. How do you plan to get through them?"

"We don't. We go under. There's an extensive system of service ways underlying the city; another detail which I believe has escaped the corporal's notice."

"You'll be heading for the port?"

"Yes—eventually. First, we have a few small chores to see to. Sozier has quite a number of our technical men working at gun point to keep various services going."

Retief nodded. "It won't be easy breaking them out. I made a fast tour of the city this afternoon. Locked doors, armed guards—"

"Oh, the locks are power-operated, too. Our fellows will know what to do when the power fails. I think the sudden darkness will eliminate any problem from the guards."

The lights flickered and died. The whine of the turbines was suddenly noticeable, descending. Faint cries sounded from outside.

Corasol switched on a small portable lantern. "All ready, gentlemen?" he called, rising. "Let's move out. We want to complete this operation before dawn."

*

Four hours later, Retief stood with Corasol in a low-ceilinged tunnel, white-tiled, brilliantly lit by a central glare strip, watching as the last of the column of men released from forced labor in the city's utilities installations filed past. A solidly-built man with pale blond hair came up, breathing hard.

"How did it go, Taine?" Corasol asked.

"They're beginning to catch on, Mr. Corasol. We had a brisk time of it at Station Four. Everybody's clear now. No one killed, but we had a few injuries."

Corasol nodded. "The last few crews in have reported trouble. Ah—what about—"

Taine shook his head. "Sorry, sir. No trace. No one's seen them. But they're probably at the port ahead of us, hiding out. They'd know we'd arrive eventually."

"I suppose so. You sent word to them well in advance . . . . "

"Suppose I stand by here with a few men. We'll patrol the tunnels in case they show up. We have several hours before daylight."

"Yes. I'll go along and see to the preparations at Exit Ten. We'll make our sortie at oh-five-hundred. If you haven't seen anything of them by then . . . . "

"I'm sure they're all right."

"They'd better be." Corasol said grimly "Let's be off, Retief."

"If it's all the same to you, Mr. Manager-General, I'll stay here with Taine. I'll join you later."

"As you wish. I don't imagine there'll be any trouble—but if there is, having a CDT observer along will lend a certain air to the operation." He smiled, shook Retief's hand and moved off along the tunnel. The echo of feet and voices grew faint, faded to silence. Taine turned to the three men detailed to him, conversed briefly, sent them off along branching corridors. He glanced at Retief.

"Mr. Retief, you're a diplomat. This errand is not a diplomatic one."

"I've been on a few like that, too, Mr. Taine."

Taine studied Retief's face. "I can believe that," he said. "However, I think you'd better rejoin the main party."

"I might be of some use here, if your missing men arrive under fire."

"Missing men?" Taine's mouth twisted in a sour smile. "You fail to grasp the picture, Mr. Retief. There'll be no missing men arriving."

"Oh? I understood you were waiting here to meet them."

"Not men, Mr. Retief. It happens that Corasol has twin daughters, aged nineteen. They haven't been seen since the trouble began."

V

Half an hour passed. Retief leaned against the tunnel wall, arms folded, smoking a cigar in silence. Taine paced, ten yards up the corridor, ten yards back . . . .

"You seem nervous, Mr. Taine," Retief said.

Taine stopped pacing, eyed Retief coldly. "You'd better go along now," he said decisively. "Just follow the main tunnel. It's about a mile."

"Plenty of time yet, Mr. Taine." Retief smiled and drew on his cigar. "Your three men are still out."

"They won't be back here. We'll rendezvous at Exit Ten."

"Am I keeping you from something, Taine?"

"I can't be responsible for your safety if you stay here."

"Oh? You think I might fall victim to an accident?"

Taine narrowed his eyes. "It could happen," he said harshly.

"Where were the girls last seen?" Retief asked suddenly.

"How would I know?"

"Weren't you the one who got word to them?"

"Maybe you'd better keep out of this."

"You sent your men off; now you're eager to see me retire to a safe position. Why the desire for solitude, Taine? You wouldn't by any chance have plans?"

"That's enough," Taine snapped. "On your way. That's an order!"

"There are some aspects of this situation that puzzle me, Mr. Taine. Mr. Corasol has explained to me how he and his Division Chiefs—including you—were surprised in the executive suite at Planetary Central by a crowd of Sozier's bully-boys. They came in past the entire security system without an alarm. Corasol and the others put up a surprisingly good fight and made it to the service elevators—and from there to the sub-station. There was even time to order an emergency alert to the entire staff—but somehow, they were all caught at their stations and kept on the job at gun point. Now, I should think that you, as Chief of Security as well as Communications, should have some ideas as to how all this came about."

"Are you implying—"

"Let me guess, Taine. You have a deal with Sozier. He takes over, ousts the legal owners, and sets himself up to live off the fat of the land, with you as his technical chief. Then, I imagine, you'd find it easy enough to dispose of Sozier—and you'd be in charge."

*

Without warning Taine put his head down and charged. Retief dropped his cigar, side-stepped and planted a solid right on Taine's jaw. He staggered, went to his hands and knees.

"I suppose you'd like to get word to Sozier that his work force is arriving at the port at oh-five-hundred," Retief said. "Of course, he'll want to have a good-sized reception committee on hand as they come out."

Taine plunged to his feet, threw a vicious left that went past Retief's ear, then abruptly dropped, clamped a lock on Retief's leg, twisted—

The two men rolled, came to rest with Taine on top, Retief face-down, his arm bent back and doubled. Taine, red-faced and puffing, grunted as he applied pressure.

"You know a lot about me," he grated, "but you overlooked the fact that I've been Glavian Judo champion for the past nine years."

"You're a clever man, Taine," Retief said between clenched teeth. "Too clever to think it will work."

"It will work. Glave's never had a CDT mission here before. We're too small. Corasol invited your Embassy in because he had an idea there was something in the wind. That forced my hand. I've had to move hastily. But by the time I invite observers in to see for themselves, everything will be running smoothly. I can even afford to let Corasol and the others go—I'll have hostages for his good behavior."

"You've been wanting to boast about it to someone who could appreciate your cleverness, I see. Sozier must be an unappreciative audience."

"Sozier's a filthy pig—but he had his uses."

"What do you plan to do now?"

"I've been wondering that myself—but I think the best solution is to simply break your arm for now. You should be easy to control then. It's quite simple. I merely apply pressure, thus . . . . "

"Judo is a very useful technique," Retief said. "But in order to make it work, you have to be a pretty good man . . . . " He moved suddenly, shifting his position. Taine grabbed, holding Retief's arm by the wrist and elbow, his own arm levering Retief's back, back . . . . Retief twisted onto his side, then his back. Taine grunted, following the movement, straining. Slowly, Retief sat up against Taine's weight. Then, with a surge, he straightened his arm. Taine's grip broke. Retief came to his feet. Taine scrambled up in time to meet a clean uppercut that snapped him onto his back—out cold.

*

"Ah, there you are," Retief said as Taine's eyes fluttered and opened. "You've had a nice nap—almost fifteen minutes. Feeling better?"

Taine snarled, straining against the bonds on his wrists.

"Gold braid has its uses," Retief commented. "Now that you're back, perhaps you can answer a question for me. What's the Birthday Cake?"

Taine spat. Retief went to stand over him.

"Time is growing short, Mr. Taine. It will be dawn in another two hours. I can't afford the luxury of coaxing you."

"You won't get away with this."

Retief looked at the glowing end of his cigar. "This won't be subtle, I agree—but it will work."

"You're bluffing."

Retief leaned closer. "In my place—would you hesitate?" he asked softly.

Taine cursed, struggled to break free, eyes on the cigar.

"What kind of diplomat are you?" he snarled.

"The modern variety. Throat-cutting, thumb-screws, poison and stiletto work were popular in Machiavelli's time; nowadays we go in more for the administrative approach—but the cigar-end still has its role."

"Look, we can come to an agreement—"

"What's the Birthday Cake?" Retief snapped.

"I'm in a position to do a lot for you!"

"Last chance—"

"It's the official Residence of the Manager-General!" Taine screeched, writhing away from the cigar.

"Where is it? Talk fast!"

"You'll never get close! There's a seven-foot wall and by this time the grounds are swarming with Sozier's men."

"Nevertheless, I want to know where it is—and the information had better be good. If I don't come back, you'll have a long wait."

Taine groaned. "All right. Put that damned cigar away. I'll tell you what I can . . . . "

*

Retief stood in the shadow of a vine-grown wall, watching the relief of the five-man guard detail at the main gate to the Residence grounds. The bluish light of the Glavian satellite reflected from the rain-pocked street, glinted from the leaves of a massive tree ten yards from the gate. The chill in the air cut through Retief's wet clothes. The men at the gate huddled, hands in pockets, coat collars turned up, backs to the wind—and to Retief. He moved silently forward, caught a low branch of the tree, pulled himself up.

The men at the gate exchanged muttered remarks. One lit a cigarette. Retief waited, then moved higher. The guards talked in low voices, edged closer to the shelter of the gate-house. Retief lowered himself onto the wall, dropped down onto the sodden lawn, crouched, waiting. There was no alarm.

Through the trees the dark shape of the house loomed up, its top storey defiantly ablaze with lights. Retief moved off silently, from the shadow of one tree to the next, swinging in an arc that would bring him to the rear of the great round structure. He froze as the heavy footfalls of one of Sozier's pickets slogged past five yards from him, then moved on. The glow of a campfire flickered near the front of the house. Retief could make out the shapes of men around it—a dozen or two, at least. Probably as many more warmed themselves at each of the other fires visible on the grounds—and most of the rest had doubtless found dryer shelter in the lee of the house itself.

Retief reached the conservatory at the rear of the house, studied the dark path leading to the broad terrace, picked out the squat shape of the utilities manifold behind a screen of shrubbery. So far, Taine's information had been accurate. The next step was to—

There was a faint sound from high above, followed by a whoosh! Then with a sharp crack! a flare appeared overhead, rocking gracefully, floating down gently under a small parachute. Below it, inky shadows rocked in unison.

In the raw white light, Retief counted eighteen men clinging to handholds on the side of the house, immobile in the pitiless glare. Above them, a face appeared, then a second, peering over the edge of the fourth-storey gallery. Both figures rose, unlimbering four-foot bows, fitting arrows to strings—

Whok! Whok! Two men lost their holds and fell, yelling, to slam into the heavy shrubbery. A second flight of arrows found marks. Retief watched from the shadows as man after man dropped to flounder in the wet foliage. Several jumped before the deadly bows were turned on them. As the flare faded, the last of the men plunged down to crash among their fellows. Retief stepped out, ran swiftly to the manifold, forcing his way among the close-growing screen, scrambled to its top. His hand fell on a spent arrow. He picked it up.

It was a stout wooden shaft twenty inches long, terminating in a rubber suction cup. Retief snorted, dropped the arrow and started up.

VI

Twenty feet above ground level, the wide windows of the third floor sun terrace presented a precarious handhold as Retief swung back a foot and kicked in a panel. Inside, he dimly made out the shape of a broad carpeted room, curving out of sight in both directions. There were wide-leaved tropical plants in boxes, groups of padded chairs, low tables with bowls of fruit. Retief made his way past them, found an inner door, went into a dark hall. At the far end, voices exchanged shouted questions. Feet pounded. A flicker of light from a hand lantern splashed across the wall, disappeared. Retief found a stair, went up it noiselessly. According to Taine, the elevator to the top floor apartment should be to the left—

Retief flattened himself to the wall. Footsteps sounded near at hand. He moved quickly to a doorway. There was a murmur of voices, the wavering light of lanterns. A party of uniformed men tiptoed past a cross corridor, struggling under the weight of a massive log two feet in diameter and twelve feet long.

" . . . on signal, hit it all together. Then . . . " someone was saying.

Retief waited, listening. There was the creak of a door, the fumbling of awkwardly laden feet on a stair, hoarse breathing, a muffled curse.

" . . . got my fingers, you slob!" a voice snarled.

"Shaddup!" another voice hissed.

There was a long moment of silence, then a muffled command—followed an instant later by a thunderous crash, a shout—cut off abruptly by a ponderous *blam!* followed instantly by a roar like a burst dam, mingled with yells, thumps, crashes. A foamy wash of water surged along the cross corridor, followed a moment later by a man sliding on his back, then another, two more, the log, fragments of a door, more men.

In the uproar, Retief moved along to the elevator, felt over the control panel, located a small knurled button. He turned it. The panel came away. He fumbled cautiously, found a toggle switch, flipped it. A light sprang up in the car. Instantly Retief flipped the light switch; the glow faded. He waited. No alarm. Men were picking themselves up, shouting.

" . . . them broads dropped a hundred-gallon bag of water . . . " Someone complained.

" . . . up there fast, men. We got the door okay!"

Feet thumped. Yells sounded.

"No good, Wes! They got a safe or something in the way!"

RETIEF: THE DIRTY DOZEN

Retief silently closed the lift door, pressed the button. With a sigh, the car slid upward, came to a gentle stop. He eased the door open, looked out into a dim-lit entrance hall. Footsteps sounded beyond a door. He waited; the clack of high heels crossing a floor. Retief stepped out of the car, went to the door, glanced into a spacious lounge with rich furniture, deep rugs, paintings, a sweep of glass, and in an alcove at the far side, a bar. Retief crossed the room, poured a stiff drink into a paper-thin glass and drained it.

The high-heeled steps were coming back now. A door opened. Two leggy young women in shorts, with red-gold hair bound back by ribbons—one green, one blue—stepped into the room. One girl held a coil of insulated wire; the other, a heavy-looking gray-enameled box eight inches on a side.

"Now, see if you can tinker that generator to get a little more juice, Lyn," the girl with the wire said. "I'll start stringing . . . . "

Her voice died as she caught sight of Retief. He raised his glass. "My compliments, ladies. I see you're keeping yourselves amused."

*

"Who . . . who are you?" Lyn faltered.

"My name's Retief. Your father sent me along to carry your bags. It's lucky I arrived when I did, before any of those defenseless chaps outside were seriously injured."

"You're not . . . one of them?"

"Of course he's not, Lyn," the second girl said. "He's much too good-looking."

"That's good," Lyn said crisply. "I didn't want to have to use this thing." She tossed a bright-plated 2 mm needler onto a chair and sat down. "Dad's all right, isn't he?"

"He's fine, and we've got to be going. Tight schedule, you know. And you'd better get some clothes on. It's cold outside."

Lyn nodded. "Environmental Control went off the air six hours ago. You can already feel snow coming."

"Don't you suppose we have time to just rig up one little old circuit?" the other twin wheedled. "Nothing serious; just enough to tickle."

"We planned to wire all the window frames, the trunk we used to block the stair, the lift shaft—"

"And then we thought we'd try to drop a loop down and pick up the gallery guard rail, and maybe some of that wrought-iron work around the front of the house—"

226

"Sorry, girls; no time."

Five minutes later, the twins were ready, wrapped in fur robes. Retief had exchanged his soaked blazer for a down-lined weatherproof.

"The lift will take us all the way down, won't it?" he asked.

Lyn nodded. "We can go out through the wine cellar."

Retief picked up the needler and handed it to Lyn. "Hang on to this," he said. "You may need it yet."

*

A cold wind whipped the ramp as dawn lightened the sky.

"It's hard to believe," Corasol said. "What made him do it?"

"He saw a chance to own it all."

"He can have it," Corasol's communicator beeped. He put it to his ear. "Everything's ship-shape and ready to lift," a tiny voice said.

Corasol turned to Retief. "Let's go aboard."

"Hold it," Retief said. "There's someone coming."

Corasol spoke into the communicator. "Keep him covered."

The man slogging across the concrete was short, wrapped in heavy garments. Over his head a white cloth fluttered from a stick.

"From the set of those bat-ears, I'd say it was the good corporal."

"I wonder what he wants."

Sozier stopped twenty feet from Retief and Corasol.

"I want to . . . ah . . . talk to you, Corasol," he said.

"Certainly, General. Go right ahead."

"Look here, Corasol. You can't do this. My men will freeze. We'll starve. I've been thinking it over, and I've decided that we can reach an understanding."

Corasol waited.

"I mean, we can get together on this thing. Compromise. Maybe I acted a little hasty." Sozier looked from Corasol to Retief. "You're from the CDT. You tell him. I'll guarantee his people full rights . . . . "

Retief puffed at his cigar in silence. Sozier started again.

"Look, I'll give you a full voice in running things. A fifty-fifty split. Whatta you say?"

"I'm afraid the proposal doesn't interest me, General," Corasol said.

"Never mind the General stuff," Sozier said desperately. "Listen, you can run it. Just give me and my boys a little say-so."

"Sorry." Corasol shook his head. "Not interested, General."

"Okay, okay! You win! Just come on back and get things straightened out! I got a belly full of running things!"

"I'm afraid I have other plans, General. For some time I've wanted to transfer operations to a world called Las Palmas on which we hold a charter. It has a naturally delightful climate, and I'm told the fishing is good. I leave Glave to the Free Electorate with my blessing. Good-by, General." He turned to the ship.

"You got to stay here!" Sozier howled. "We'll complain to the CDT! And don't call me General! I'm a Corporal—"

"You're a General now—whether you like it or not." Corasol said bluntly. He shivered. There was a hint of ice in the air. "If you or any of your men ever decide to go to work, General, I daresay we can train you for employment on Las Palmas. In the meantime—Long Live the Revolution!"

"You can't do this! I'll sue!"

"Calm down, Sozier," Retief said. "Go back to town and see if you can get your radio working. Put in a call for Mr. Magnan aboard the CDT vessel. Tell him your troubles. It will make his day. And a word of advice: Mr. Magnan hates a piker—so ask for plenty."

*

"My boy, I'm delighted," Ambassador Sternwheeler boomed. "A highly professional piece of work. A stirring testimonial to the value of the skilled negotiator!"

"You're too kind, Mr. Ambassador." Retief said, glancing at his watch.

"And Magnan tells me that not only will the Mission be welcomed, and my job secure for another year—that is, I shall have an opportunity to serve—but a technical mission has been requested as well. I shall look forward to meeting General Sozier. He sounds a most reasonable chap."

"Oh, you'll like him, Mr. Ambassador. A true democrat, willing to share all you have."

Counsellor of Embassy Magnan tapped and entered the office.

"Forgive the intrusion, Mr. Ambassador," he said breathlessly, "but I must—"

"Well, what is it, man? The deal hasn't gone sour?"

"Oh, far from it! I've been exploring General Sozier's economic situation with him via scope, and it seems he'll require a loan."

"Yes, yes? How much?"

Magnan inhaled proudly. "Twenty. Million. Credits."

"No!"

"Yes!"

"Magnificent! Good lord, Magnan, you're a genius! This will mean promotions all around. Why, the administrative load alone—"

"I can't wait to make planetfall, Mr. Ambassador. I'm all a-bubble with plans. I hope they manage to get the docking facilities back in operation soon."

"Help is on the way, my dear Magnan. I'm assured the Environmental Control installations will be coming back in operation again within a year or two."

"My, didn't those ice-caps form quickly. And in the open sea."

"Mere scum ice. As my Counsellor for Technical Affairs, you'll be in charge of the ice-breaking operation once we're settled in. I imagine you'll want to spend considerable time in the field. I'll be expecting a record of how every credit is spent."

"I'm more the executive type," Magnan said. "Possibly Retief—"

A desk speaker hummed. "Mr. Corasol's lighter has arrived to ferry Mr. Retief across to the Company ship . . . . "

"Sorry you won't be with us, Retief," Sternwheeler said heartily. He turned to Magnan. "Manager-General Corasol has extended Retief an exequatur as Consul General to Las Palmas."

*

Retief nodded. "Much as I'd like to be out in that open boat with you, breaking ice, I'm afraid duty calls elsewhere."

"Your own post? I'm not sure he's experienced enough, Mr. Ambassador. Now, I—"

"He was requested by name, Magnan. It seems the Manager-General's children took a fancy to him."

"Eh? How curious. I never thought you were particularly interested in infant care, Retief."

"Perhaps I haven't been, Mr. Magnan." Retief draped his short blue cape over his left arm and turned to the door. "But remember the diplomat's motto: be adaptable . . . . "

DIPLOMAT-AT-ARMS

Retief had just one job on Northroyal—to save the galaxy from madness and war. So with a frayed cloak and an old horse and a packet in his saddlebags—not to mention blood, guts, and brains he set out.

The cold white sun of Northroyal glared on pale dust and vivid colors in the narrow raucous street. Retief rode slowly, unconscious of the huckster's shouts, the kaleidoscope of smells, the noisy milling crowd. His thoughts were on events of long ago on distant worlds; thoughts that set his features in narrow-eyed grimness. His bony, powerful horse, unguided, picked his way carefully, with flaring nostrils, wary eyes alert in the turmoil.

The mount sidestepped a darting gamin and Retief leaned forward, patted the sleek neck. The job had some compensations, he thought; it was good to sit on a fine horse again, to shed the grey business suit . . .

A dirty-faced man pushed a fruit cart almost under the animal's head; the horse shied, knocked over the cart. At once a muttering crowd began to gather around the heavy-shouldered grey-haired man. He reined in and sat scowling, an ancient brown cape over his shoulders, a covered buckler slung at the side of the worn saddle, a scarred silver-worked claymore strapped across his back in the old cavalier fashion.

Retief hadn't liked this job when he had first heard of it. He had gone alone on madman's errands before, but that had been long ago a phase of his career that should have been finished. And the information he had turned up in his background research had broken his professional detachment. Now the locals were trying an old tourist game on him; ease the outlander into a spot, then demand money . . .

Well, Retief thought, this was as good a time as any to start playing the role; there was a hell of a lot here in the quaint city of Fragonard that needed straightening out.

"Make way, you rabble!" he roared suddenly, "or by the chains of the sea-god I'll make a path through you!" He spurred the horse; neck arching, the mount stepped daintily forward.

The crowd made way reluctantly before him. "Pay for the merchandise you've destroyed," called a voice.

"Let peddlers keep a wary eye for their betters," snorted the man loudly, his eye roving over the faces before him. A tall fellow with long yellow hair stepped squarely into his path.

"There are no rabble or peddlers here," he said angrily. "Only true cavaliers of the Clan Imperial . . . "

The mounted man leaned from his saddle to stare into the eyes of the other. His seamed brown face radiated scorn. "When did a true cavalier turn to commerce? If you were trained to the Code you'd know a gentleman doesn't soil his hands with penny-grubbing, and that the Emperor's highroad belongs to the mounted knight. So clear your rubbish out of my path, if you'd save it."

"Climb down off that nag," shouted the tall young man, reaching for the bridle. "I'll show you some practical knowledge of the Code. I challenge you to stand and defend yourself. "

In an instant the thick barrel of an antique Imperial Guards power gun was in the grey-haired man's hand. He leaned negligently on the high pommel of his saddle with his left elbow, the pistol laid across his forearm pointing unwaveringly at the man before him.

The hard old face smiled grimly. "I don't soil my hands in street brawling with new-hatched nobodies," he said. He nodded toward the arch spanning the street ahead. "Follow me through the arch, if you call yourself a man and a Cavalier." He moved on then; no one hindered him. He rode in silence throagh the crowd, pulled up at the gate barring the street. This would be the first real test of his cover identity. The papers which had gotten him through Customs and Immigration at Fragonard Spaceport the day before had been burned along with the civilian clothes. From here on he'd be getting by on the uniform and a cast-iron nerve.

A purse-mouthed fellow wearing the uniform of a Lieutenant-Ensign in the Household Escort Regiment looked him over, squinted his eyes, smiled sourly.

"What can I do for you, Uncle?" He spoke carelessly, leaning against the engraved buttress mounting the wrought-iron gate. Yellow and green sunlight filtered down through the leaves of the giant linden trees bordering the cobbled street.

The grey-haired man stared down at him. "The first thing you can do, Lieutenant-Ensign," he said in a voice of cold steel, "is come to a position of attention."

The thin man straightened, frowning. "What's that?" His . expression hardened. "Get down off that beast and let's have a look at your papel'Sif you've got any."

The mounted man didn't move. "I'm making" allowances for the fact that your regiment is made up of idlers who've never learned to soldier," he said quietly. "But having had your attention called to it, even you should recognize the insignia of a Battle Commander."

The officer stared, glancing over the drab figure of the old man. Then he saw the tarnished gold thread worked into the design of a dragon rampant, almost invisible against the faded color of the heavy velvet cape.

He licked his lips, cleared his throat, hesitated. What in name of the Tormented One would a top-ranking battle officer be doing on this thin old horse, dressed in plain worn clothing? "Let me see your papers Commander," he said.

The Commander flipped back the cape to expose the ornate butt of the power pistol.

"Here are my credentials," he said. "Open the gate."

"Here," the Ensign spluttered,

"What's this . . . "

"For a man who's taken the Emperor's commission," the old man said, "you're criminally ignorant of the courtesies due a general officer. Open the gate or I'll blow it open. You'll not deny the way to an Imperial Battle officer." He drew the pistol.

The Ensign gulped, thought fleeting of sounding the alarm signal, of insisting on seeing papers . . . Then as the pistol came up, he closed the switch, and the gate swung open. The heavy hooves of the gaunt horse clattered past him; he caught a glimpse of a small brand on the lean flank. Then he was staring after the retreating back of the terrible old man. Battle Commander indeed! The old fool was wearing a fortune in valuable antiques, and the animal bore the brand of a thoroughbred battle-horse. He'd better report this . . . He picked up the communicator, as a tall young man with an angry face came up to the gate.

Retief rode slowly down the narrow street lined with the stalls of suttlers, metalsmiths, weapons technicians, freelance squires. The first obstacle was behind him. He hadn't played it very suavely, but he had been in no mood for bandying words. He had been angry ever since he had started this job; and that, he told himself, wouldn't do. He was beginning to regret his high-handedness with the crowd outside the gate. He should save the temper for those responsible, not the bystanders; and in any event, an agent of the Corps should stay cool at all times. That was essentially the same criticism that Magnan had handed him along with the assignment, three months ago.

"The trouble with you, Retief," Magnan had said, "is that you are unwilling to accept the traditional restraints of the Service; you conduct yourself too haughtily, too much in the manner of a free agent . . . "

KEITH LAUMER

His reaction, he knew, had only proved the accuracy of his superior's complaint. He should have nodded penitent agreement, indicated that improvement would be striven for earnestly; instead, he had sat expressionless, in a silence which inevitably appeared antagonistic. He remembered how Magnan had moved uncomfortably, cleared his throat, and frowned at the papers before him. "Now, in the matter of your next assignment," he said, "we have a serious situation to deal with in an area that could be critical."

Retief almost smiled at the recollection. The man had placed himself in an amusing dilemma. It was necessary to emphasize the great importance of the job at hand, and simultaneously to avoid letting Retief have the satisfaction of feeling that he was to be intrusted with anything vital; to express the lack of confidence the Corps felt in him while at the same time invoking his awareness of the great trust he was receiving. It was strange how Magnan could rationalize his personal dislike into a righteous concern for the best interests of the Corps.

Magnan had broached the nature of the assignment obliquely, mentioning his visit as a tourist to Northroyal, a charming, backward little planet settled by Cavaliers, refugees from the breakup of the Empire of the Lily.

Retief knew the history behind Northroyal's tidy, proud, tradition-bound society. When the Old Confederation broke up, dozens of smaller governments had grown up among the civilized worlds. For a time, the Lily Empire had been among the most vigorous of them, comprising Twenty-one worlds, and supporting an excellent military force under the protection of which the Lilyan merchant fleet had carried trade to a thousand far-flung worlds.

When the Concordiat had come along, organizing the previously sovereign states into a new Galactic jurisdiction, the Empire of the Lily had resisted, and had for a time held the massive Concordiat fleets at bay. In the end, of course, the gallant but outnumbered Lilyan forces had been driven back to the gates of the home world. The planet of Lily had been saved catastrophic bombardment only by a belated truce which guaranteed self-determination to Lily on the cessation of hostilities, disbandment of the Lilyan fleet, and the exile of the entire membership of the Imperial Suite, which, under the Lilyan clan tradition, had numbered over ten thousand individuals. Every man, woman, and child who could claim even the most distant blood relationship to the Emperor, together with their servants, dependents, retainers, and proteges, were included. The move took weeks to complete, but at the end of it the Cavaliers, as they were known, had been transported to an

233

uninhabited, cold, sea-world, which they named Northroyal. A popular bit of lore in connection with the exodus had it that the ship bearing the Emperor himself had slipped away en route to exile, and that the ruler had sworn that he would not return until the day he could come with an army of liberation. He had never been heard from again.

The land area of the new world, made up of innumerable islands, totaled half a million square miles. Well stocked with basic supplies and equipment, the cavaliers had set to work and turned their rocky fief into a snug, well integrated if tradition ridden society, and today exported sea-foods, fine machinery, and tourist literature.

It was in the latter department that Northroyal was best known. Tales of the pomp and color, the quaint inns and good food, the beautiful girls, the brave display of royal cavalry, and the fabulous annual Tournament of the Lily attracted a goodly number of sightseers, and the Cavalier Line was now one of the planet's biggest foreign-exchange earners.

Magnan had spoken of Northroyal's high industrial potential, and her well-trained civilian corps of space navigators.

"The job of the Corps," Retief interrupted, "is to seek out and eliminate threats to the peace of the Galaxy. How does a little story-book world like Northroyal get into the act?"

"More easily than you might imagine," Magnan said. "Here you have a close-knit society, proud, conscious of a tradition of military power, empire. A clever rabble-rouser using the right appeal would step into a ready-made situation there. It would take only an order on the part of the planetary government to turn the factories to war production, and convert the merchant fleet into a war fleet and we'd be faced with a serious power imbalance a storm center."

"I think you're talking nonsense, Mr. Minister," Retief said bluntly. "They've got more sense than that. They're not so far gone on tradition as to destroy themselves. They're a practical people."

Magnan drummed his fingers on the desk top. "There's one factor 1 haven't covered yet," he said. "There has been what amounts to a news blackout from Northroyal during the last six months . . . "

Retief snorted. "What news?"

Magnan had been enjoying the suspense. "Tourists have been having great difficulty, getting to Northroyal," he said. "Fragonard, the capital, is completely closed to outsiders. We managed, however, to get an agent in." He paused, gazing at Retief. "It seems," he went on, "that the rightful Emperor has turned up."

Retief narrowed his eyes. "What's that?" he said sharply.

Magnan drew back, intimidated by the power of Retief's tone, annoyed by his own reaction. In his own mind, Magnan was candid enough to know that this was the real basis for his intense dislike for his senior agent. It was an instinctive primitive fear of physical violence. Not that Retief had ever assaulted anyone; but he had an air of mastery that made Magnan feel trivial.

"The Emperor;" Magnan repeated. "The traditional story is that he was lost on the voyage to Northroyal. There was a legend that he had slipped out of the hands of the Concordiat in order to gather new support for a counter-offensive, hurl back the invader, all that sort of thing."

"The Concordiat collapsed of its own weight within a century," Retief "aid. "There's no invader to hurl back. Northroyal is free and independent like every other world."

"*Of* course, of course," Magnan said. "But you're missing the emotional angle. Retief. It's all very well to be independent; but what about the dreams of Empire, the vanished glory, Destiny, et cetera?"

"What about them?"

"That's all our agent heard; it's everywhere. The news strips are full of it. Video is playing it up; everybody's talking it. The returned Emperor seems to be a clever propagandist; the next step will be a full scale mobilization. And we're not equipped to handle that."

"What am I supposed to do about all this?"

"Your orders are, and I quote, to proceed to Fragonard and there employ such measures as shall be appropriate to negate the present trend toward an expansionist sentiment among the populace." Magnan passed a document across the desk to Retief for his inspection.

The orders were brief, and wasted no wordage on details. As an officer of the Corps with the rank of Counsellor, Retief enjoyed wide latitude, and broad powers and corresponding responsibility in the event of failure. Retief wondered how this assignment had devolved on him, among the thousands of Corps agents scattered through the Galaxy. Why was one man being handed a case which on the face of it should call for a full mission? "This looks like quite an undertaking for a single agent, Mr. Minister," Reticf said.

"Well, of course, if You don't feel you can handle it . . . " Magnan looked solemn.

Retief looked at him, smiling faintly. Magnan's tactics had been rather obvious. Here was one of those nasty jobs which could easily pass in reports as routine if all went well; but even a slight mistake could mean complete failure, and failure meant war; and the agent who had let it happen would be finished in the Corps.

There was danger in the scheme for Magnan, too. The blame might reflect back on him. Probably he had plans for averting disaster after Retief had given up. He was too shrewd to leave himself out in the open. And for that matter, Retief reflected, too good an agent to let the situation get out of hand.

No, it was merely an excellent opportunity to let Retief discredit himself, with little risk of any great credit accruing to him in the remote event of success.

Retief could, of course, refuse the assignment, but that would be the end of his career. He would never be advanced to the rank of Minister, and age limitations would force his retirement in a year or two. That would be an easy victory for Magnan.

Retief liked his work as an officer-agent of the Diplomatic Corps, that ancient supranational organization dedicated to the contravention of war. He had made his decision long ago, and he had learned to accept his life as it was, with all its imperfections. It was easy enough to complain about the petty intrigues, the tyranies of rank, the small inequities. But these were merely a part of the game, another challenge to be met and dealt with. The overcoming of obstacles was Jame Retief's specialty. Some of the obstacles were out in the open, the recognized difficulties inherent in any tough assignment. Others were concealed behind a smoke-screen of personalities and efficiency reports; and both were equally important. You did your job in the field, and then you threaded your way through the maze of Corps politics. And if you couldn't handle the job any part of it you'd better find something else to do.

He had accepted the assignment of course, after letting Magnan wonder for a few minutes; and then for two months he had buried himself in research, gathering every scrap of information, direct and indirect, that the massive files of the Corps would yield. He had soon found himself immersed in the task, warming to its challenge, fired with emotions ranging from grief to rage as he ferreted out the hidden pages in the history of the exiled Cavaliers.

He had made his plan, gathered a potent selection of ancient documents and curious objects; a broken chain of gold, a tiny key, a small silver box. And now he was here, inside the compound of the Grand Corrida.

Everything here in these ways surrounding and radiating from the Field of the Emerald Crown the arena itself was devoted to the servicing and supplying of the thousands of First Day contenders in the Tournament of the Lily, and the housing and tending of the dwindling number of winners who stayed on for the following days. There were tiny eating places, taverns, inns; all consciously antique in style, built in imitation of their counterparts left behind long ago on far off Lily.

"Here you are, pop, firstclass squire," called a thin red-haired fellow.

"Double up and save credits," called a short dark man. "First-day contract . . . " Shouts rang back and forth across the alley-like street as the stall keepers scented a customer. Retief ignored them, moved on toward the looming wall of the arena. Ahead, a slender youth stood with folded arms before his stall, looking toward the approaching figure on the black horse. He leaned forward, watching Retief intently, then straightened, turned and grabbed up a tall narrow body shield from behind him. He raised the shield over his head, and as Retief came abreast, called "Battle officer!"

Retief reined in the horse, looked down at the youth. "At your service, sir," the young man said. He stood straight and looked Retief in the eye. Retief looked back. The horse minced, tossed his head.

"What is your name, boy?" Retief asked.

"Fitzraven, sir."

"Do you know the Code?"

"I know the Code, sir."

Retief stared at him, studying his face, his neatly cut uniform of traditional Imperial green, the old but well oiled leather of his belt and boots.

"Lower your shield, Fitzraven," he said. "You're engaged." He swung down from his horse. "The first thing I want is care for my mount. His name is Danger-by-Night. And then I want an inn for myself."

"I'll care for the horse myself, Commander," Fitzraven said. "And the Commander will find good lodging at the sign of the Phoenix-in-Dexter-Chief; quarters are held ready for my client." The squire took the bridle, pointing toward the inn a few doors away.

Two hours later, Retief came back to the stall, a thirty-two ounce steak and a bottle of Neauveau Beaujolais having satisfied a monumental appetite induced by the long ride down from the spaceport north of Fragonard. The plain banner he had carried in his saddlebag fluttered now from the staff above the stall. He moved through the narrow room to a courtyard behind, and stood in the doorway watching as Fitzraven curried the dusty hide of the lean black horse. The saddle and fittings were laid out on a heavy table, ready for cleaning. There was clean straw in the stall where the horse stood, and an empty grain bin and water bucket indicated the animal had been well fed and watered.

Retief nodded to the squire, and strolled around the courtyard staring up at the deep blue sky of early evening above the irregular line of roofs and chimneys, noting the other squires, the variegated mounts stabled here, listening to the hubbub of talk, the clatter of crockery from the kitchen of the inn. Fitzraven finished his work and came over to his new employer.

"Would the Commander like to sample the night life in the Grand Corrida?"

"Not tonight," Retief said. "Let's go up to my quarters; 1 want to learn a little more about what to expect."

Retief's room, close under the rafters on the fourth floor of the inn, was small but adequate, with a roomy wardrobe and a wide bed. The contents of his saddlebags were already in place in the room.

Retief looked around. "Who gave you permission to open my saddlebags?"

Fitzraven flushed slightly. "I thought the Commander would wish to have them unpacked," he said stiffly.

"I looked at the job the other squires were doing on their horses," Retief said. "You were the only one who was doing a proper job of tending the animal. Why the special service?"

"I was trained by my father," Fitzraven said. "I serve only true knights, and I perform my duties honorably. If the Commander is dissatisfied. . ."

"How do you know I'm a true knight?"

"The Commander wears the uniform and weapons of one of the oldest Imperial Guards Battle Units, the Iron Dragon," Fitzraven said. "And the Commander rides a battle , horse, true bred."

"How do you know I didn't steal them?"

Fitzraven grinned suddenly. "They fit the Commander too well."

Retief smiled. "All right, son, you'll do," he said. "Now brief me on the First Day. I don't want to miss anything. And you may employ the personal pronoun."

For an hour Fitzraven discussed the order of events for the elimination contests of the First Day of the Tournament of the Lily, the strategies that a clever contender could employ to husband his strength, the pitfalls into which the unwary might fall.

The tournament was the culmination of a year of smaller contests held throughout the equatorial chain of populated islands. The North-royalans had substituted various forms of armed combat for the sports practiced on most worlds; a compensation for the lost empire, doubtless, a primitive harking-back to an earlier, more glorious day.

Out of a thousand First Day entrants, less than one in ten would come through to face the Second Day. Of course, the First Day events were less lethal than those to be encountered farther along in the three day tourney, Retief learned; there would be a few serious injuries in the course of the opening day, and those would be largely due to the clumsiness or ineptitude on the part of the entrants.

There were no formal entrance requirements, Fitzraven said, other than proof of minimum age and status in the Empire. Not all the entrants were natives of Northroyal; many came from distant worlds, long scattered descendants of the citizens of the shattered Lily Empire. But all competed for the same prizes; status in the Imperial peerage, the honors of the Field of the Emerald crown, and Imperial grants of land, wealth to the successful.

"Will you enter the First Day events, sir," Fitzraven asked, "or do you have a second or third day certification?"

"Neither," Retief said. "We'll sit on the sidelines and watch."

Fitzraven looked surprised. It had somehow not occurred to him that the old man was not to be a combatant. And it was too late to get seats . . .

"How . . . " Fitzraven began, after a pause.

"Don't worry," Retief said. "We'll have a place to sit." Fitzraven fell silent, tilted his head to one side, listening. Loud voices, muffled by walls, the thump of heavy feet.

"Something is up," Fitzraven said. "Police." He looked at Retief.

"I wouldn't be surprised," Retief said, "if they were looking for me. Let's go find out."

"We need not meet them," the squire said. "There is another way . . ."

"Never mind," Retief said, "as well now as later." He winked at Fitzraven and turned to the door.

Retief stepped off the lift into the crowded common room, Fitzraven at his heels. Half a dozen men in dark blue tunics and tall shakos moved among the patrons, staring at faces. By the door Retief saw the thin-mouthed Ensign he had overawed at the gate. The fellow saw him at the same moment and plucked at the sleeve of the nearest policeman, pointing.

The man dropped a hand to his belt, and at once the other policeman turned, followed his glance to Retief. They moved toward him with one accord. Retief stood waiting.

The first cop planted himself before Retief, looking him up and down. "Your papers!" he snapped.

Retief smiled easily. "I am a peer of the Lily and a Battle officer of the Imperial forces," he said. "On what pretext are you demanding papers of me, Captain ?"

The cop raised his eyebrows. "Let's say you are charged with unauthorized entry into the controlled area of the Grand Corrida, and with impersonating an Imperial officer," he said. "You didn't expect to get away with it, did you grandpa?" The fellow smiled sardonically.

"Under the provisions of the Code," Retief said, "the status of a peer may not be questioned, nor his actions interfered with except by Imperial Warrant. Let me see yours, Captain. And I suggest you assume a more courteous tone when addressing your superior officer." Retief's voice hardened to a whip crack with the last words.

The policeman stiffened, scowled. His hand dropped to the nightstick at his belt.

"None of your insolence, old man," he snarled. "Papers! Now!"

Retief's hand shot out, gripped the officer's hand over the stick. "Raise that stick," he said quietly," and I'll assuredly beat out your brains with it." He smiled calmly into the captain's bulging eyes. The captain was a strong man. He threw every ounce of his strength into the effort to bring up his arm, to pull free of the old man's grasp. The crowd of customers, the squad of police, stood silently, staring, uncertain of what was going on. Retief stood steady; the officer strained, reddened. The old man's arm was like cast steel.

"I see you are using your head, Captain," Retief said. "Your decision not to attempt to employ force against a peer was an intelligent one."

The cop understood. He was was being offered an opportunity to save a little face. He relaxed slowly.

"Very well, uh, sir," he said stiffly. "I will assume you can establish your identity properly; kindly call at the commandant's office in the morning."

Retief released his hold and the officer hustled his men out, shoving the complaining Ensign ahead. Fitzraven caught Retief's eye and grinned.

"Empty pride is a blade with no hilt," he said. "A humble man would have yelled for help."

Retief turned to the barman. "Drinks for all," he called. A happy shout greeted this announcement. They had all enjoyed seeing the police outfaced.

"The cops don't seem to be popular here," the old man said.

Fitzraven sniffed. "A lawabiding subjct parks illegally for five minutes, and they are on him like flies after dead meat; but let his car be stolen by lawless hoodlums they are nowhere to be seen."

"That has a familiar sound," Retief said. He poured out a tumbler of vodka, looked at Fitzraven.

"Tomorrow," he said. "A big day."

A tall blonde young man near the door looked after him with bitter eyes.

"All right, old man," he muttered. "We'll see then."

The noise of the crowd came to Retief's ears as a muted rumble through the massive pile of the amphitheater above. A dim light filtered from the low-ceilinged corridor into the cramped office of the assistant Master of the Games.

"If you know your charter," Retief said, "you will recall that a Battle Commander enjoys the right to observe the progress of the games from the official box. I claim that privilege."

"I know nothing of this," the cadaverous official replied impatiently. "You must obtain an order from the Master of the Games before I can listen to you." He turned to another flunkey, opened his mouth to speak. A hand seized him by the shoulder, lifted him bodily from his seat. The man's mouth remained open in shock.

Retief held the stricken man at arms length, then drew him closer. His eyes blazed into the gaping eyes of the other. His face was white with fury.

"Little man," he said in a strange, harsh voice, "I go now with my groom to take my place in the official box. Read your Charter well before you interfere with me and your Holy Book as well." He dropped the fellow with a crash, saw him slide under the desk. No one made a sound. Even Fitzraven looked pale. The force of the old man's rage had been like a lethal radiation crackling in the room.

RETIEF: THE DIRTY DOZEN

The squire followed as Retief strode off down the corridor He breathed deeply, wiping his forehead. This was some old man he had met this year, for sure!

Retief slowed, turning to wait for Fitzraven. He smiled ruefully. "I was rough on the old goat," he said. "But officious pipsqueaks sting me like deerflies."

They emerged from the gloom of the passage into a well-situated box, too the best seats in the first row. Retief stared at the white glare and roiled dust of the arena, the banked thousands of faces looming above, and a sky of palest blue with one tiny white cloud. The gladiators stood in little groups, waiting. A' strange scene, Retief thought. A scene from dim antiquity, but real, complete with the odors of fear and excitement, the hot wind that ruffled his hair, the rumbling animal sound from the thousand throats of the many-headed monster. He wondered what it was they really wanted to see here today. A triumph of skill and courage, a reaffirmation of ancient virtues, the spectacle of men who laid life on the gaming table and played for a prize called glory ;or was it merely blood and death they wanted?

It was strange that this archaic ritual of the blood tournament, combining the features of the Circus of Caesar, the joust of Medieval Terran Europe, the Olympic Games, a rodeo, and a six-day bicycle race should have come to hold such an important place in a modern culture, Retief thought. In its present form it was a much distorted version of the traditional Tournament of the Lily, through whose gauntlet the nobility of the old Empire had come. It had been a device of harsh enlightenment to insure and guarantee to every man, once each year, the opportunity to prove himself against others whom society called his betters. Through its discipline, the humblest farm lad could rise by degrees to the highest levels in the Empire. For the original Games had tested every facet of a man, from his raw courage to his finesse in strategy, from his depths of endurance under mortal stress to the quickness of his intellect, from his instinct for truth to his wilyness in eluding a complex trap of violence.

In the two centuries since the fall of the Empire, the Games had gradually become a tourist spectacle, a free-for-all, a celebration with the added spice of danger for those who did not shrink back, and fat prizes to a few determined finalists. The Imperial Charter was still invoked at the opening of the Games, the old Code reaffirmed; but there were few who knew or cared what the Charter and Code actually said, what terms existed there. The popular mind left such details to the regents of the tourney. And in recent months, with the once sought-after tourists suddenly and inexplicably turned away, it seemed the Games were being perverted to a purpose even less admirable . . .

Well, thought Retief, perhaps I'll bring some of the fine print into play, before I'm done.

Bugle blasts sounded beyond the high bronze gate. Then with a heavy clang it swung wide and a nervous official stepped out nodding jerkily to the front rank of today's contenders.

The column moved straight out across the field, came together with other columns to form a square before the Imperial box. High above, Retief saw banners fluttering, a splash of color from the uniforms of ranked honor guards. The Emperor himself was here briefly to open the Tournament.

Across the field the bugles rang out again; Retief recognized the *Call to Arms* and the *Imperial Salute.* Then an amplified voice began the ritual reading of the Terms of the Day.

". . . by the clement dispensation of his Imperial Majesty, to be conducted under the convention of Fragonard, and there be none dissenting . . . " The voice droned on.

It finished at last, and referees moved to their positions. Retief looked at Fitzraven. "The excitement's about to begin."

Referees handed out heavy whips, gauntlets and face shields. The first event would be an unusual one.

Retief watched as the yellow- haired combatant just below the box drew on the heavy leather glove which covered and protected the left hand and forearm, accepted the fifteen-foot lash of braided ox-hide. He flipped it tentatively, laying the length out along the ground and recalling it with an effortless turn of the wrist, the frayed tip snapping like a pistol shot. The thing was heavy, Retief noted, and clumsy; the leather had no life to it.

The box had filled now; no one bothered Retief and the squire. The noisy crowd laughed and chattered, called to acquaintances in the stands and on the field below.

A bugle blasted peremptorily nearby, and white-suited referees darted among the milling entrants, shaping them into groups of five. Retief watched the blonde youth, a tall frowning man, and three others of undistinguished appearance.

Fitzraven leaned toward him. "The cleverest will hang back and let the others eliminate each other," he said in a low voice, "so that his first encounter will be for the set."

Retief nodded. A man's task here was to win his way as high as possible; every stratagem was important. He saw the blonde fellow inconspicuously edge back as a hurrying referee paired off the other four, called to him to stand by, and led the others to rings marked off on the dusty turf. A whistle blew suddenly, and over the arena the roar of sound changed tone. The watching crowd leaned forward as the hundreds of keyed up gladiators laid on their lashes in frenzied effort. Whips cracked, men howled, feet shuffled; here the crowd laughed as some clumsy fellow sprawled, yelping; there they gasped in excitement as two surly brutes flogged each other in all-out offense.

Retief saw the tip of one man's whip curl around his opponent's ankle, snatch him abruptly off his feet. The other pair circled warily, rippling their lashes uncertainly. One backed over the line unnoticing and was led away expostulating, no blow having been struck.

The number on the field dwindled away to half within moments. Only a few dogged pairs, now bleeding from cuts, still contested the issue. A minute longer and the whistle blew as the last was settled.

The two survivors of the group below paired off now, and as the whistle blasted again, the tall fellow, still frowning, brought the other to the ground with a single sharp flick of the lash. Retief looked him over. This was a man to watch.

More whistles, and a field now almost cleared; only two men left out of each original five; the blond moved out into the circle, stared across at the other. Retief recognized him suddenly as the fellow who had challenged him outside the gate, over the spilled fruit. So he had followed through the arch.

The final whistle sounded and a hush fell over the watchers. Now the shuffle of feet could be heard clearly, the hissing breath of the weary fighters, the creak and slap of leather.

The blonde youth flipped his lash out lightly, saw it easily evaded, stepped aside from a sharp counter-blow. He feinted, reversed the direction of his cast, and caught the other high on the chest as he dodged aside. A welt showed instantly. He saw a lightning-fast riposte on the way, sprang back. The gauntlet came up barely in time. The lash wrapped around the gauntlet, and the young fellow seized the leather, hauled sharply. The other stumbled forward. The blond brought his whip across the fellow's back in a tremendous slamming blow that sent a great fragment of torn shirt flying. Somehow the man stayed on his feet, backed off, circled. His opponent followed up, laying down one whistling whip-crack after another, trying to drive the

244

other over the line. He had hurt the man with the cut across the back, and now was attempting to finish him easily.

He leaned away from a sluggish pass, and then Retief saw agony explode in his face as a vicious cut struck home. The blonde youth reeled in a drunken circle, out on his feet. Slow to follow up, the enemy's lash crashed across the circle; the youth, steadying quickly, slipped under it, struck at the other's stomach. The leather cannoned against the man, sent the remainder of his shirt fluttering in a spatter of blood. With a surge of shoulder and wrist that made the muscles creak, the blonde reversed the stroke, brought the lash back in a vicious cut aimed at the same spot. It struck, smacking with a wet explosive crack. And he struck again, again, as the fellow tottered back, fell over the line.

The winner went limp suddenly, staring across at the man who lay in the dust, pale now, moving feebly for a moment, then slackly still. There was a great deal of blood, and more blood. Retief saw with sudden shock that the man was disemboweled. That boy, thought Retief, plays for keeps.

The next two events constituting the First Day trials were undistinguished exhibitions of a two-handed version of old American Indian wrestling and a brief bout of fencing with blunt-tipped weapons. Eighty men were certified for the Second Day before noon, and Retief and Fitzraven were back in the inn room a few minutes later. "Take some time off now while I catch up on my rest," Retief said. "Have some solid food ready when I wake." Then he retired for the night.

*

With his master breathing heavily in a profound sleep, the squire went down to the common room and found a table at the back, ordered a mug of strong ale, and sat alone, thinking.

This was a strange one he had met this year. He had seen at once that he was no idler from some high-pressure world, trying to lose himself in a fantasy of the old days. And no more was he a Northroyalan; there was a grim force in him, a time-engraved stamp of power that was alien to the neat well-ordered little world. And yet there was no doubt that there was more in him of the true Cavalier than in a Fragonard-born courtier. He was like some ancient warrior noble from the days of the greatness of the Empire. By the two heads, the old man was strange, and terrible in anger!

Fitzraven listened to the talk around him.

"I was just above," a blacksmith at the next table was saying. "He gutted the fellow with the lash! It was monstrous! I'm glad I'm not one of the fools who want to play at warrior. Imagine having your insides drawn out by a rope of dirty leather!"

"The games have to be tougher now," said another. "We've lain dormant here for two centuries, waiting for something to come some thing to set us on our way again to power and wealth . . . "

"Thanks, I'd rather go on living quietly as a smith and enjoying a few of the simple pleasures there was no glory in that fellow lying in the dirt with his belly torn open you can be sure of that."

"There'll be more than torn bellies to think about, when we mount a battle fleet for Grimwold and Tania," said another.

"The Emperor has returned," snapped the war-like one. "Shall we hang back where he leads ?"

The smith muttered. "His is a tortured genealogy, by my judgment. I myself trace my ancestry by three lines into the old Place at Lily."

"So do we all. All the more reason we should support our Emperor."

"We live well here; we have no quarrel with other worlds. Why not leave the past to itself?"

"Our Emperor leads; we will follow. If you disapprove, enter the Lily Tournament next year and win a high place; then your advice will be respected."

"No thanks. I like my insides to stay on the inside."

Fitzraven thought of Retief. The old man had said that he held his rank in his own right, citing no genealogy. That was strange indeed. The Emperor had turned up only a year ago, presenting the Robe, the Ring, the Seal, the crown jewels, and the Imperial Book which traced his descent through five generations from the last reigning Emperor of the Old Empire.

How could it be that Retief held a commission in his own right, dated no more than thirty years ago? And the rank of Battle Commander, That was a special rank, Fitzraven remembered, a detached rank for a distinguished noble and officer of proven greatness, assigned to no one unit, but dictating his own activities.

Either Retief was a fraud . . . but Fitzraven pictured the old man, his chiseled features that time had not disguised, his soldier's bearing, his fantastic strength, his undoubtedly authentic equipage. Whatever the explanation, he was a true knight. That was enough.

*

Retief awoke refreshed, and ravenous. A great rare steak and a giant tankard of autumn ale were ready on the table. He ate, ordered more and ate again. Then he stretched, shook himself, no trace of yesterday's fatigue remaining. His temper was better, too, he realized. He was getting too old to exhaust himself.

"It's getting late, Fitzraven," he said. "Let's be going."

They arrived at the arena and took their places in the official box in time to watch the first event, a cautious engagement with swords.

After four more events and three teams of determined but colorless competition, only a dozen men were left on the field awaiting the next event, including the tall blonde youth who Retief had been watching since he had recognized him. He himself, he reflected, was the reason for the man's presence here; and he had acquitted himself well.

Retief saw a burly warrlor carrying a two-handed sword paired off now against the blonde youth. The fellow grinned as he moved up to face the other.

This would be a little different, the agent thought watching; this fellow was dangerous. Yellow-hair moved in, his weapon held level across his chest. The big man lashed out suddenly with the great sword, and the other jumped back, then struck backhanded at his opponent's shoulder, nicked him lightly, sliding back barely in time to avoid a return swing. The still grinning man moved in, the blade chopping the air before him in a whistling figure eight. He pressed his man back, the blade never pausing.

There was no more room; the blonde fellow jumped sideways, dropping the point of his sword in time to intercept a vicious cut. He back stepped; he couldn't let that happen again. The big man was very strong.

The blade was moving again now, the grin having faded a little. He'll have to keep away from him, keep circling, Retief thought. The big fellow's pattern is to push his man back to the edge, then pick him off as he tries to sidestep. He'll have to keep space between them.

The fair-haired man backed, watching for an opening. He jumped to the right, and as the other shifted to face him, leaped back to the left and catching the big man at the end of his reach to the other side, slashed him across the ribs and kept moving. The man roared, twisting around in vicious cuts at the figure that darted sideways, just out of range. Then the blond brought his claymore across in a low swing that struck solidly across the back of the other's legs, with a noise like a butcher separating ribs with a cleaver.

RETIEF: THE DIRTY DOZEN

Like a marionette with his strings cut, the man folded to his knees, sprawled. The other man stepped back, as surgeons men swarmed up to tend the fallen fighter. There were plenty of them available now; so far the casualties had been twice normal. On the other mounds in view, men were falling. The faint-hearted had been eliminated; the men who were still on their feet were determined, or desperate. There would be no more push-overs.

"Only about six left," Fitzraven called.

"This has been a rather unusual tournament so far," Retief said. "That young fellow with the light hair seems to be playing rough, forcing the pace."

"I have never seen such a businss-like affair," Fitzraven said. "The weak-disposed have been frightened out, and the fighters cut down with record speed. At this rate there will be none left for the Third Day."

There was delay on the field, as referees and other officials hurried back and forth; then an announcement· boomed out. The Second Day was officially concluded. The six survivors would be awarded Second Day certificates, and would be eligible for the Third and Last Day tomorrow.

Retief and Fitzraven left the box, made their way through the crowd back to the inn.

"See that Danger-by-Night is well fed and exercised," Retief said to the squire. "And check over all of my gear thoroughly. I wish to put on my best appearance tomorrow; it will doubtless be my last outing of the kind for some time."

Fitzraven hurried away to tend his chores, while Reticf ascended to his room to pore over the contents of his dispatch case far into the night.

*

The Third Day had dawned grey and chill, and an icy wind whipped across the arena. The weather had not discouraged the crowd, however. The stands were packed and the overflow of people stood in the aisles, perched high on the back walls, crowding every available space. Banners flying from the imperial box indicated the presence of the royal party. This was the climactic day. The field, by contrast, was almost empty; two of the Second Day winners had not re-entered for today's events, having apparently decided that they had had enough honor for one year. They would receive handsome prizes, and respectable titles; that was enough.

The four who had come to the arena today to stake their winning and their lives on their skill at arms would be worth watching Retief thought. There was the blonde young fellow, still unmarked; a great swarthy ruffian; a tall broad man of perhaps thirty; and a squat bowlegged fellow with enormous shoulders and long arms. They were here to win or die.

From the officials' box Retief and Fitzraven had an excellent view of the arena, where a large circle had been marked out. The officials seated nearby had given them cold glances as they entered, but no one had attempted to interfere. Apparently, they had accepted the situation. Possibly, Retief thought, they had actually studied the charter. He hoped they had studied it carefully. It would make things easier.

Announcements boomed, officials moved about, fanfares blasted, while Retief sat absorbed in thought. The scene reminded him of things he had long forgotten, days long gone, of his youth, when he had studied the martial skills, serving a long apprenticeship under his world's greatest masters. It had been his father's conviction that nothing so trained the eye and mind and body as fencing, judo, savete, and the disciplines of the arts of offense, and defense.

He had abandoned a priceless education when he had left his home to seek his fortune in the main stream of galactic culture, but it had stood him in good stead on more than one occasion. An agent of the Corps could not afford to let himself decline into physical helplessness, and Retief had maintained his skills as well as possible. He leaned forward now, adjusting his binoculars as the bugles rang out. Few in the crowd were better qualified than Retief to judge today's performance. It would be interesting to see how the champions handled themselves on the field.

The first event was about to begin, as the blonde warrior was paired off with the bowlegged man. The two had been issued slender foils, and now faced each other, blades crossed. A final whistle blew, and blade clashed on blade. The squat man was fast on his feet, bouncing around in a semi-circle before his taller antagonist, probing his defense with great energy. The blonde man backed away slowly, fending off the rain of blows with slight motions of his foil. He jumped back suddenly, and Retief saw a red spot grow on his thigh. The ape-like fellow was more dangerous than he had appeared.

Now the blonde man launched his attack, beating aside the weapon of the other and striking in for the throat, only to have his point deflected at the last instant. The short man backed now, giving ground reluctantly. Suddenly he dropped into a grotesque crouch, and lunged under the other's defense in a desperate try for a quick kill. It was a mistake; the taller man whirled aside, and his blade flicked delicately once. The bowlegged man slid out flat on his face.

RETIEF: THE DIRTY DOZEN

"What happened ?" Fitzraven said, puzzled. "I didn't see the stroke that nailed him."

"It was very pretty," Retief said thoughtfully, lowering the glasses. "Under the fifth rib and into the heart."

Now the big dark man and the tall broad fellow took their places. The bugles and whistles sounded, and the two launched a furious exchange, first one and then the other forcing his enemy back before losing ground in turn. The crowd roared its approval as the two stamped and thrust, parried and lunged.

"They can't keep up this pace forever," Fitzraven said. "They'll have to slow down."

"They're both good," Retief said. "And evenly matched."

Now the swarthy fellow leaped back, switched the foil to his left hand, then moved quickly in to the attack. Thrown off his pace, the other man faltered, let the blade nick him on the chest, again in the arm. Desperate, he back-pedaled, fighting defensively now. The dark man followed up his advantage, pressing savagely, and a moment later Retief saw a foot of bright steel projecting startlingly from the tall man's back. He took two steps, then folded, as the foil was wrenched from the dark man's hand. Wave upon wave of sound rolled across the packed stands. Never had they seen such an exhibition as this! It was like the legendary battle of the heroes of the Empire, the fighters who had carried the Lily banner half across the galaxy.

"I'm afraid that's all," Fitzraven said. "These two can elect either to share the victory of the Tourney now, or to contend for sole honors, and in the history of the Tournament on Northroyal, there have never been fewer than three to share the day."

"It looks as though this is going to be the first time, then," Retief said. "They're getting ready to square off."

Below on the field, a mass of officials surrounded the dark man and the fair one, while the crowd outdid itself. Then a bugle sounded in an elaborate salute.

"That's it," Fitzraven said excitedly. "Heroes' Salute. They're going to do it."

"You don't know how glad I am to hear that," Retief said.

"What will the weapon be?" the squire wondered aloud.

"My guess is, something less deadly than the foil," Retief replied.

Moments later the announcement came. The two champions of the day would settle the issue with bare hands. This, thought Retief, would be something to see.

The fanfares and whistles rang out again, and the two men moved cautiously together. The dark man swung an open-handed blow, which smacked harmlessly against the other's shoulder. An instant later the blonde youth feinted a kick, instead drove a hard left to the dark man's chin, staggering him. He followed up, smashing two blows to the stomach, then another to the head. The dark man moved back, suddenly reached for the blonde man's wrist as he missed a jab, whirled, and attempted to throw his opponent. The blonde man slipped aside, and locked his right arm over the dark man's head, seizing his own right wrist with his left hand. The dark man twisted, fell heavily on the other man, reaching for a headlock of his own.

The two rolled in the dust, then broke apart and were on their feet again. The dark man moved in, swung an openhanded slap which popped loudly against the blonde man's face. It was a device, Retief saw, to enrage the man, dull the edge of his skill.

The blonde man refused to be rattled, however; he landed blows against the dark man's head, evaded another attempt to grapple. It was plain that he preferred to avoid the other's bear-like embrace. He boxed carefully, giving ground, landing a blow as the opportunity offered. The dark man followed doggedly, seemingly unaffected by the pounding. Suddenly he leaped, took two smashing blows full in the face, and crashed against the blonde man, knocking him to the ground. There was a flying blur of flailing arms and legs as the two rolled across the turf, and as they came to rest, Retief saw that the dark man had gotten his break. Kneeling behind the other, he held him in a rigid stranglehold, his back and shoulder muscles bulging with the effort of holding his powerful adversary immobilized.

"It's all over," Fitzraven said tensely.

"Maybe not," Retief replied. "Not if he plays it right, and doesn't panic."

The blonde man strained at the arm locked at his throat, twisting it fruitlessly. Instinct drove him to tear at the throttling grip, throw off the smothering weight. But the dark man's grip was solid, his position unshakable. Then the blond stopped struggling abruptly and the two seemed as still as an image in stone. The crowd fell silent, fascinated.

"He's given up," Fitzraven said.

"No, watch," Retief said. "He's starting to use his head."

The blonde man's arms reached up now, his hands moving over the other's head, seeking a grip. The dark man pulled his head in, pressing against his victim's back, trying to elude his grip. Then the hands found a hold, and the blonde man bent suddenly forward, heaving with a tremendous surge. The dark man came up; flipped high, his grip slipping. The blond rose as the other went over his head, shifted his grip in midair, and as the dark man fell heavily in front of him, the snap of the spine could be heard loud in the stillness. The battle was over, and the blonde victor rose to his feet amid a roar of applause.

Retief turned to Fitzraven. "Time for us to be going, Fitz," he said.

The squire jumped up. "As you command, sir; but the ceremony is quite interesting . . ."

"Never mind that; let's go." Retief moved off, Fitzraven following, puzzled.

*

Retief descended the steps inside the stands, turned and started down the corridor.

"This way, sir," Fitzraven called. "That leads to the arena."

"I know it," Retief said. "That's where I'm headed."

Fitzraven hurried up alongside. What was the old man going to do now? "Sir," he said, "no one may enter the arena until the tourney has been closed, except the gladiators and the officials. I know this to be an unbreakable law."

"That's right, Fitz," Retief said. "You'll have to stop at the grooms' enclosure."

"But you, sir," Fitzraven gasped."

"Everything's under control," Retief said. "I'm going to challenge the Champion."

*

In the Imperial box, the Emperor Rolan leaned forward, fixing his binoculars on a group of figures at the officials' gate. There seemed to be some sort of disturbance there. This was a piece of damned impudence, just as the moment had arrived for the Imperial presentation of the Honors of the Day. The Emperor turned to an aide.

"What the devil's going on down there?" he snapped.

The courtier murmured into a communicator, listened.

"A madman, Imperial Majesty," he said smoothly. "He wished to challenge the champion."

"A drunk, more likely," Rolan said sharply. "Let him be removed at once. And tell the Master of the Games to get on with the ceremony!"

The Emperor turned to the slim dark girl at his side.

"Have you found the Games entertaining, Monica?"

"Yes, sire," she replied unemotionally.

"Don't call me that, Monica," he said testily. "Between us there is no need of formalities."

"Yes, Uncle," the girl said.

"Damn it, that's worse," he said. "To you I am simply Rolan." He placed his hand firmly on her silken knee. "And now if they'll get on with this tedious ceremony, I should like to be on the way. I'm looking forward with great pleasure to showing you my estates at Snowdahl."

The Emperor drummed his fingers, stared down at the field, raised the glasses only to see the commotion again.

"Get that fool off the field," he shouted, dropping the glasses. "Am I to wait while they haggle with this idiot? It's insufferable . . . "

Courtiers scurried, while Rolan glared down from his seat.

Below, Retief faced a cluster of irate referees. One, who had attempted to haul Retief bodily backward, was slumped on a bench, attended by two surgeons.

"I claim the right to challenge, under the Charter," Retief repeated. "Nobody here will be so foolish, I hope, as to attempt to deprive me of that right, now that I have reminded you of the justice of my demand."

From the control cage directly below the Emperor's high box, a tall seam-faced man in black breeches and jacket emerged, followed by two armed men. The officials darted ahead, stringing out between the two, calling out. Behind Retief, on the other side of the barrier, Fitzraven watched anxiously. The old man was full of surprises, and had a way of getting what he wanted; but even if he had the right to challenge the Champion of the Games, what purpose could he have in doing so? He was as strong as a bull, but no man his age could be a match for the youthful power of the blonde fighter. Fitzraven was worried; he was fond of this old warrior. He would hate to see him locked behind the steel walls of Fragonard Keep for thus disturbing the order of the Lily Tournament. He moved closer to the barrier, watching.

The tall man in black strode through the chattering officials, stopped before Retief, motioned his two guards forward.

He made a dismissing motion toward Retief. "Take him off the field," he said brusquely. The guards stepped up, laid hands on Retief's arms. He let them get a grip, then suddenly stepped back and brought his arms together. The two men cracked heads, stumbled back. Retief looked at the black-clad man.

"If you are the Master of the Games," he said clearly, "you are well aware that a decorated Battle Officer has the right of challenge, under the Imperial Charter. I invoke that prerogative now, to enter the lists against the man who holds the field."

"Get out, you fool," the official hissed, white with fury. "The Emperor himself has commanded . . . "

"Not even the Emperor can override the Charter, which predates his authority by four hundred years," Retief said coldly. "Now do your duty."

"There'll be no more babble of duties and citing of technicalities while the Emperor waits," the official snapped. He turned to one of the two guards who hung back now, eyeing Retief. "You have a pistol; draw it. "If I give the command, shoot him between the eyes."

Retief reached up and adjusted a tiny stud set in the stiff collar of his tunic. He tapped his finger lightly against the cloth. The sound boomed across the arena. A command microphone of the type authorized a Battle Commander was a very efficient device.

"I have claimed the right to challenge the champion," he said slowly. The words rolled out like thunder. "This right is guaranteed under the Charter to any Imperial Battle officer who wears the Silver Star."

The Master of the Games stared at him aghast. This was getting out of control. Where the devil had the old man gotten a microphone and a P. A. system? The crowd was roaring now like a gigantic surf. This was something new!

Far above in the Imperial box the tall gray-eyed man was rising, turning toward the exit. "The effrontery," he said in a voice choked with rage. "That I should sit awaiting the pleasure . . . "

The girl..at his side hesitated, hearing the amplified voice booming across the arena.

"Wait, . . . Rolan," she said. "Something is happening . . . "

The man looked back. "A trifle late," he snapped.

"One of the contestants is disputing something," she said. "There was an announcement—something about an Imperial officer challenging the champion."

The Emperor Rolan turned to an aide hovering nearby.

"What is this nonsense?"

The courtier bowed. "It is merely a technicality, Majesty. A formality lingering on from earlier times."

"Be specific," the Emperor snapped.

The aide lost some of his aplomb. "Why, it means, ah, that an officer of the Imperial forces holding a battle commission and certain high decorations may enter the lists at any point, without other qualifying conditions. A provision never invoked under modern . . . "

The Emperor turned to the girl. "It appears that someone seeks to turn the entire performance into a farcical affair, at my expense," he said bitterly. "We shall see just how far . . . "

"I call on you, Rolan," Retief's voice boomed, "to enforce the Code."

"What impertinence is this?" Rolan growled. "Who is the fool at the microphone?" The aide spoke into his communicator, listened.

"An old man from the crowd, sire. He wears the insignia of a Battle-Commander, and a number of decorations, including the Silver Star. According to the Archivist, he has the legal right to challenge."

"I won't have it," Rolan snapped. "A fine reflection on me that would be. Have them take the fellow away; he's doubtless crazed." He left the box, followed by his entourage.

"Rolan," the girl said, "wasn't that the way the Tourneys were, back in the days of the Empire?"

"*These* are the days of the Empire, Monica. And I am not interested in what used to be done. This is today. Am I to present the spectacle of a doddering old fool being hacked to bits, in my name? I don't want the timid to be shocked by butchery. It might have unfortunate results for my propaganda program. I'm currently emphasizing the glorious aspects of the coming war, not the sordid ones. There has already been too much bloodshed today; an inauspicious omen for my expansion plan."

On the field below, the Master of the Games stepped closer to Retief. He felt the cold eyes of the Emperor himself boring into his back. This old devil could bring about his Ruin . . .

"I know all about you," he snarled. "I've checked on you, since you forced your way into an official area; I interviewed two officers . . . you overawed them with glib talk and this threadbare finery you've decked yourself in. Now you attempt to ride rough-shod over me. Well, I'm not so easily thrust aside. If you resist arrest any further, I'll have you shot where you stand !"

Retief drew his sword.

"In the name of the Code you are sworn to serve," he said, his voice ringing across the arena, "I will defend my position." He reached up and flipped the stud at his throat to full pick-up.

"To the Pit with your infernal Code!" bellowed the Master, and blanched in horror as his words boomed sharp and clear across the field to the ears of a hundred thousand people. He stared around, then whirled back to Retief. "Fire," he screamed.

A pistol cracked, and the guard spun, dropped. Fitzraven held the tiny power gun leveled across the barrier at the other guard. "What next, sir?" he asked brightly.

The sound of the shot, amplified, smashed deafeningly across the arena, followed by a mob roar of excitement, bewilderment, shock. The group around Retief stood frozen, staring at the dead man. The Master of the Games made a croaking sound, eyes bulging. The remaining guard cast a glance at the pistol, then turned and ran.

There were calls from across the field; then a troop of brown uniformed men emerged from an entry, trotted toward the group. The officer at their head carried a rapid fire shock gun in his hand. He waved his squad to a halt as he reached the fringe of the group. He stared at Retief's drab uniform, glanced at the corpse. Retief saw that the officer was young, determined looking, wearing the simple insignia of a Battle Ensign.

The Master of the Games found his voice. "Arrest this villain!" he screeched, pointing at Retief. Shoot the murderer!"

The ensign drew himself to attention, saluted crisply.

"Your orders, sir," he said.

"I've told you!" the Master howled. "Seize this malefactor!" The ensign turned to the black-clad official. "Silence, sir, or I shall be forced to remove you," he said sharply. He looked at Retief. "I await the Commander's orders."

Retief smiled, returned the young officer's salute with a wave of his sword, then sheathed it. "I'm glad to see a little sense displayed here, at last, Battle-Ensign," he said. "I was beginning to fear I'd fallen among Concordiatists."

The outraged Master began an harangue which was abruptly silenced by two riot police. He was led away, protesting. The other officials disappeared like a morning mist, carrying the dead guard.

"I've issued my challenge, Ensign," Retief said. "I wish it to be conveyed to the champion-apparent at once." He smiled. "And I'd like you to keep your men around to see that nothing interferes with the orderly progress of the Tourney in accordance with the Charter in its original form."

The ensign's eyes sparkled. Now here was a battle-officer who sounded like a fighting man; not a windbag like the commandant of the Household Regiment from whom the ensign took his orders. He didn't know where the old man came from, but any battle-officer outranked any civilian or flabby barracks-soldier, and this was a Battle Commander, a general officer, and of the Dragon Corps!

Minutes later, a chastened Master of the Games announced that a challenge had been issued. It was the privilege of the champion to accept, or to refuse the challenge if he wished. In the latter event, the challenge would automatically be met the following year.

"I don't know what your boys said to the man," Retief remarked, as he walked out to the combat circle, the ensign at his left side and slightly to the rear, "but they seem to have him educated quickly."

"They can be very persuasive, sir," the young officer replied.

They reached the circle, stood waiting. Now, thought Retief, I've got myself in the position I've been working toward. The question now is whether I'm still man enough to put it over.

He looked up at the massed stands, listening to the mighty roar of the crowd. There would be no easy out for him now. Of course, the new champion might refuse to fight; he had every right to do so, feeling he had earned his year's rest and enjoyment of his winnings. But that would be a defeat for Retief as final as death on the dusty ground of the arena. He had come this far by bluff, threat, and surprise. He would never come this close again.

It was luck that he had clashed with this young man outside the gate, challenged him to enter the lists. That might give the challenge the personal quality that would elicit an angry acceptance.

The champion was walking toward Retief now, surrounded by referees. He stared at the old man, eyes narrowed. Retief returned the look calmly.

"Is this dodderer the challenger?" the blonde youth asked scathingly. "It seems to me I have met his large mouth before?"

"Never mind my mouth, merchant," Retief said loudly. "It is not talk I offer you, but the bite of steel."

The yellow-haired man reddened, then laughed shortly.

"Small glory I'd win out of skewering you, old graybeard."

"You'd get even less out of showing your heels," Retief said.

"You will not provoke me into satisfying your perverted ambition to die here," the other retorted.

"It's interesting to note," Retief said, "how a peasant peddler wags his tongue to avoid a fight. Such rabble should not be permitted on honorable ground." He studied the other's face to judge how this line of taunting was going on. It was distasteful to have to embarrass the young fellow; he seemed a decent sort. But he had to enrage him to the point that he would discard his wisdom and throw his new-won prize on the table for yet another cast of the dice. And his sore point seemed to be mention of commerce.

"Back to your cabbages, then, fellow," Retief said harshly, "before I whip you there with the flat of my sword."

The young fellow looked at him, studying him. His face was grim. "All right," he said quietly. "I'll meet you in the circle."

Another point gained, Retief thought, as he moved to his position at the edge of the circle. Now, if I can get him to agree to fight on horseback . . .

He turned to a referee. "I wish to suggest that this contest be conducted on horseback if the peddler owns a horse and is not afraid."

The point was discussed between the referee and the champion's attendants, with many glances at Retief, and much waving of arms. The official returned. "The champion agrees to meet you by day or by night, in heat or cold, on foot or on horseback."

"Good," said Retief. "Tell my groom to bring out my mount."

It was no idle impulse which prompted this move. Retief had no illusions as to what it would take to win a victory over the champion. He knew that his legs, while good enough for most of the business of daily life, were his weakest point. They were no longer the nimble tireless limbs that had once carried him up to meet the outlaw Mal de Di alone in Bifrost Pass. Nine hours later he had brought the bandit's two hundred and ten pound body down into the village on his back, his own arm broken. He had been a mere boy then, younger than this man he was now to meet. He had taken up Mal de Di's standing challenge to any unarmed man who would come alone to the high pass, to prove that he, was not too young to play a man's part. Perhaps now he was trying to prove he was not too old . . .

An official approached leading Danger-by-Night. It took **an** expert to appreciate the true worth of the great gaunt animal, Retief knew. To the uninitiated eye, he presented a sorry appearance, but Retief would rather have had this mount with the imperial brand on his side, than a paddock full of show horses.

A fat white charger was led out to the blonde champion. It looked like a strong animal, Retief thought, but slow. His chances were looking better, things were going well.

A ringing blast of massed trumpets cut through the clamor of the crowd. Retief mounted, watching his opponent. A referee came to his side, handed up a heavy club, studded with long projecting spikes. "Your weapon, sir," he said.

Retief took the thing. It was massive, clumsy; he had never before handled such a weapon. He knew no subtleties of technique with this primitive bludgeon. The blonde youth had surprised him, he admitted to himself, smiling slightly. As the challenged party, he had the choice of weapons, of course. He had picked an unusual one.

Retief glanced across at Fitzraven, standing behind the inner barrier, jaw set, a grim expression on his face. That boy, thought Retief, doesn't have much confidence in my old bones holding out.

The whistle blew. Retief moved toward the other man at a trot, the club level at his side. He had decided to handle it like a shortsword, so long as that seemed practical. He would have to learn by experience.

The white horse cantered past him swerving, and the blond fellow whirled his club at Retief's head. Automatically, Retief raised his club, fended off the blow, cut at the other's back, missed. This thing is too short, Retief thought, whirling his horse. I've got to get in closer. He charged at the champion as the white horse was still in mid-turn, slammed a heavy blow against his upraised club, rocking the boy; then he was past, turning again. He caught the white horse shorter this time, barely into his turn, and aimed a swing at the man who first twisted to face him, then spurred, leaped away. Retief pursued him, yelping loudly. Get him rattled, he thought. Get him good and mad!

The champion veered suddenly, veered again, then reared his horse high, whirling, to bring both forefeet down in a chopping attack. Retief reined in, and Danger-by-Night sidestepped disdainfully, as the heavy horse crashed down facing him.

That was a pretty maneuver, Retief thought; but slow, too slow.

His club swung in an overhand cut; the white horse tossed his head suddenly, and the club smashed down across the animal's skull. With a shuddering exhalation, the beast collapsed, and the blonde man sprang clear.

Retief reined back, dismayed. He hadn't wanted to kill the animal. He had the right, now, to ride the man down from the safety of the saddle. When gladiators met in mortal combat, there were no rules except those a man made for himself. If he dismounted, met his opponent on equal terms, the advantage his horse had given him would be lost. He looked at the man standing now, facing him, waiting, blood on his face from the fall. He thought of the job he had set himself, the plan that hinged on his victory here. He reminded himself that he was old, too old to meet youth on equal terms; but even as he did so, he was reining the lean battle stallion back, swinging down from the saddle. There were some things a man had to do, whether logic was served or not. He couldn't club the man down like a mad dog from the saddle.

There was a strange expression on the champion's face. He sketched a salute with the club he held. "All honor to you, old man," he said. "Now I will kill you." He moved in confidently. Retief stood his ground, raising his club to deflect a blow, shifting an instant ahead of the pattern of the blonde man's assault. There was a hot exchange as the younger man pressed him, took a glancing blow on the temple, stepped back breathing heavily. This wasn't going as he had planned. The old man stood like a wall of stone, not giving an inch; and when their weapons met, it was like flailing at a granite boulder. The young fellow's shoulder ached from the shock. He moved sideways, circling cautiously.

Retief moved to face him. It was risky business, standing up to the attack, but his legs were not up to any fancy footwork. He had no desire to show his opponent how stiff his movements were, or to tire himself with skipping about. His arms were still as good as any man's, or better. They would have to carry the battle.

The blonde jumped in, swung a vicious cut; Retief leaned back, hit out in a one-handed blow, felt the club smack solidly against the other's jaw. He moved now, followed up, landed again on the shoulder. The younger man backed, shaking his head. Retief stopped, waited. It was too bad he couldn't follow up his advantage, but he couldn't chase the fellow all over the arena. He had to save his energy for an emergency. He lowered his club, leaned on it. The crowd noises waxed and waned, unnoticed. The sun beat down in unshielded whiteness, and fitful wind moved dust across the field.

KEITH LAUMER

"Come back, peddler," he called. "I want you to sample more of my wares." If he could keep the man angry, he would be careless; and Retief needed the advantage.

The yellow-haired man charged suddenly, whirling the club. Retief raised his, felt the shock of the other's weapon against his. He whirled as the blonde darted around shifted the club to his left hand in time to ward off a wild swing. Then the fingers of his left hand exploded in fiery agony, and the club flew from his grasp. His head whirled, vision darkening, at the pain from his smashed fingers. He tottered, kept his feet, managed to blink away the faintness, to stare at this hand. Two fingers were missing, pulped, unrecognizable. He had lost his weapon; he was helpless now before the assault of the other.

His head hummed harshly, and his breath came like hot sand across an open wound. He could feel a tremor start and stop in his leg, and his whole left arm felt as though it had been stripped of flesh in a shredding machine. He had not thought it would be as bad as this. His ego, he realized, hadn't aged gracefully.

Now is the hour, old man, he thought. There's no help for you to call on, no easy way out. You'll have to look within yourself for some hidden reserve of strength and endurance and will; and you must think well now, wisely, with a keen eye and a quick hand, or lose your venture. With a moment stiffened by the racking pain-shock, he drew his ceremonial dagger, a jewel-encrusted blade ten inches long. At the least he would die with a weapon in his hand and his face to the enemy.

The blonde youth moved closer, tossed the club aside. "Shall a peddler be less capable of the *beau geste* than the arrogant knight?" He laughed, drawing a knife from his belt. "Is your head clear, old man?" he asked. "Are you ready?"

"A gesture . . . you can . . . ill afford," Retief managed. Even breathing hurt. His nerves were shrieking their message of shock at the crushing of living flesh and bone. His forehead was pale, wet with cold sweat.

The young fellow closed, struck out, and Retief evaded. the point by an inch, stepped back. His body couldn't stand pain as once it had, he was realizing. He had grown soft, sensitive. For too many years he had been a Diplomat, an operator by manipulation, by subtlety and finesse. Now, when it was man to man, brute strength against brute strength, he was failing.

But he had known when he started that strength was not enough, not without agility; it was subtlety he should be relying on now, his skill at trickery, his devious wit.

Retief caught a glimpse of staring faces at the edge of the field, heard for a moment the mob roar, and then he was again wholly concentrated on the business at hand.

He breathed deeply, struggling for clear-headedness. He had to inveigle the boy into a contest in which he stood a chance. If he could put him on his mettle, make him give up his advantage of tireless energy, quickness . . .

"Are you an honest peddler, or a dancing master," Retief managed to growl. "Stand and meet me face to face."

The blonde man said nothing, feinting rapidly, then striking out. Retief was ready, nicked the other's wrist.

"Gutter fighting is one thing," Retief said. "But you are afraid to face the old man's steel, right arm against right arm." If he went for that, Retief thought, he was even younger than he looked.

"I have heard of the practice," the blonde man said, striking at Retief, moving aside from a return cut. "It was devised for old men who did not wish to be made ridiculous by more agile men. I understand that you think you can hoodwink me, but I can beat you at your own game . . . "

"My point awaits your pleasure," Retief said.

The younger man moved closer, knife held before him. Just a little closer, Retief thought. Just a little closer.

The blonde man's eyes were on Retief's. Without warning, Retief dropped his knife and in a lightning motion caught the other's wrist.

"Now struggle, little fish," he said. "I have you fast."

The two men stood chest to chest, staring into each other's eyes. Retief's breath, came hard, his heart pounded almost painfully. His left arm was a great pulsating weight of pain. Sweat ran down his dusty face into his eyes. But his grip was locked solidly. The blonde youth strained in vain

With a twist of his wrist Retief turned the blade, then forced the youth's arm up. The fellow struggled to prevent it, throwing all his weight into his effort, fruitlessly. Retief smiled.

"I won't kill you," he said,

"but I will have to break your arm. That way you cannot be expected to continue the fight."

"I want no favors from you, old man," the youth panted.

"You won't consider this a favor until the bones knit," Retief said. "Consider this a fair return for my hand."

He pushed the arm up, then suddenly turned it back, levered the upper arm over his forearm, and yanked the tortured member down behind the blonde man's back. The bones snapped audibly, and the white-faced youth gasped, staggered as Retief released him.

There were minutes of confusion as referees rushed in, announcements rang out, medics hovered, and the crowd roared its satisfaction, after the fickle nature of, crowds. They were satisfied.

An official pushed through to Retief. He wore the vivid colors of the Review regiment. Retief reached up and set the control on the command mike.

"I have the honor to advise you, sir, that you have won the field, and the honors of the day." He paused, startled at the booming echoes, then went on. The bystanders watched curiously, as Retief tried to hold his concentration on the man, to stand easily while blackness threatened to move in over him. The pain from the crushed hand swelled and focused, then faded, came again. The great dry lung-fulls of air he drew in failed to dispel the sensation of suffocation. He struggled to, understand the words that seemed to echo from a great distance.

"And now in the name of the Emperor for crimes against the peace and order of the Empire, I place you under. arrest for trial before the High Court at Fragonard."

Retief drew a deep breath, gathered his thoughts to speak.

"Nothing," he said, "could possibly please me more."

*

The room was vast and ornate, and packed with dignitaries, high officials, peers of the Lily. Here in the great chamber known as the Blue Vault, the High Court sat in silent ranks, waiting.

The charges had been read, the evidence presented. The prisoner, impersonating a peer of the Lily and an officer of an ancient and honored Corps, had flaunted the law of Northroyal and the authority of the Emperor, capping his audacity with murder, done by the hand of his servant sworn. Had the prisoner anything to say?

Retief, alone in the prisoner's box in the center of the room, his arm heavily bandaged and deadened with dope, faced the court. This would be the moment when all his preparations would be put to the ultimate test. He had laid long plans toward this hour. The archives of the Corps were beyond comparison in the galaxy, and he had spent weeks there, absorbing every detail of the fact that had been recorded on the world of Northroyal, and on the Old Empire which had preceded it. And to the lore of the archives, he had added facts known to himself, data from his own wide experience. But would those tenuous threads of tradition, hearsay, rumor, and archaic record hold true now? That was the gamble on which his mission was staked. The rabbits had better be in the hat.

He looked at the dignitaries arrayed before him. It had been a devious route, but so far he had succeeded; he had before him the highest officials of the world, the High Justices, the Imperial Archivist, the official keepers of the Charter and the Code, and of the protocols and rituals of the tradition on which this society was based. He had risked everything on his assault on the sacred stasis of the Tournament, but how else could he have gained the ears of this select audience, with all Northroyal tuned in to hear the end of the drama that a hundred thousand had watched build to its shattering climax?

Now it was his turn to speak. It had better be good. "Peers of the realm," Retief said, speaking clearly and slowly, "the basis of the charges laid against me is the assumption that I have falsified my identity. Throughout, I have done no more than exercise the traditional rights of a general officer and of a Lilyan peer, and, as befits a Cavalier, I have resisted all attempts to deprive me of those honored prerogatives. While it is regrettable that the low echelon of officials appears to be ignorant of the status of a Lilyan Battle Commander, it is my confident assumption that here, before the ranking nobles of the Northroyalan peerage, the justice of my position will be recognized."

As Retief paused, a dour graybeard spoke up from the Justices' bench.

"Your claims are incoherent to this court. You are known to none of us: and if by chance you claim descent from some renegade who deserted his fellow cavaliers at the time of the Exile, you will find scant honor among honest men here. From this, it is obvious that you delude yourself in imagining that you can foist your masquerade on this court successfully."

"I am not native to Northroyal," Retief said, "nor do I claim to be. Nor am I a descendant of renegades. Are you gentlemen not overlooking the fact that there was one ship which did not accompany the cavaliers into exile, but escaped Concordiat surveillance and retired to rally further opposition to the invasion?"

There was a flurry of muttered comment, putting together of heads, and shuffling of papers. The High Justice spoke.

"This would appear to be a reference to the vessel bearing the person of the Emperor Roquelle and his personal suite . . . "

"That is correct," Retief said.

"You stray farther than ever from the credible," a justice snapped. "The entire royal household accompanied the Emperor Rolan on the happy occasion of his rejoining his subjects here at Northroyal a year ago."

"About that event, I will have more to say later," Retief said coolly. "For the present, suffice it to say that I am a legitimate descendant . . . "

"It does indeed NOT suffice to say!" barked the High Justice. "Do you intend to instruct this court as to what evidence will be acceptable ?"

"A figure of speech, Milord," Retief said. "I am quite able to prove my statement."

"Very well," said the High Justice. "Let us see your proof, though I confess I cannot conceive of a satisfactory one."

Retief reached down, unsnapped the flat despatch case at his belt, drew out a document.

"This is my proof of my bona fides," he said. "I present it in evidence that I have committed no fraud. 1 am sure that you will recognize an authentic commission-in-patent of the Emperor Roquelle. Please note that the seals are unbroken." He passed the paper over.

A page took the heavy paper, looped with faded red ribbon and plastered with saucer-sized seals, trotted over to the Justices' bench and handed it up to the High Justice. He took it, gazed at it, turning it over, then broke the crumbling seals. The near by Justices leaned over to see this strange exhibit. It was a heavily embossed document of the Old Empire type, setting forth genealogy and honors, and signed in sprawling letters with the name of an emperor two centuries dead, sealed with his tarnished golden seal. The Justices stared in amazement. The document was worth a fortune.

"I ask that the lowermost paragraph be read aloud," Retief said. "The amendment of thirty years ago."

The High Justice hesitated, then waved a page to him, handed down the document.

"Read the lowermost paragraph aloud," he said.

The page read in a clear, well-trained voice.

RETIEF: THE DIRTY DOZEN

"KNOW ALL MEN BY THESE PRESENTS THAT WHEREAS: THIS OUR LOYAL SUBJECT AND PEER OF THE IMPERIAL LILY JAME JARL FREELORD OF THE RETIEF; OFFICER IMPERIAL OF THE GUARD; OFFICER OF BATTLE; HEREDITARY LEGIONNAIRE OF HONOR; CAVALIER OF THE LILY; DEFENDER OF SALIENT WEST; BY IMPERIAL GRACE OFFICER OF THE SILVER STAR; HAS BY HIS GALLANTRY FIDELITY AND SKILL BROUGHT HONOR TO THE IMPERIAL LILY: AND WHEREAS WE PLACE SPECIAL CONFIDENCE AND ESTEEM IN THIS SUBJECT AND PEER: WE DO THEREFORE APPOINT AND COMMAND THAT HE SHALL FORTHWITH ASSUME AND HENCEFORTH BEAR THE HONORABLE RANK OF BATTLE COMMANDER: AND THAT HE SHALL BEAR THE OBLIGATIONS AND ENJOY THE PRIVILEGES APPERTAINING THEREUNTO: AS SHALL HIS HEIRS FOREVER."

There was a silence in the chamber as the page finished reading. All eyes turned to Retief, who stood in the box, strange expression on his face.

The page handed the paper back up to the High Justice, who resumed his perusal.

"I ask that my retinal patterns now be examined, and matched to those coded on the amendment," Retief said. The High Justice beckoned to a Messenger, and the court waited a restless five minutes until the arrival of an expert who quickly made the necessary check. He went to the Justice's bench, handed up a report form, and left the court room. The magistrate glanced at the form, turned again to the document. Below Roquelle's seal were a number of amendments, each in turn signed and sealed. The justices spelled out the unfamiliar names.

"Where did you get this?" the High Justice demanded uncertainly.

"It has been the property of my family for nine generations," Retief replied.

Heads nodded over the document, gray beards wagged.

"How is it," asked a Justice, "that you offer in evidence a document bearing amendments validated by signatures and seals completely unknown to us? In order to impress this court, such a warrant might well bear the names of actual former emperors, rather than of fictitious ones. I note the lowermost amendment, purporting to be a certification of high military rank dated only thirty years ago is signed Ronare."

"I was at that time attached to the Imperial Suite-in-Exile," Retief said. "I commanded the forces of the Emperor Ronare."

The High Justice and a number of other members of the court snorted openly.

"This impertinence will not further your case," the old magistrate said sharply. "Ronare, indeed. You cite a nonexistent authority. At the alleged time of issue of this warrant, the father of our present monarch held the Imperial fief at Trallend."

"At the time of the issue of this document," Retief said in ringing tones, "the father of your present ruler held the bridle when the Emperor mounted!"

An uproar broke out from all sides. The Master-at-arms pounded in vain for silence. At length a measure of order was restored by a gangly official who rose and shouted for the floor. The roar died down, and the stringy fellow, clad in russet velvet with the gold chain of the Master of the Seal about his neck, called out, "Let the court find the traitor guilty summarily and put an end to this insupportable insolence . . . ."

"Northroyal has been the victim of fraud," Retief said loudly in the comparative lull. "But not on my part. The man Rolan is an imposter."

A tremendous pounding of gavels and staffs eventually brought the outraged dignitaries to grim silence. The Presiding Justice peered down at Retief with doom in his lensed eyes. "Your knowledge of the Lilyan tongue and of the forms of court practice as well as the identity of your retinal patterns with those of the warrant tend to substantiate your origin in the Empire. Accordingly, this court is now disposed to recognize in you that basest of offenders, a renegade of the peerage." He raised his voice. "Let it be recorded that one Jame Jarl, a freelord of the Imperial Lily and officer Imperial of the Guard has by his own words disavowed his oath and his lineage." The fiery old man glared around at his fellow jurists. "Now let the dog of a broken officer be sentenced!"

"I have proof of what I say," Retief called out. "Nothing has been proven against me. I have acted by the Code, and by the Code I demand my hearing!"

"You have spurned the Code," said a fat dignitary.

"I have told you that a usurper sits on the Lily throne," Retief said. "If I can't prove it, execute me."

There was an icy silence.

"Very well," said the High Justice. "Present your proof."

"When the man, Rolan, appeared," Retief said, "he presented the Imperial seal and ring, the ceremonial robe, the major portion of the crown jewels, and the Imperial Geneology."

"That is correct."

"Was it noted, by any chance, that the seal was without its chain, that the robe was stained, that the most important of the jewels, the ancient Napoleon Emerald, was missing; that the ring bore deep scratches, and that the lock on the book had been forced ?"

A murmur grew along the high benches of the court. Intent eyes glared down at Retief.

"And was it not considered strange that the Imperial signet was not presented by this would-be Emperor, when that signet alone constitutes the true symbol of the Empire?"

Retief's voice had risen to a thunderous loudness.

The High Justice stared now with a different emotion in his eyes.

"What do you know of these matters?" he demanded, but without assurance.

Retief reached into a tiny leather bag at his side, drew out something which he held out for inspection.

This a broken chain," he said. "It was cut when the seal was stolen from its place in Suite-in-Exile." He placed the heavy links on the narrow wainscot before him. "This," he said, "is the Napoleon Emerald, once worn by the legendary Bonaparte in a ring. It is unique in the galaxy, and easily proved genuine." There was utter stillness now. Retief placed a small key beside the chain and the gem. "This key will open the forced lock of the Imperial Genealogical Record."

Retief brought out an ornately wrought small silver casket and held it in view.

"The stains on the robe are the blood of the Emperor Ronare, shed by the knife of a murderer. The ring is scratched by the same knife, used to sever the finger in order to remove the ring." A murmur of horrified comment ran round the room now. Retief waited. letting all eyes focus on the silver box in his hand. It contained a really superb copy of the Imperial Signet; like the chain, the key and the emerald, the best that the science of the Corps could produce, accurate even in its internal molecular structure. It had to be, if it were to have a chance of acceptance. It would be put to the test without delay, matched to an electronic matrix with which it would, if acceptable, resonate perfectly, The copy had been assembled on the basis of some excellent graphic records; the original signet, as Retief knew, had been lost irretrievably in a catastrophic palace fire, a century and a half ago.

He opened the box, showed the magnificent wine-red crystal set in platinum. Now was the moment. "This is the talisman which alone would prove the falseness of the imposter Rolan," Retief said. "I call upon the honorable High Court to match it to the matrix; and while that is being done, I ask that the honorable Justices study carefully the genealogy included in the Imperial patent which I have presented to the court."

A messenger was dispatched to bring in the matrix while the Justices adjusted the focus of their corrective lenses and clustered over the document. The chamber buzzed with tense excitement. This was a fantastic development indeed!

The High Justice looked up as the massive matrix device was wheeled into the room. He stared at Retief. "This genealogy "he began.

A Justice plucked at his sleeve, indicated the machine, whispering something. The High Justice nodded.

Retief handed the silver box down carefully to a page, watched as the chamber of the machine was opened, the great crystal placed in position. He held his breath as technicians twiddled controls, studied dials, then closed a switch. There was a sonorous musical tone from the machine.

The technician looked up. "The crystal," he said, "does match the matrix."

Amid a burst of exclamations which died as he faced the High Justice, Retief spoke.

"My lords, peers of the Imperial Lily," he said in a ringing voice, "know by this signet that we, Retief, by the grace of God Emperor, do now claim our rightful throne."

And just as quickly as the exclamations had died, they rose once more a mixture of surprise and awe.

Epilogue

"A brilliant piece of work, Mr. Minister, and congratulations on your promotion," the Ambassador-at-large said warmly. "You've shown what individualism and the unorthodox approach can accomplish where the academic viewpoint would consider the situation hopeless."

RETIEF: THE DIRTY DOZEN

"Thank you, Mr. Ambassador," Retief replied, smiling. "I was surprised myself when it was all over, that my gamble paid off. Frankly, I hope I won't ever be in a position again to be quite so inventive."

"I don't mind telling you now," the Ambassador said, "that when I saw Magnan's report of your solo assignment to the case, I seriously attempted to recall you, but it was too late. It was a nasty piece of business sending a single agent in on a job with the wide implications of this one. Mr. Magnan had been under a strain, I'm afraid. He is having a long rest now . . . "

Retief understood perfectly. His former chief had gotten the axe, and he himself had emerged clothed in virtue. That was the one compensation of desperate ventures; if you won, they paid well. In his new rank, he had a long tenure ahead. He hoped the next job would be something complex and far removed from Northroyal. He thought back over the crowded weeks of his brief reign there as Emperor. It had been a stormy. scene when the bitterly resisting Rolan had been brought to face the High Court. The man had been hanged an hour before sunrise on the following day, still protesting his authenticity. That, at least, was a lie. Retief was grateful that he had proof that Rolan was a fraud, because he would have sent him to the gallows on false evidence even had he been the true heir.

His first act after his formal enthronement had been the abolition in perpetuity the rite of the tourney, and the formal cancellation of all genealogical requirements for appointments public private. He had ordered the release and promotion of the Battle Ensign who had ignored Rolan's arrest order and had been himself imprisoned for his pains. Fitzraven he had seen appointed to the Imperial War College his future assured.

Retief smiled as he remembered the embarrassment of the young fellow who had been his fellow-finalist in the tourney. He had offered him satisfaction on the field of honor as soon as his arm healed, and had been asked in return for forgetfulness of poor judgment. He had made him a Captain of the Guard and a peer of the realm. He had the spirit for it.

There had been much more to do, and Retief's days had been crowded with the fantastically complex details of disengaging a social structure from the crippling reactionary restraints of ossified custom and hallowed tradition. In the end, he had produced a fresh and workable new constitution for the kingdom which he hoped would set the world on an enlightened and dynamic path to a productive future.

The memory of Princess Monica lingered pleasantly; a true princess of the Lily, in the old tradition. Retief had abdicated in her favor; her genealogy had been studded with enough Imperial forebears to satisfy the crustiest of the Old Guard peerage; of course, it could not compare with the handsome document he had displayed showing his own descent in the direct line through seven—or was it eight—generations of Emperors-in-exile from the lost monarch of the beleaguered Lily Empire, but it was enough to justify his choice. Rolan's abortive usurpation had at least had the effect of making the Northroyalans appreciate an enlightened ruler.

At the last, it had not been easy to turn away forever from the seat of Empire which he so easily sat. It had not been lightly that he had said good-by to the lovely Monica, who had reminded him of another dark beauty of long ago.

A few weeks in a modern hospital had remedied the harsher after-effects of his short career as a gladiator, and he was ready now for the next episode that fate and the Corps might have in store. But he would not soon forget Northroyal . . .

" . . . magnificent ingenuity," someone was saying. "You must have assimilated your indoctrination on the background unusually thoroughly to have been able to prepare in advance just those artifacts and documents which would prove most essential. And the technical skill in the production itself. Remarkable. To think that you were able to hoodwink the high priests of the cult in the very sanctum sanctorum."

"Merely the result of careful research," Retief said modestly. "I found all I needed on late developments, buried in our files. The making of the Signet was quite a piece of work; but credit for that goes to our own technicians."

"I was even more impressed by that document," a young counselor said. "What a knowledge of their psychology, and of technical detail that required."

Retie smiled faintly. The others had all gone into the hall now, amid a babble of conversation. It was time to be going. He glanced at the eager junior agent.

"No," he said, "I can't claim much credit there. I've had that document for many years; it, at least, was perfectly genuine."

CPSIA information can be obtained
at www.ICGtesting.com
Printed in the USA
LVHW092303050820
662514LV00010B/159